PoPuLarMMOs

PAT + JEN, the stars of PopularMMOS, are two of the most popular YouTubers in the world. With over 16.9 million subscribers and 14 billion combined views, their Minecraft-inspired channel is one of the most-watched channels on YouTube. To learn more, visit Pat and Jen on YouTube @PopularMMOS and @GamingwithJen.

To Hazel and Ezra —D.J.

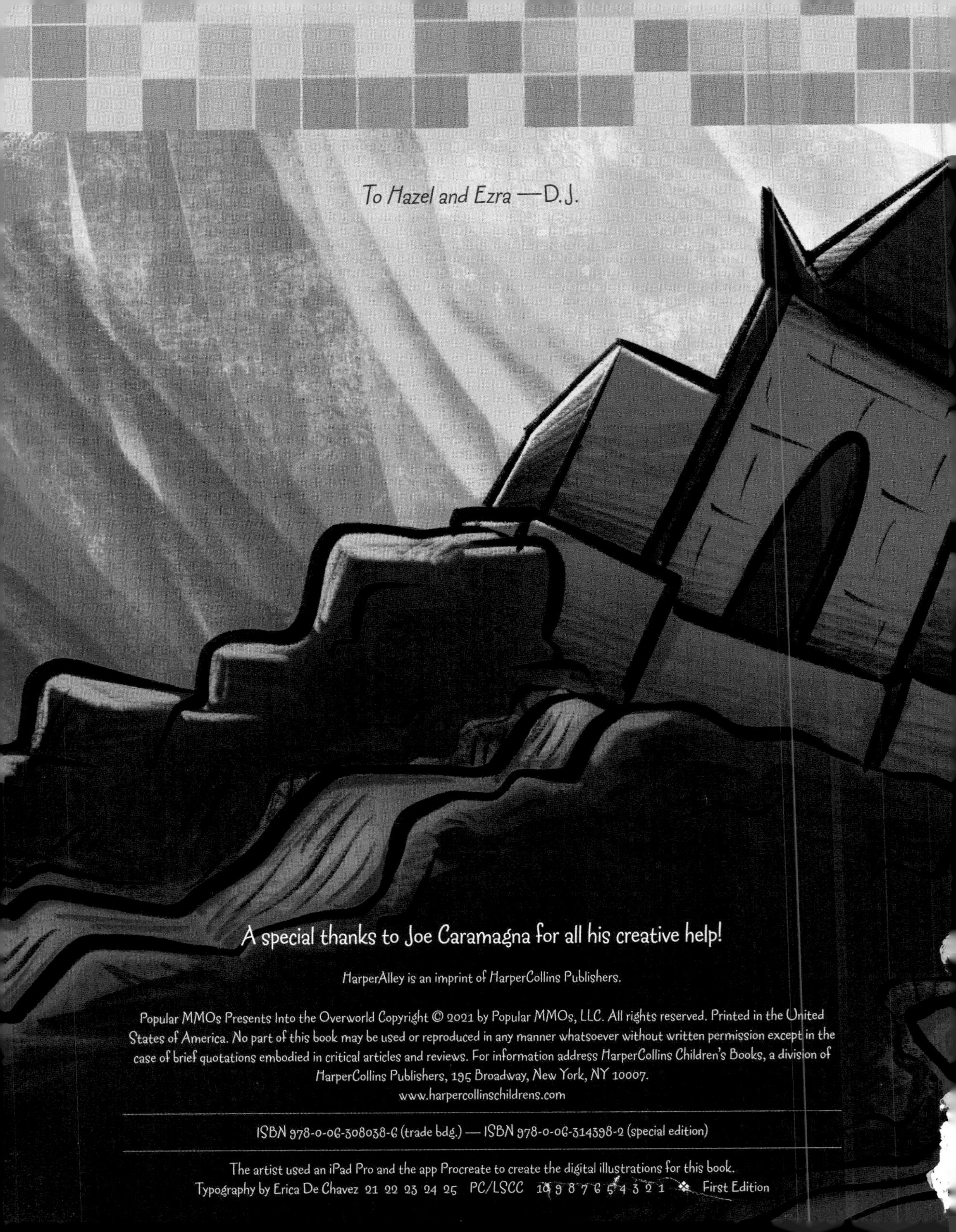

A special thanks to Joe Caramagna for all his creative help!

HarperAlley is an imprint of HarperCollins Publishers.

 For information address HarperCollins Children's Books, a division of HarperCollins Publishers, 195 Broadway, New York, NY 10007.
www.harpercollinschildrens.com

ISBN 978-0-06-308038-6 (trade bdg.) — ISBN 978-0-06-314398-2 (special edition)

The artist used an iPad Pro and the app Procreate to create the digital illustrations for this book.
Typography by Erica De Chavez 21 22 23 24 25 PC/LSCC 10 9 8 7 6 5 4 3 2 1 ❖ First Edition

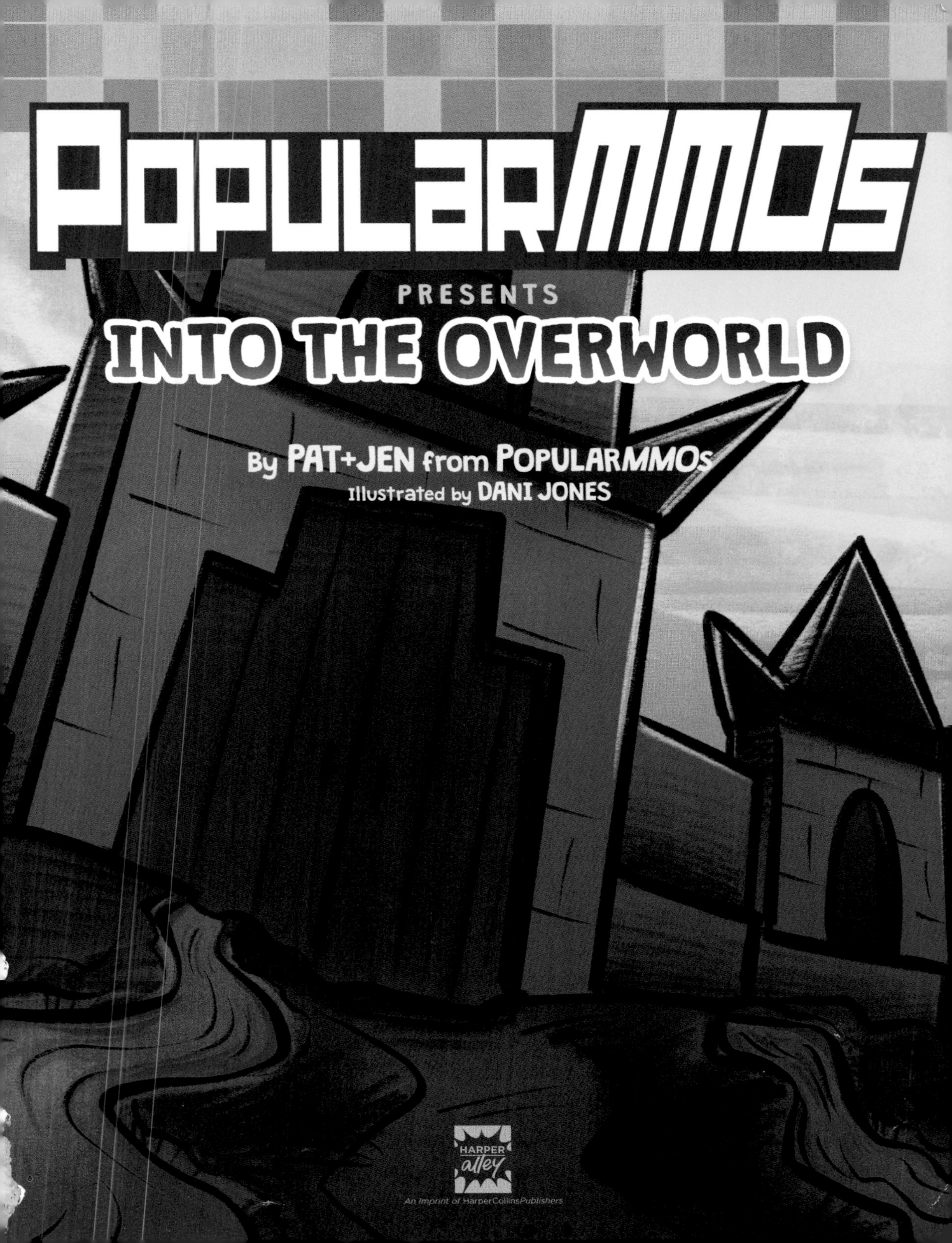

POPULARMMOs

PRESENTS

INTO THE OVERWORLD

By PAT+JEN from POPULARMMOs
Illustrated by DANI JONES

HARPER alley
An Imprint of HarperCollinsPublishers

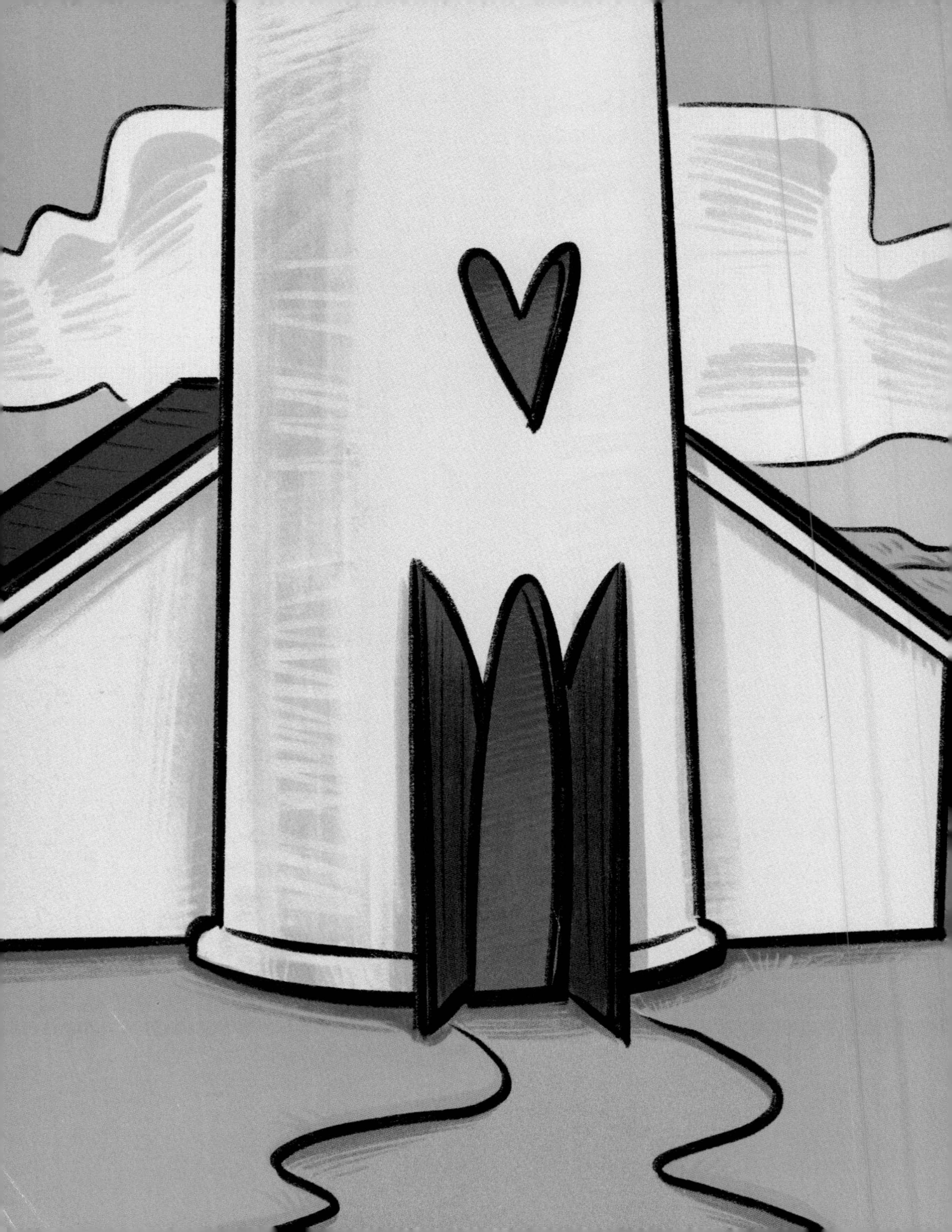

Hey, what's going on, guys!

It's Pat and Jen, and we're so thrilled that you're reading our fourth book! A lot has changed since *A Hole New World* first came out. Jen's discovered that she has a sister! (Spoiler alert: it's Evil Jen!) And she's off on a new quest to unlock the deep, dark secrets about the rest of her family. It's an adventure filled with unexpected revelations, daring double crosses, and all your favorite PopularMMOs characters, from Bomby to Herobrine to Honey Boo Boo.

But most of all, what means the world to us is your continued support. Honestly, when we first started writing this series, we only had the vaguest sense of where it would all go. But the places it's taken us to and the things we've discovered along the way— it's more than we could have imagined when we started out. If you haven't read *A Hole New World*, *Enter the Mine*, or *Zombie's Day Off* yet, we highly recommend you do. They're good fun and all available now in paperback and all the craziness will mean so much more if you come along for the full ride!

Anyway, it's been a crazy adventure. Even we didn't expect the twists and turns that happen here. Have fun! Read on! We think you'll be surprised by what happens next.

And, as always, thanks for being a fan.

We love you!

Pat + Jen

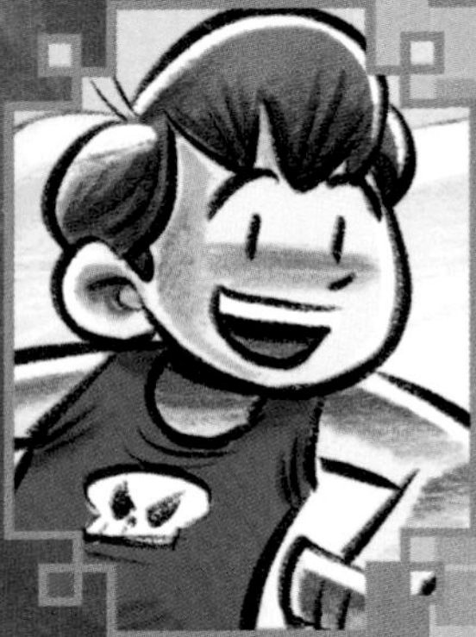

PAT & JEN

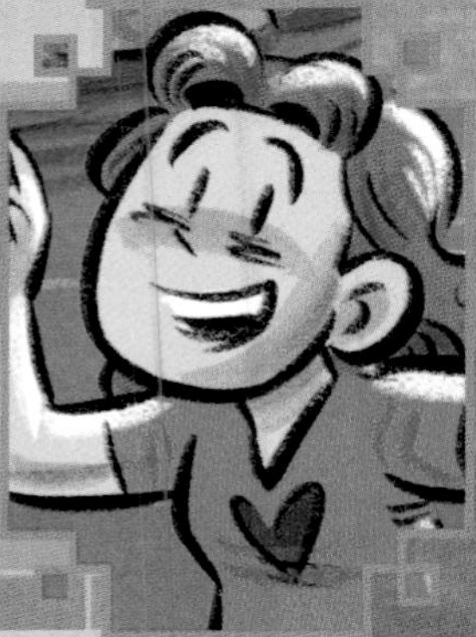

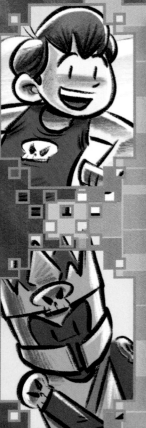

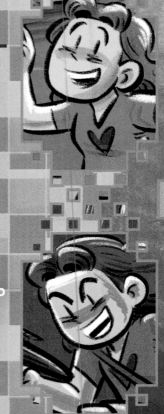

Pat is an awesome dude who's always looking for an epic adventure with his partner, Super Gamer Jen. Pat loves to have fun with his friends and take control of every situation with his cool weapons and can-do attitude. Jen is the sweetest person in the world and loves to laugh, but don't let her cheeriness fool you—she's also fierce. In fact, she could be an even greater adventurer than Pat . . . if she weren't so clumsy. Even when they go on their own separate adventures they—along with their savage cat, Cloud—have a bond that can never be broken.

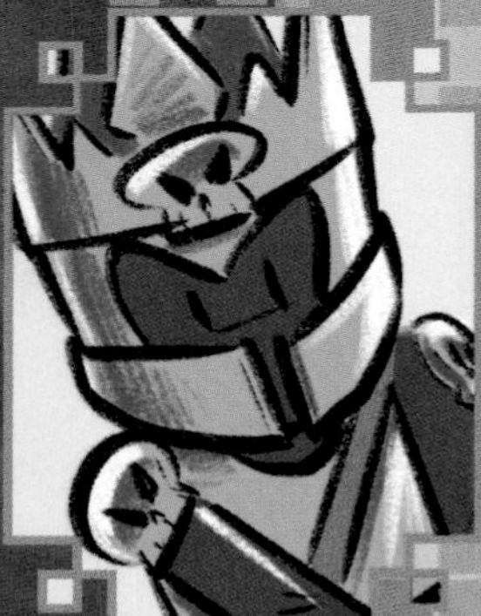

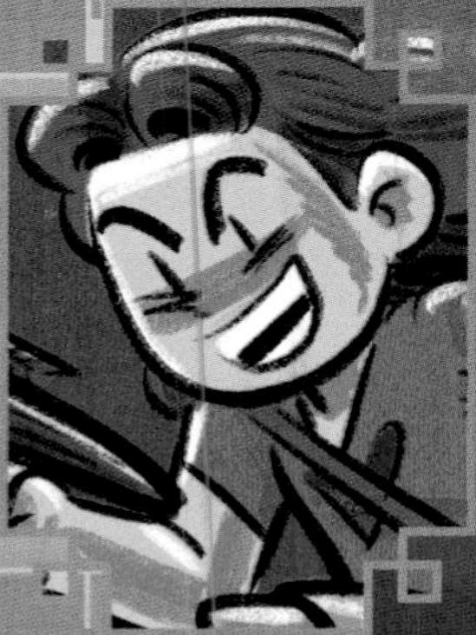

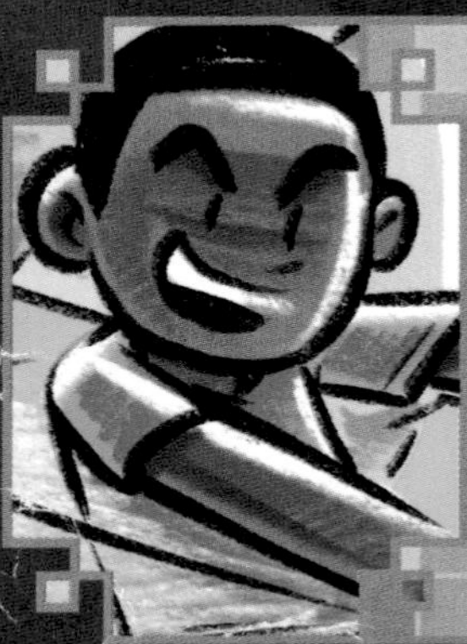

CARTER

Carter is Jen's best friend and her biggest fan, but he doesn't seem to like Pat very much at all. Carter is also not very smart and sometimes carries a pickle that he uses as a sword!

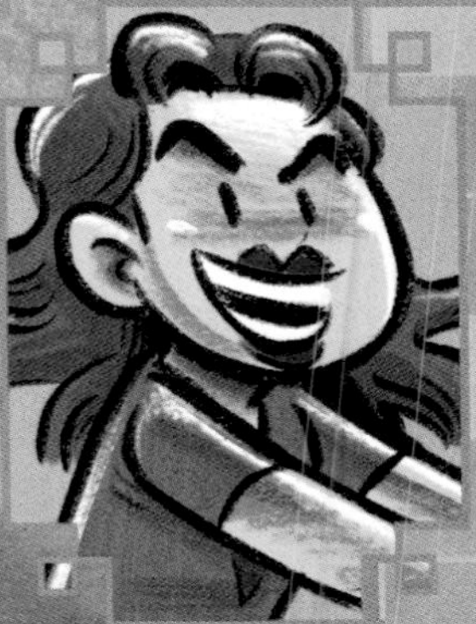

EVIL JEN

Evil Jen's favorite thing is chaos. She lives for wreaking havoc on the world. What makes her truly evil, however, is that she would take someone as sweet as her twin sister, Jen, and enjoy being an evil version of her.

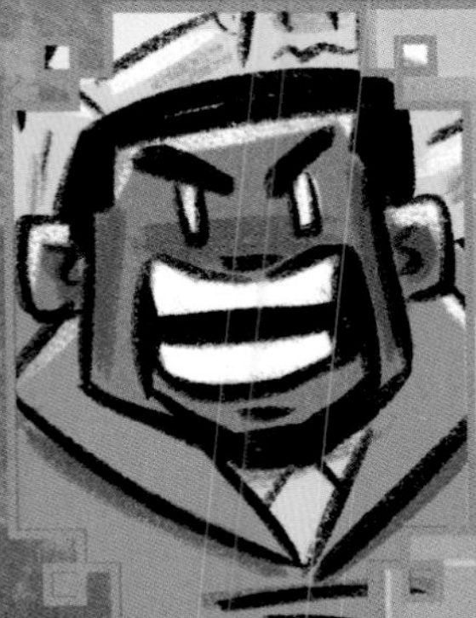

HEROBRINE

Herobrine longs to be the king of all realms. He's as evil as evil gets, and he'll stop at nothing to get what he wants. It has been revealed recently that Herobrine is Jen and Evil Jen's father. But he also has another secret that will change everything for Pat and Jen.

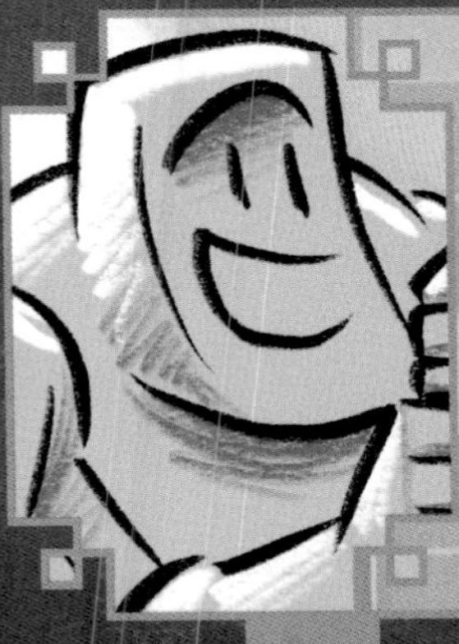

HONEY BOO BOO

Honey Boo Boo is a golem of iron on the outside, but is all softy on the inside!

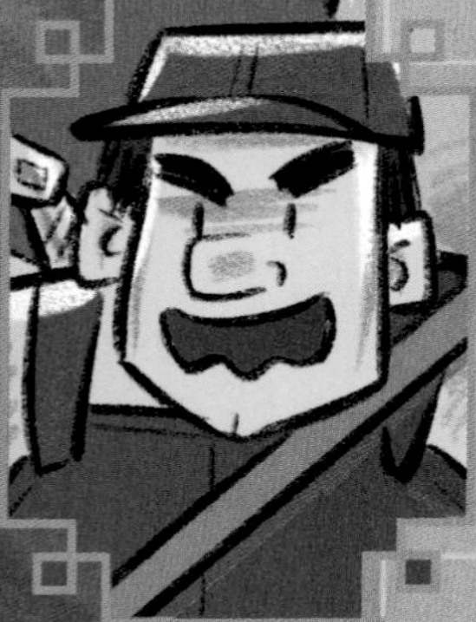

BOB

Bob is the former best friend of Valentine, the archer elf. He has been locked away with Valentine in Herobrine's dungeon, but Herobrine has other plans.

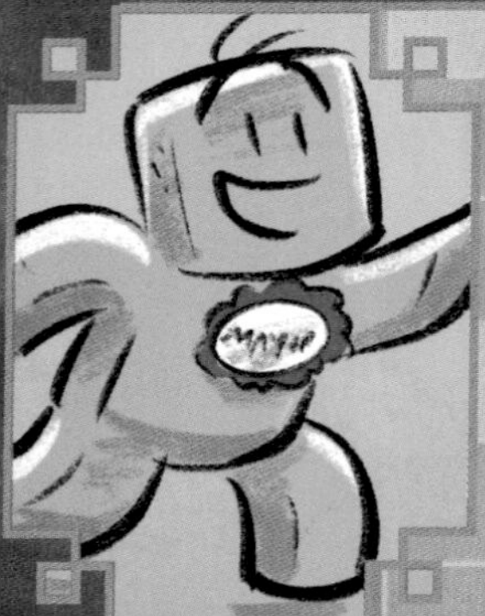

BOMBY

Bomby is somewhat of a pet to Pat and Jen but also Pat's best friend. He's loyal to Pat and always ready to step in for his friend when he's needed.

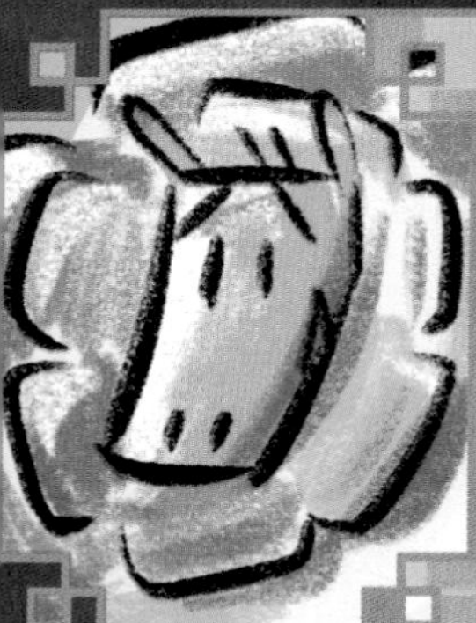

MR. RAINBOW

Mr. Rainbow is a magical sheep whose wool can appear to be any color of the rainbow. He has vowed to bring Jen and Evil Jen to meet their mother, but Mr. Rainbow is keeping a deep, dark secret. . . .

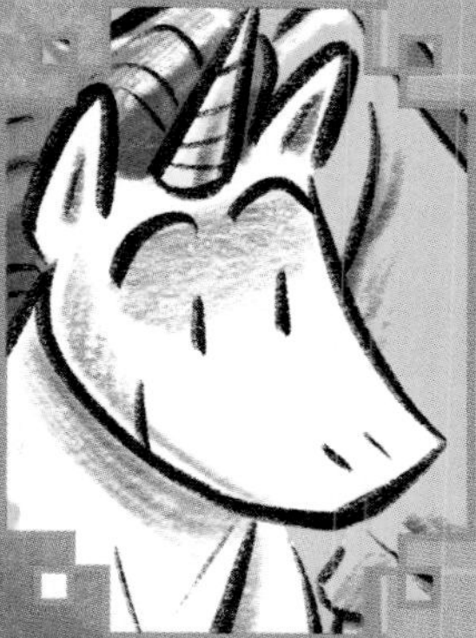

GIZMO

Gizmo is a magical unicorn who leaves a trail of rainbows wherever he goes. Mr. Rainbow will do anything to keep Gizmo safe.

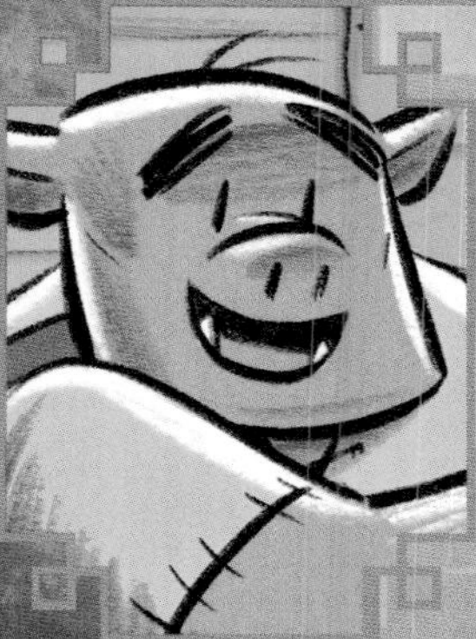

JUMBLISFOIWTHOWEWUWUWASHESUSOSH

This Pigman is Gizmo's cellmate and an expert on healing diseases. To make it easy, let's just call him Jim.

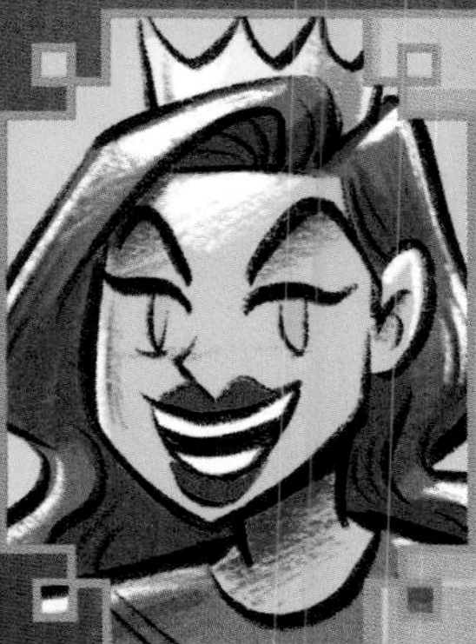

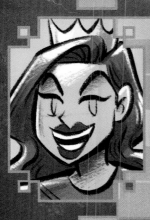

ZOMBIE QUEEN

Jen and Evil Jen's mother is the zombie queen of the Overworld. She holds a grudge against her former partner, Herobrine, and will stop at nothing to get revenge on him!

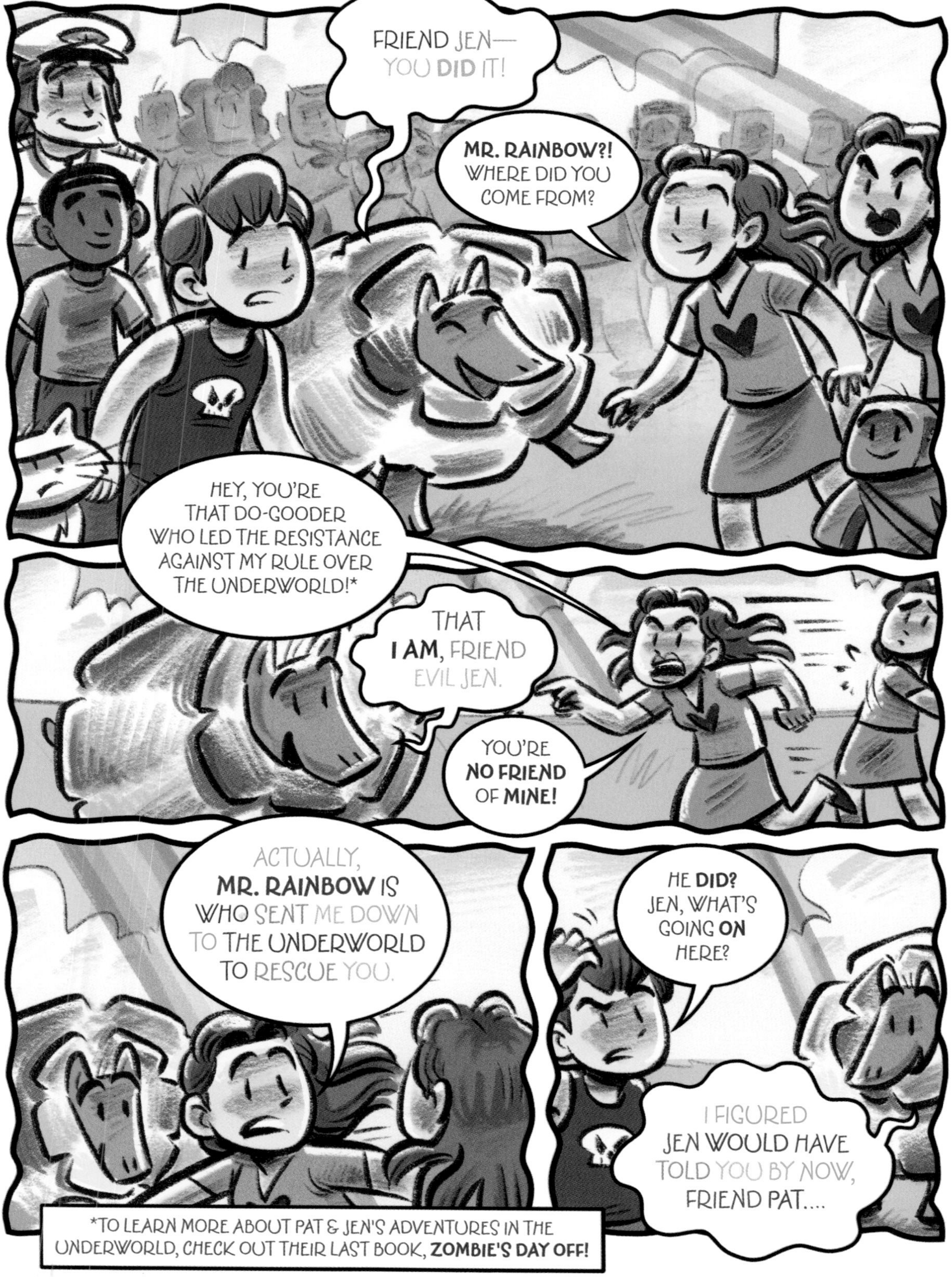
FRIEND JEN— YOU DID IT!
MR. RAINBOW?! WHERE DID YOU COME FROM?
HEY, YOU'RE THAT DO-GOODER WHO LED THE RESISTANCE AGAINST MY RULE OVER THE UNDERWORLD!*
THAT I AM, FRIEND EVIL JEN.
YOU'RE NO FRIEND OF MINE!
ACTUALLY, MR. RAINBOW IS WHO SENT ME DOWN TO THE UNDERWORLD TO RESCUE YOU.
HE DID? JEN, WHAT'S GOING ON HERE?
I FIGURED JEN WOULD HAVE TOLD YOU BY NOW, FRIEND PAT....

*TO LEARN MORE ABOUT PAT & JEN'S ADVENTURES IN THE UNDERWORLD, CHECK OUT THEIR LAST BOOK, **ZOMBIE'S DAY OFF!**

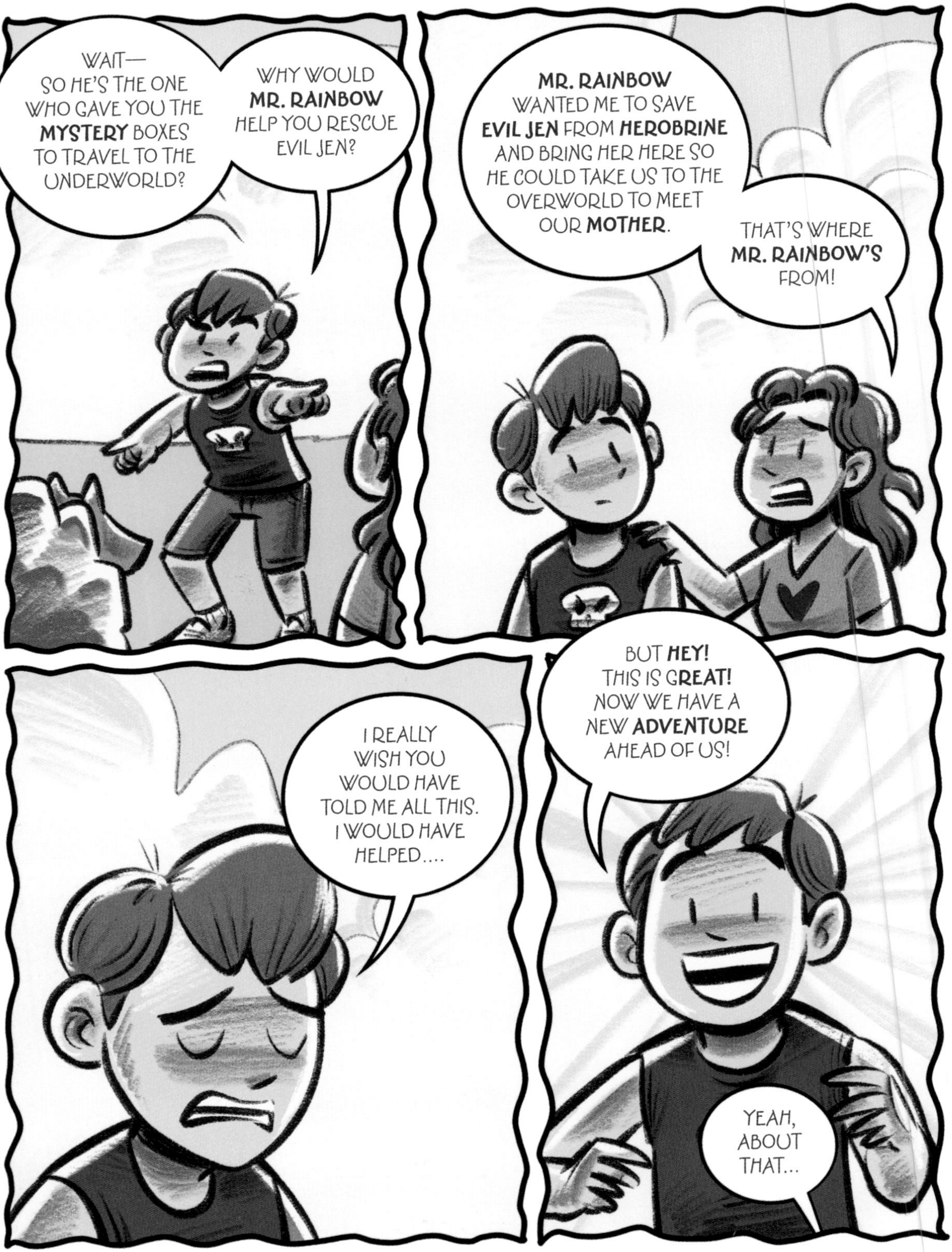
WAIT—
SO HE'S THE ONE WHO GAVE YOU THE MYSTERY BOXES TO TRAVEL TO THE UNDERWORLD?
WHY WOULD MR. RAINBOW HELP YOU RESCUE EVIL JEN?
MR. RAINBOW WANTED ME TO SAVE EVIL JEN FROM HEROBRINE AND BRING HER HERE SO HE COULD TAKE US TO THE OVERWORLD TO MEET OUR MOTHER.
THAT'S WHERE MR. RAINBOW'S FROM!
I REALLY WISH YOU WOULD HAVE TOLD ME ALL THIS. I WOULD HAVE HELPED....
BUT HEY! THIS IS GREAT! NOW WE HAVE A NEW ADVENTURE AHEAD OF US!
YEAH, ABOUT THAT...

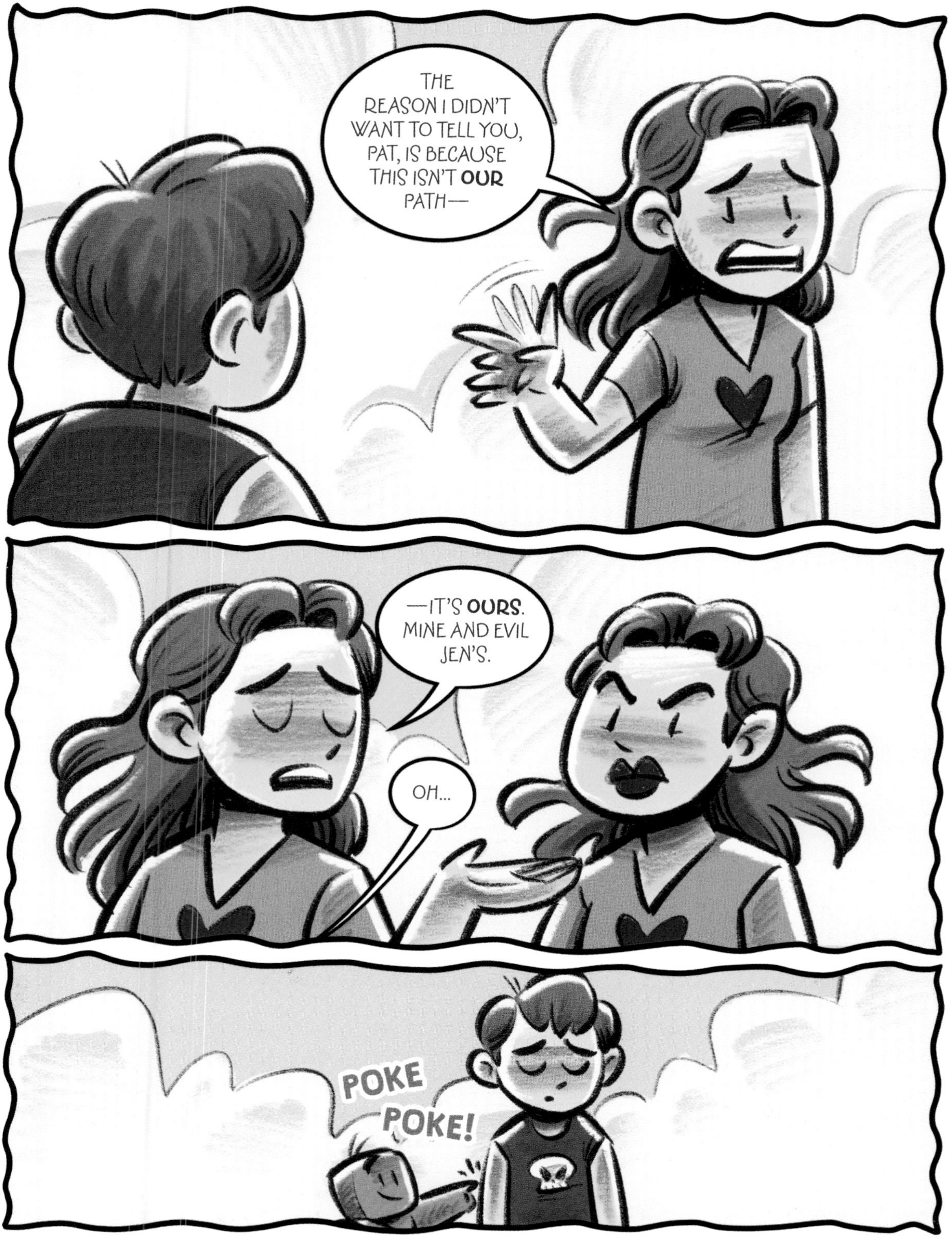
THE REASON I DIDN'T WANT TO TELL YOU, PAT, IS BECAUSE THIS ISN'T **OUR** PATH—
—IT'S **OURS**. MINE AND EVIL JEN'S.
OH...
POKE
POKE!

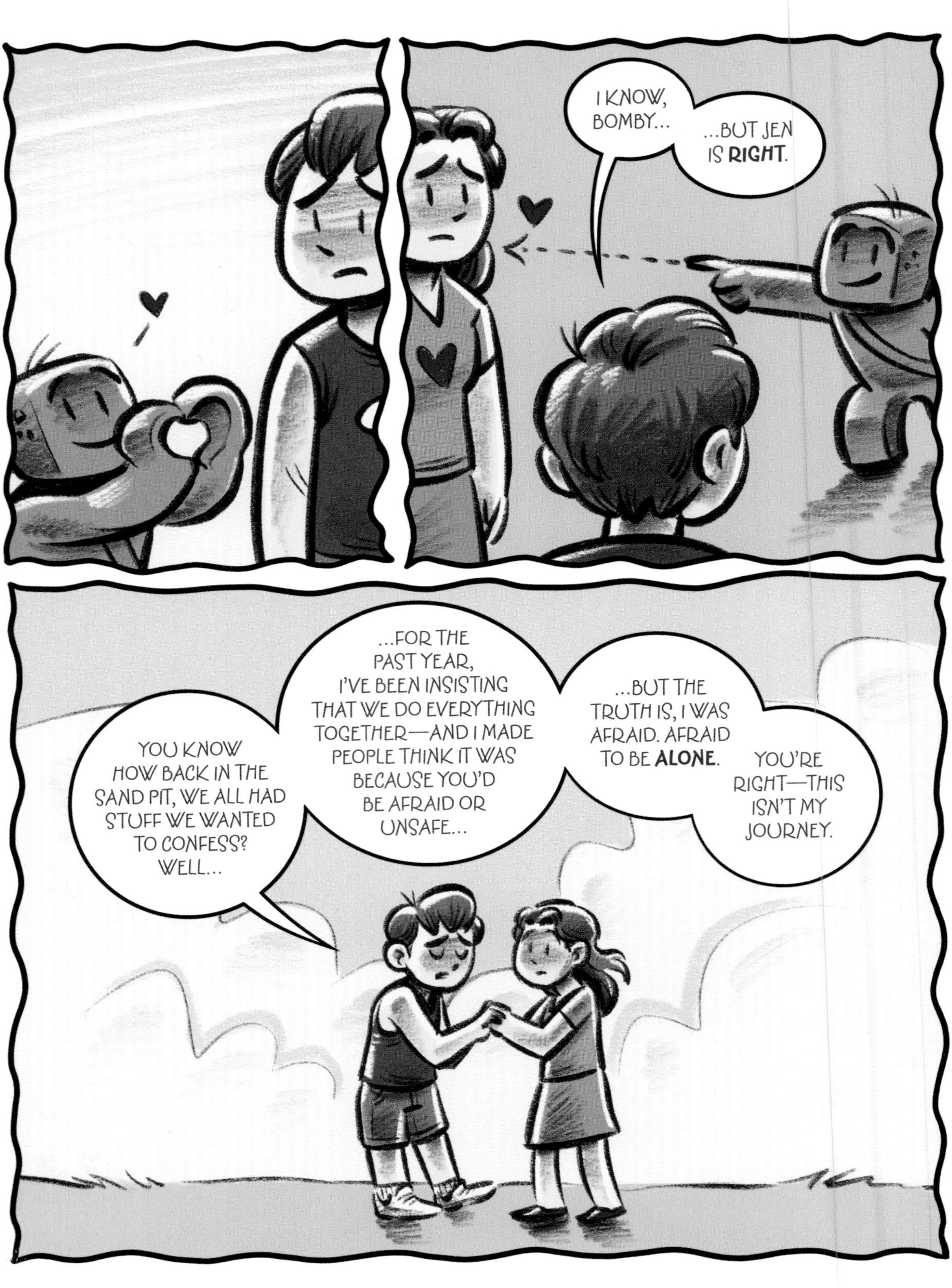
I KNOW, BOMBY...
...BUT JEN IS **RIGHT**.
YOU KNOW HOW BACK IN THE SAND PIT, WE ALL HAD STUFF WE WANTED TO CONFESS? WELL...
...FOR THE PAST YEAR, I'VE BEEN INSISTING THAT WE DO EVERYTHING TOGETHER—AND I MADE PEOPLE THINK IT WAS BECAUSE YOU'D BE AFRAID OR UNSAFE...
...BUT THE TRUTH IS, I WAS AFRAID. AFRAID TO BE **ALONE**.
YOU'RE RIGHT—THIS ISN'T MY JOURNEY.

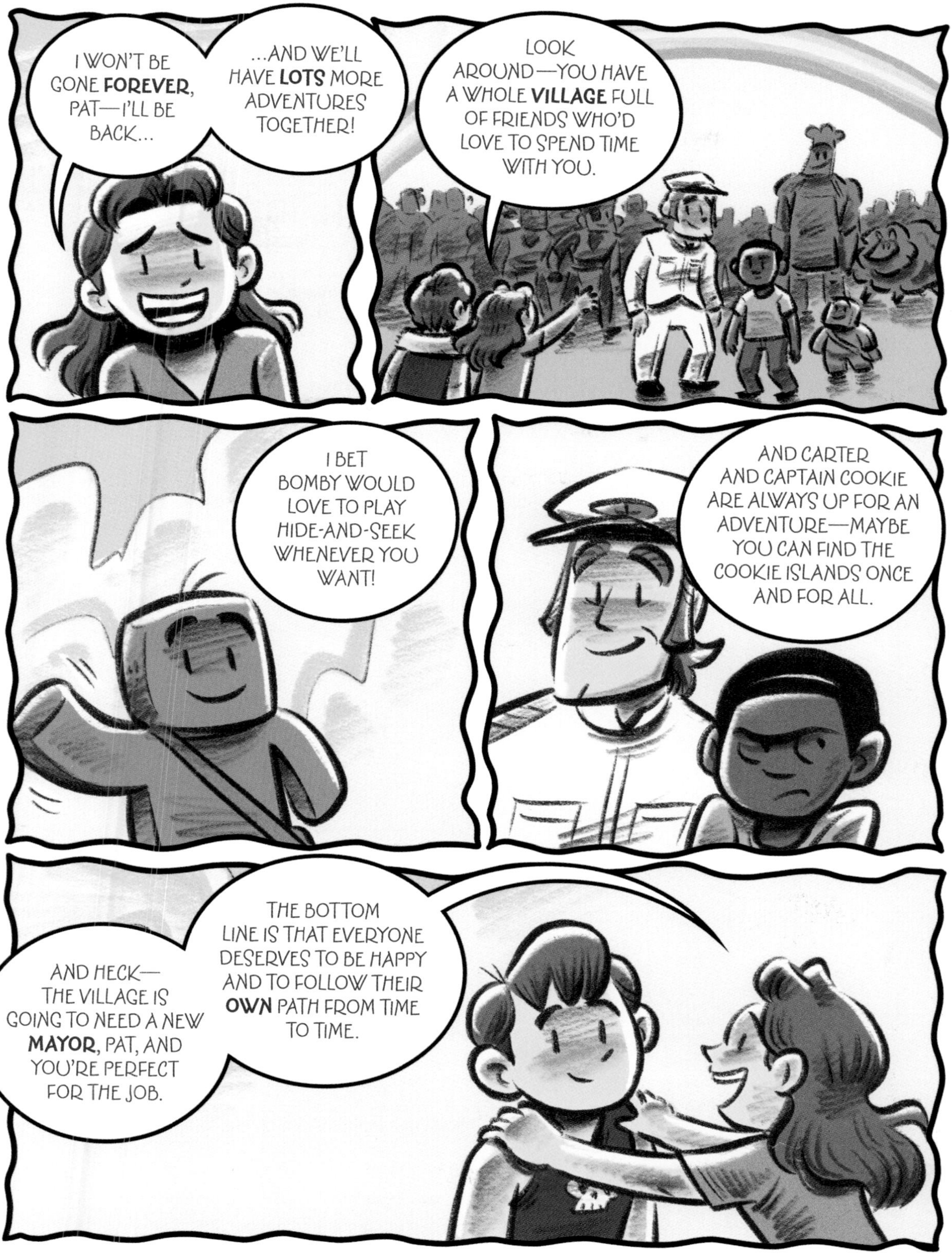
I WON'T BE GONE **FOREVER**, PAT—I'LL BE BACK...
...AND WE'LL HAVE **LOTS** MORE ADVENTURES TOGETHER!
LOOK AROUND—YOU HAVE A WHOLE **VILLAGE** FULL OF FRIENDS WHO'D LOVE TO SPEND TIME WITH YOU.
I BET BOMBY WOULD LOVE TO PLAY HIDE-AND-SEEK WHENEVER YOU WANT!
AND CARTER AND CAPTAIN COOKIE ARE ALWAYS UP FOR AN ADVENTURE—MAYBE YOU CAN FIND THE COOKIE ISLANDS ONCE AND FOR ALL.
THE BOTTOM LINE IS THAT EVERYONE DESERVES TO BE HAPPY AND TO FOLLOW THEIR **OWN** PATH FROM TIME TO TIME.
AND HECK—THE VILLAGE IS GOING TO NEED A NEW **MAYOR**, PAT, AND YOU'RE PERFECT FOR THE JOB.

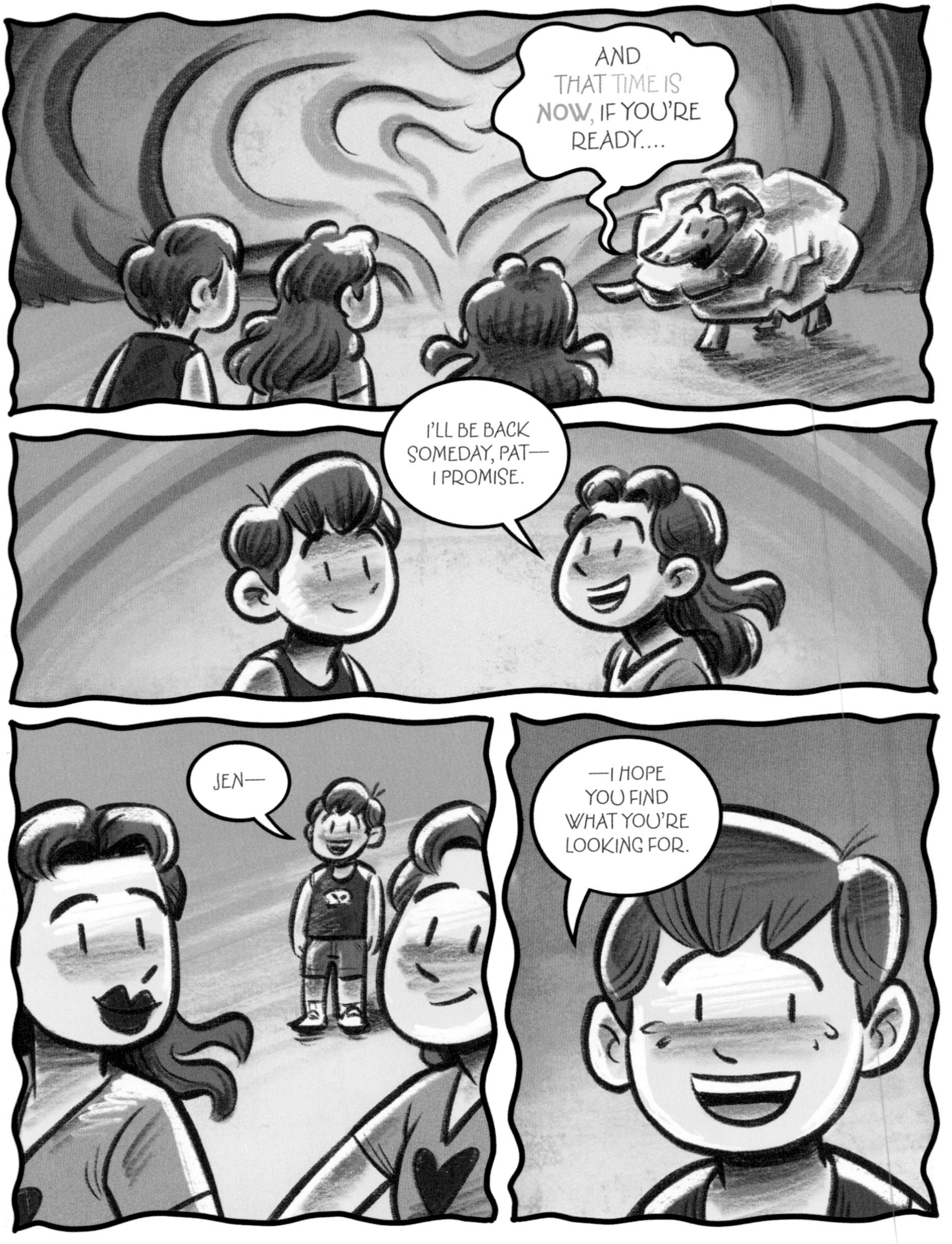
AND THAT TIME IS NOW, IF YOU'RE READY....
I'LL BE BACK SOMEDAY, PAT— I PROMISE.
JEN—
—I HOPE YOU FIND WHAT YOU'RE LOOKING FOR.

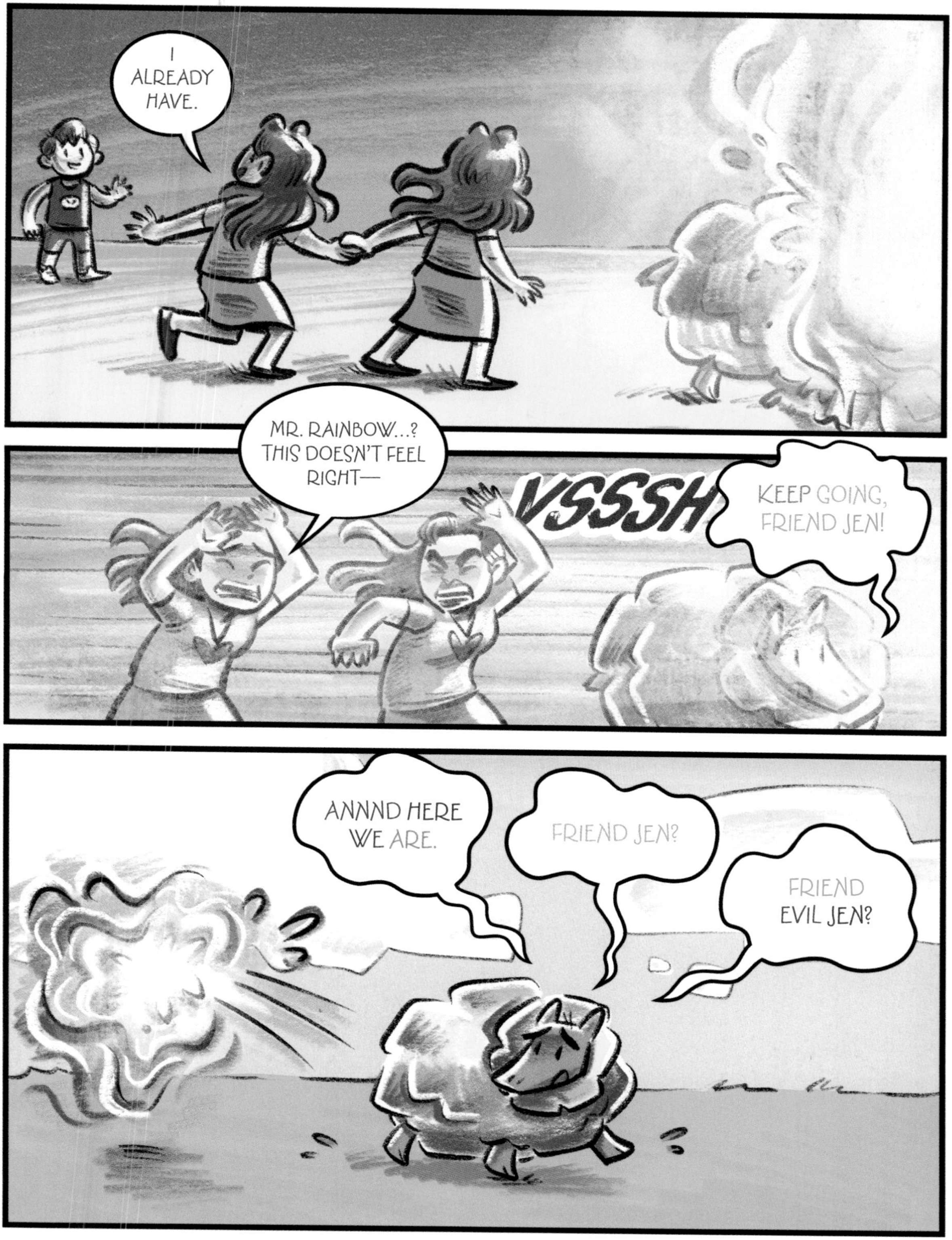
I ALREADY HAVE.
MR. RAINBOW...? THIS DOESN'T FEEL RIGHT—
VSSSH
KEEP GOING, FRIEND JEN!
ANNND HERE WE ARE.
FRIEND JEN?
FRIEND EVIL JEN?

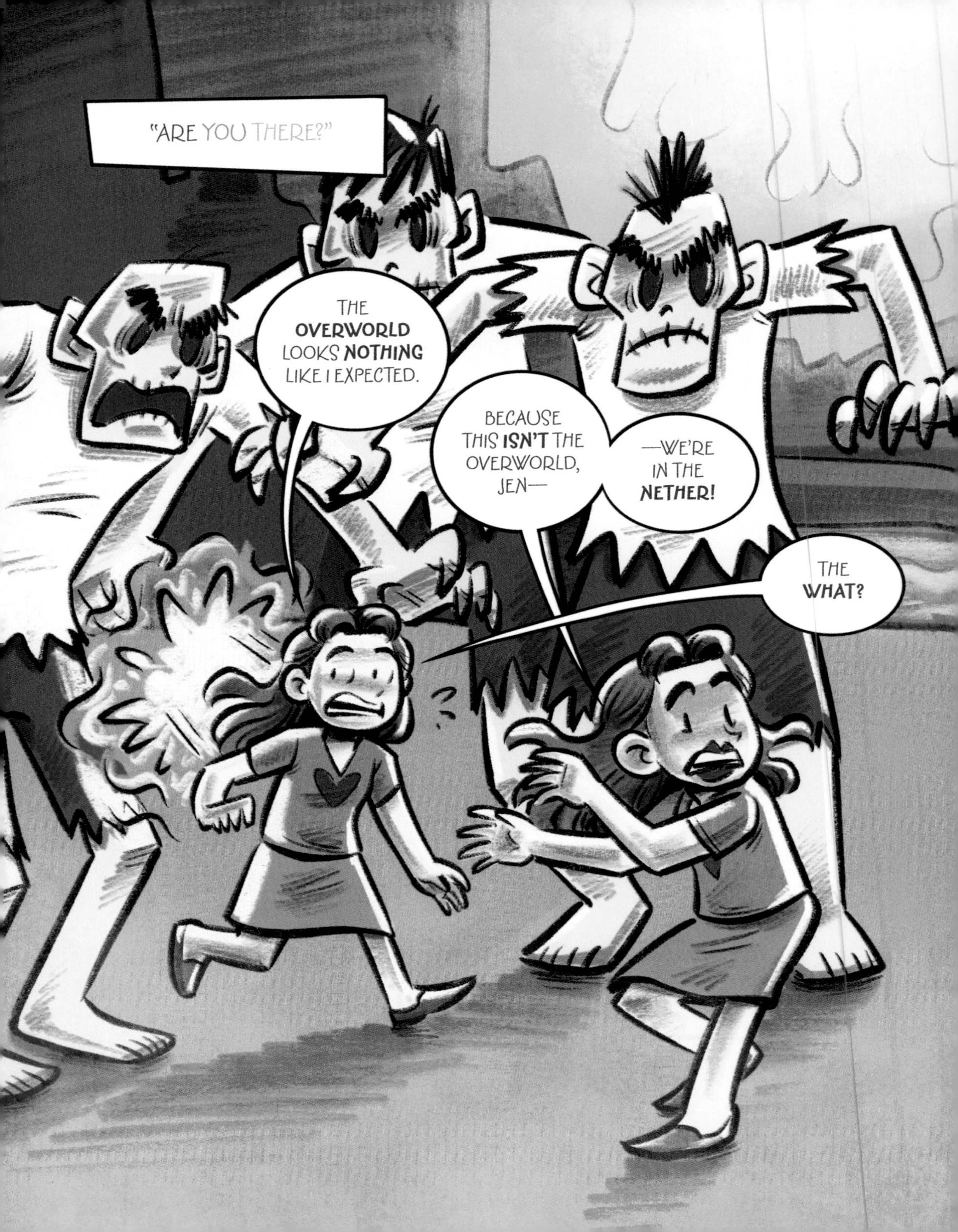
"ARE YOU THERE?"
THE OVERWORLD LOOKS NOTHING LIKE I EXPECTED.
BECAUSE THIS ISN'T THE OVERWORLD, JEN—
—WE'RE IN THE NETHER!
THE WHAT?

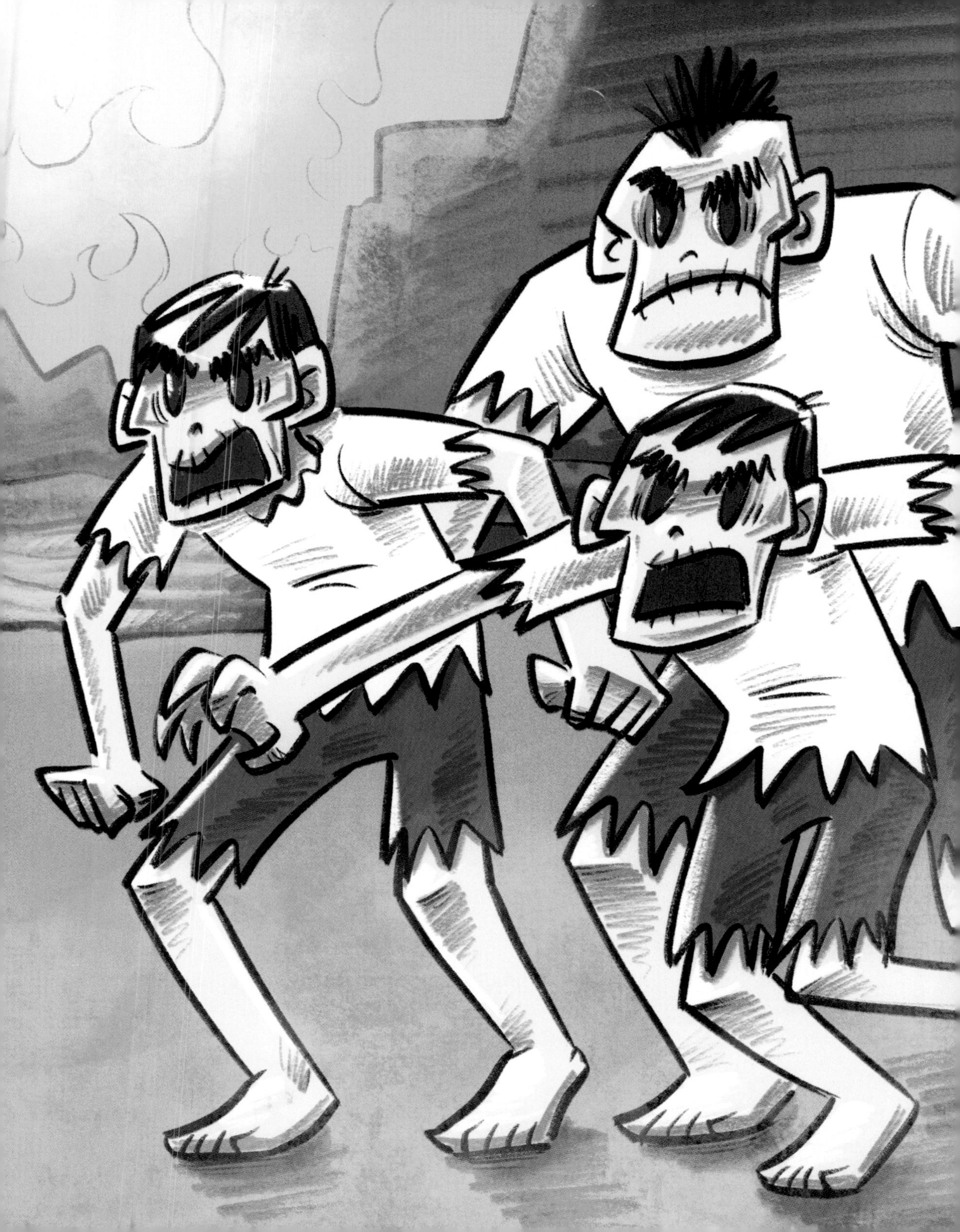

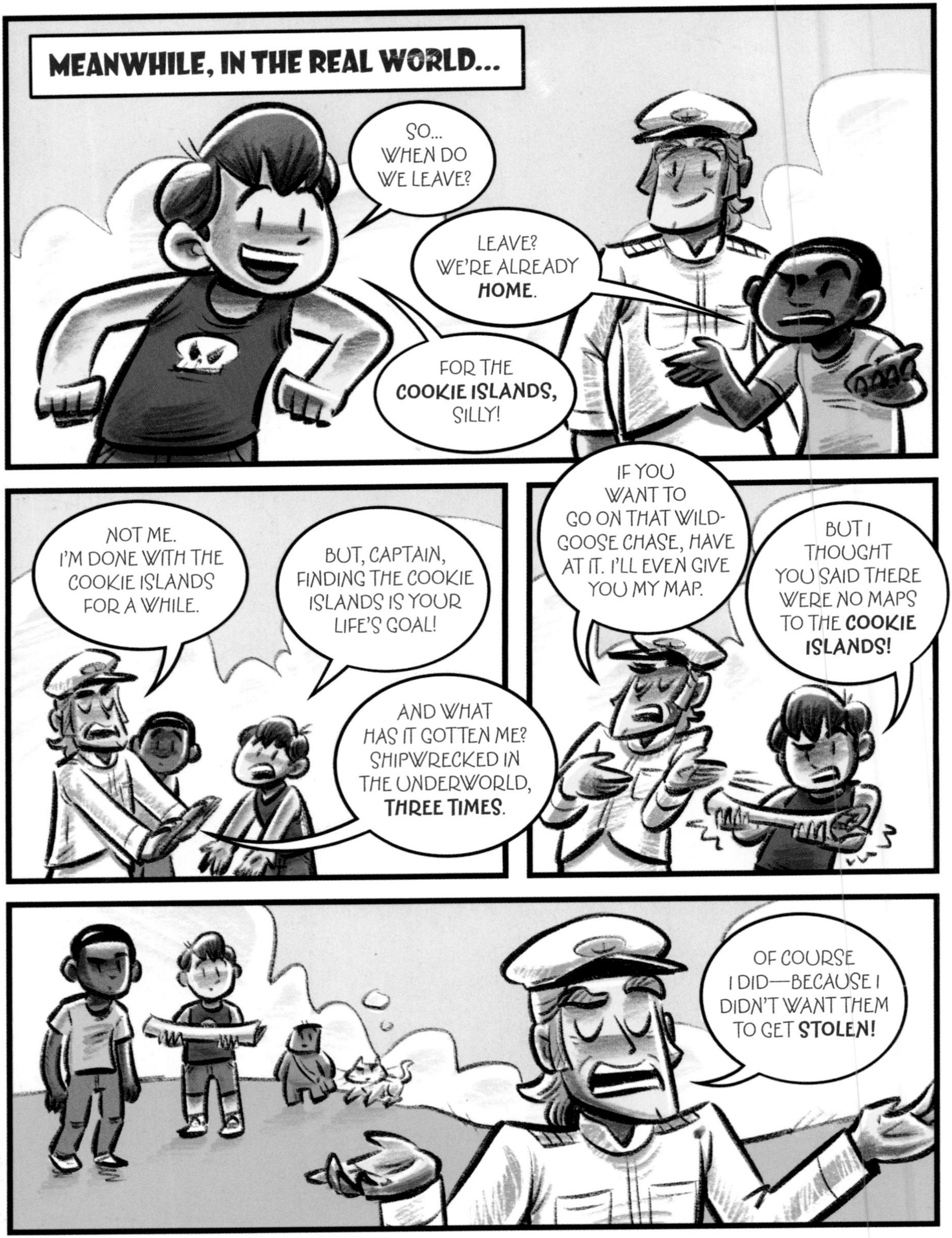
MEANWHILE, IN THE REAL WORLD...
SO... WHEN DO WE LEAVE?
FOR THE COOKIE ISLANDS, SILLY!
LEAVE? WE'RE ALREADY HOME.
NOT ME. I'M DONE WITH THE COOKIE ISLANDS FOR A WHILE.
BUT, CAPTAIN, FINDING THE COOKIE ISLANDS IS YOUR LIFE'S GOAL!
AND WHAT HAS IT GOTTEN ME? SHIPWRECKED IN THE UNDERWORLD, THREE TIMES.
IF YOU WANT TO GO ON THAT WILD-GOOSE CHASE, HAVE AT IT. I'LL EVEN GIVE YOU MY MAP.
BUT I THOUGHT YOU SAID THERE WERE NO MAPS TO THE COOKIE ISLANDS!
OF COURSE I DID—BECAUSE I DIDN'T WANT THEM TO GET STOLEN!

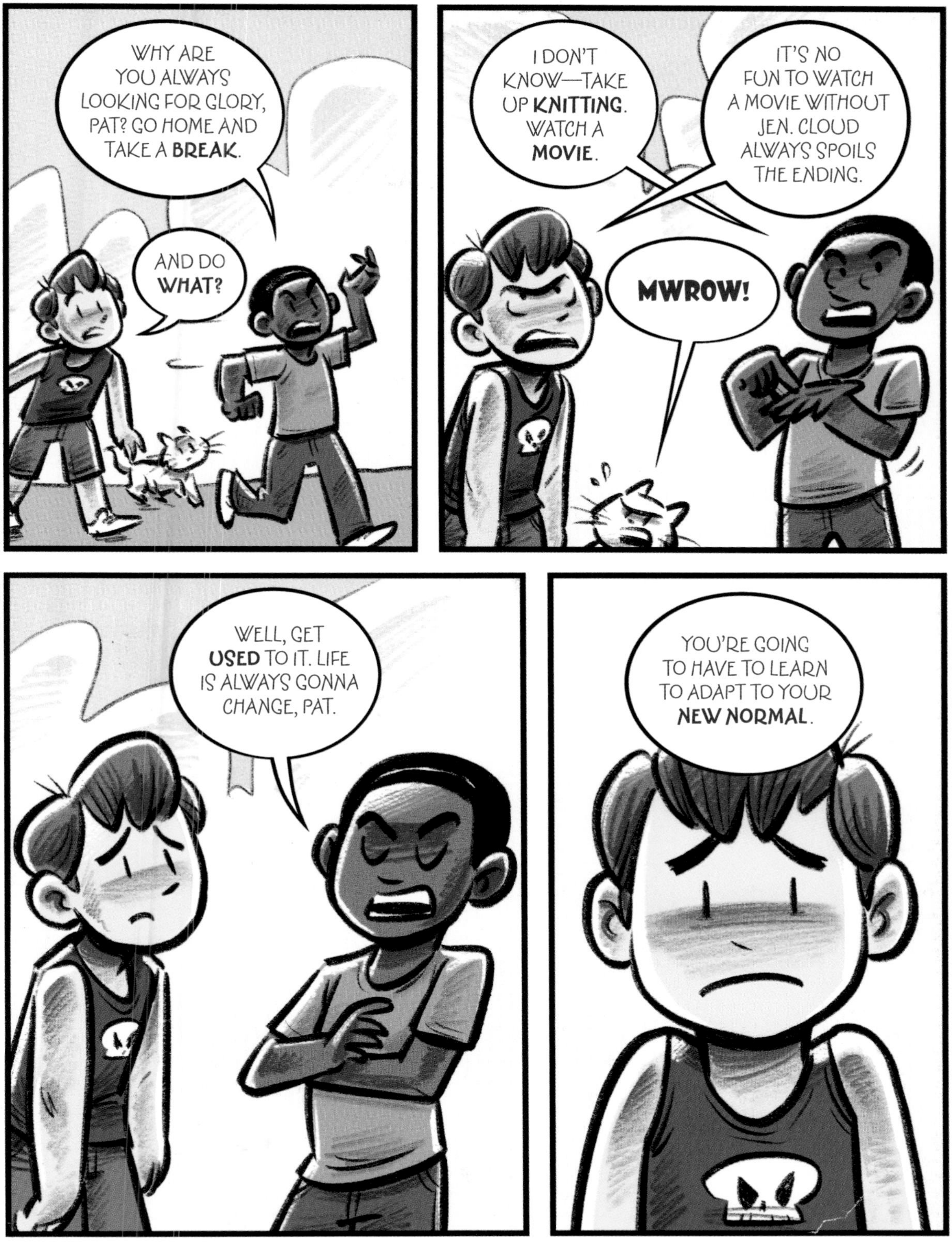
WHY ARE YOU ALWAYS LOOKING FOR GLORY, PAT? GO HOME AND TAKE A BREAK.
AND DO WHAT?
I DON'T KNOW—TAKE UP KNITTING. WATCH A MOVIE.
IT'S NO FUN TO WATCH A MOVIE WITHOUT JEN. CLOUD ALWAYS SPOILS THE ENDING.
MWROW!
WELL, GET USED TO IT. LIFE IS ALWAYS GONNA CHANGE, PAT.
YOU'RE GOING TO HAVE TO LEARN TO ADAPT TO YOUR NEW NORMAL.

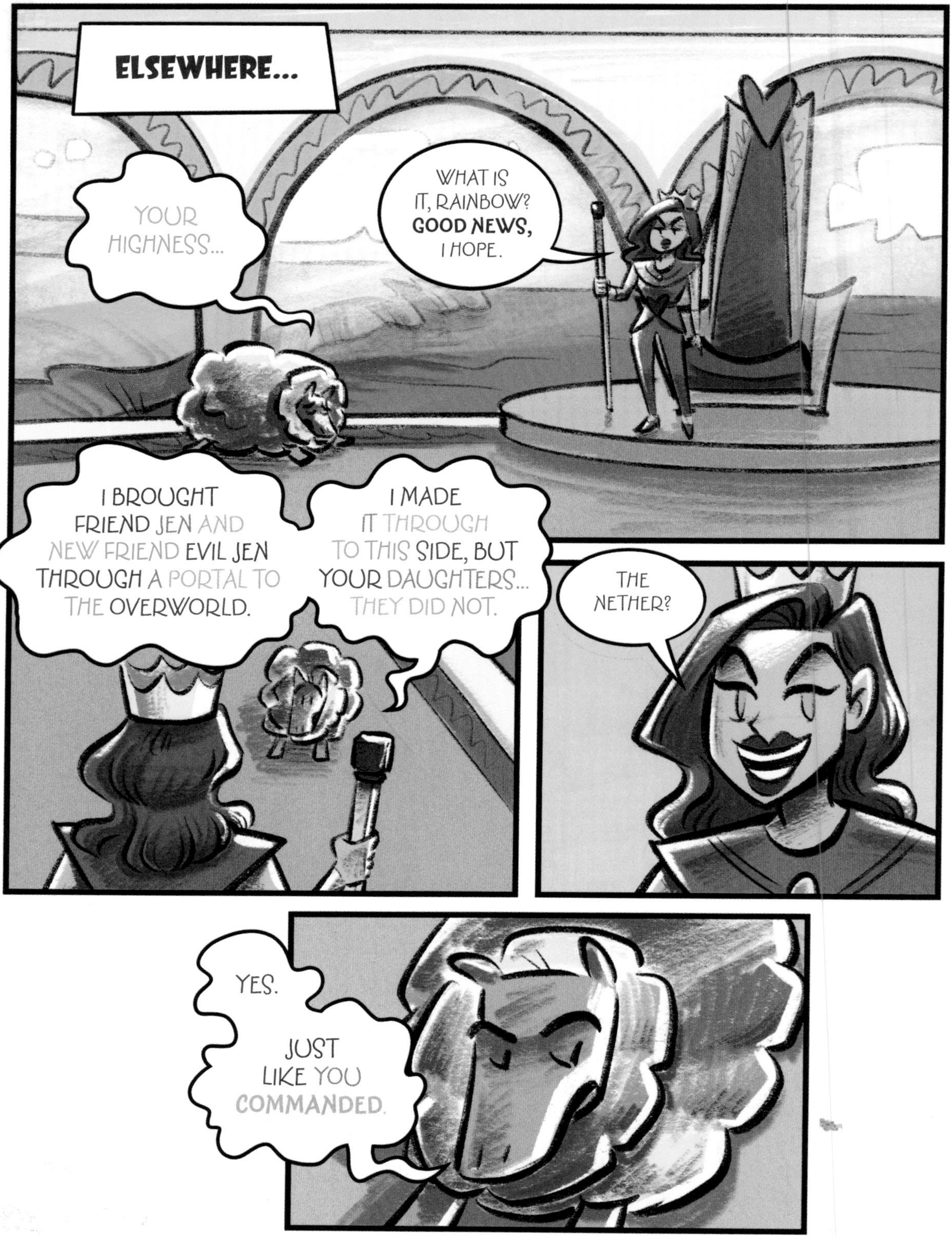
ELSEWHERE...
YOUR HIGHNESS...
WHAT IS IT, RAINBOW? GOOD NEWS, I HOPE.
I BROUGHT FRIEND JEN AND NEW FRIEND EVIL JEN THROUGH A PORTAL TO THE OVERWORLD.
I MADE IT THROUGH TO THIS SIDE, BUT YOUR DAUGHTERS... THEY DID NOT.
THE NETHER?
YES.
JUST LIKE YOU COMMANDED.

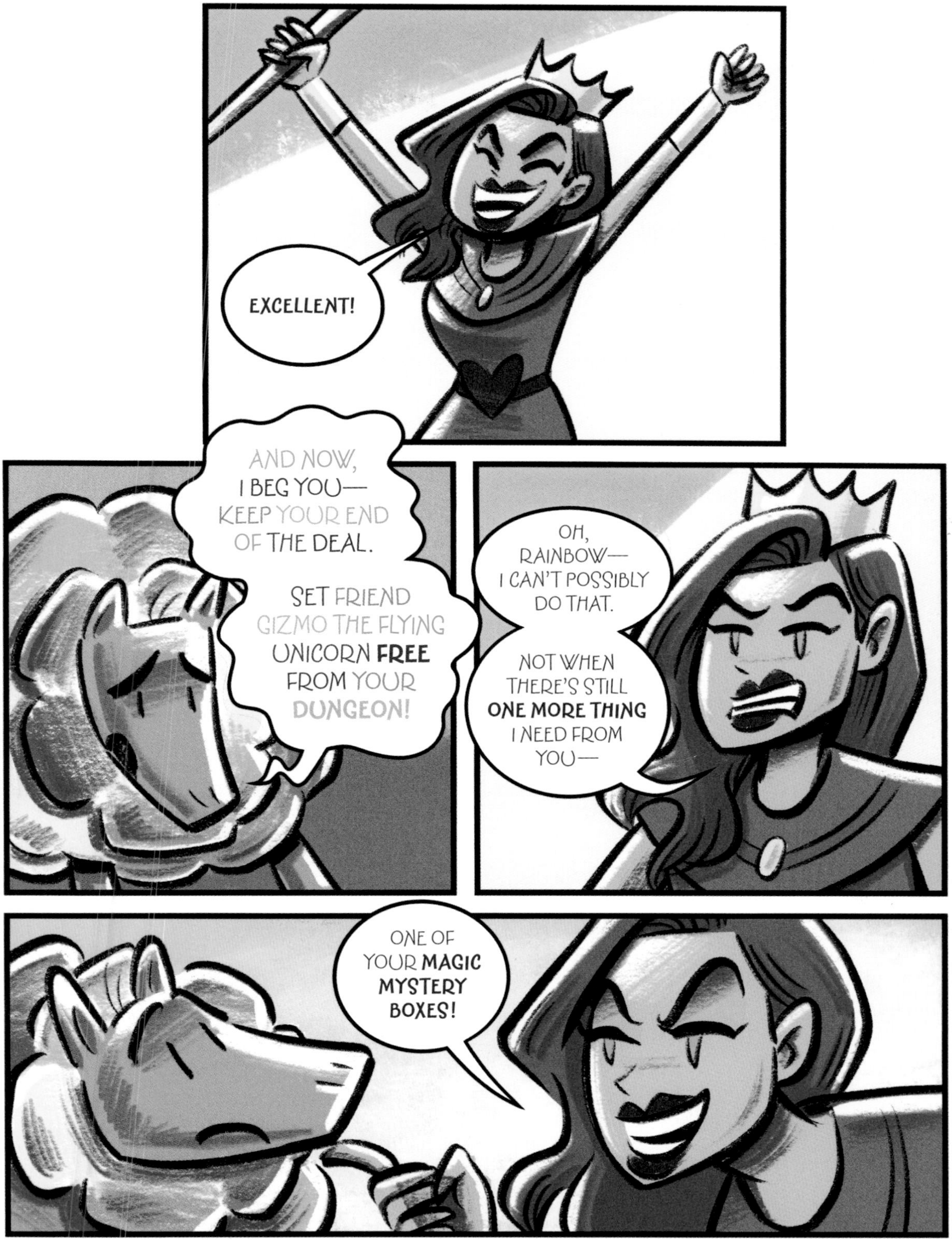
EXCELLENT!
AND NOW, I BEG YOU— KEEP YOUR END OF THE DEAL.
SET FRIEND GIZMO THE FLYING UNICORN FREE FROM YOUR DUNGEON!
OH, RAINBOW— I CAN'T POSSIBLY DO THAT.
NOT WHEN THERE'S STILL ONE MORE THING I NEED FROM YOU—
ONE OF YOUR MAGIC MYSTERY BOXES!

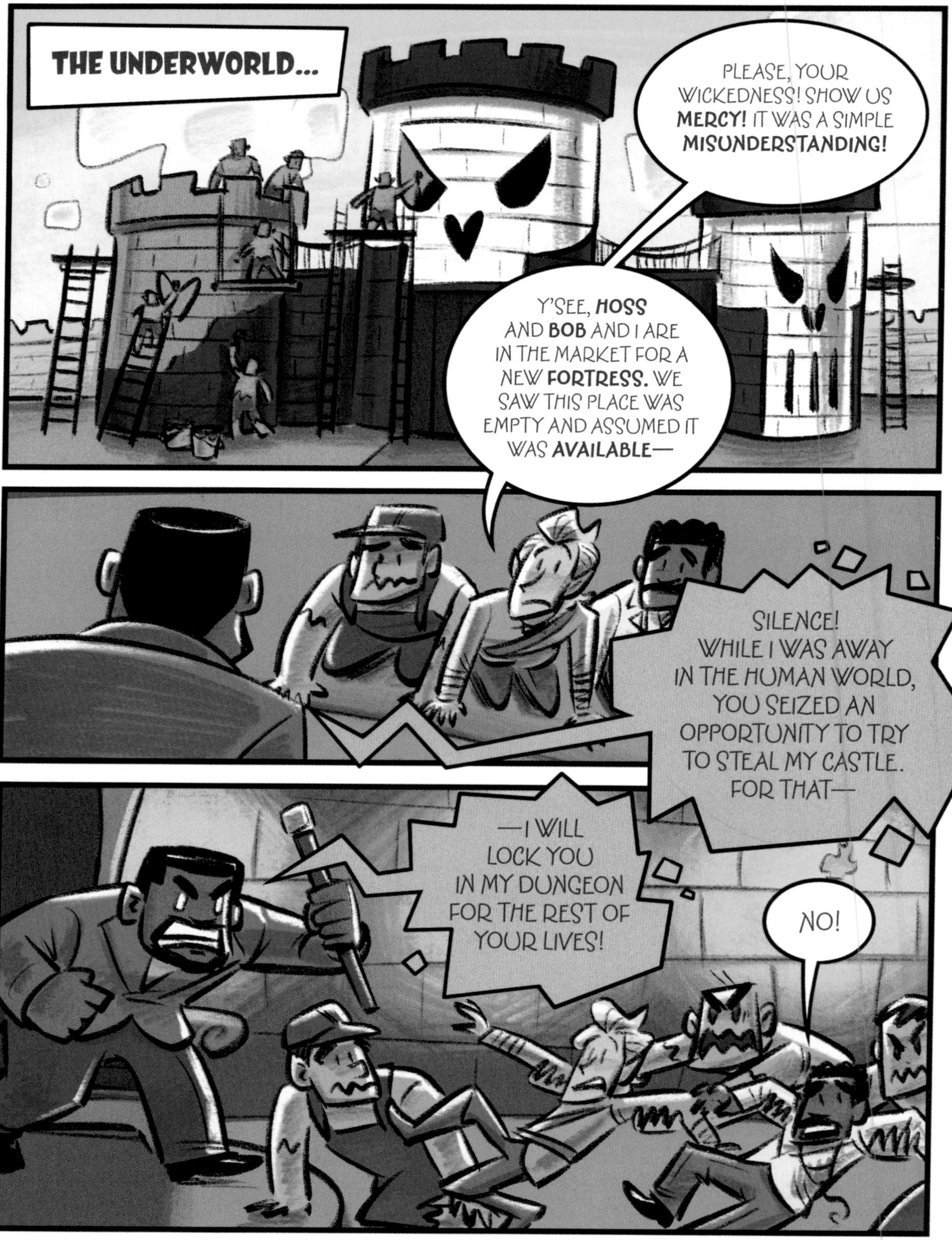
THE UNDERWORLD...
PLEASE, YOUR WICKEDNESS! SHOW US MERCY! IT WAS A SIMPLE MISUNDERSTANDING!
Y'SEE, HOSS AND BOB AND I ARE IN THE MARKET FOR A NEW FORTRESS. WE SAW THIS PLACE WAS EMPTY AND ASSUMED IT WAS AVAILABLE—
SILENCE! WHILE I WAS AWAY IN THE HUMAN WORLD, YOU SEIZED AN OPPORTUNITY TO TRY TO STEAL MY CASTLE. FOR THAT—
—I WILL LOCK YOU IN MY DUNGEON FOR THE REST OF YOUR LIVES!
NO!

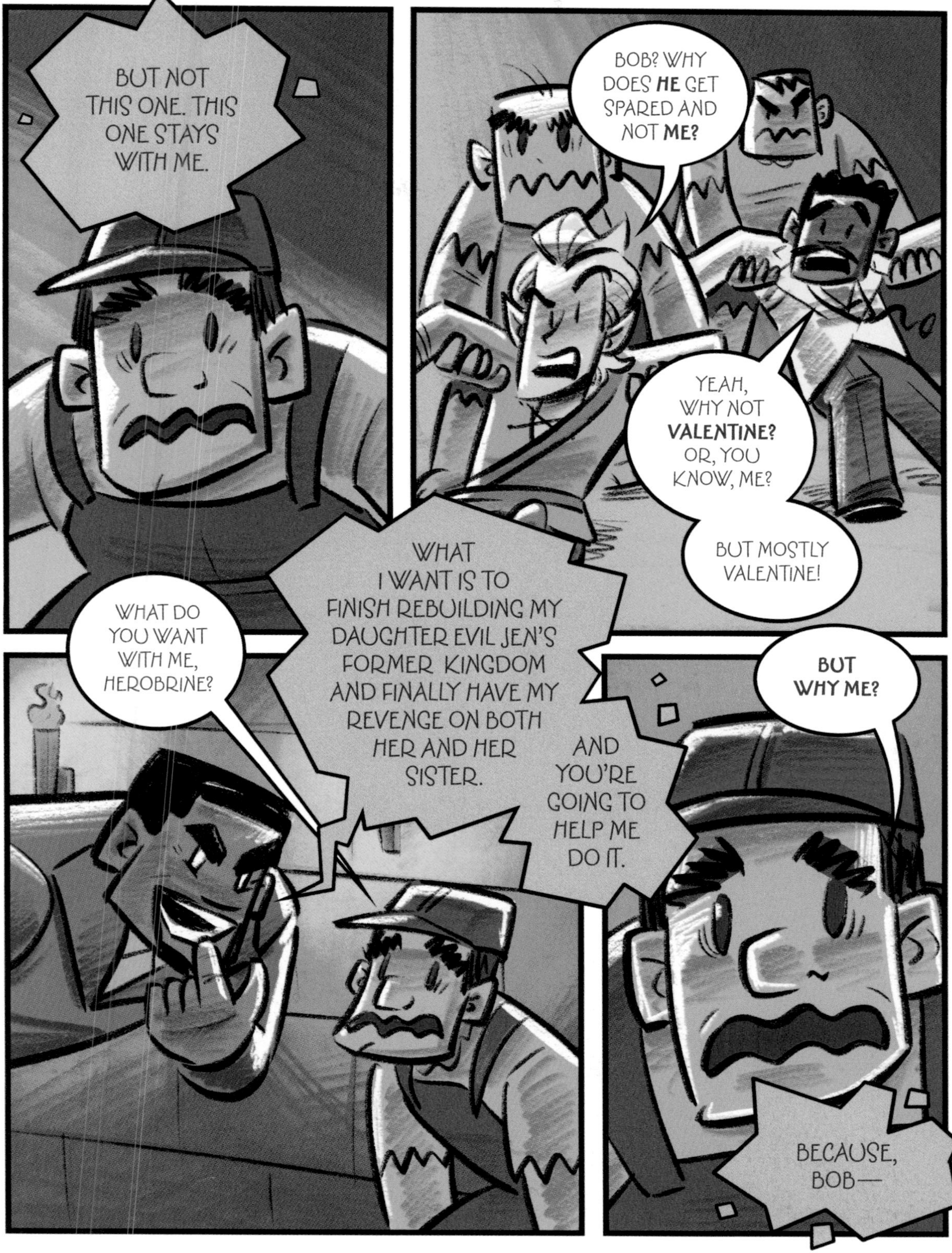
BUT NOT THIS ONE. THIS ONE STAYS WITH ME.
BOB? WHY DOES **HE** GET SPARED AND NOT **ME?**
YEAH, WHY NOT **VALENTINE?** OR, YOU KNOW, ME?
BUT MOSTLY VALENTINE!
WHAT DO YOU WANT WITH ME, HEROBRINE?
WHAT I WANT IS TO FINISH REBUILDING MY DAUGHTER EVIL JEN'S FORMER KINGDOM AND FINALLY HAVE MY REVENGE ON BOTH HER AND HER SISTER.
AND YOU'RE GOING TO HELP ME DO IT.
BUT WHY ME?
BECAUSE, BOB—

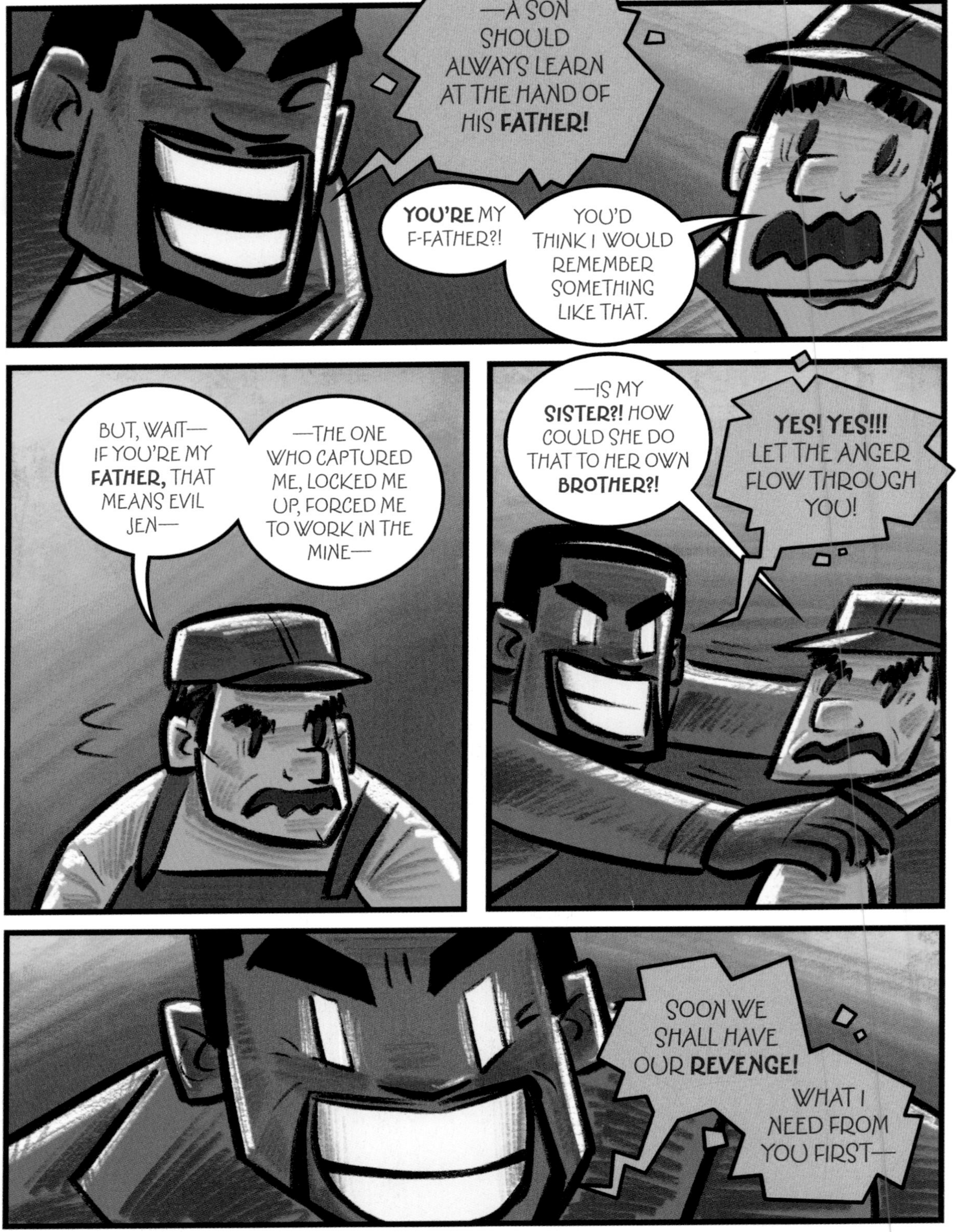
—A SON SHOULD ALWAYS LEARN AT THE HAND OF HIS **FATHER!**
YOU'RE MY F-FATHER?!
YOU'D THINK I WOULD REMEMBER SOMETHING LIKE THAT.
BUT, WAIT— IF YOU'RE MY **FATHER,** THAT MEANS EVIL JEN—
—THE ONE WHO CAPTURED ME, LOCKED ME UP, FORCED ME TO WORK IN THE MINE—
—IS MY **SISTER?!** HOW COULD SHE DO THAT TO HER OWN **BROTHER?!**
YES! YES!!! LET THE ANGER FLOW THROUGH YOU!
SOON WE SHALL HAVE OUR **REVENGE!**
WHAT I NEED FROM YOU FIRST—

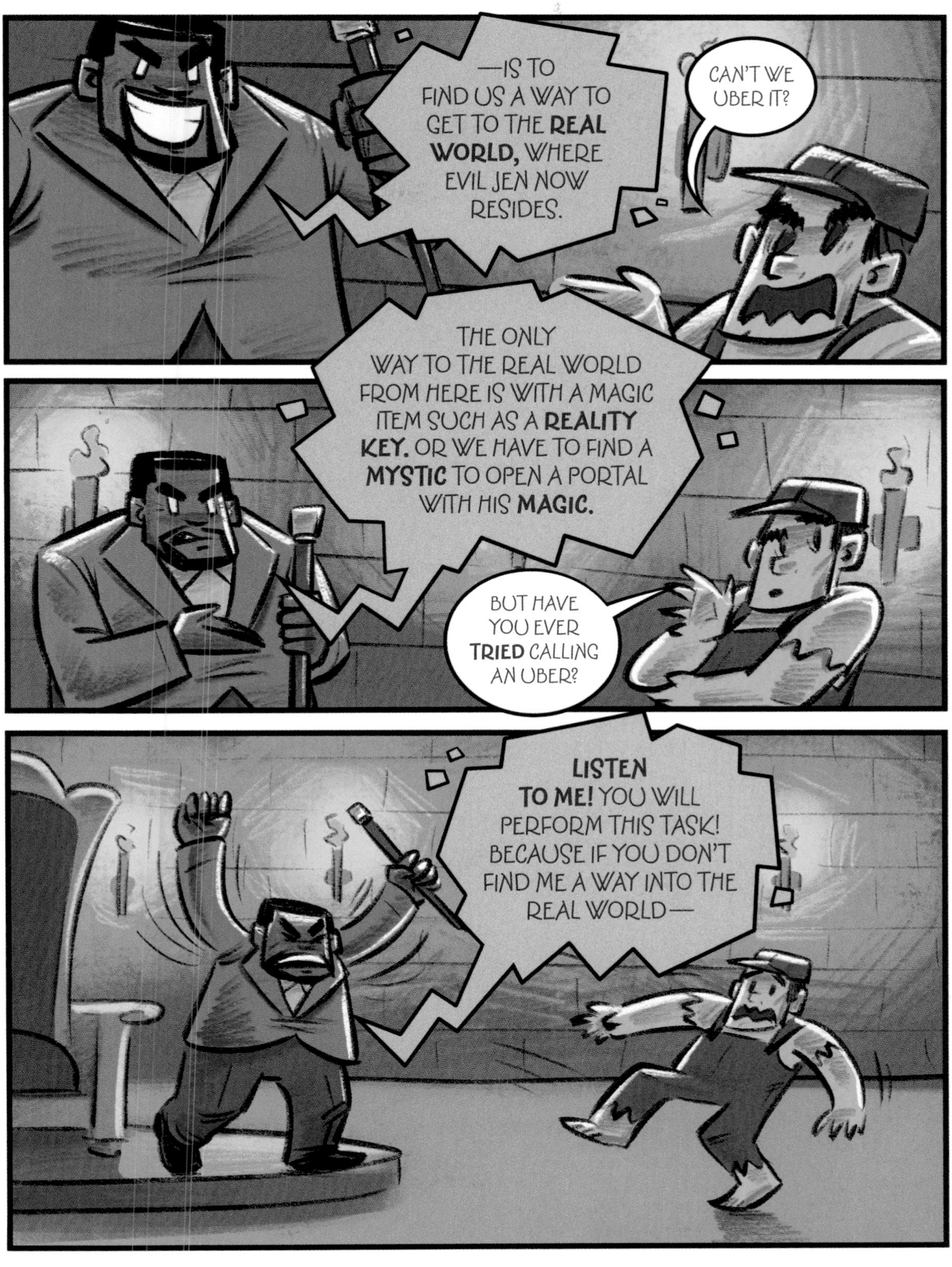
—IS TO FIND US A WAY TO GET TO THE **REAL WORLD,** WHERE EVIL JEN NOW RESIDES.
CAN'T WE UBER IT?
THE ONLY WAY TO THE REAL WORLD FROM HERE IS WITH A MAGIC ITEM SUCH AS A **REALITY KEY.** OR WE HAVE TO FIND A **MYSTIC** TO OPEN A PORTAL WITH HIS **MAGIC.**
BUT HAVE YOU EVER **TRIED** CALLING AN UBER?
LISTEN TO ME! YOU WILL PERFORM THIS TASK! BECAUSE IF YOU DON'T FIND ME A WAY INTO THE REAL WORLD—

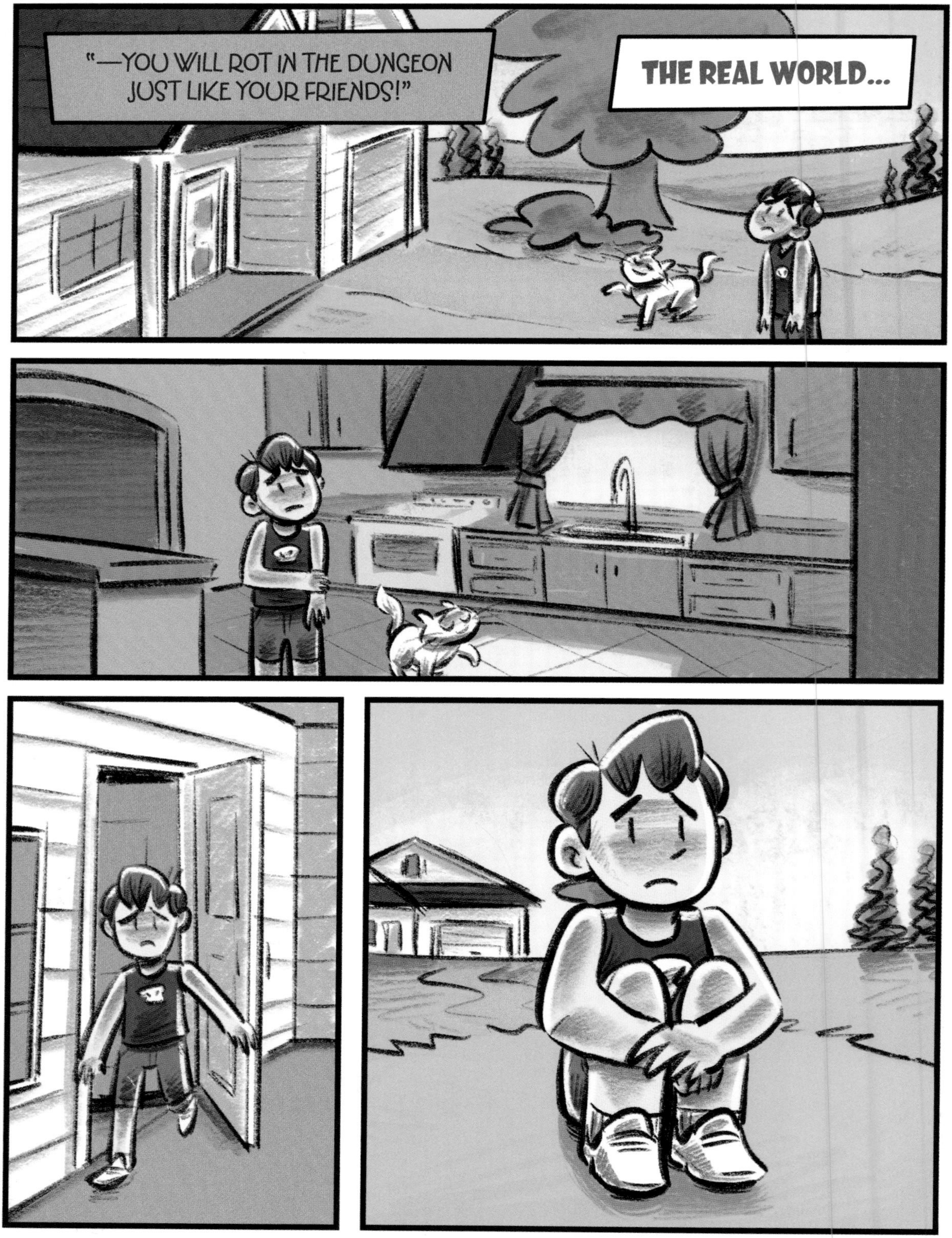
"—YOU WILL ROT IN THE DUNGEON JUST LIKE YOUR FRIENDS!"
THE REAL WORLD...

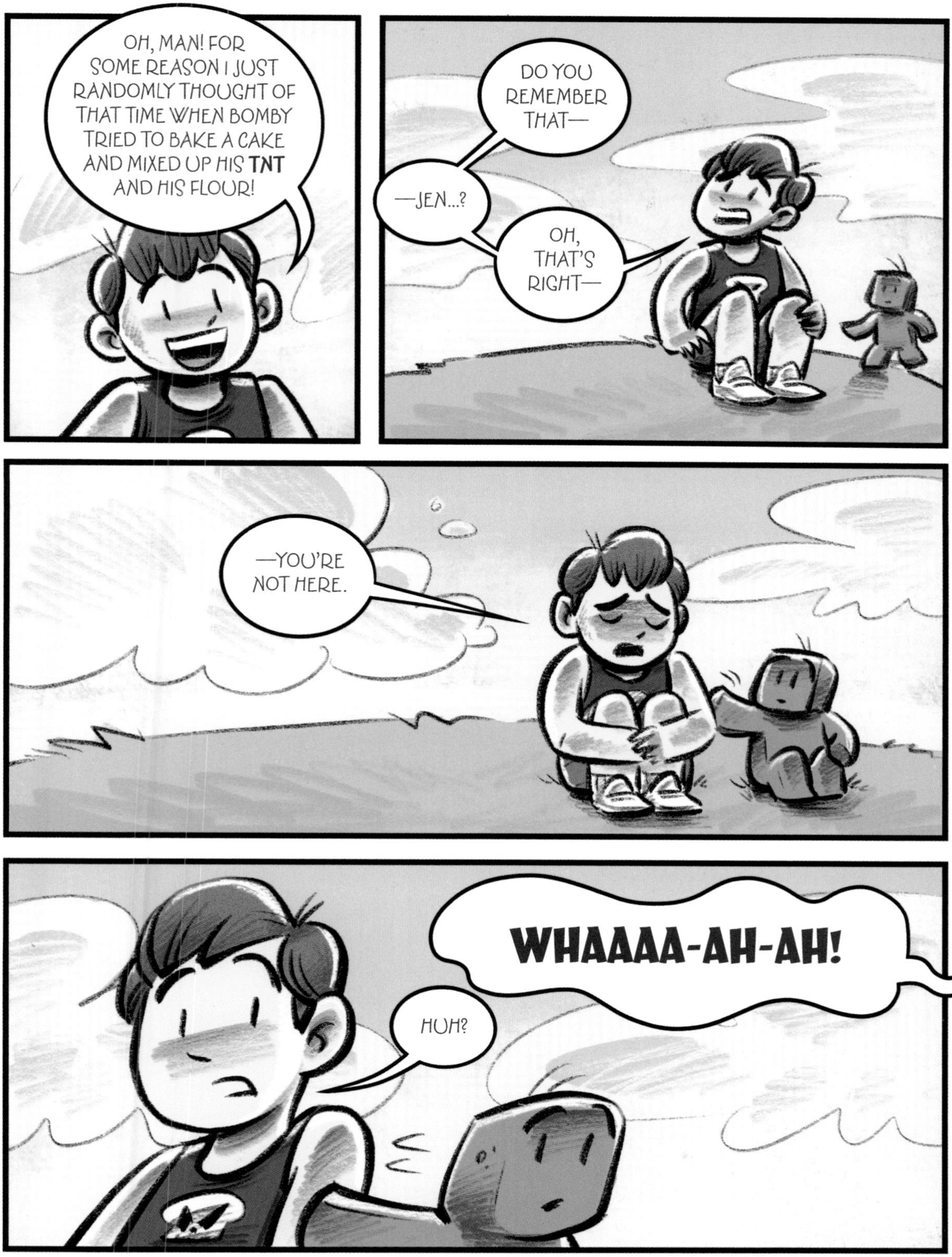
OH, MAN! FOR SOME REASON I JUST RANDOMLY THOUGHT OF THAT TIME WHEN BOMBY TRIED TO BAKE A CAKE AND MIXED UP HIS **TNT** AND HIS FLOUR!
DO YOU REMEMBER THAT—
—JEN...?
OH, THAT'S RIGHT—
—YOU'RE NOT HERE.
WHAAAA-AH-AH!
HUH?

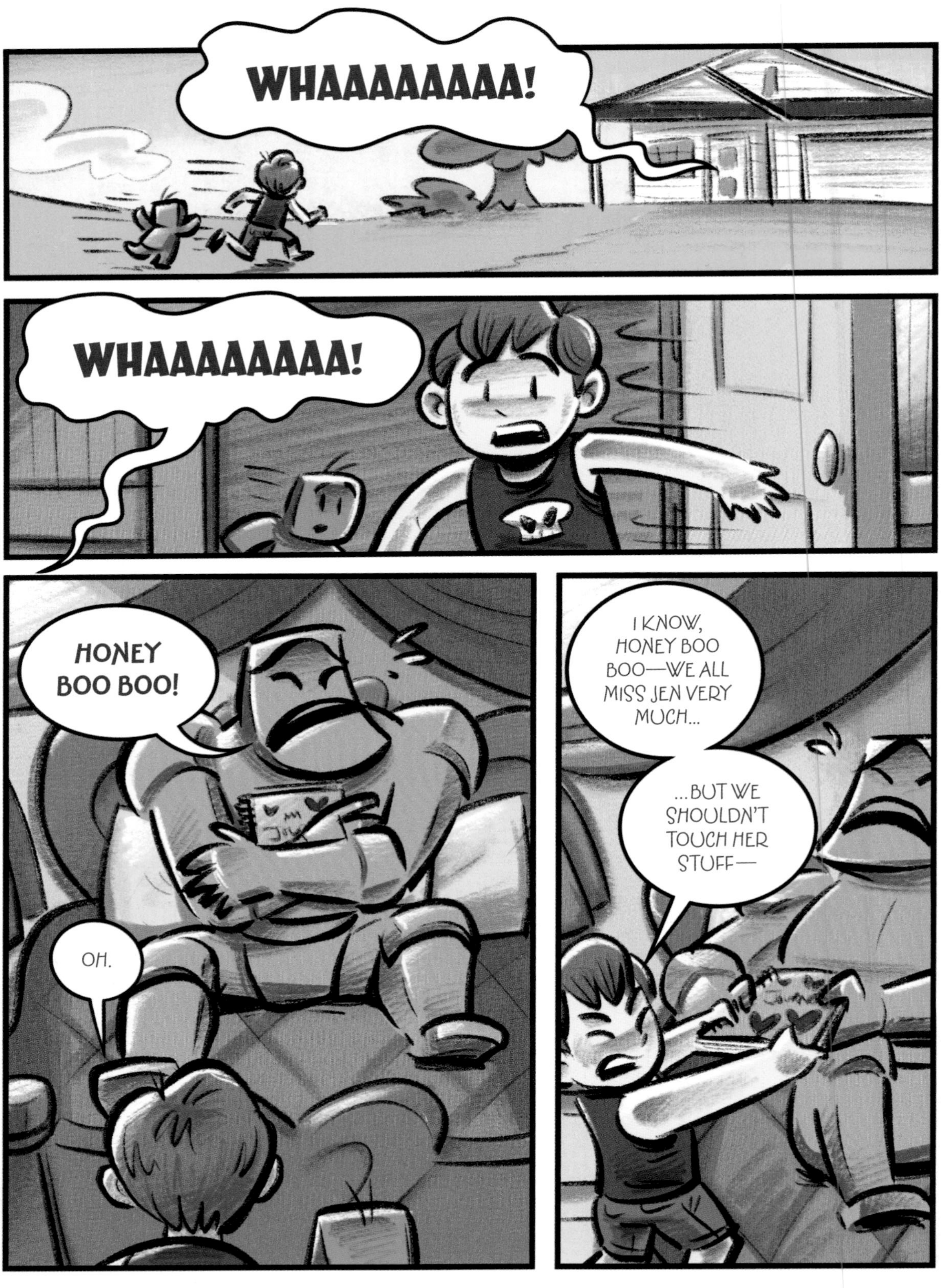
WHAAAAAAAA!
WHAAAAAAAAA!
HONEY BOO BOO!
OH.
I KNOW, HONEY BOO BOO—WE ALL MISS JEN VERY MUCH...
...BUT WE SHOULDN'T TOUCH HER STUFF—

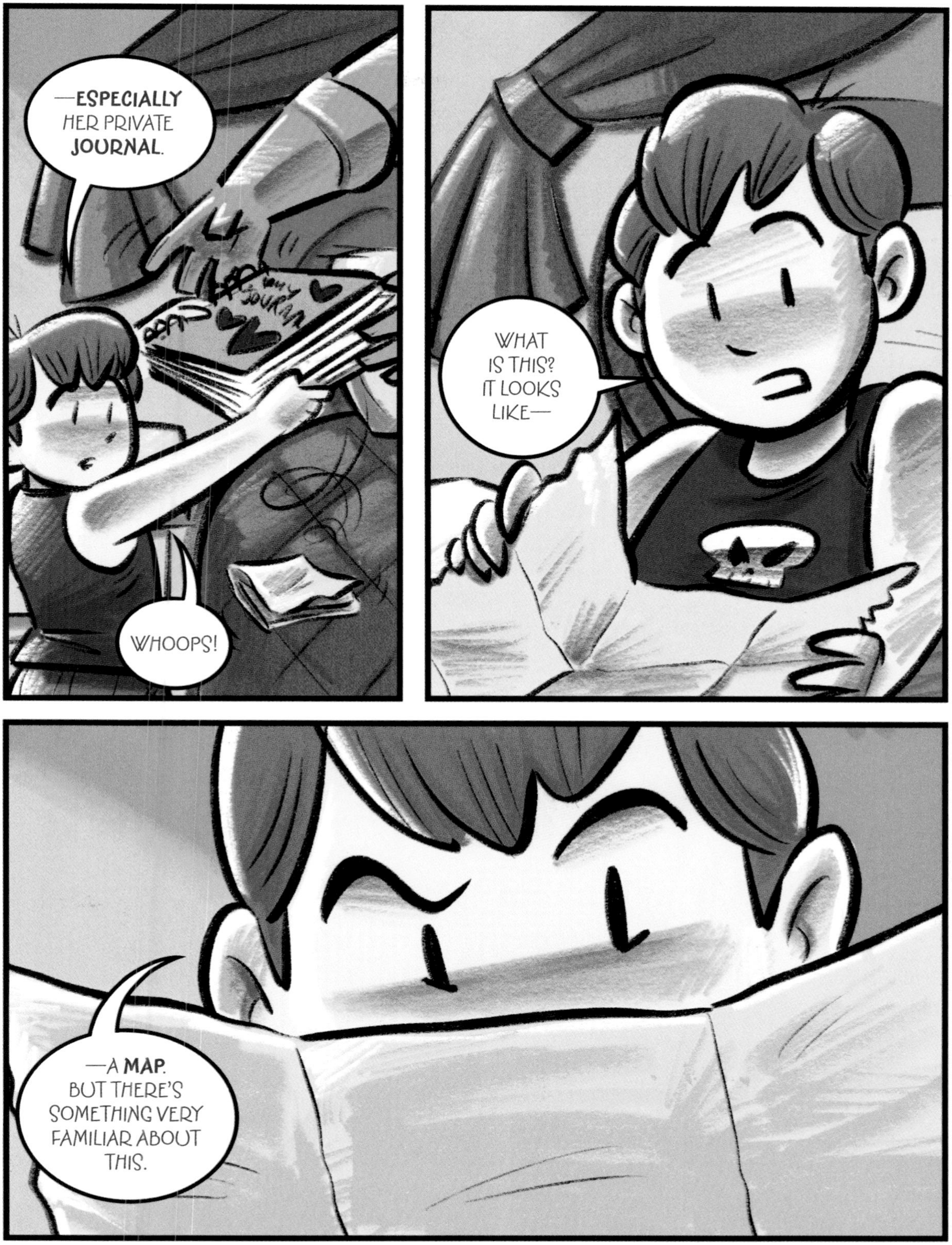
—ESPECIALLY HER PRIVATE JOURNAL.
WHOOPS!
WHAT IS THIS? IT LOOKS LIKE—
—A MAP. BUT THERE'S SOMETHING VERY FAMILIAR ABOUT THIS.

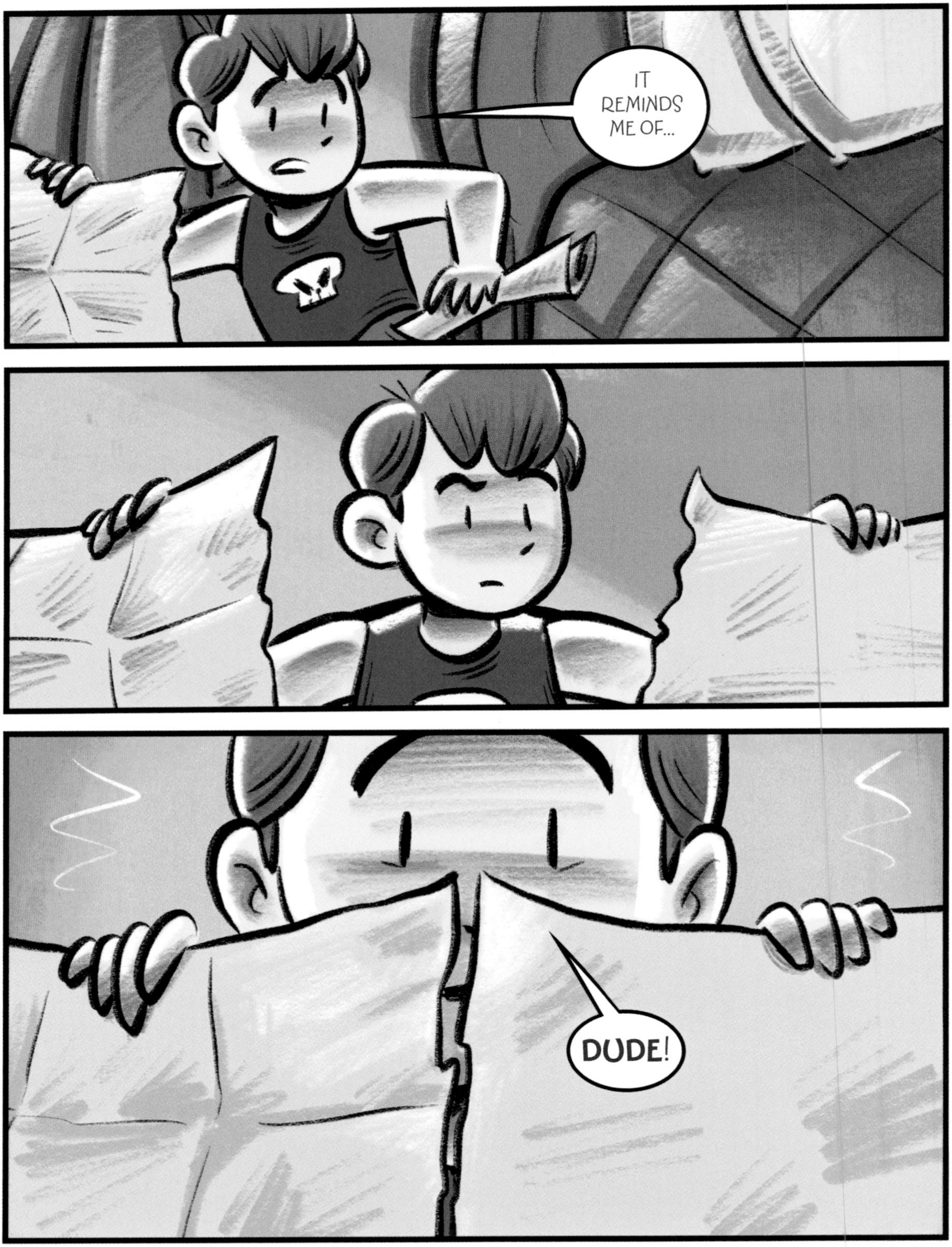
IT REMINDS ME OF...
DUDE!

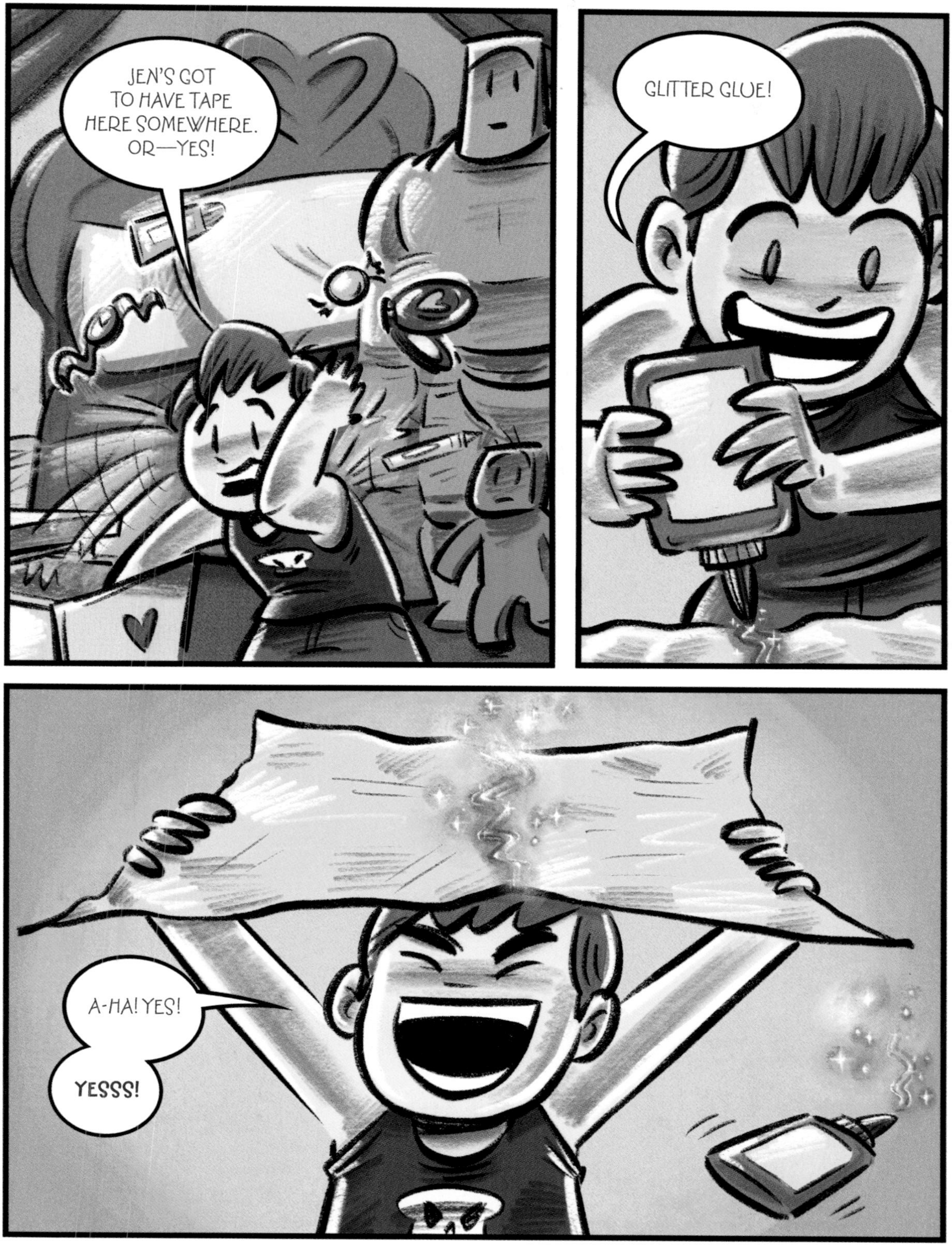
JEN'S GOT TO HAVE TAPE HERE SOMEWHERE. OR—YES!
GLITTER GLUE!
A-HA! YES!
YESSS!

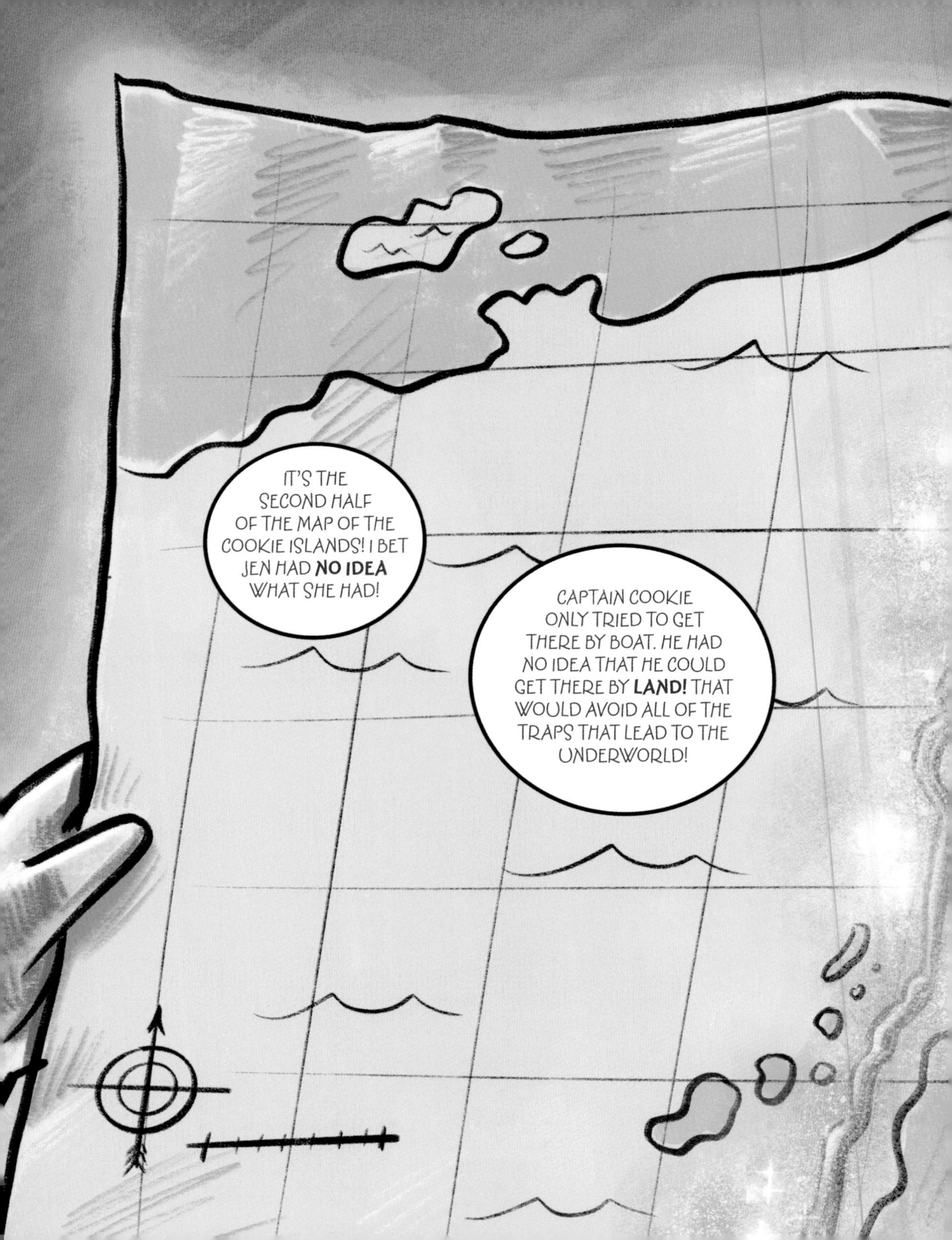
IT'S THE SECOND HALF OF THE MAP OF THE COOKIE ISLANDS! I BET JEN HAD **NO IDEA** WHAT SHE HAD!
CAPTAIN COOKIE ONLY TRIED TO GET THERE BY BOAT. HE HAD NO IDEA THAT HE COULD GET THERE BY **LAND!** THAT WOULD AVOID ALL OF THE TRAPS THAT LEAD TO THE UNDERWORLD!

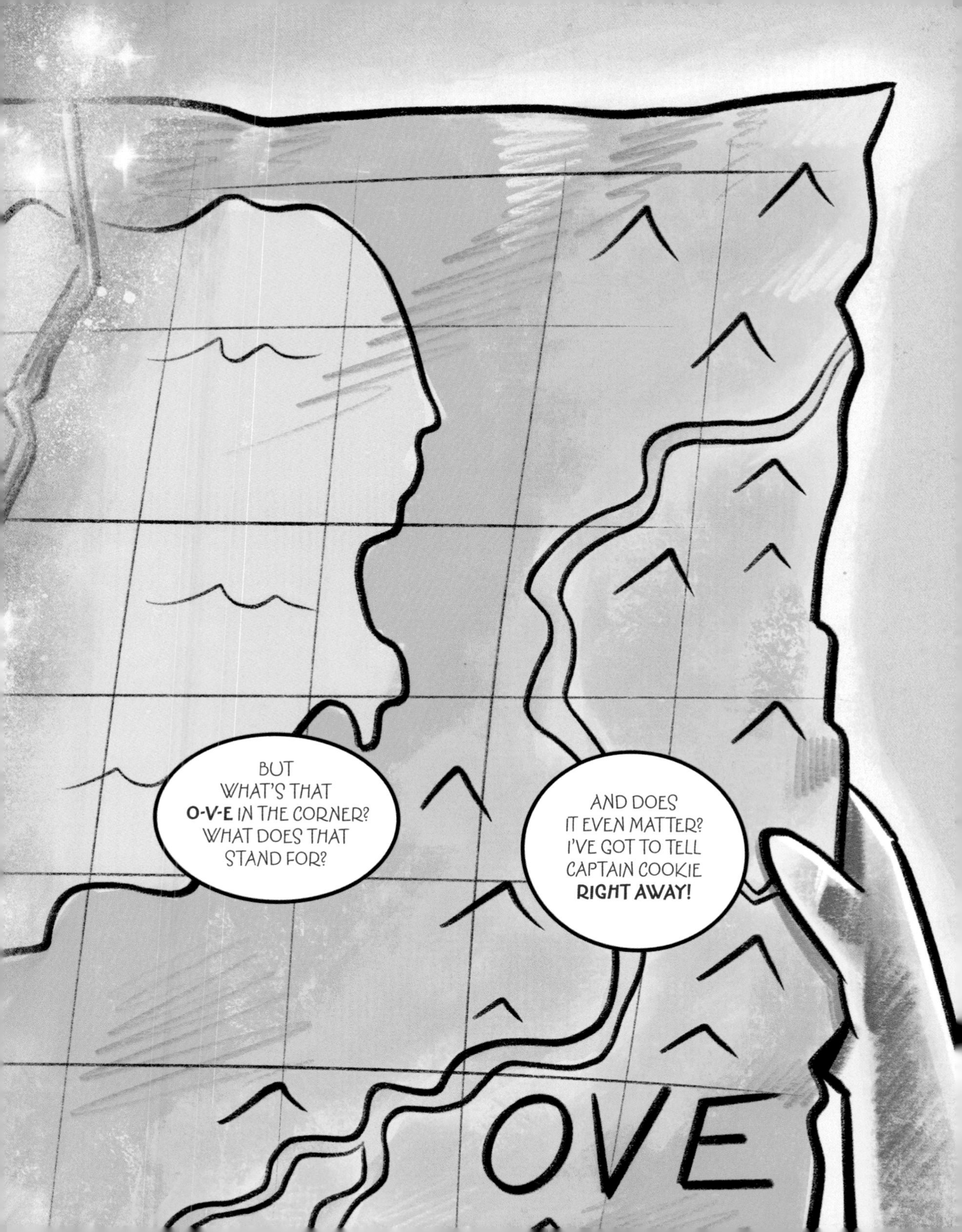
BUT WHAT'S THAT **O-V-E** IN THE CORNER? WHAT DOES THAT STAND FOR?
AND DOES IT EVEN MATTER? I'VE GOT TO TELL CAPTAIN COOKIE **RIGHT AWAY!**
OVE

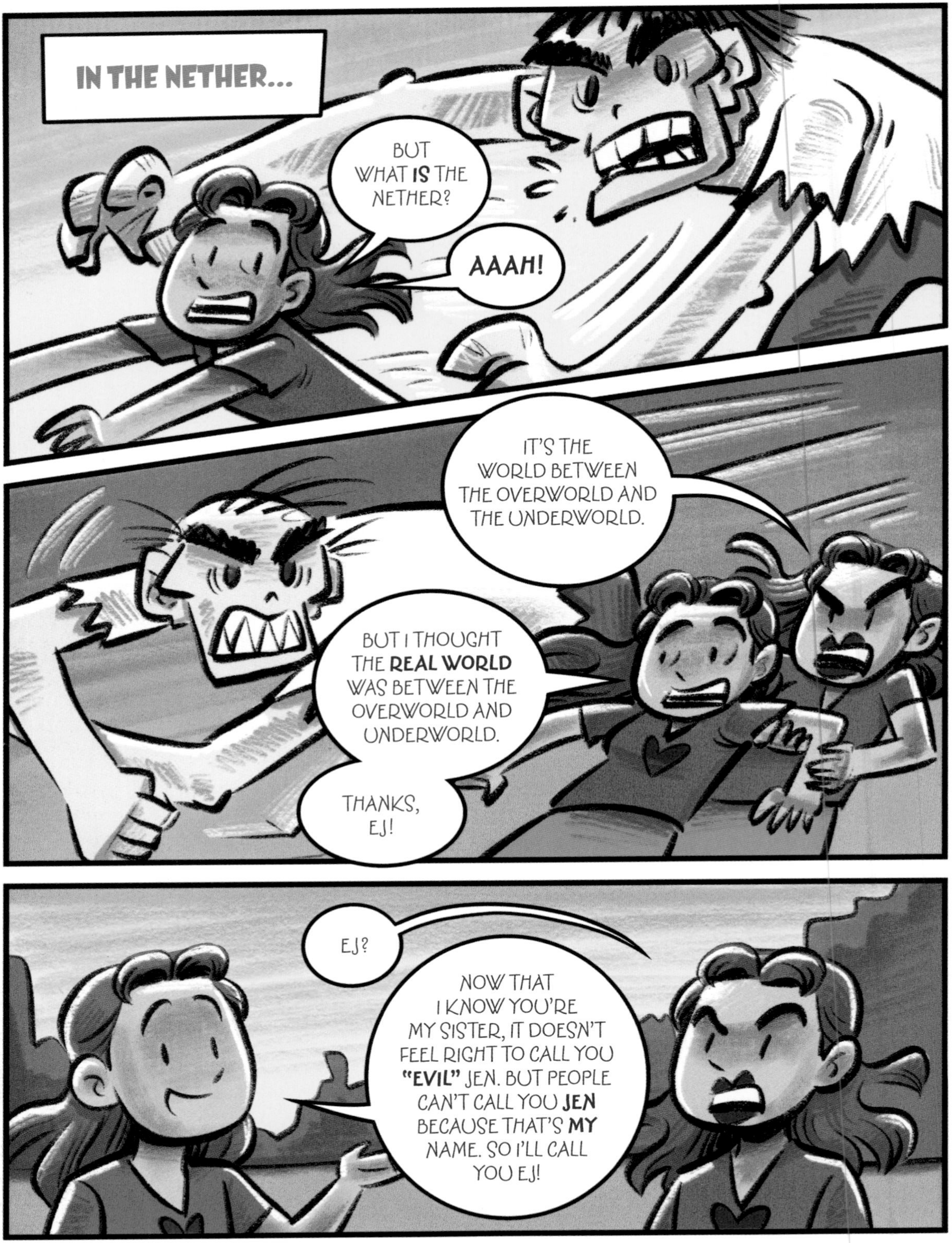
IN THE NETHER...
BUT WHAT **IS** THE NETHER?
AAAH!
IT'S THE WORLD BETWEEN THE OVERWORLD AND THE UNDERWORLD.
BUT I THOUGHT THE **REAL WORLD** WAS BETWEEN THE OVERWORLD AND UNDERWORLD.
THANKS, EJ!
EJ?
NOW THAT I KNOW YOU'RE MY SISTER, IT DOESN'T FEEL RIGHT TO CALL YOU **"EVIL"** JEN. BUT PEOPLE CAN'T CALL YOU **JEN** BECAUSE THAT'S **MY** NAME. SO I'LL CALL YOU EJ!

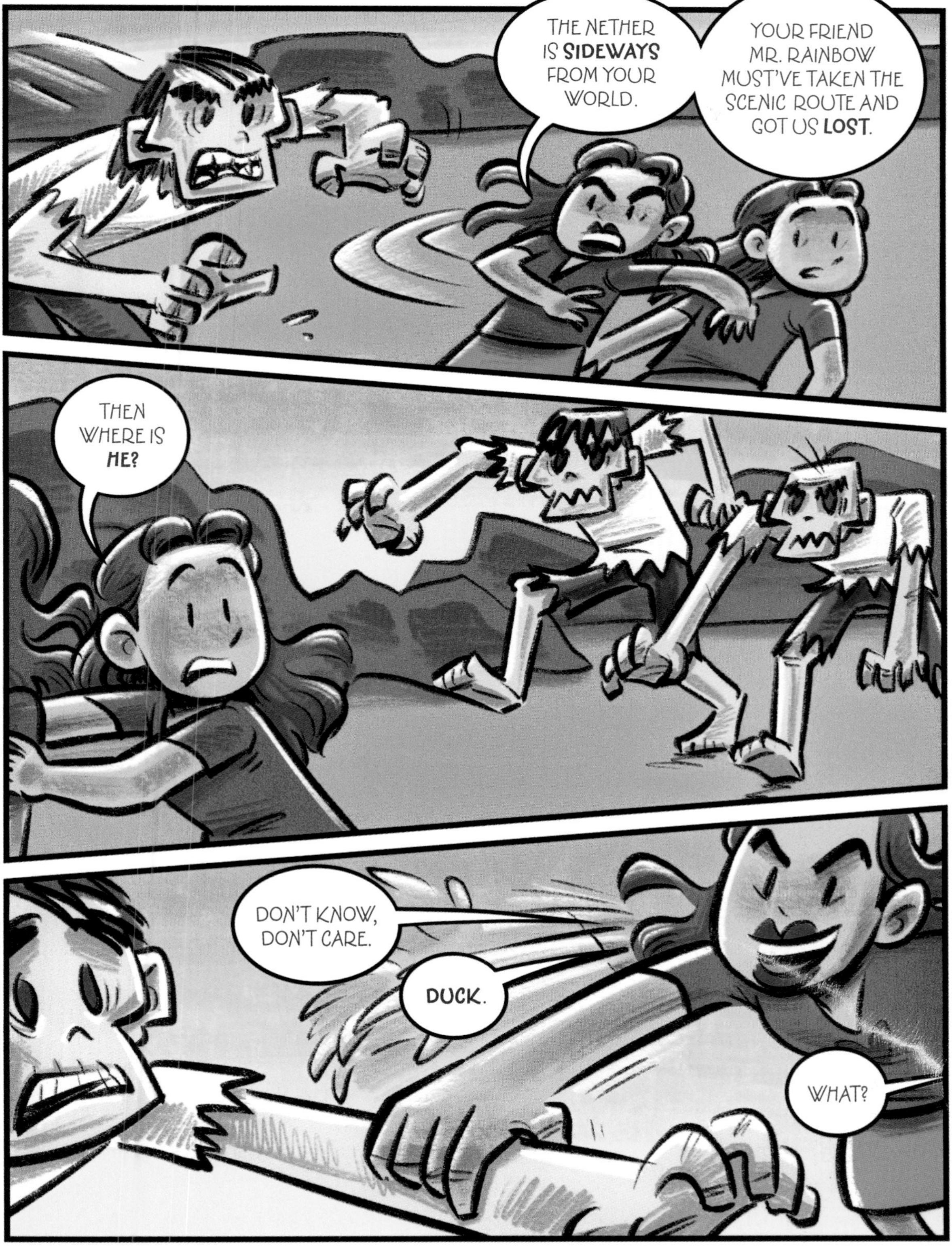
THE NETHER IS **SIDEWAYS** FROM YOUR WORLD.
YOUR FRIEND MR. RAINBOW MUST'VE TAKEN THE SCENIC ROUTE AND GOT US **LOST**.
THEN WHERE IS **HE?**
DON'T KNOW, DON'T CARE.
DUCK.
WHAT?

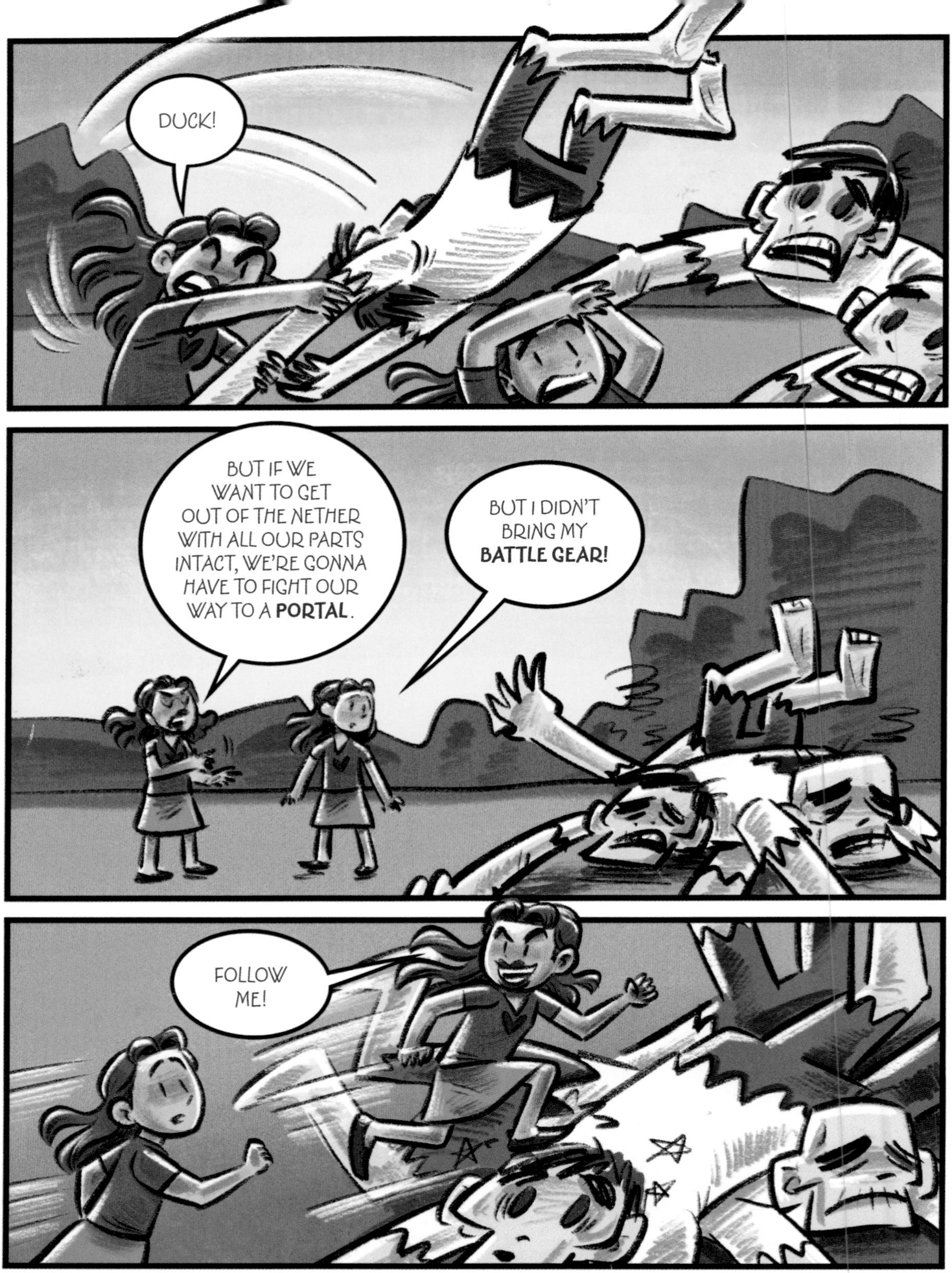
DUCK!
BUT IF WE WANT TO GET OUT OF THE NETHER WITH ALL OUR PARTS INTACT, WE'RE GONNA HAVE TO FIGHT OUR WAY TO A **PORTAL**.
BUT I DIDN'T BRING MY **BATTLE GEAR!**
FOLLOW ME!

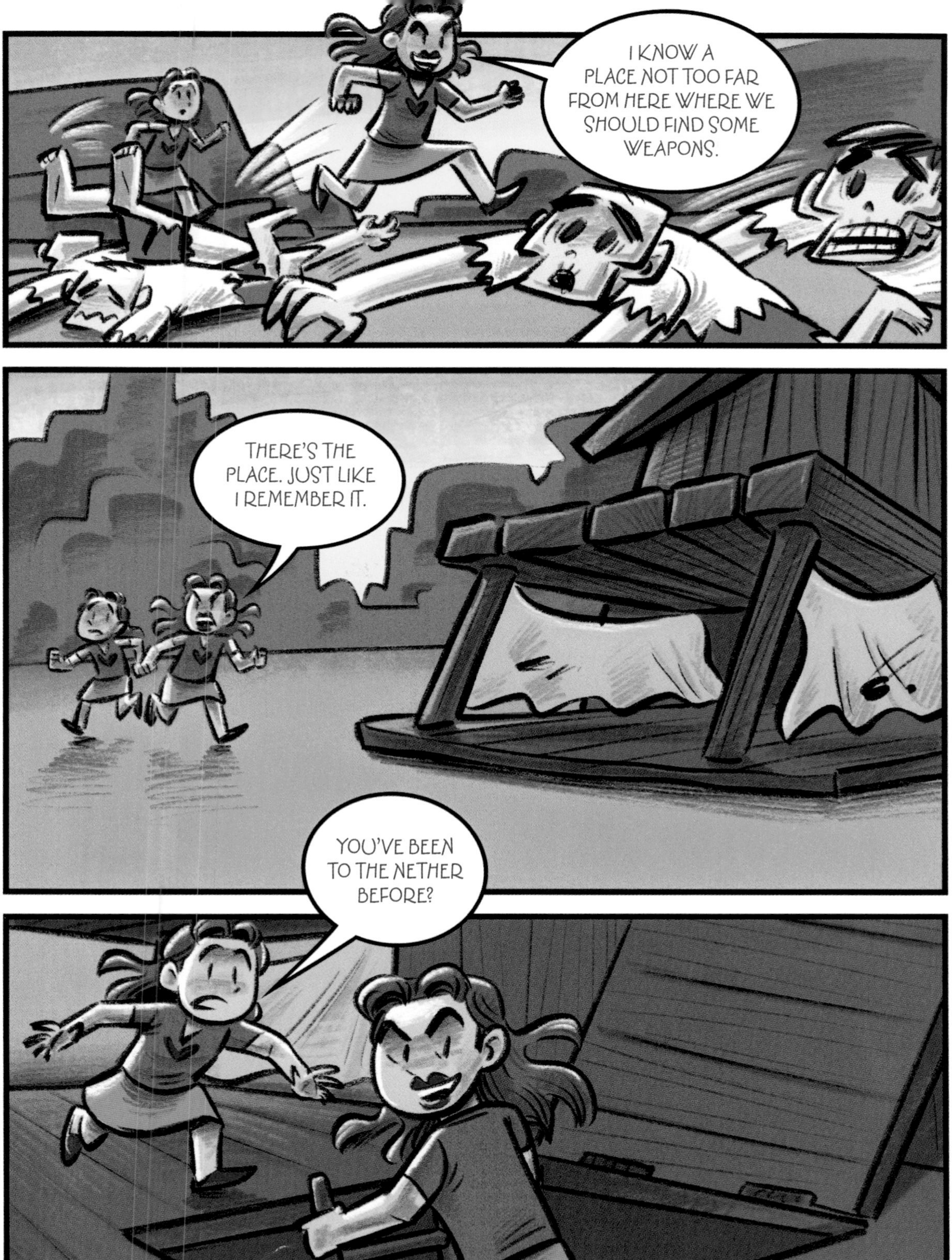
I KNOW A PLACE NOT TOO FAR FROM HERE WHERE WE SHOULD FIND SOME WEAPONS.
THERE'S THE PLACE. JUST LIKE I REMEMBER IT.
YOU'VE BEEN TO THE NETHER BEFORE?

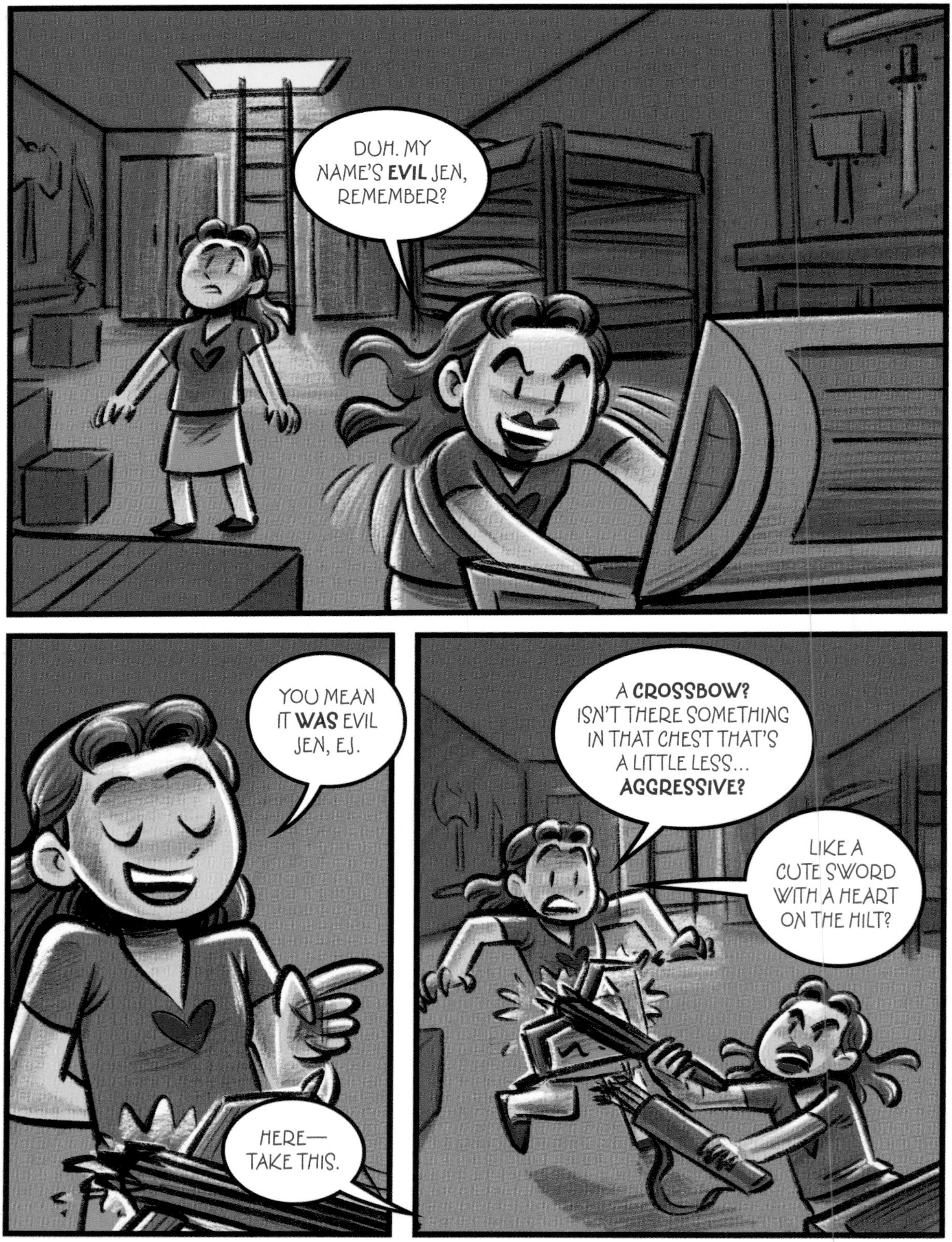
DUH. MY NAME'S **EVIL** JEN, REMEMBER?
YOU MEAN IT **WAS** EVIL JEN, EJ.
HERE— TAKE THIS.
A **CROSSBOW?** ISN'T THERE SOMETHING IN THAT CHEST THAT'S A LITTLE LESS... **AGGRESSIVE?**
LIKE A CUTE SWORD WITH A HEART ON THE HILT?

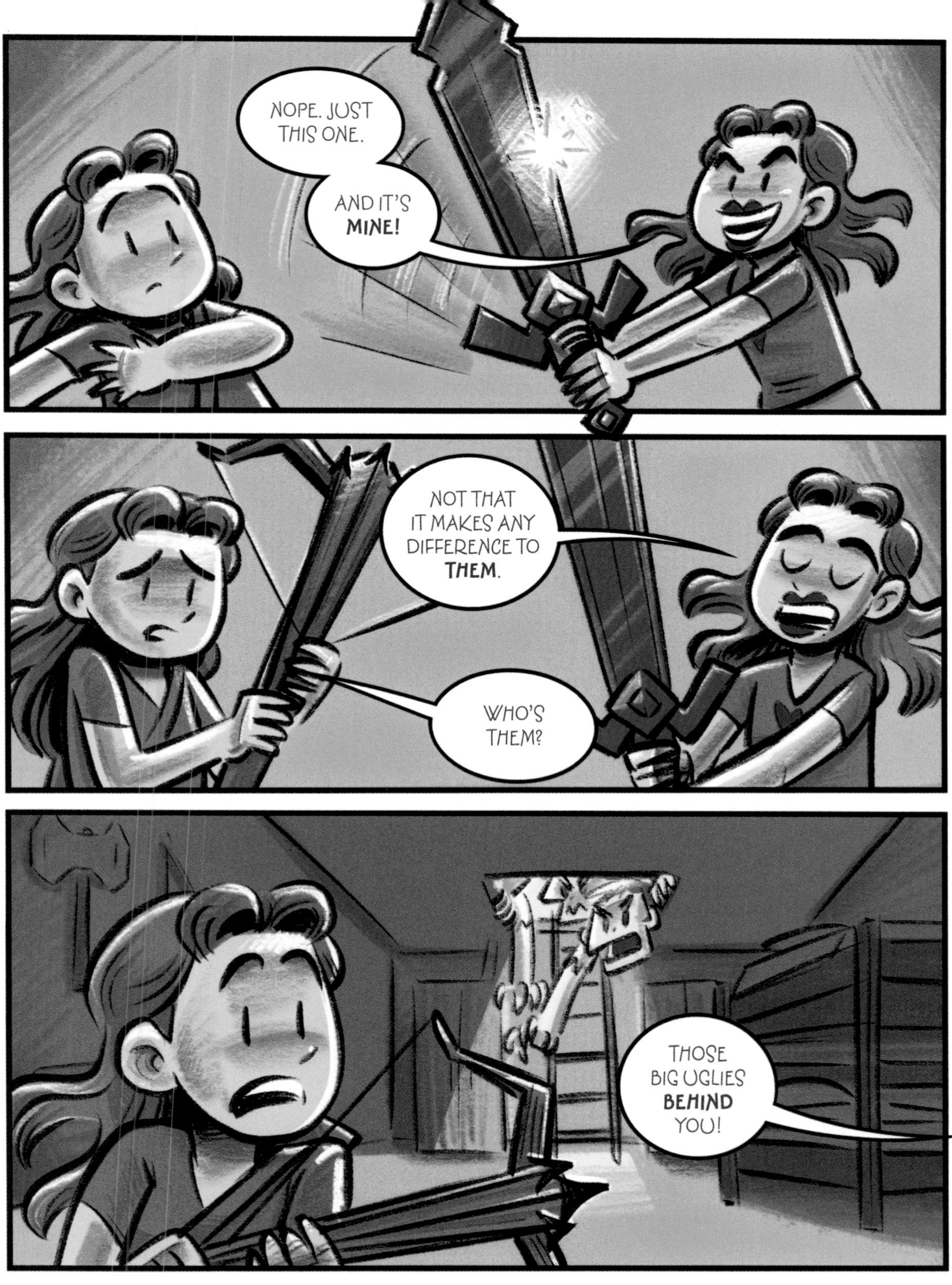
NOPE. JUST THIS ONE.
AND IT'S **MINE!**
NOT THAT IT MAKES ANY DIFFERENCE TO **THEM**.
WHO'S THEM?
THOSE BIG UGLIES **BEHIND** YOU!

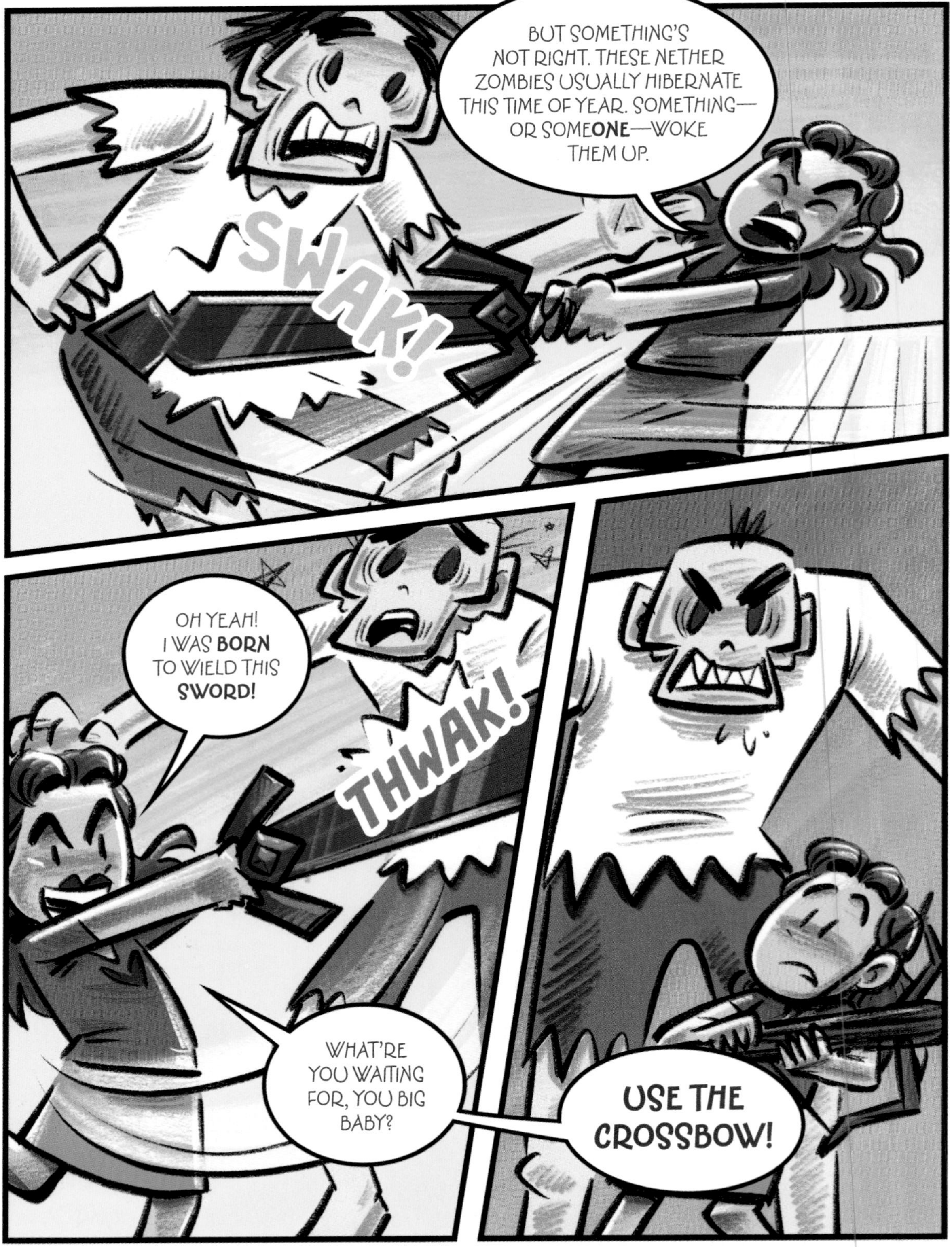
BUT SOMETHING'S NOT RIGHT. THESE NETHER ZOMBIES USUALLY HIBERNATE THIS TIME OF YEAR. SOMETHING— OR SOME**ONE**—WOKE THEM UP.
SWAK!
OH YEAH! I WAS **BORN** TO WIELD THIS **SWORD!**
THWAK!
WHAT'RE YOU WAITING FOR, YOU BIG BABY?
USE THE CROSSBOW!

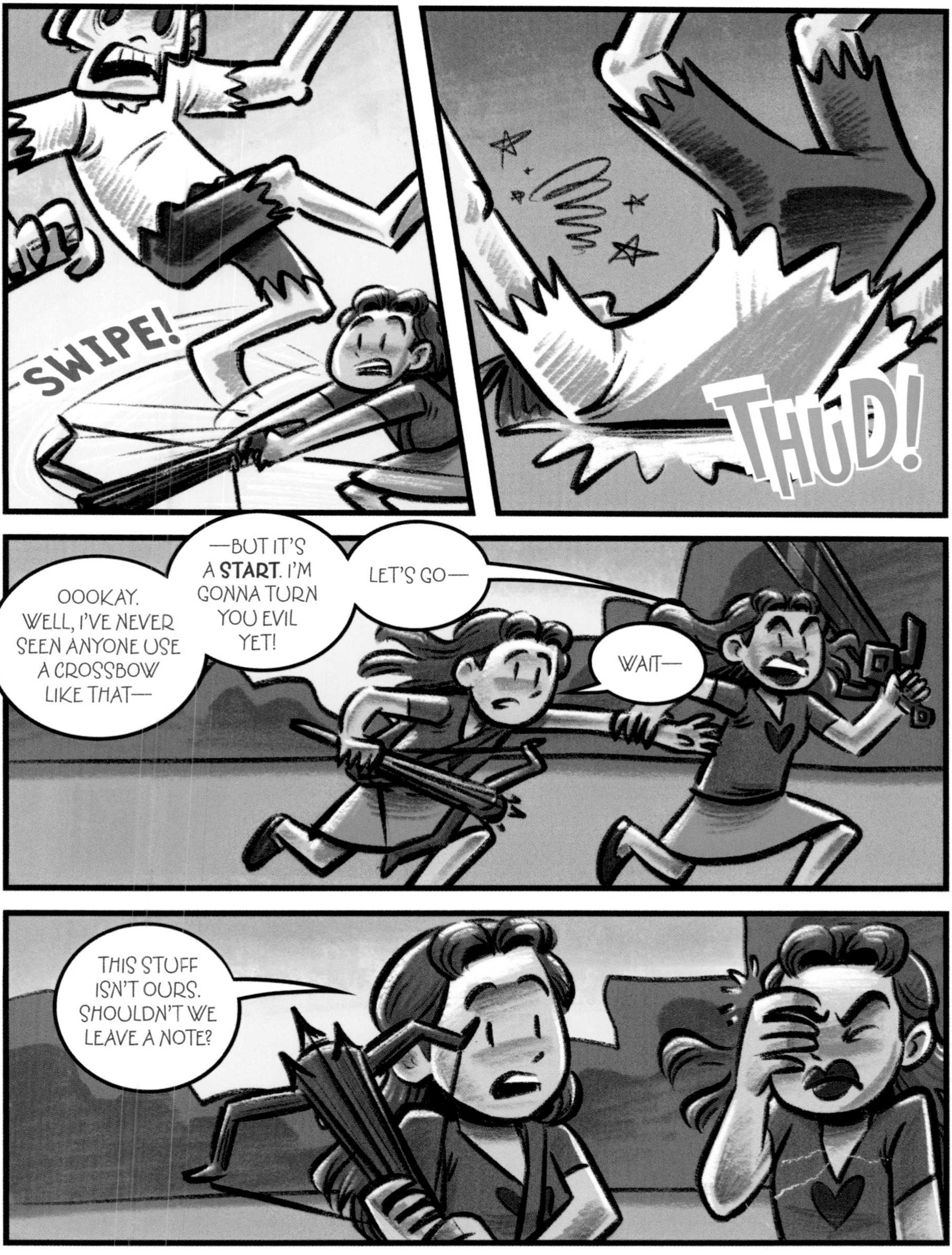
SWIPE!
THUD!
OOOKAY. WELL, I'VE NEVER SEEN ANYONE USE A CROSSBOW LIKE THAT—
—BUT IT'S A **START**. I'M GONNA TURN YOU EVIL YET!
LET'S GO—
WAIT—
THIS STUFF ISN'T OURS. SHOULDN'T WE LEAVE A NOTE?

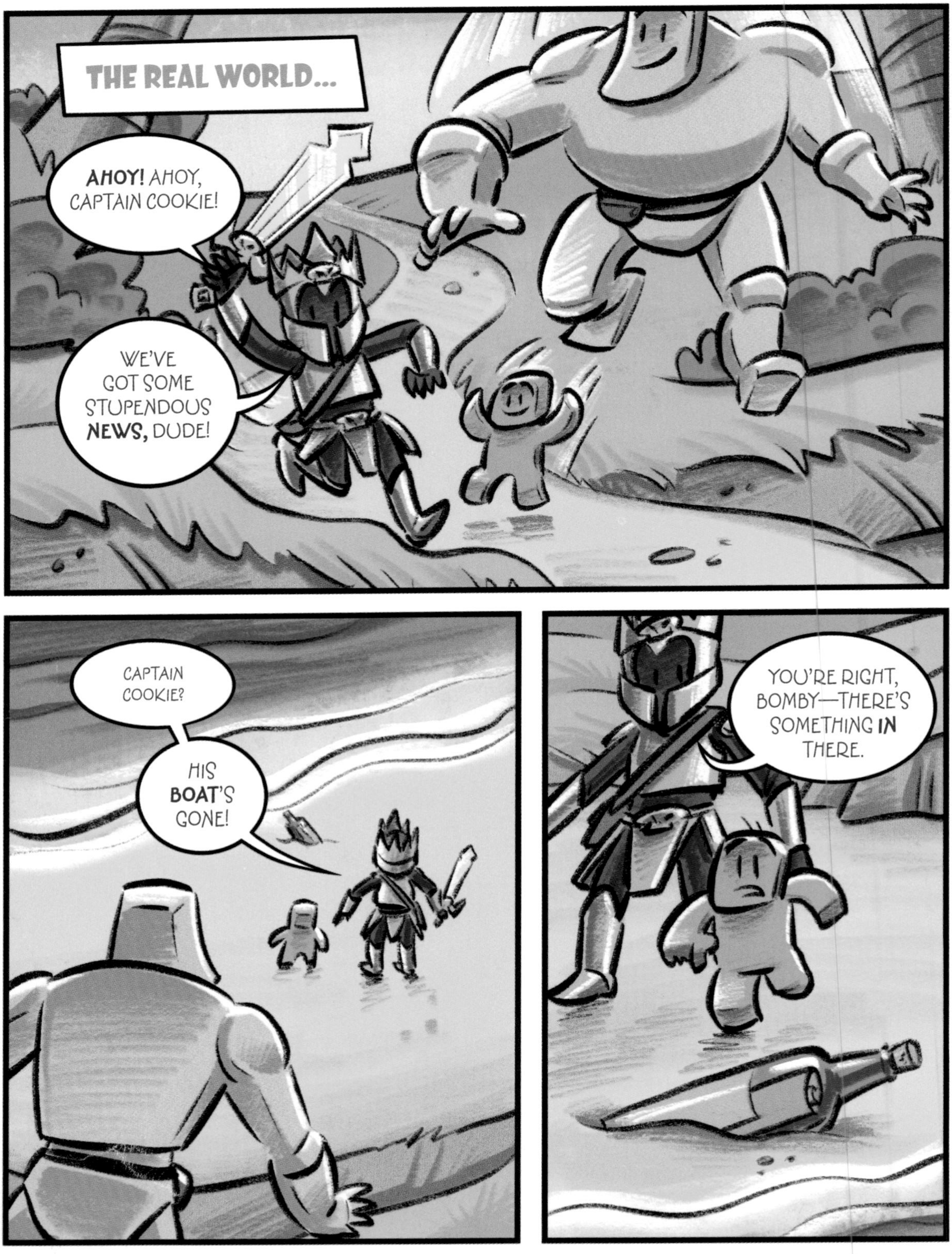
THE REAL WORLD...
AHOY! AHOY, CAPTAIN COOKIE!
WE'VE GOT SOME STUPENDOUS **NEWS,** DUDE!
CAPTAIN COOKIE?
HIS **BOAT**'S GONE!
YOU'RE RIGHT, BOMBY—THERE'S SOMETHING **IN** THERE.

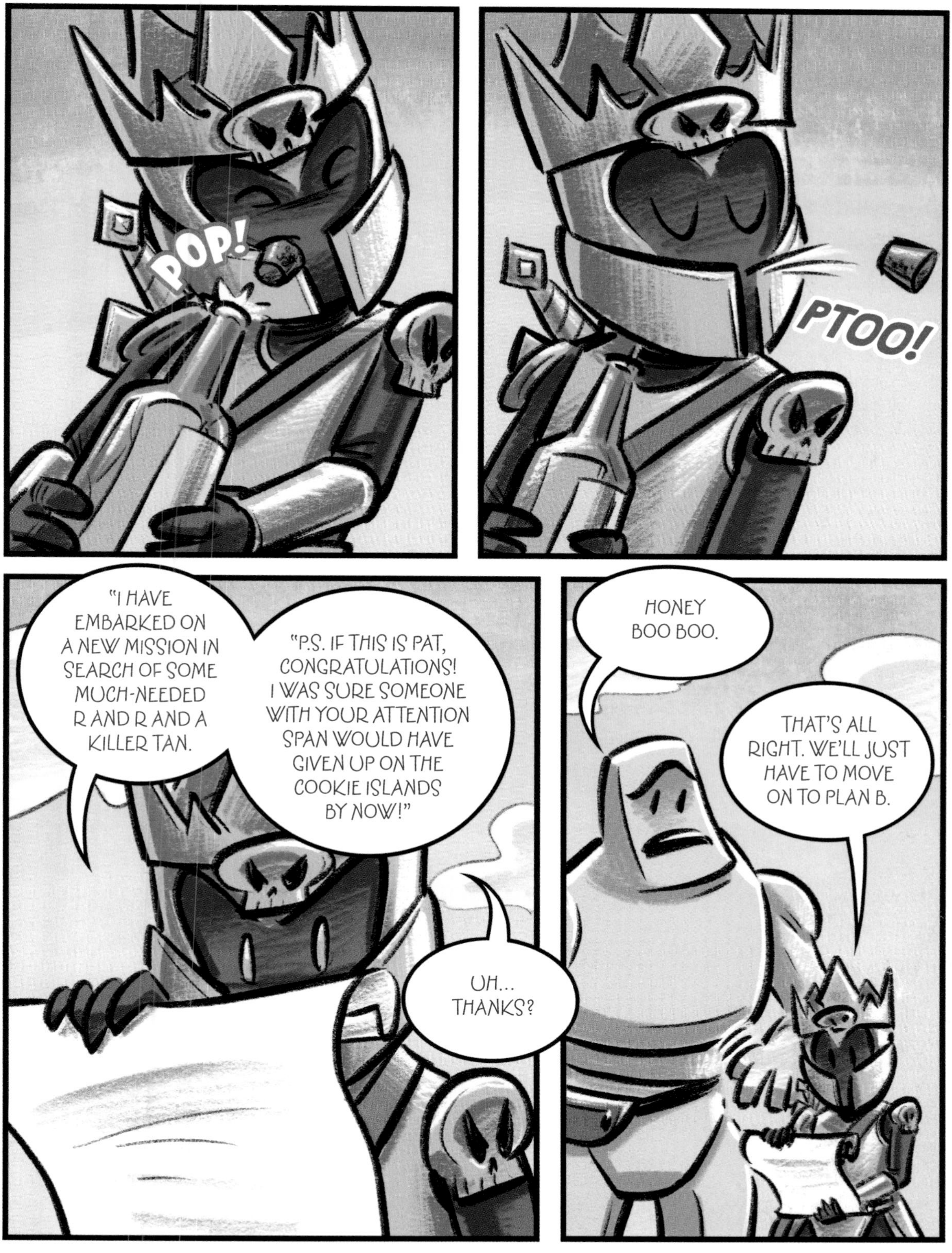
POP!
PTOO!
"I HAVE EMBARKED ON A NEW MISSION IN SEARCH OF SOME MUCH-NEEDED R AND R AND A KILLER TAN.
"P.S. IF THIS IS PAT, CONGRATULATIONS! I WAS SURE SOMEONE WITH YOUR ATTENTION SPAN WOULD HAVE GIVEN UP ON THE COOKIE ISLANDS BY NOW!"
UH... THANKS?
HONEY BOO BOO.
THAT'S ALL RIGHT. WE'LL JUST HAVE TO MOVE ON TO PLAN B.

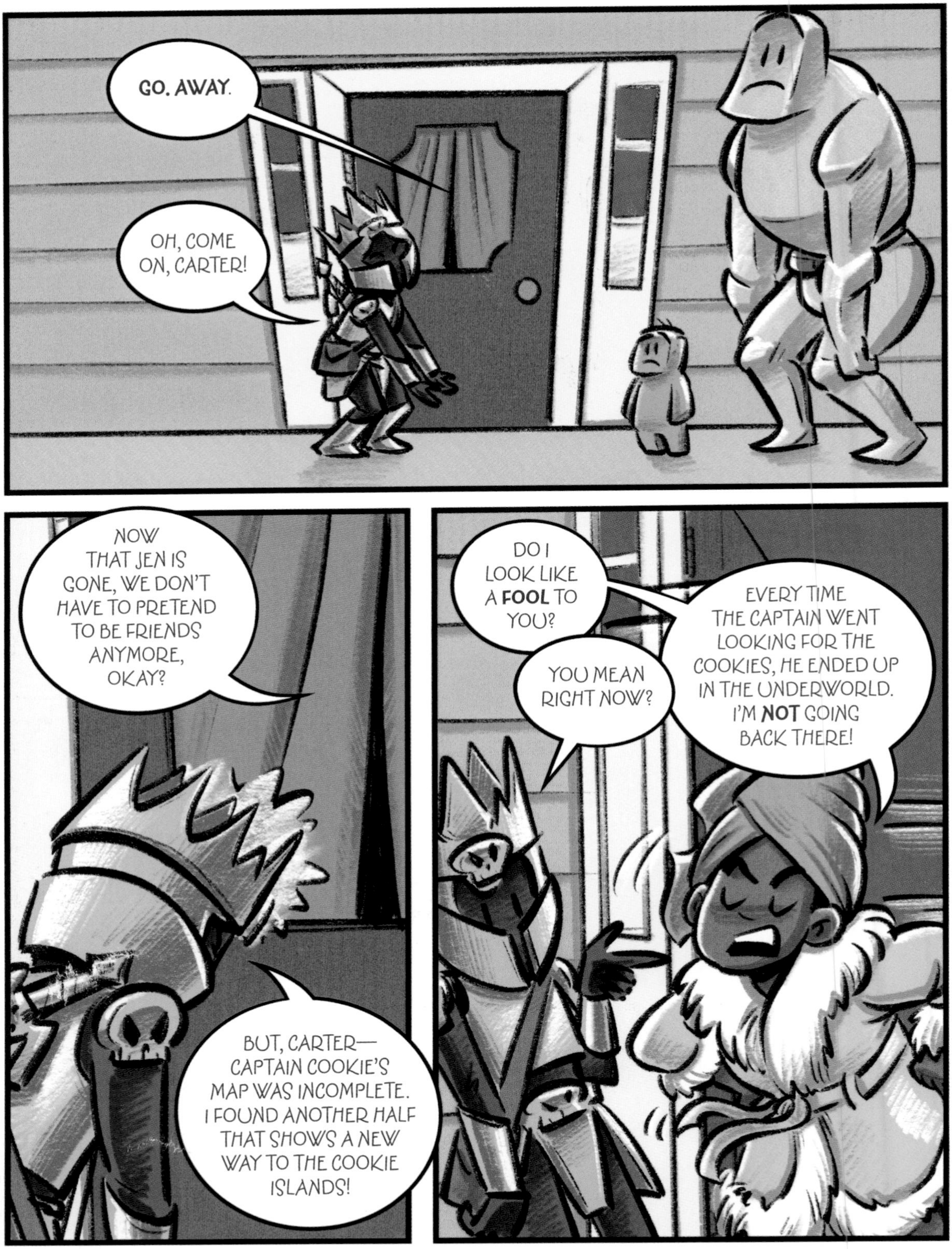
GO. AWAY.
OH, COME ON, CARTER!
NOW THAT JEN IS GONE, WE DON'T HAVE TO PRETEND TO BE FRIENDS ANYMORE, OKAY?
BUT, CARTER— CAPTAIN COOKIE'S MAP WAS INCOMPLETE. I FOUND ANOTHER HALF THAT SHOWS A NEW WAY TO THE COOKIE ISLANDS!
DO I LOOK LIKE A **FOOL** TO YOU?
YOU MEAN RIGHT NOW?
EVERY TIME THE CAPTAIN WENT LOOKING FOR THE COOKIES, HE ENDED UP IN THE UNDERWORLD. I'M **NOT** GOING BACK THERE!

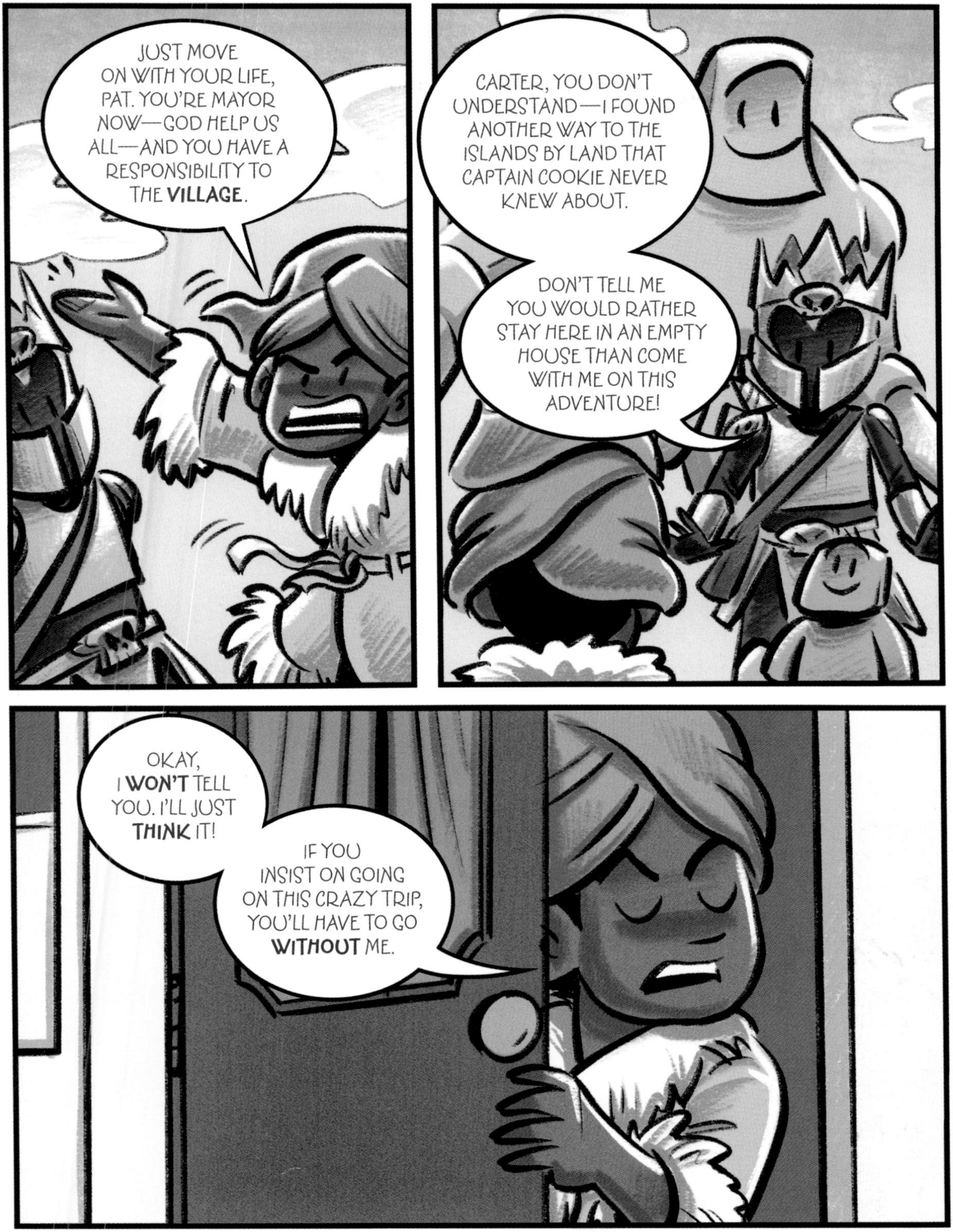
JUST MOVE ON WITH YOUR LIFE, PAT. YOU'RE MAYOR NOW—GOD HELP US ALL—AND YOU HAVE A RESPONSIBILITY TO THE **VILLAGE**.
CARTER, YOU DON'T UNDERSTAND—I FOUND ANOTHER WAY TO THE ISLANDS BY LAND THAT CAPTAIN COOKIE NEVER KNEW ABOUT.
DON'T TELL ME YOU WOULD RATHER STAY HERE IN AN EMPTY HOUSE THAN COME WITH ME ON THIS ADVENTURE!
OKAY, I **WON'T** TELL YOU. I'LL JUST **THINK** IT!
IF YOU INSIST ON GOING ON THIS CRAZY TRIP, YOU'LL HAVE TO GO **WITHOUT** ME.

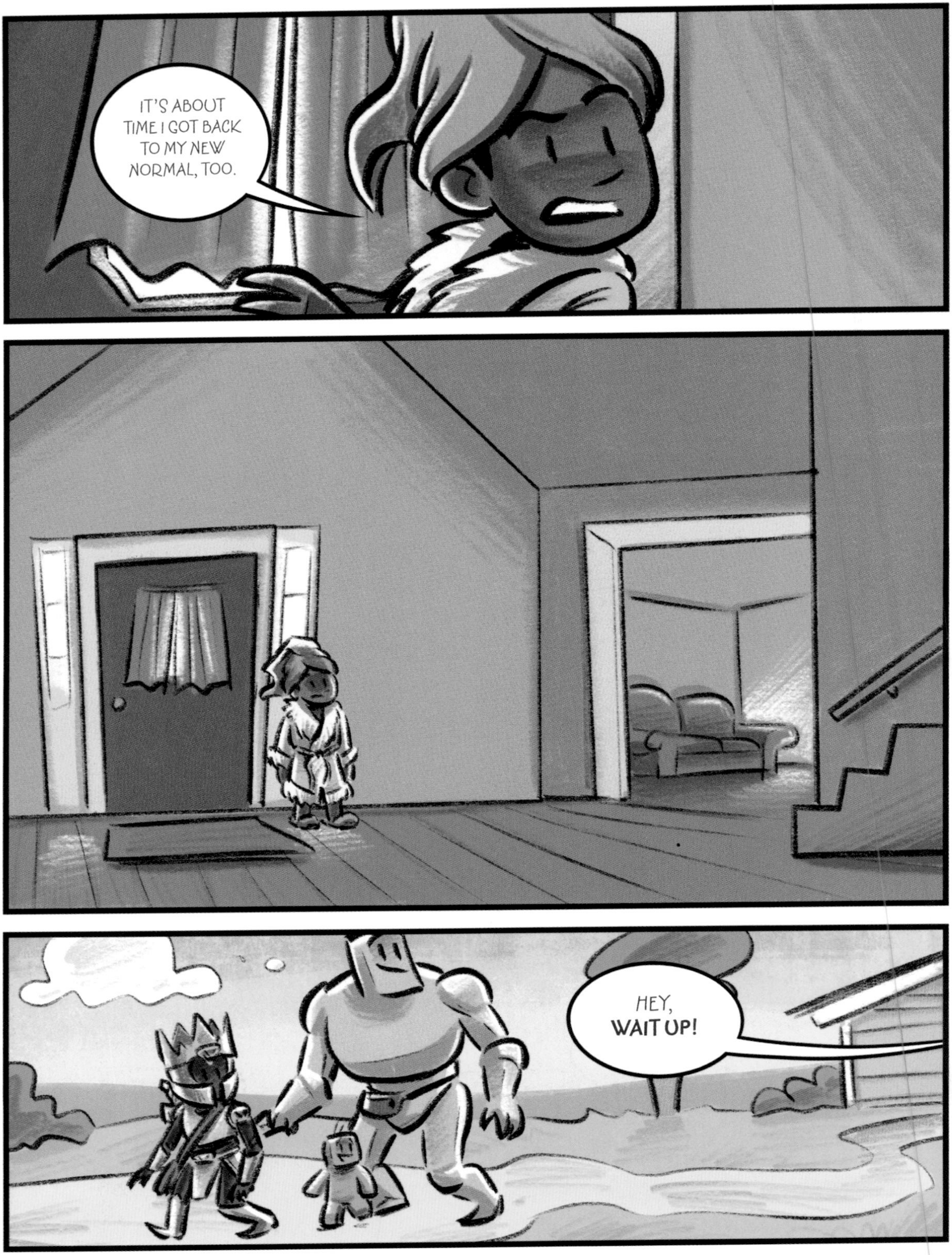
IT'S ABOUT TIME I GOT BACK TO MY NEW NORMAL, TOO.
HEY, WAIT UP!

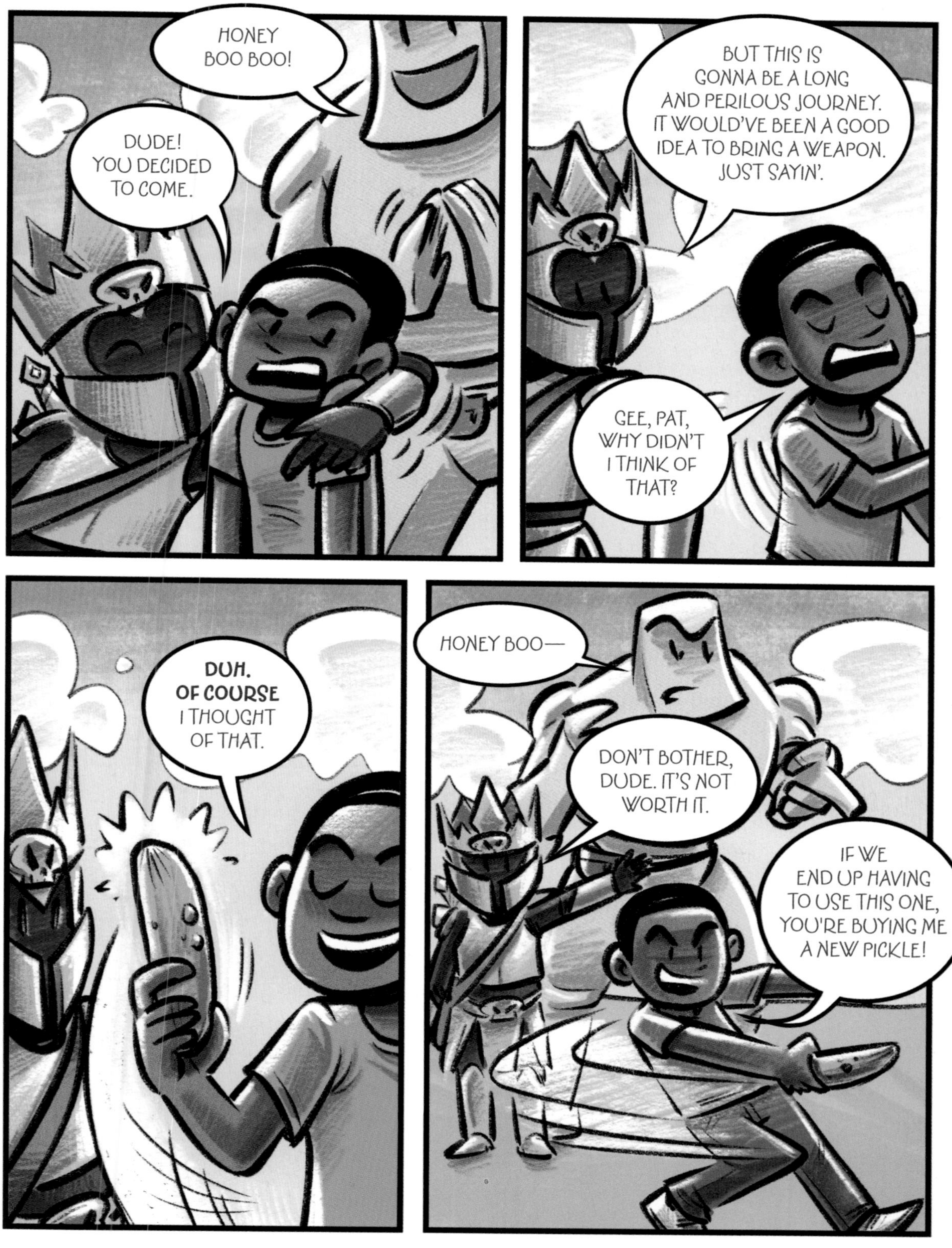
HONEY BOO BOO!
DUDE! YOU DECIDED TO COME.
BUT THIS IS GONNA BE A LONG AND PERILOUS JOURNEY. IT WOULD'VE BEEN A GOOD IDEA TO BRING A WEAPON. JUST SAYIN'.
GEE, PAT, WHY DIDN'T I THINK OF THAT?
DUH. OF COURSE I THOUGHT OF THAT.
HONEY BOO—
DON'T BOTHER, DUDE. IT'S NOT WORTH IT.
IF WE END UP HAVING TO USE THIS ONE, YOU'RE BUYING ME A NEW PICKLE!

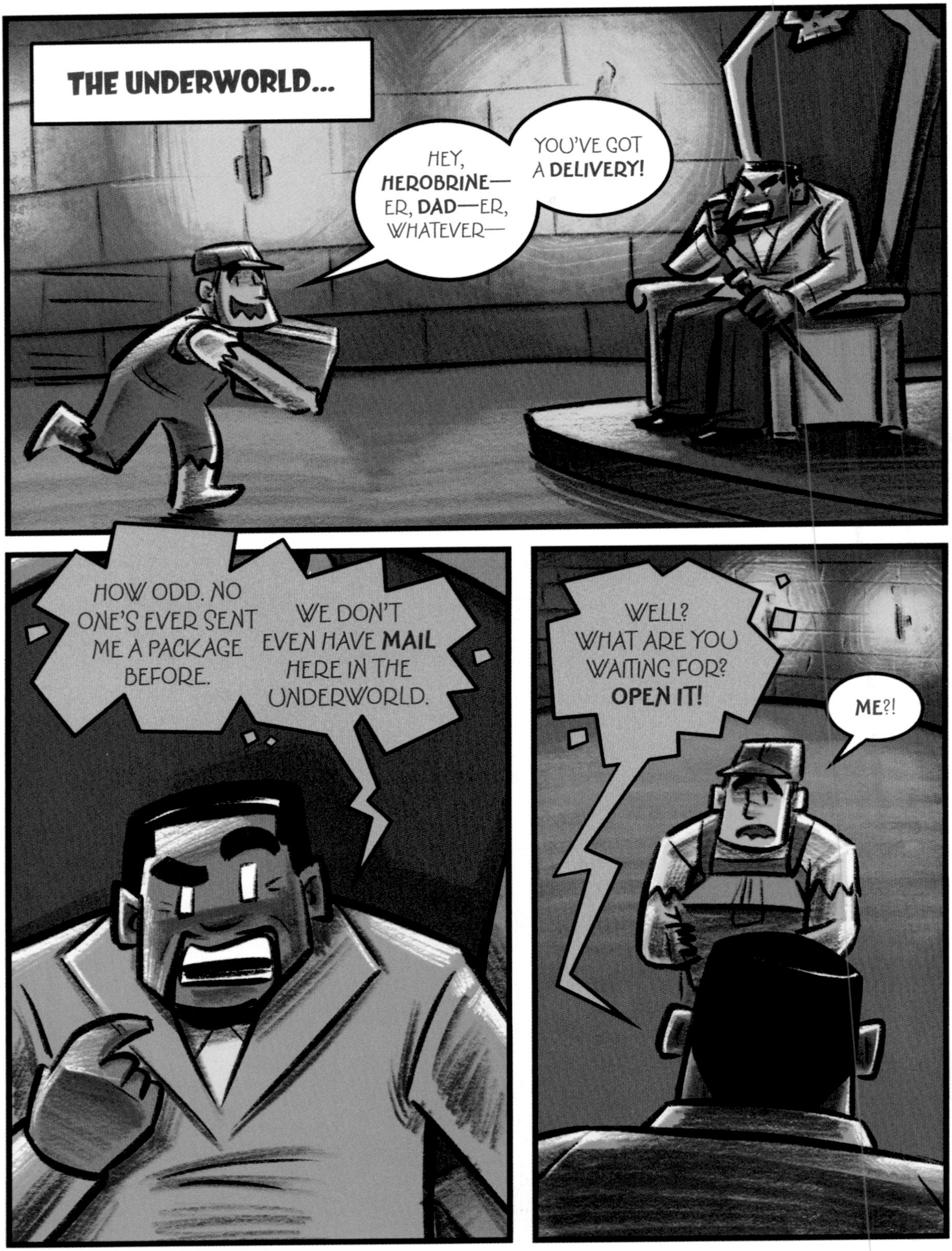
THE UNDERWORLD...
HEY, HEROBRINE— ER, DAD—ER, WHATEVER—
YOU'VE GOT A DELIVERY!
HOW ODD. NO ONE'S EVER SENT ME A PACKAGE BEFORE.
WE DON'T EVEN HAVE MAIL HERE IN THE UNDERWORLD.
WELL? WHAT ARE YOU WAITING FOR? OPEN IT!
ME?!

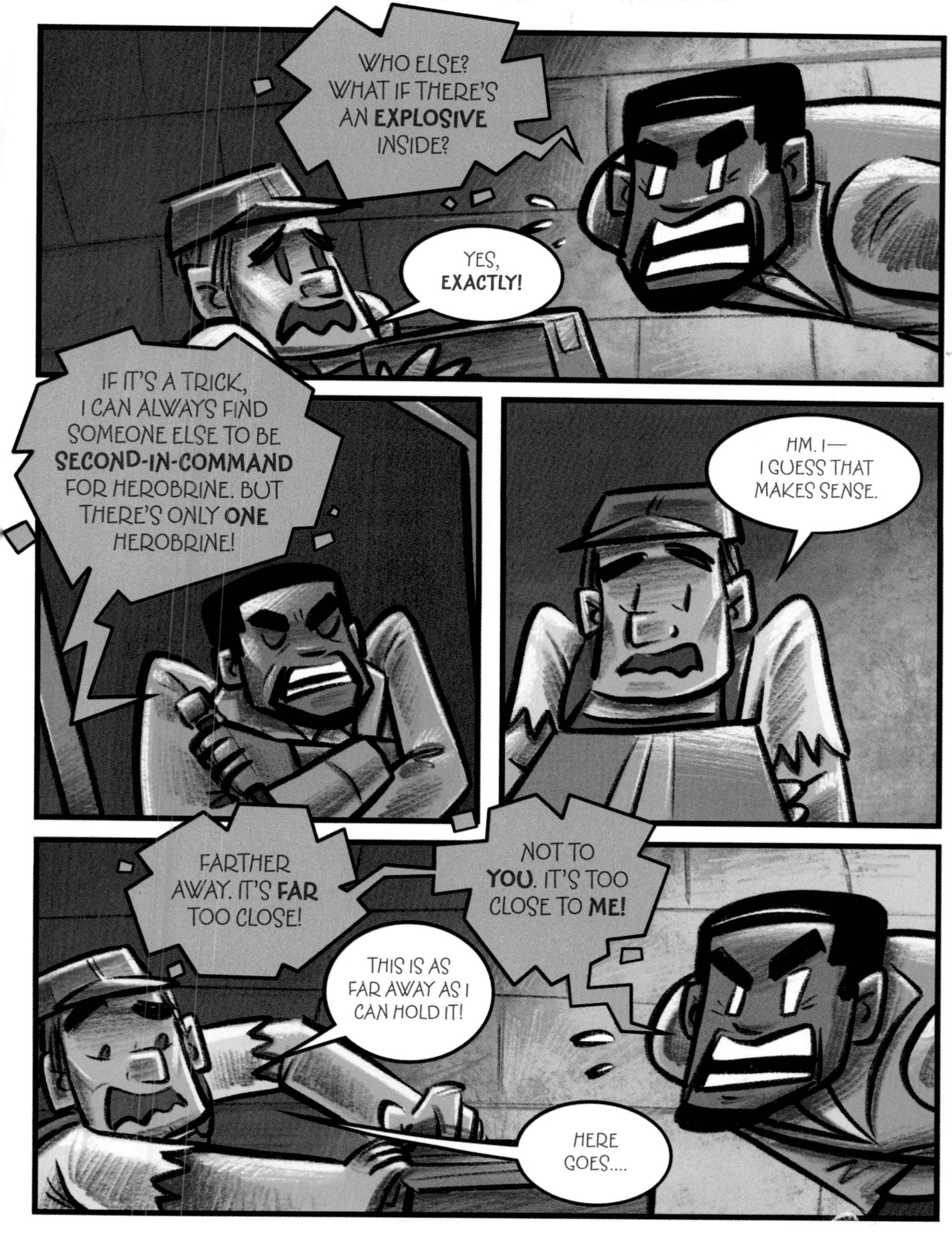
WHO ELSE? WHAT IF THERE'S AN **EXPLOSIVE** INSIDE?
YES, **EXACTLY!**
IF IT'S A TRICK, I CAN ALWAYS FIND SOMEONE ELSE TO BE **SECOND-IN-COMMAND** FOR HEROBRINE. BUT THERE'S ONLY **ONE** HEROBRINE!
HM. I— I GUESS THAT MAKES SENSE.
FARTHER AWAY. IT'S **FAR** TOO CLOSE!
NOT TO **YOU**. IT'S TOO CLOSE TO **ME!**
THIS IS AS FAR AWAY AS I CAN HOLD IT!
HERE GOES....

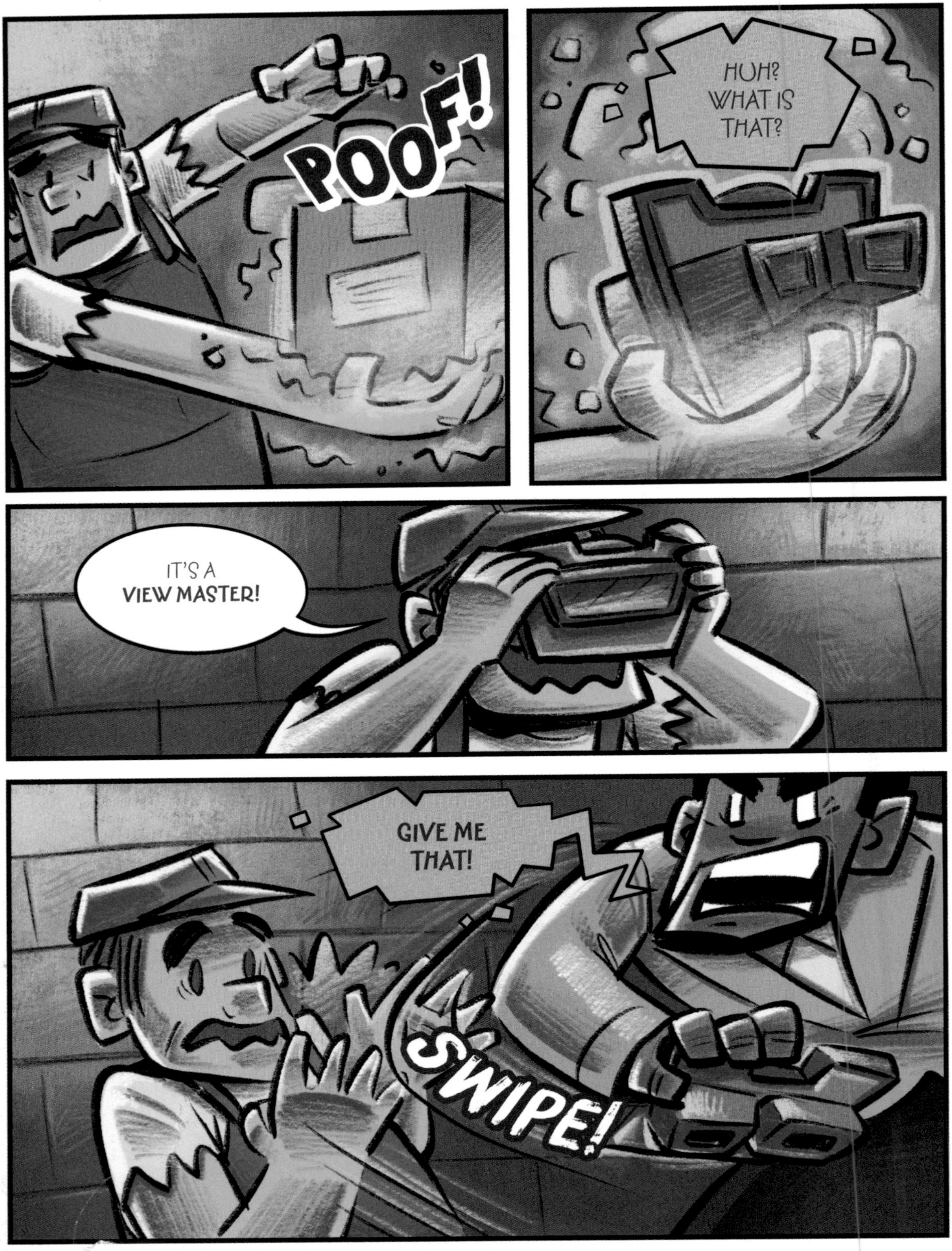
POOF!
HUH? WHAT IS THAT?
IT'S A VIEW MASTER!
GIVE ME THAT!
SWIPE!

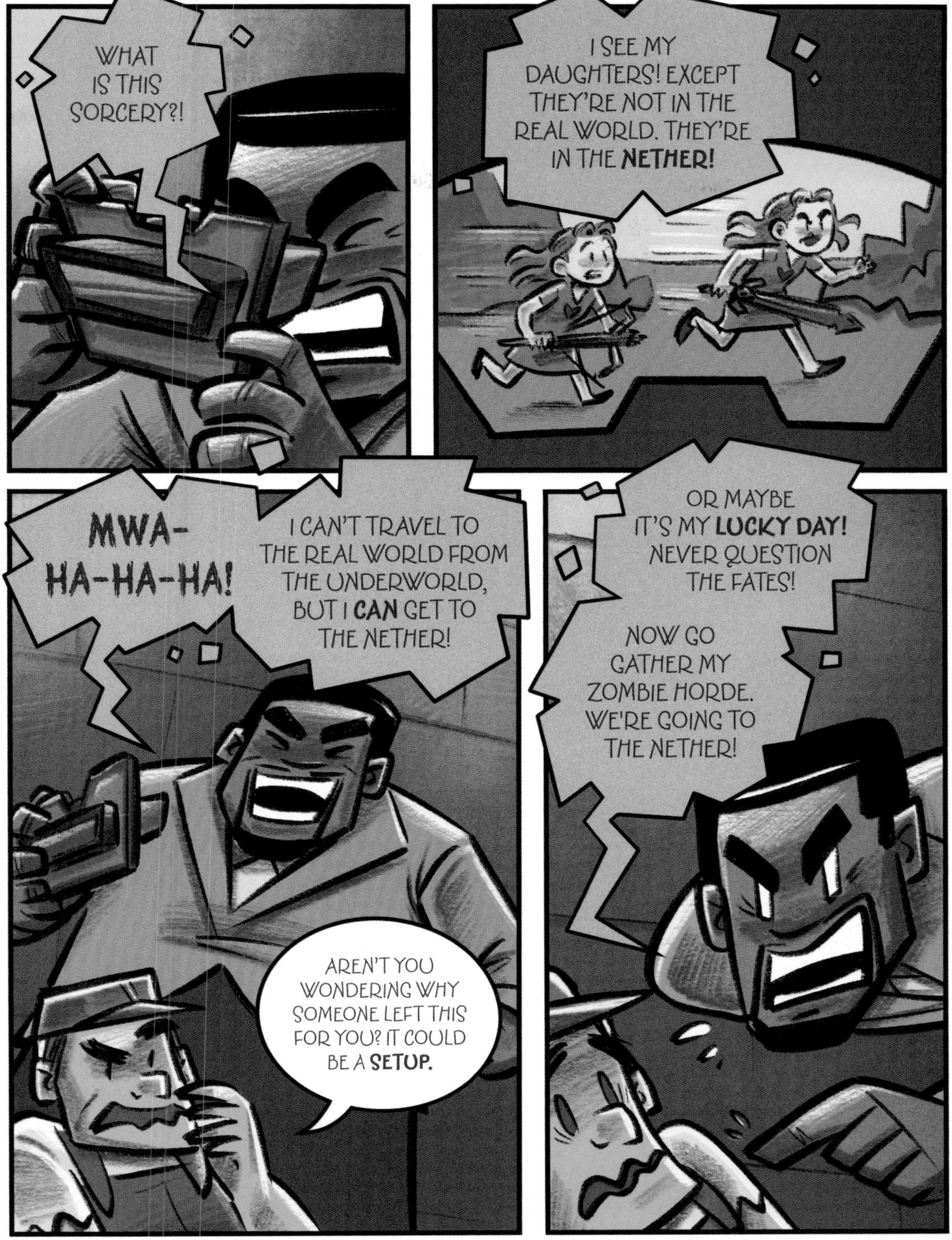
WHAT IS THIS SORCERY?!
I SEE MY DAUGHTERS! EXCEPT THEY'RE NOT IN THE REAL WORLD. THEY'RE IN THE **NETHER!**
MWA-HA-HA-HA!
I CAN'T TRAVEL TO THE REAL WORLD FROM THE UNDERWORLD, BUT I **CAN** GET TO THE NETHER!
AREN'T YOU WONDERING WHY SOMEONE LEFT THIS FOR YOU? IT COULD BE A **SETUP.**
OR MAYBE IT'S MY **LUCKY DAY!** NEVER QUESTION THE FATES!
NOW GO GATHER MY ZOMBIE HORDE. WE'RE GOING TO THE NETHER!

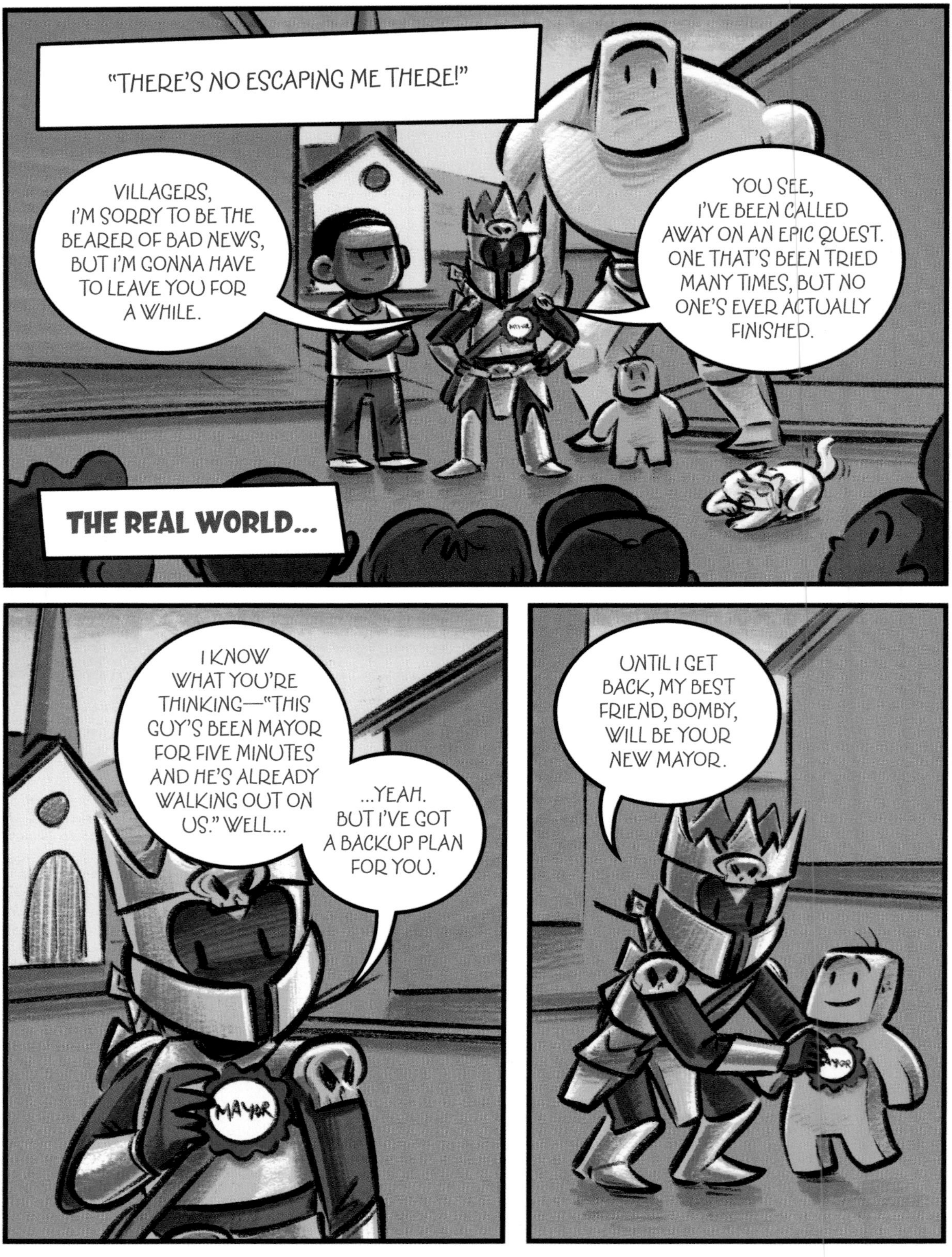
"THERE'S NO ESCAPING ME THERE!"
VILLAGERS, I'M SORRY TO BE THE BEARER OF BAD NEWS, BUT I'M GONNA HAVE TO LEAVE YOU FOR A WHILE.
YOU SEE, I'VE BEEN CALLED AWAY ON AN EPIC QUEST. ONE THAT'S BEEN TRIED MANY TIMES, BUT NO ONE'S EVER ACTUALLY FINISHED.
THE REAL WORLD...
MAYOR
I KNOW WHAT YOU'RE THINKING—"THIS GUY'S BEEN MAYOR FOR FIVE MINUTES AND HE'S ALREADY WALKING OUT ON US." WELL...
...YEAH. BUT I'VE GOT A BACKUP PLAN FOR YOU.
MAYOR
UNTIL I GET BACK, MY BEST FRIEND, BOMBY, WILL BE YOUR NEW MAYOR.
MAYOR

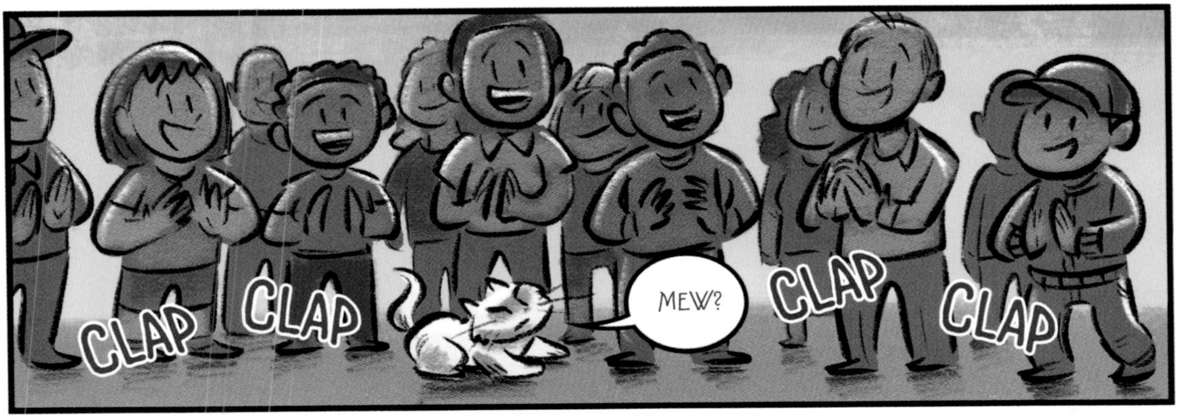
CLAP
CLAP
MEW?
CLAP
CLAP

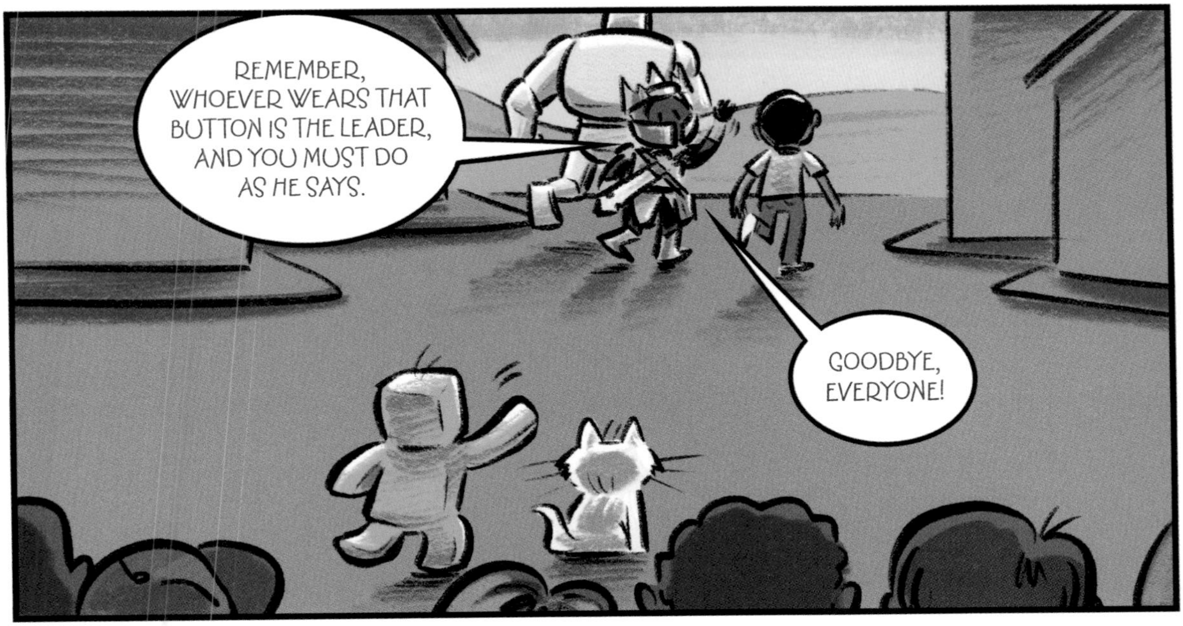
REMEMBER, WHOEVER WEARS THAT BUTTON IS THE LEADER, AND YOU MUST DO AS HE SAYS.
GOODBYE, EVERYONE!

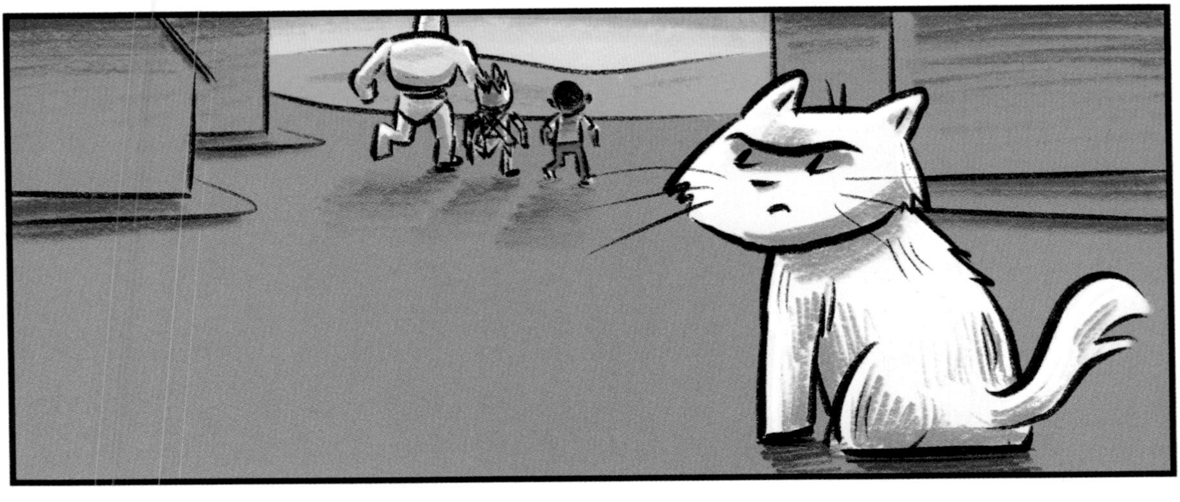

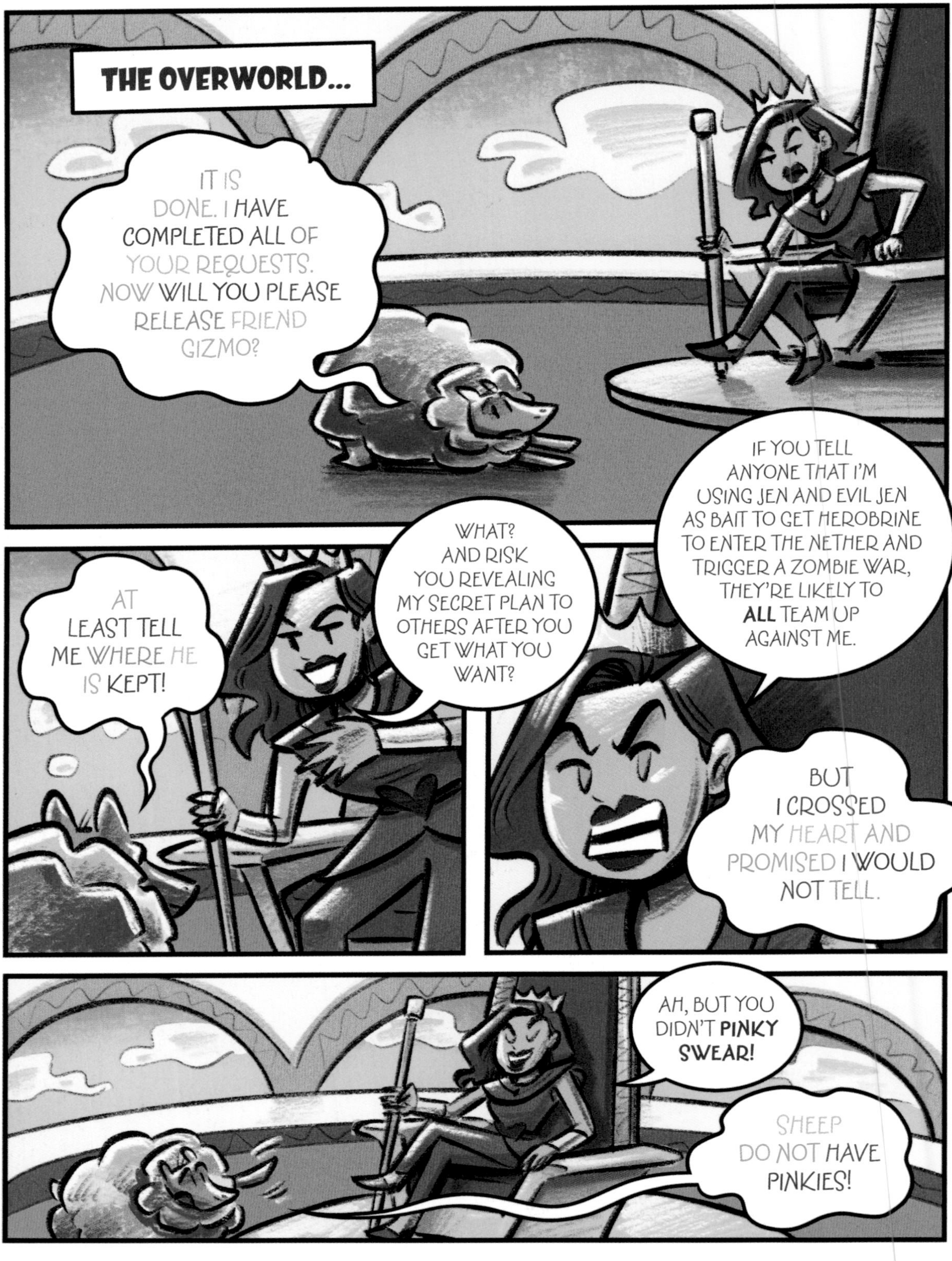
THE OVERWORLD...
IT IS DONE. I HAVE COMPLETED ALL OF YOUR REQUESTS. NOW WILL YOU PLEASE RELEASE FRIEND GIZMO?
AT LEAST TELL ME WHERE HE IS KEPT!
WHAT? AND RISK YOU REVEALING MY SECRET PLAN TO OTHERS AFTER YOU GET WHAT YOU WANT?
IF YOU TELL ANYONE THAT I'M USING JEN AND EVIL JEN AS BAIT TO GET HEROBRINE TO ENTER THE NETHER AND TRIGGER A ZOMBIE WAR, THEY'RE LIKELY TO ALL TEAM UP AGAINST ME.
BUT I CROSSED MY HEART AND PROMISED I WOULD NOT TELL.
AH, BUT YOU DIDN'T PINKY SWEAR!
SHEEP DO NOT HAVE PINKIES!

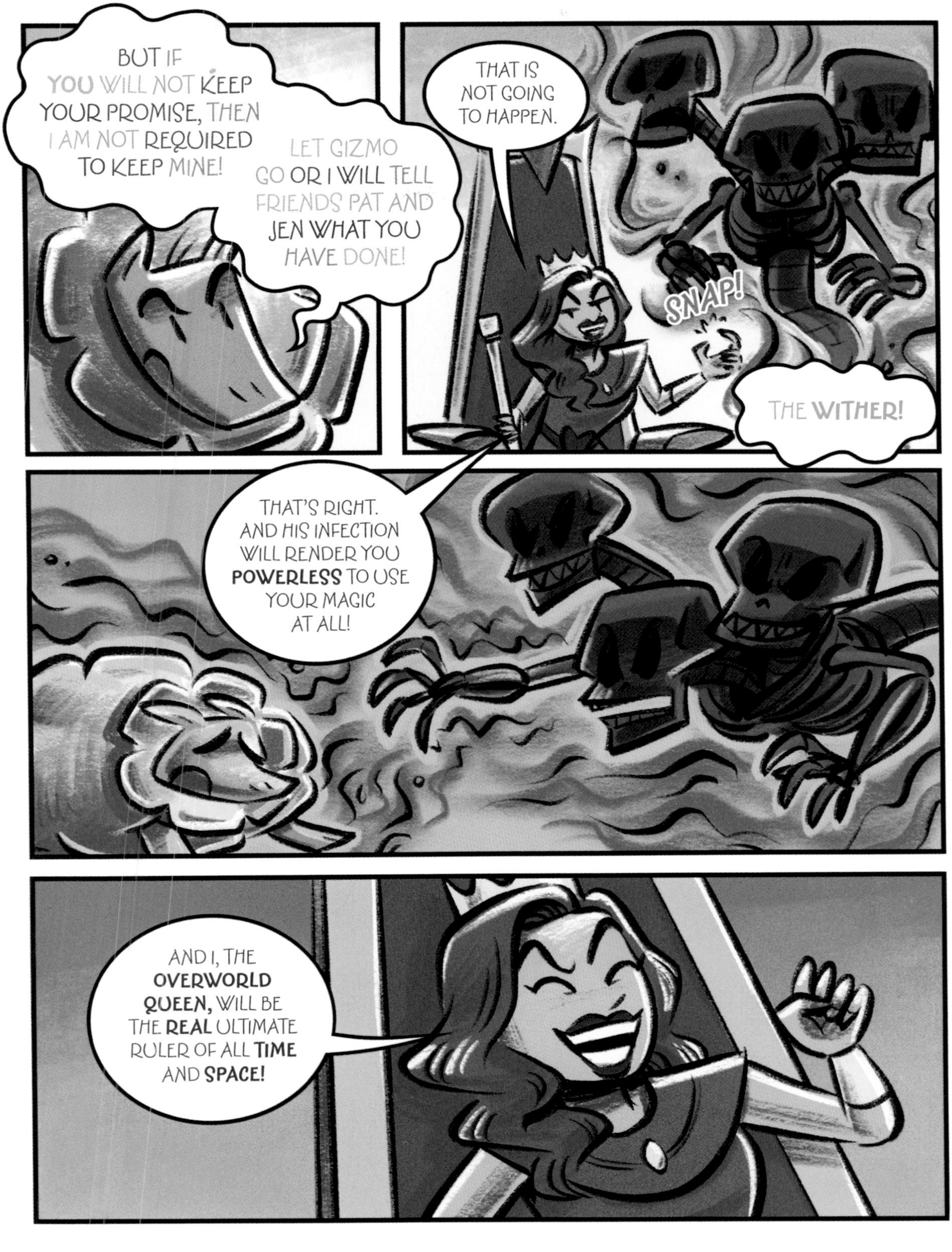
BUT IF YOU WILL NOT KEEP YOUR PROMISE, THEN I AM NOT REQUIRED TO KEEP MINE!
LET GIZMO GO OR I WILL TELL FRIENDS PAT AND JEN WHAT YOU HAVE DONE!
THAT IS NOT GOING TO HAPPEN.
SNAP!
THE WITHER!
THAT'S RIGHT. AND HIS INFECTION WILL RENDER YOU POWERLESS TO USE YOUR MAGIC AT ALL!
AND I, THE OVERWORLD QUEEN, WILL BE THE REAL ULTIMATE RULER OF ALL TIME AND SPACE!

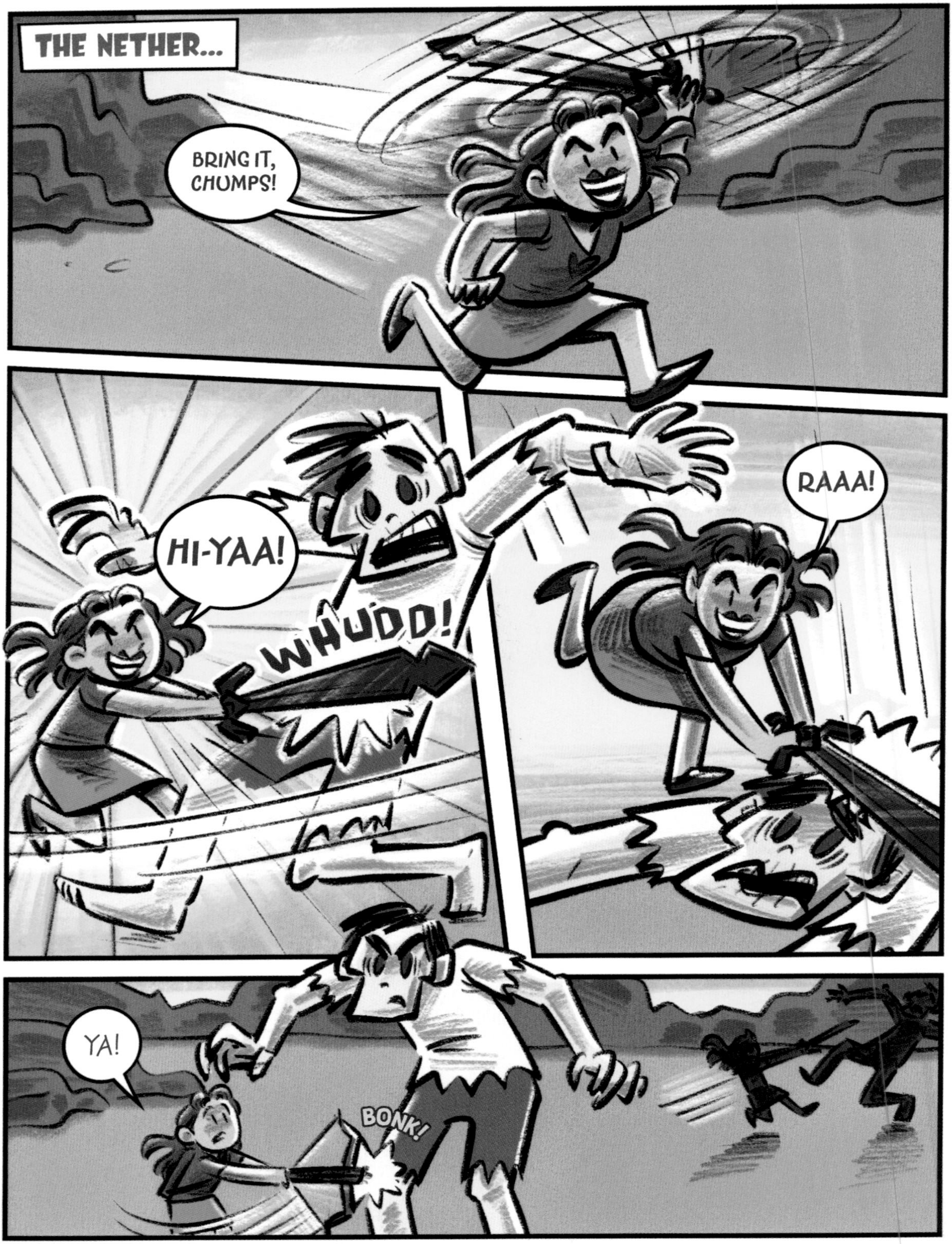
THE NETHER...
BRING IT, CHUMPS!
HI-YAA!
WHUDD!
RAAA!
YA!
BONK!

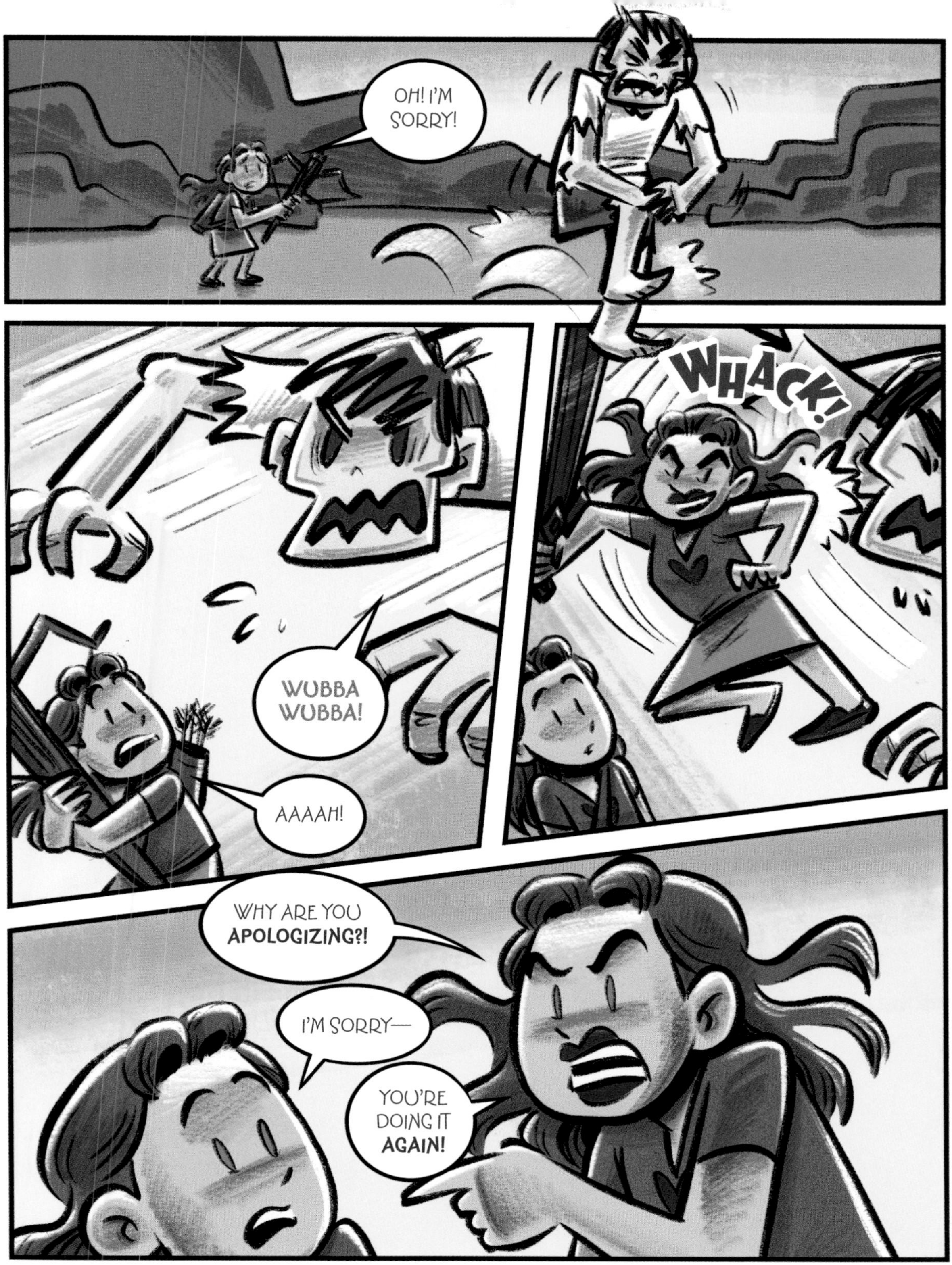
OH! I'M SORRY!
WUBBA WUBBA!
AAAAH!
WHACK!
WHY ARE YOU APOLOGIZING?!
I'M SORRY—
YOU'RE DOING IT AGAIN!

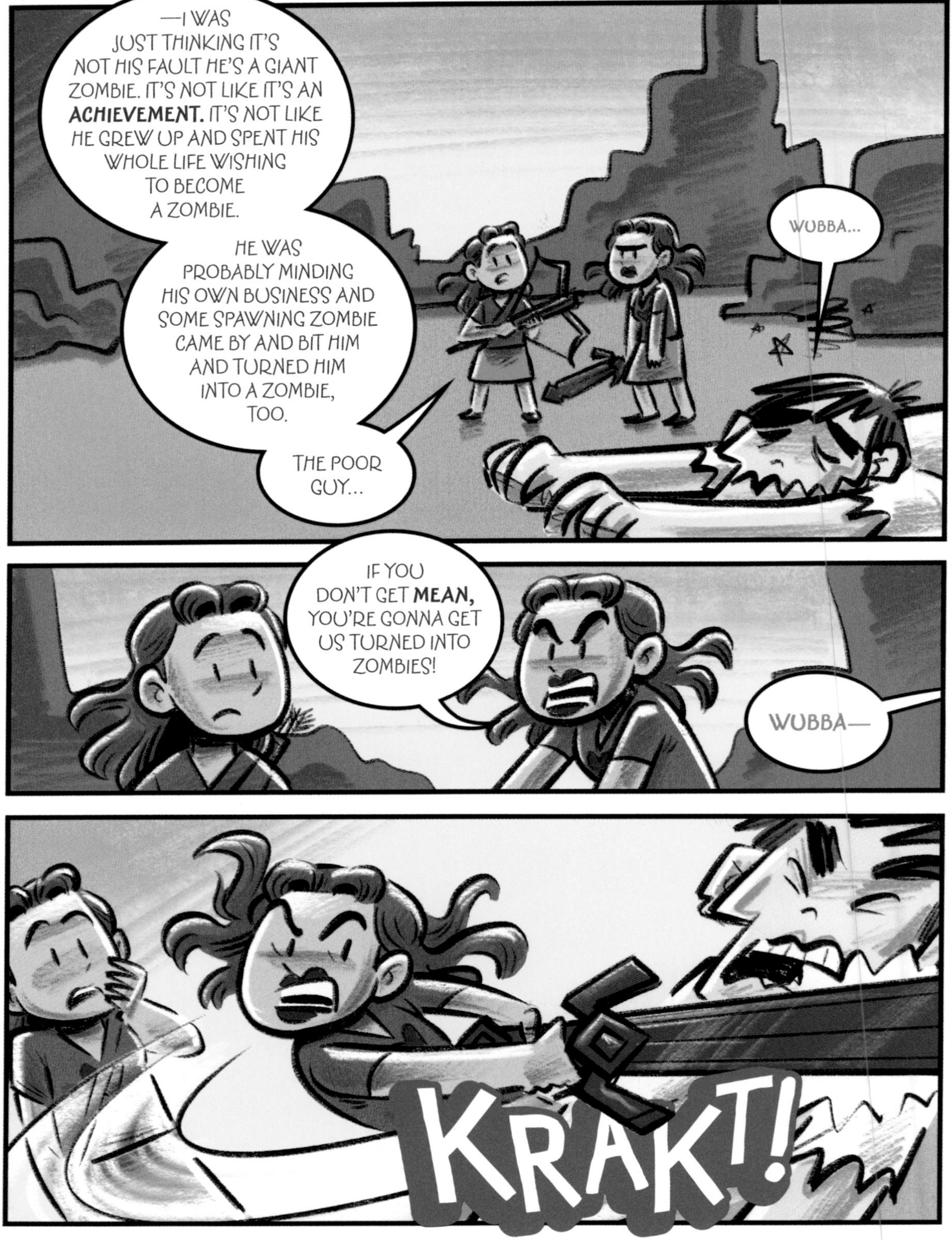
—I WAS JUST THINKING IT'S NOT HIS FAULT HE'S A GIANT ZOMBIE. IT'S NOT LIKE IT'S AN **ACHIEVEMENT.** IT'S NOT LIKE HE GREW UP AND SPENT HIS WHOLE LIFE WISHING TO BECOME A ZOMBIE.
HE WAS PROBABLY MINDING HIS OWN BUSINESS AND SOME SPAWNING ZOMBIE CAME BY AND BIT HIM AND TURNED HIM INTO A ZOMBIE, TOO.
THE POOR GUY...
WUBBA...
IF YOU DON'T GET **MEAN,** YOU'RE GONNA GET US TURNED INTO ZOMBIES!
WUBBA—
KRAKT!

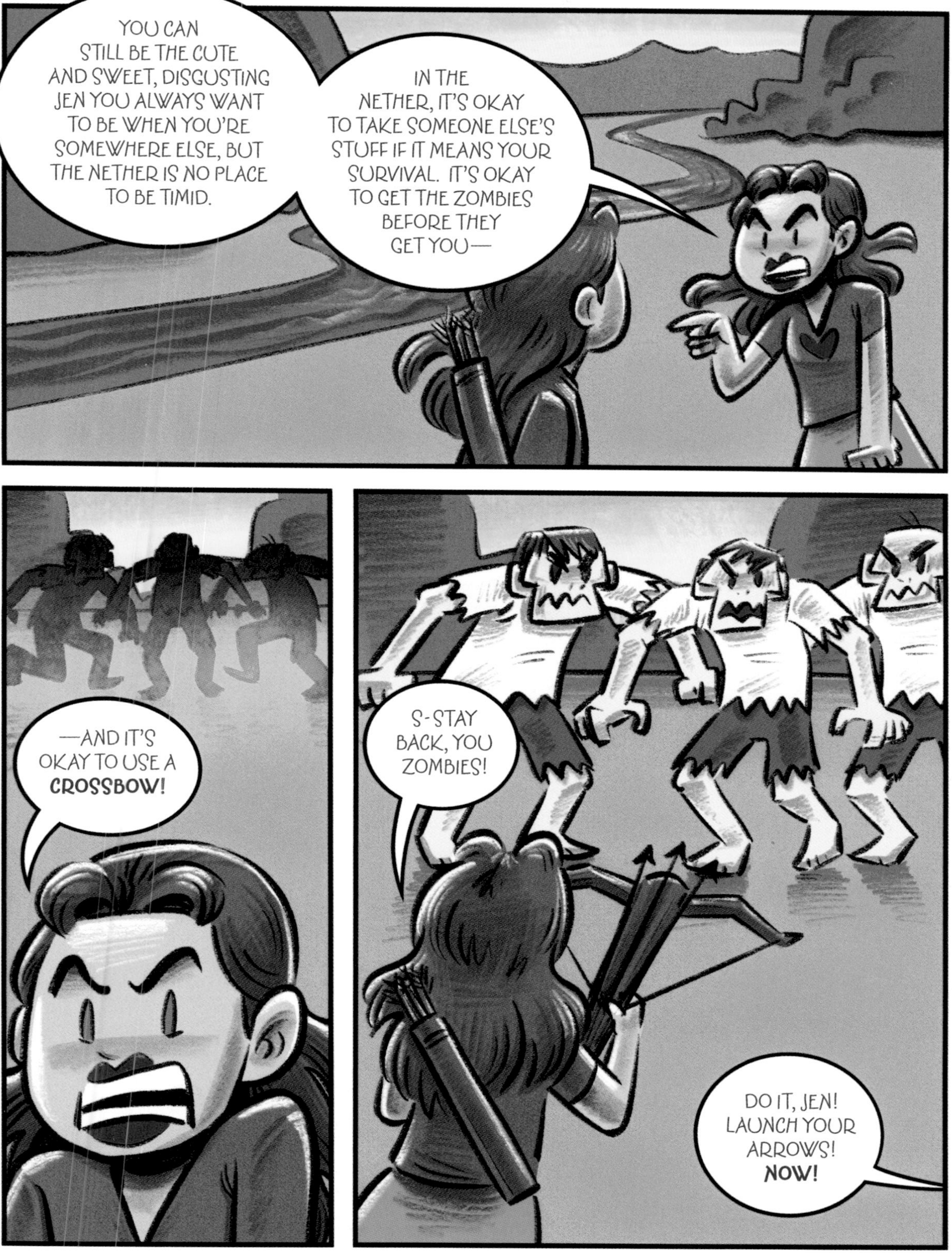
YOU CAN STILL BE THE CUTE AND SWEET, DISGUSTING JEN YOU ALWAYS WANT TO BE WHEN YOU'RE SOMEWHERE ELSE, BUT THE NETHER IS NO PLACE TO BE TIMID.
IN THE NETHER, IT'S OKAY TO TAKE SOMEONE ELSE'S STUFF IF IT MEANS YOUR SURVIVAL. IT'S OKAY TO GET THE ZOMBIES BEFORE THEY GET YOU—
—AND IT'S OKAY TO USE A **CROSSBOW!**
S-STAY BACK, YOU ZOMBIES!
DO IT, JEN! LAUNCH YOUR ARROWS! **NOW!**

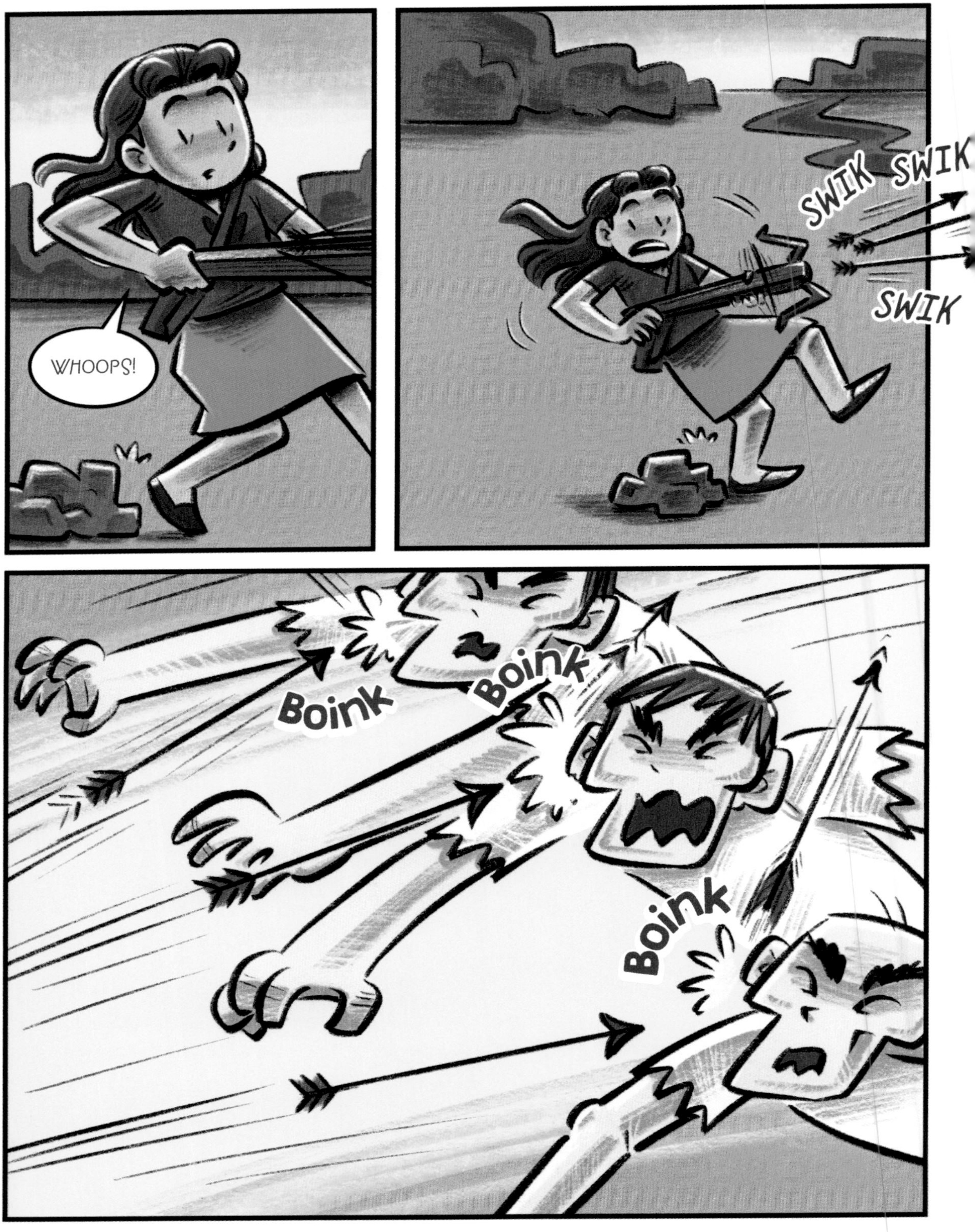
WHOOPS!
SWIK SWIK
SWIK
Boink
Boink
Boink

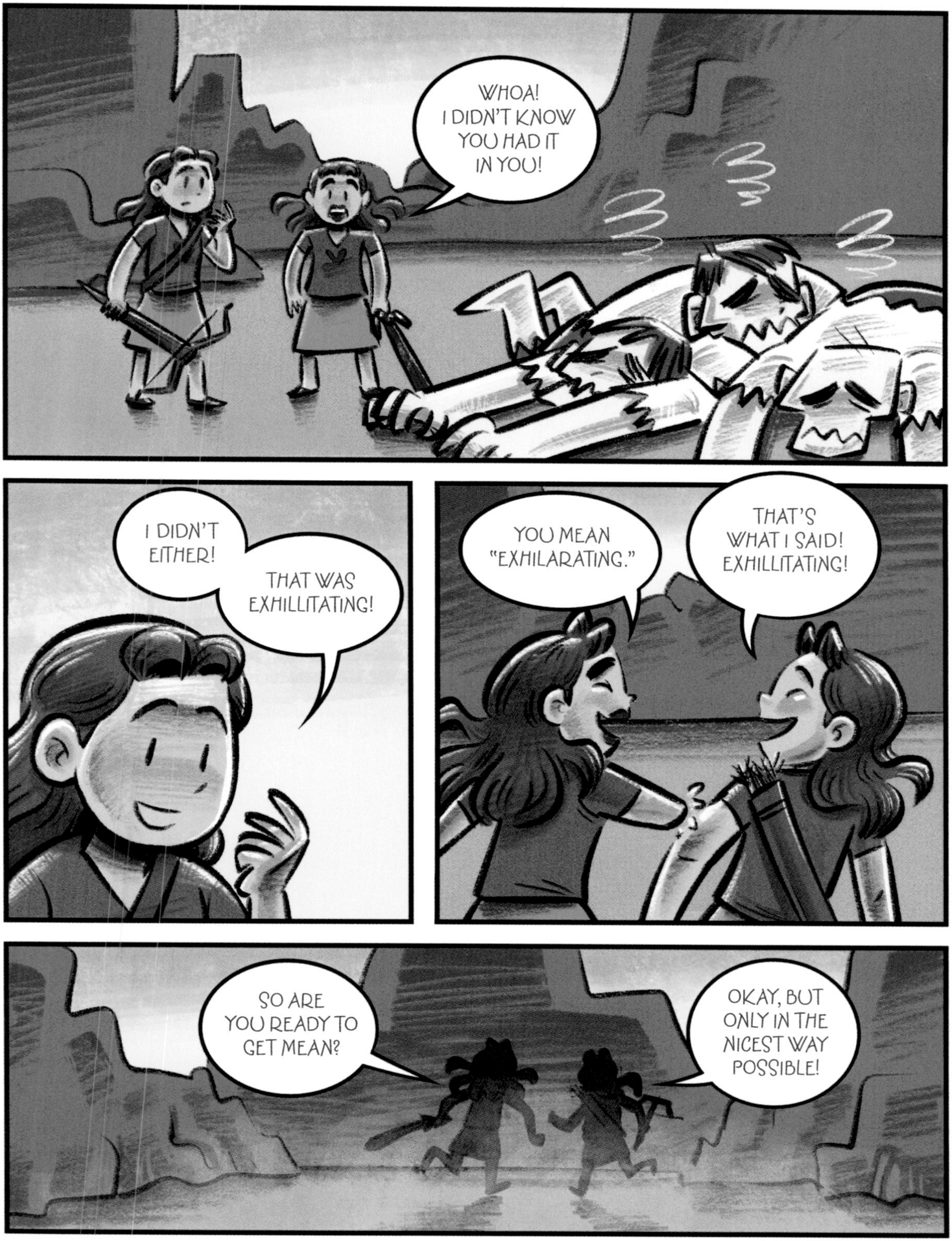
WHOA! I DIDN'T KNOW YOU HAD IT IN YOU!
I DIDN'T EITHER!
THAT WAS EXHILLITATING!
YOU MEAN "EXHILARATING."
THAT'S WHAT I SAID! EXHILLITATING!
SO ARE YOU READY TO GET MEAN?
OKAY, BUT ONLY IN THE NICEST WAY POSSIBLE!

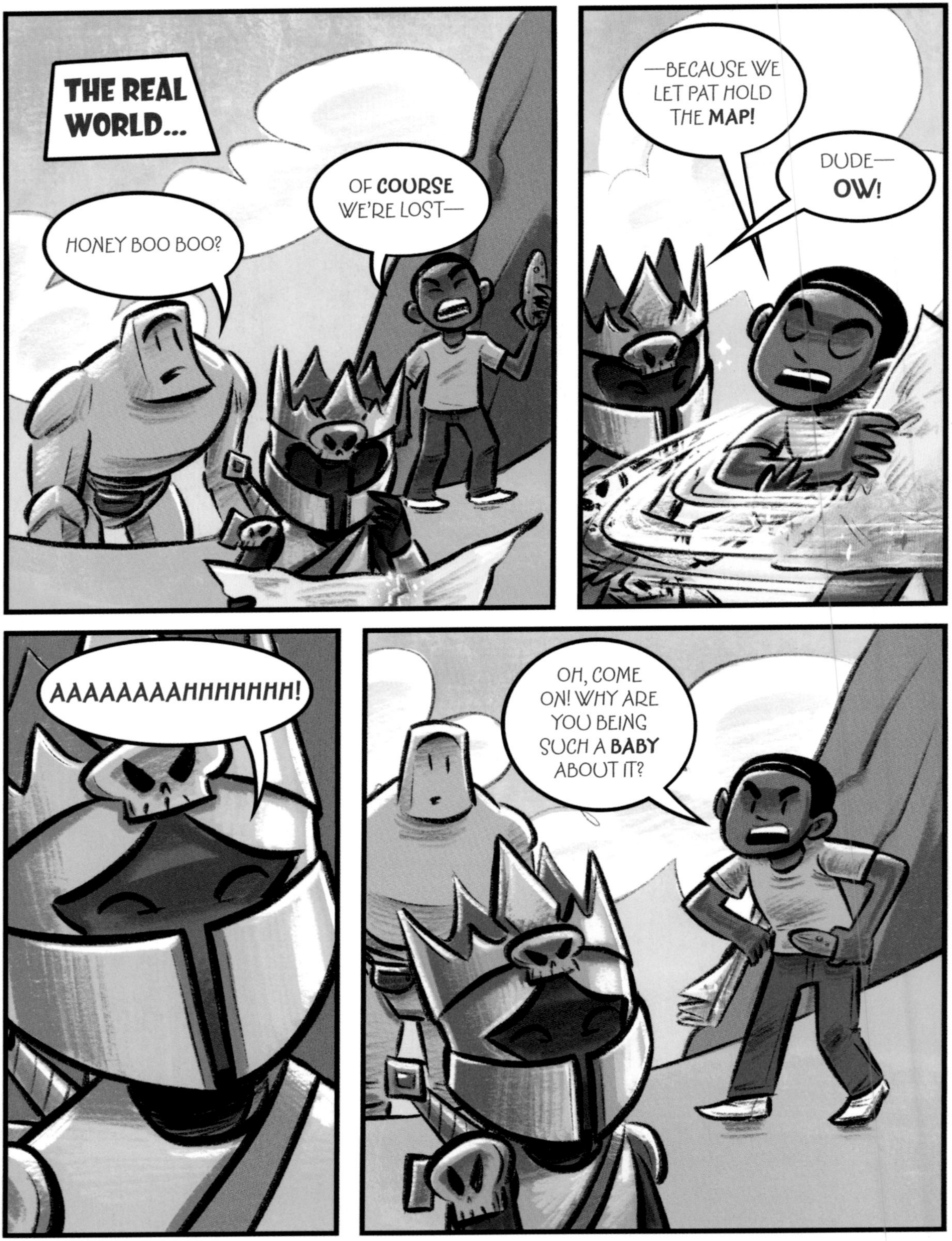
THE REAL WORLD...
HONEY BOO BOO?
OF COURSE WE'RE LOST—
—BECAUSE WE LET PAT HOLD THE MAP!
DUDE— OW!
AAAAAAAAHHHHHHH!
OH, COME ON! WHY ARE YOU BEING SUCH A BABY ABOUT IT?

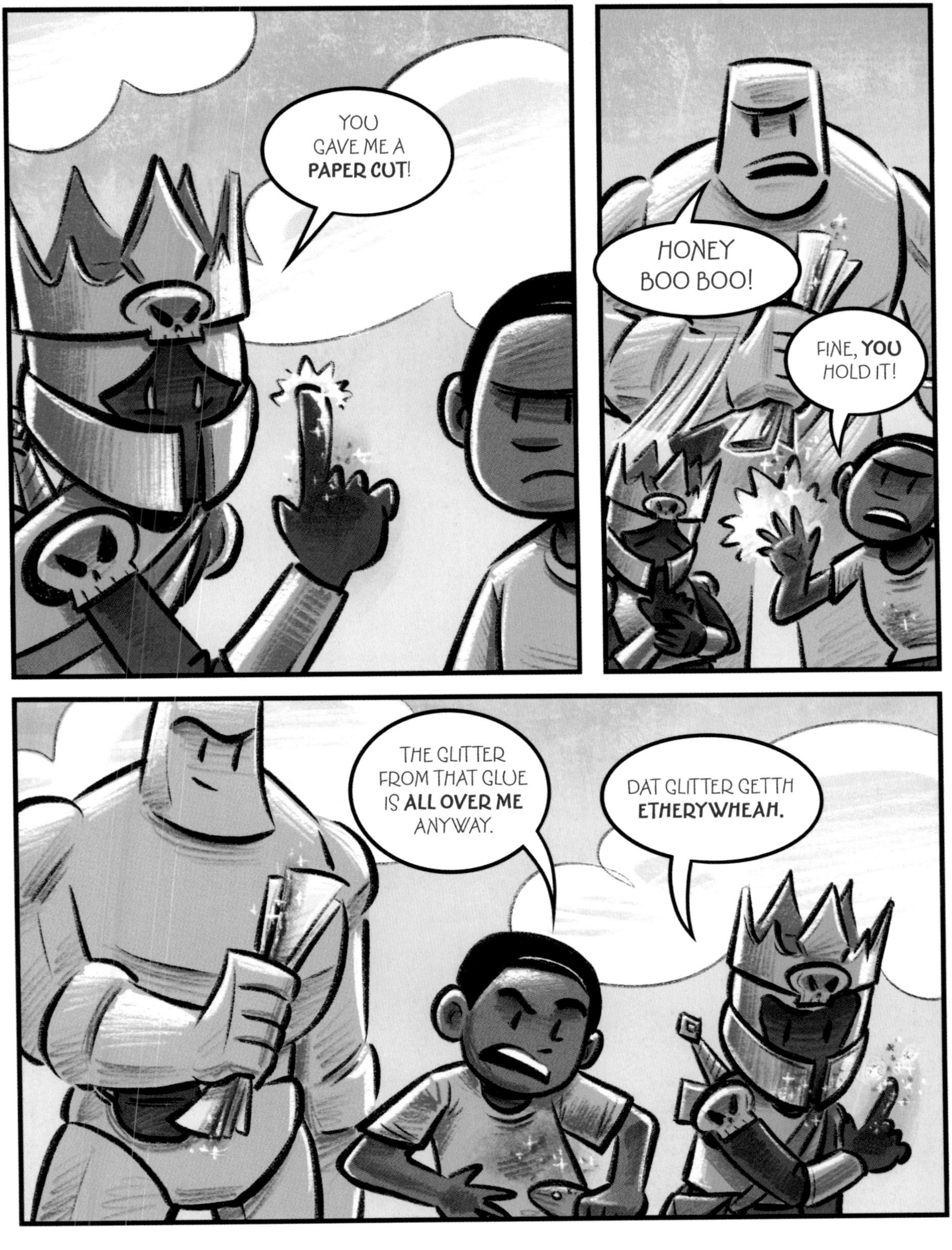
YOU GAVE ME A **PAPER CUT**!
HONEY BOO BOO!
FINE, **YOU** HOLD IT!
THE GLITTER FROM THAT GLUE IS **ALL OVER ME** ANYWAY.
DAT GLITTER GETTH **ETHERYWHEAH.**

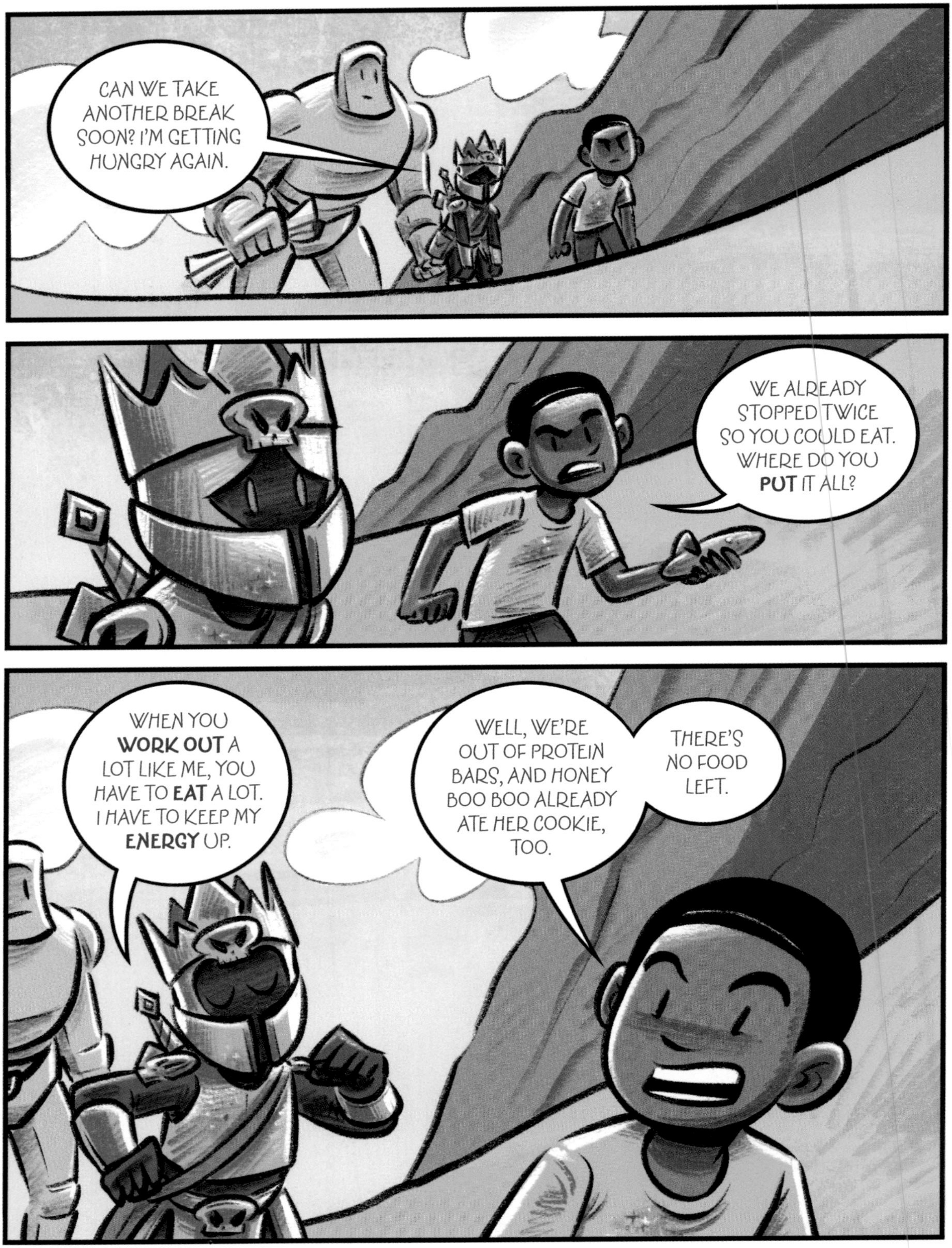
CAN WE TAKE ANOTHER BREAK SOON? I'M GETTING HUNGRY AGAIN.
WE ALREADY STOPPED TWICE SO YOU COULD EAT. WHERE DO YOU **PUT** IT ALL?
WHEN YOU **WORK OUT** A LOT LIKE ME, YOU HAVE TO **EAT** A LOT. I HAVE TO KEEP MY **ENERGY** UP.
WELL, WE'RE OUT OF PROTEIN BARS, AND HONEY BOO BOO ALREADY ATE HER COOKIE, TOO.
THERE'S NO FOOD LEFT.

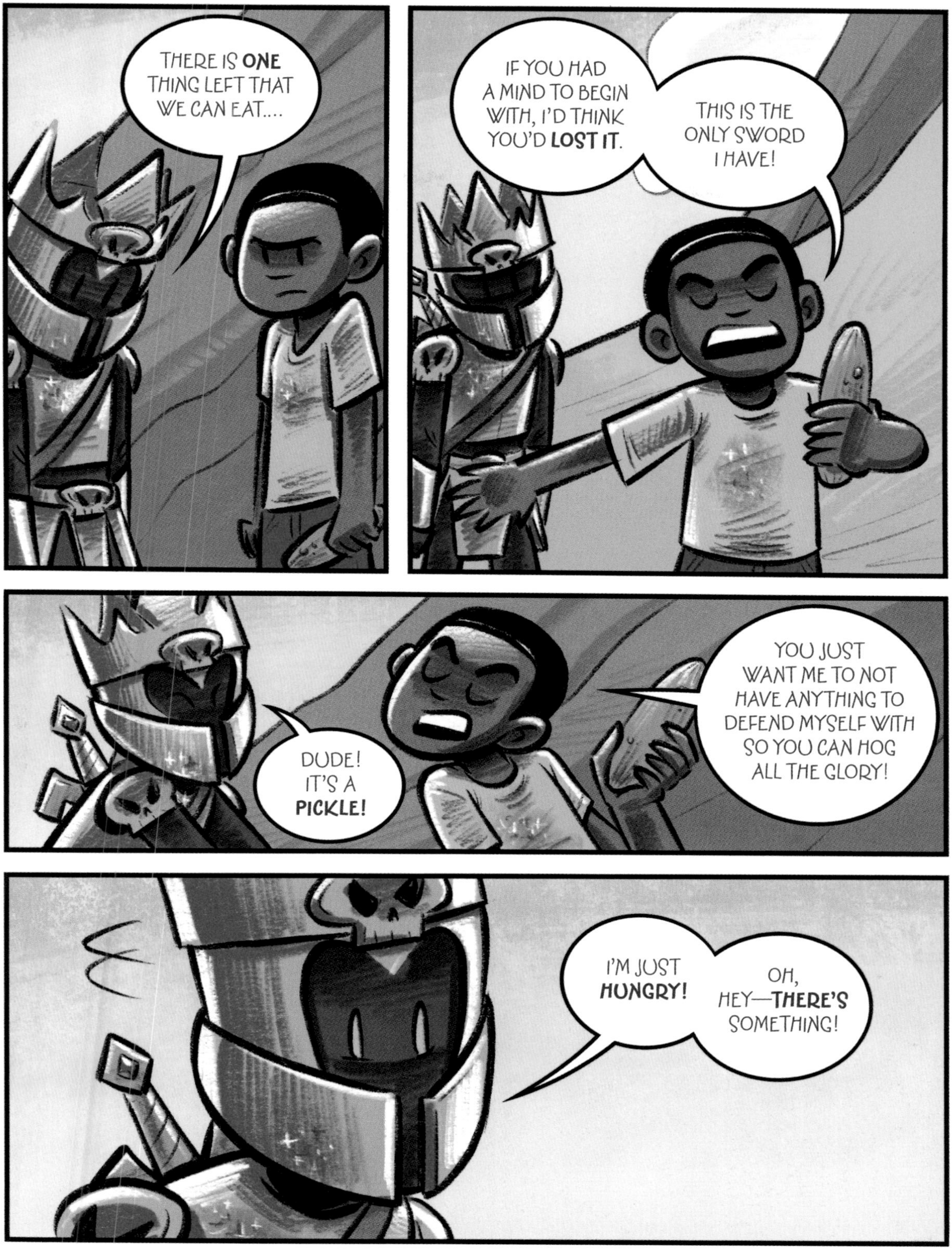
THERE IS **ONE** THING LEFT THAT WE CAN EAT....
IF YOU HAD A MIND TO BEGIN WITH, I'D THINK YOU'D **LOST IT**.
THIS IS THE ONLY SWORD I HAVE!
YOU JUST WANT ME TO NOT HAVE ANYTHING TO DEFEND MYSELF WITH SO YOU CAN HOG ALL THE GLORY!
DUDE! IT'S A **PICKLE!**
I'M JUST **HUNGRY!**
OH, HEY—**THERE'S** SOMETHING!

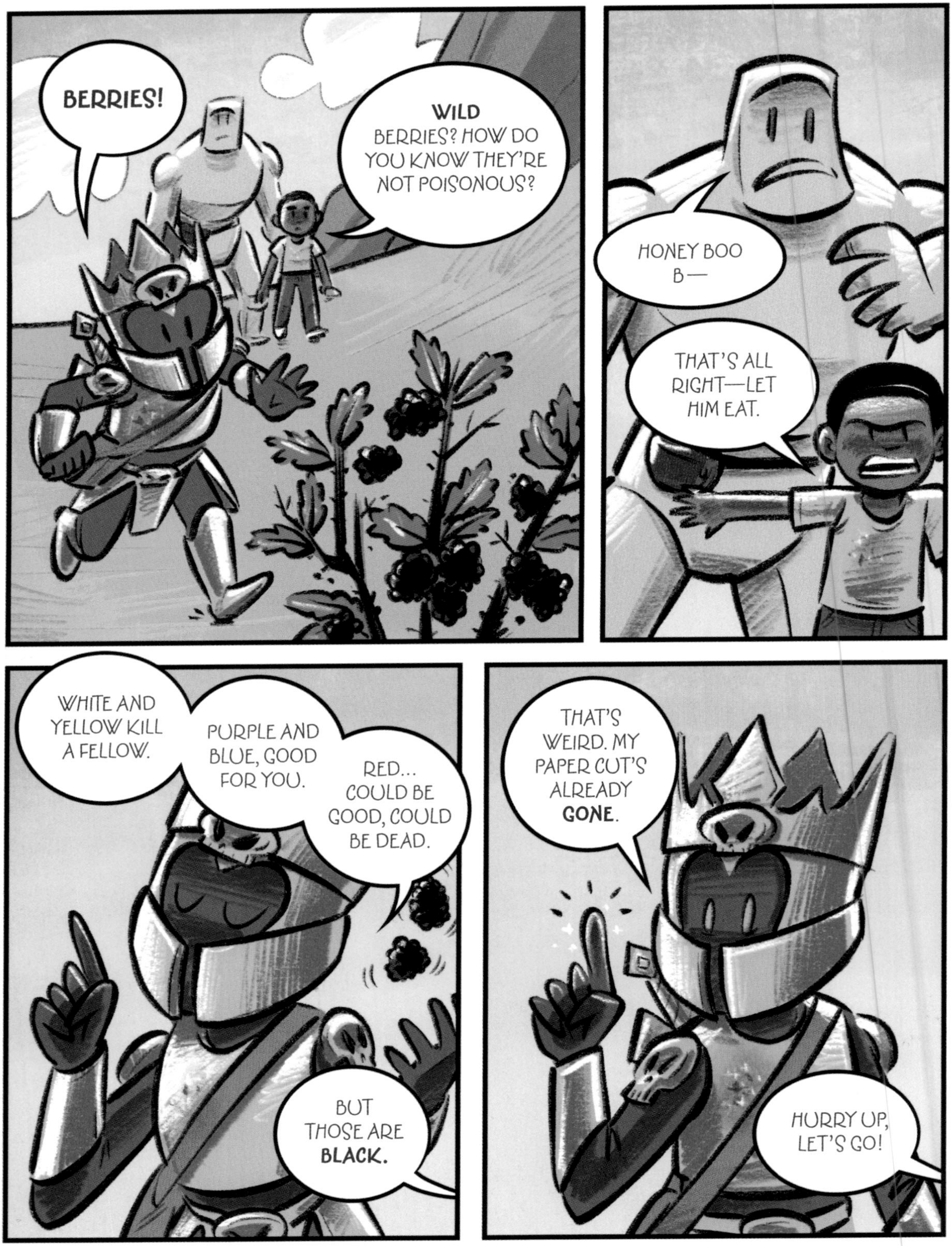

BERRIES!
WILD BERRIES? HOW DO YOU KNOW THEY'RE NOT POISONOUS?
HONEY BOO B—
THAT'S ALL RIGHT—LET HIM EAT.
WHITE AND YELLOW KILL A FELLOW.
PURPLE AND BLUE, GOOD FOR YOU.
RED... COULD BE GOOD, COULD BE DEAD.
BUT THOSE ARE BLACK.
THAT'S WEIRD. MY PAPER CUT'S ALREADY GONE.
HURRY UP, LET'S GO!

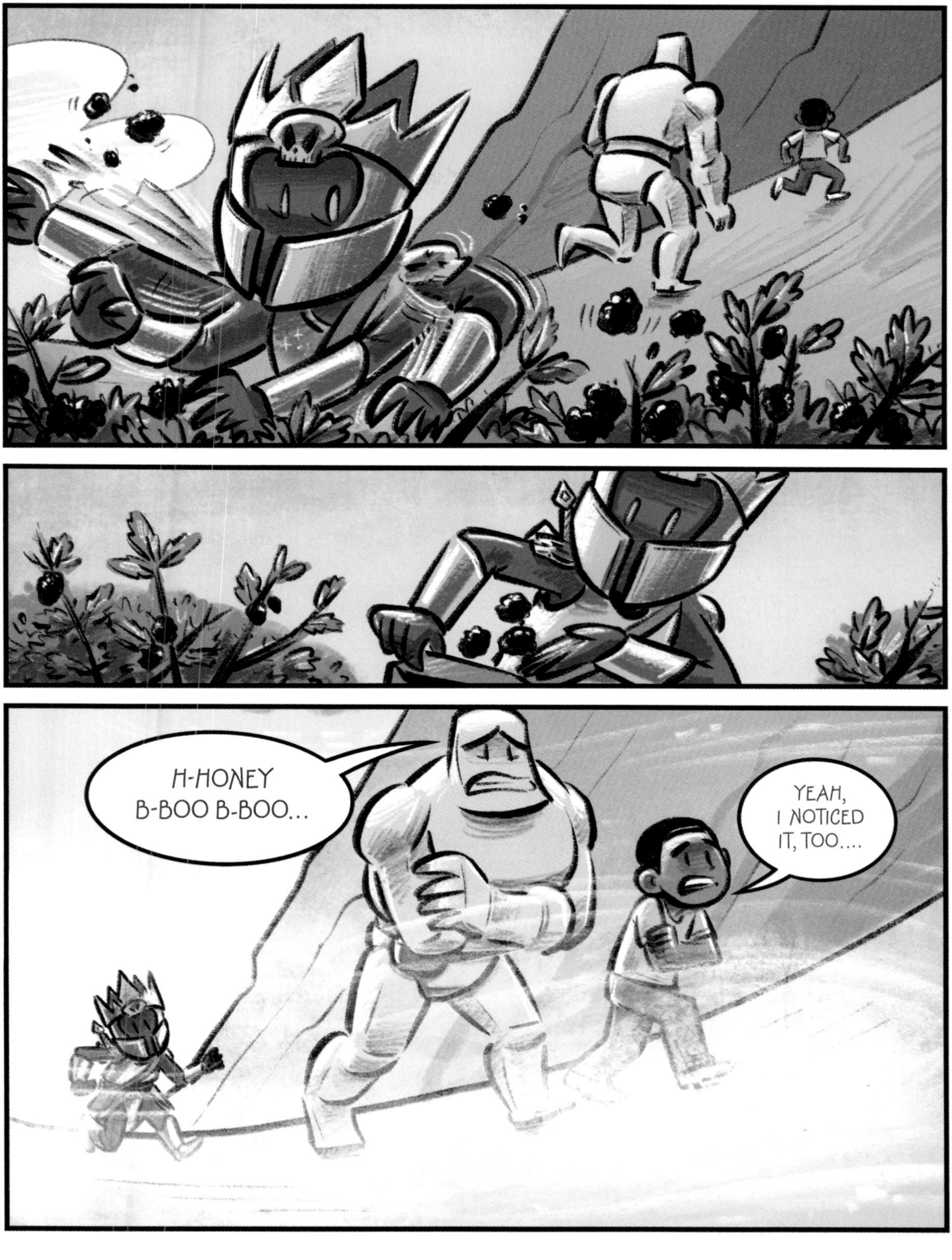
H-HONEY B-BOO B-BOO...
YEAH, I NOTICED IT, TOO....

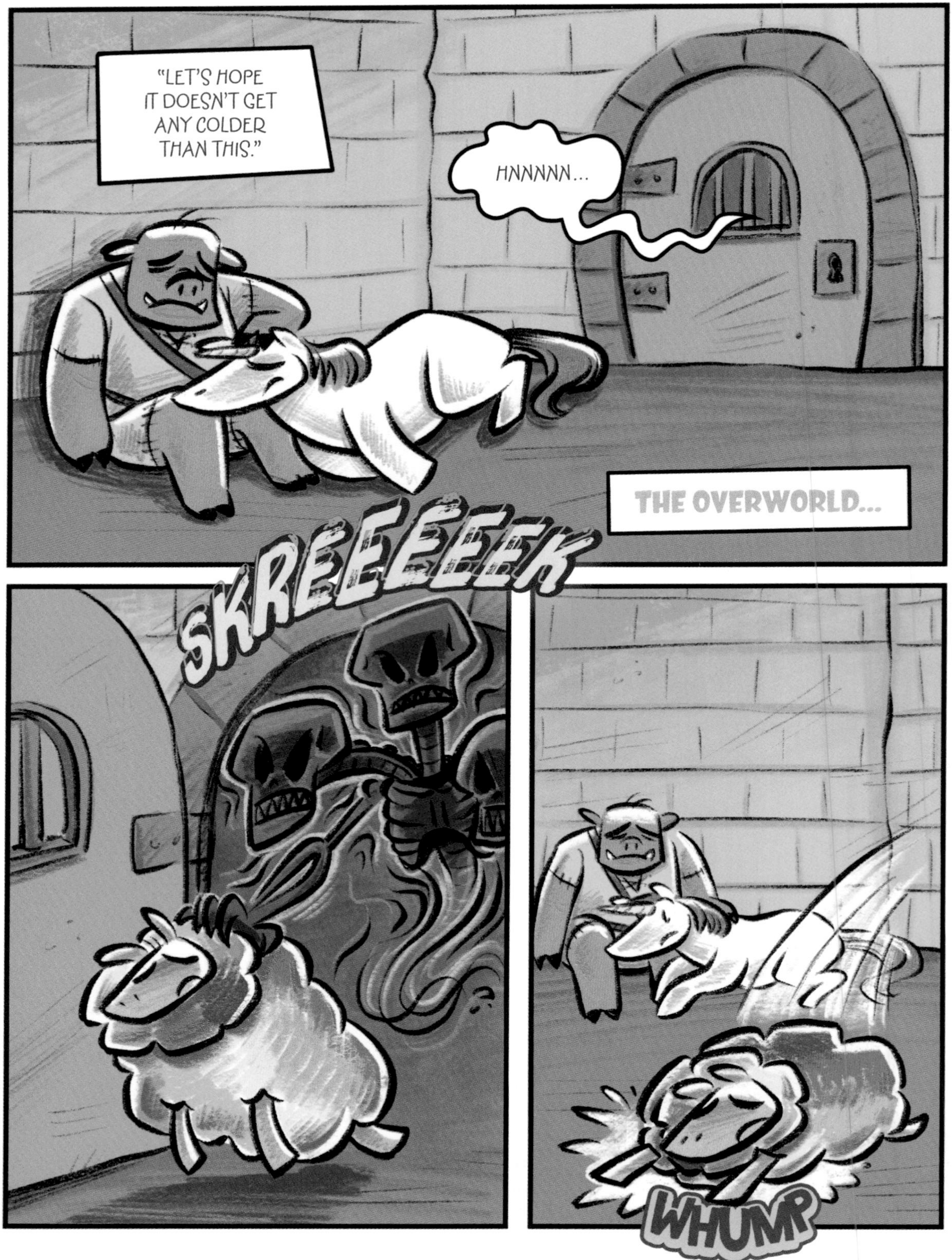
"LET'S HOPE IT DOESN'T GET ANY COLDER THAN THIS."
HNNNNN...
THE OVERWORLD...
SKREEEEEK
WHUMP

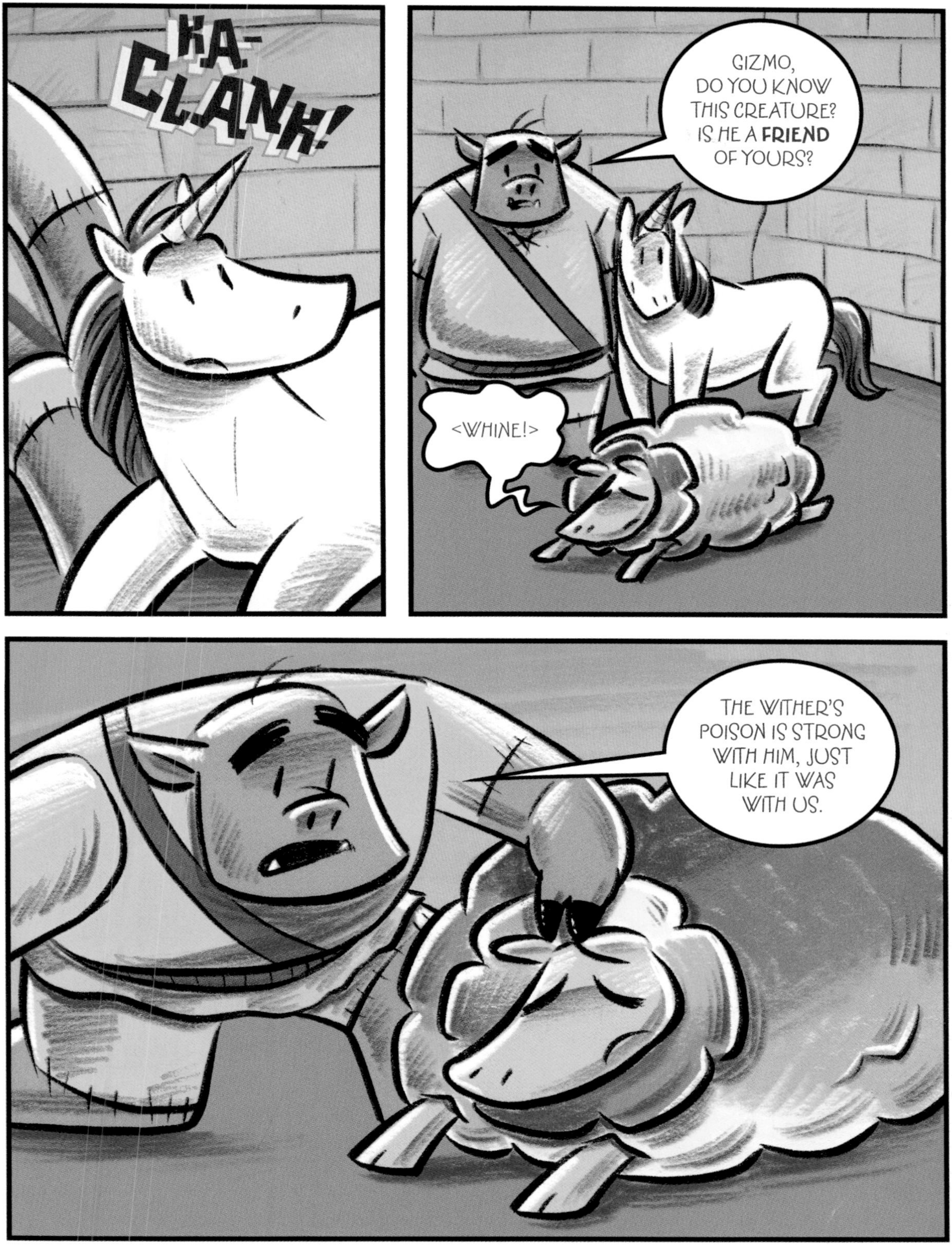
KA-CLANK!
GIZMO, DO YOU KNOW THIS CREATURE? IS HE A **FRIEND** OF YOURS?
<WHINE!>
THE WITHER'S POISON IS STRONG WITH HIM, JUST LIKE IT WAS WITH US.

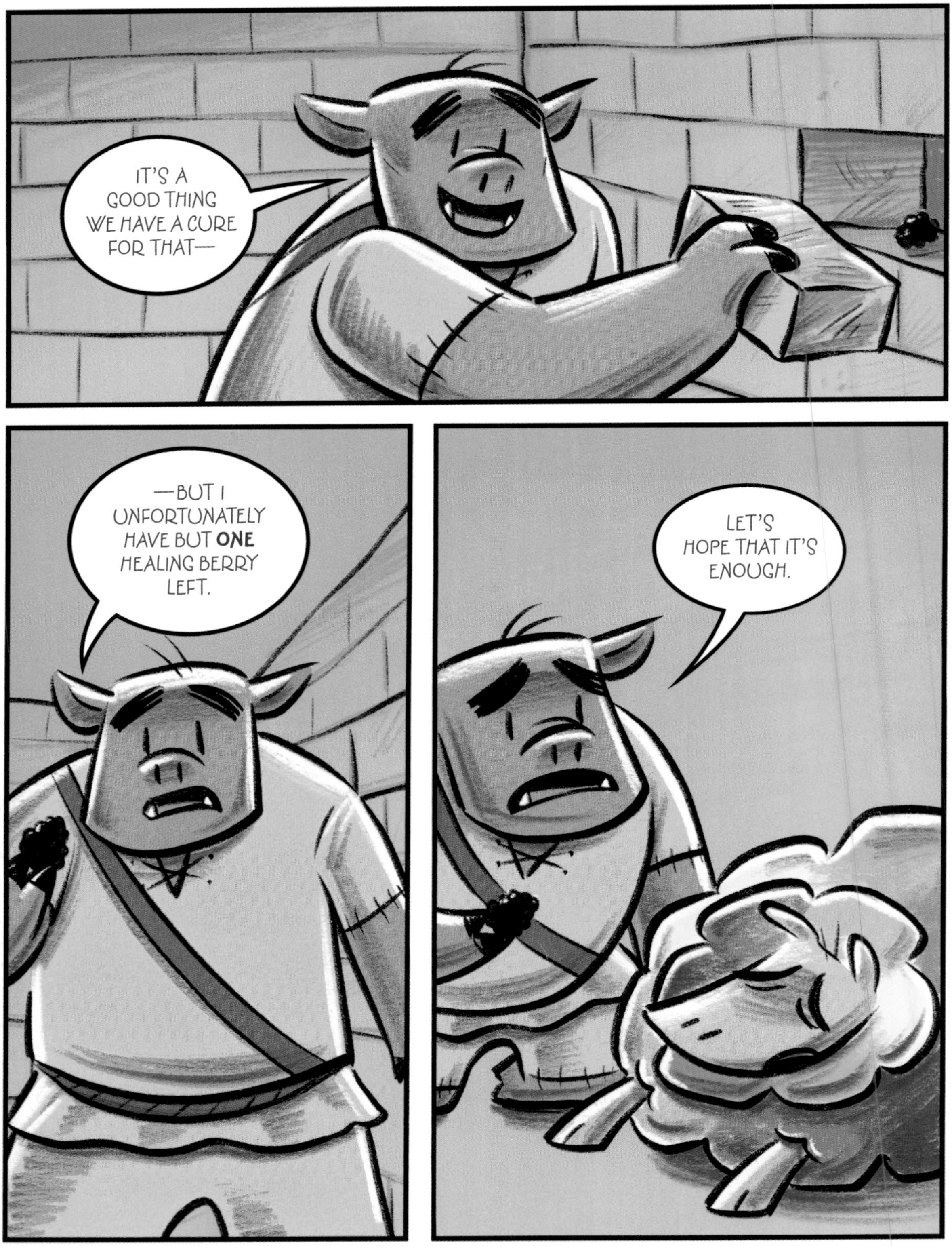
IT'S A GOOD THING WE HAVE A CURE FOR THAT—
—BUT I UNFORTUNATELY HAVE BUT **ONE** HEALING BERRY LEFT.
LET'S HOPE THAT IT'S ENOUGH.

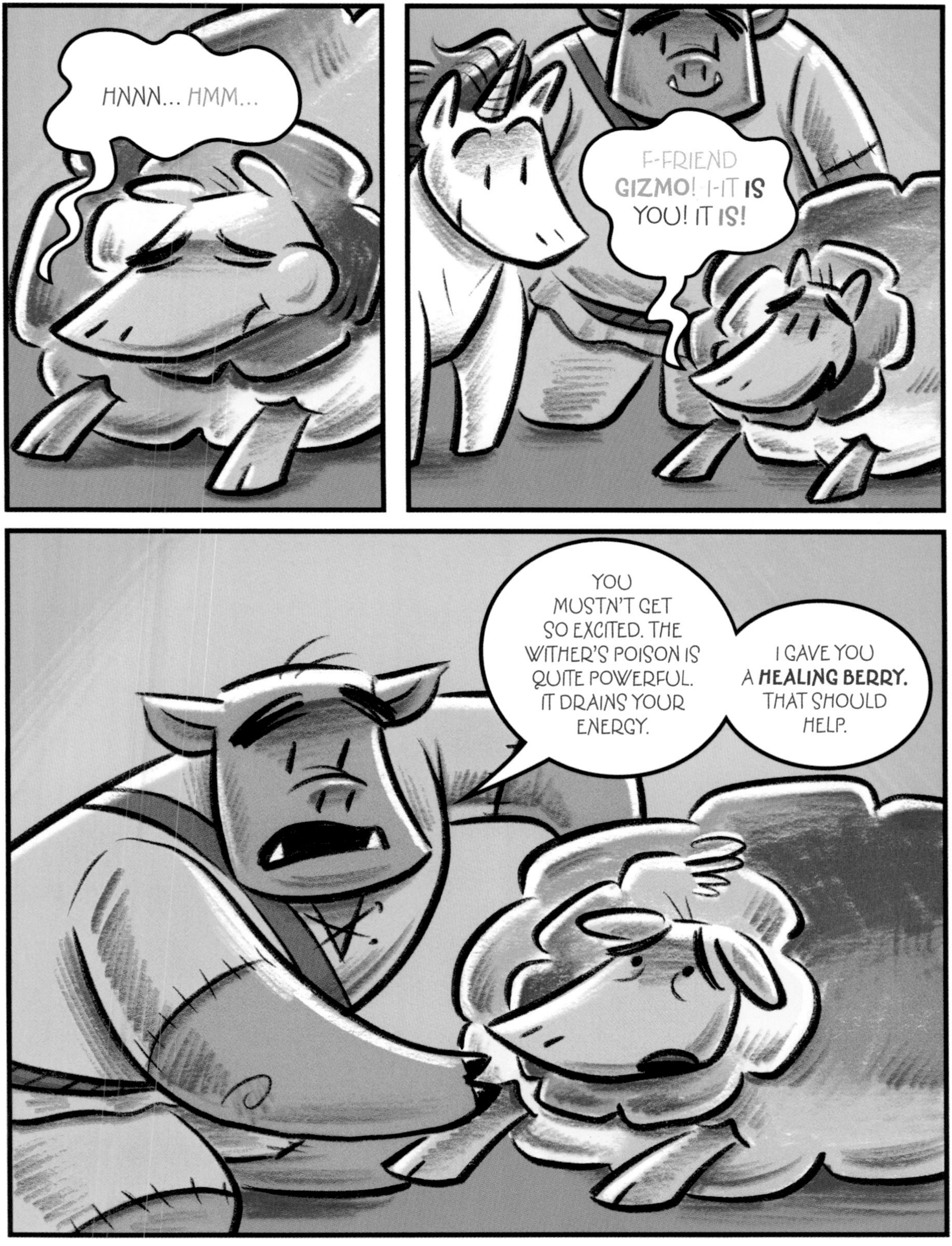
HNNN... HMM...
F-FRIEND GIZMO! I-IT IS YOU! IT IS!
YOU MUSTN'T GET SO EXCITED. THE WITHER'S POISON IS QUITE POWERFUL. IT DRAINS YOUR ENERGY.
I GAVE YOU A HEALING BERRY. THAT SHOULD HELP.

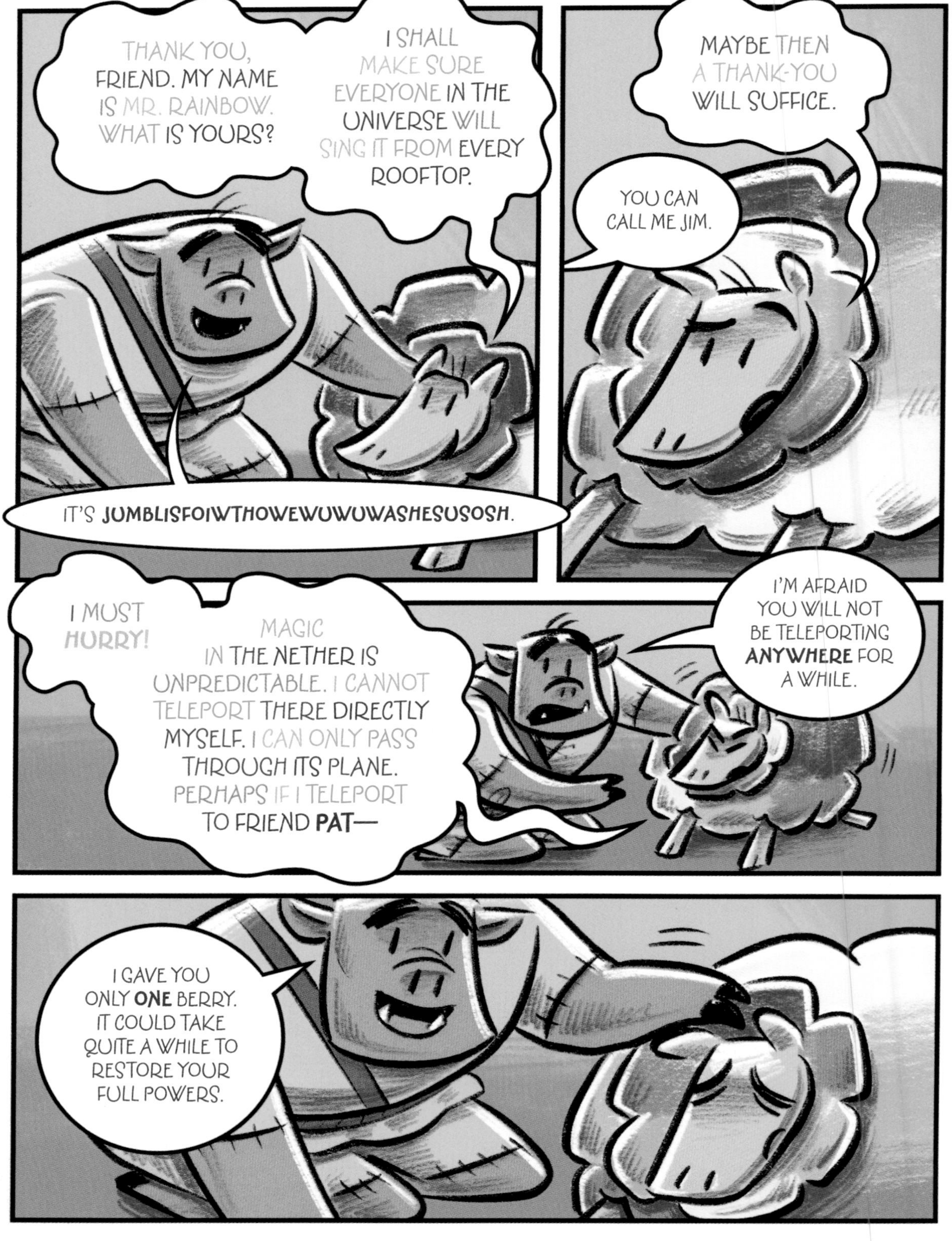

THANK YOU, FRIEND. MY NAME IS MR. RAINBOW. WHAT IS YOURS?
I SHALL MAKE SURE EVERYONE IN THE UNIVERSE WILL SING IT FROM EVERY ROOFTOP.
IT'S **JUMBLISFOIWTHOWEWUWUWASHESUSOSH**.
YOU CAN CALL ME JIM.
MAYBE THEN A THANK-YOU WILL SUFFICE.
I MUST **HURRY!**
MAGIC IN THE NETHER IS UNPREDICTABLE. I CANNOT TELEPORT THERE DIRECTLY MYSELF. I CAN ONLY PASS THROUGH ITS PLANE. PERHAPS IF I TELEPORT TO FRIEND **PAT**—
I'M AFRAID YOU WILL NOT BE TELEPORTING **ANYWHERE** FOR A WHILE.
I GAVE YOU ONLY **ONE** BERRY. IT COULD TAKE QUITE A WHILE TO RESTORE YOUR FULL POWERS.

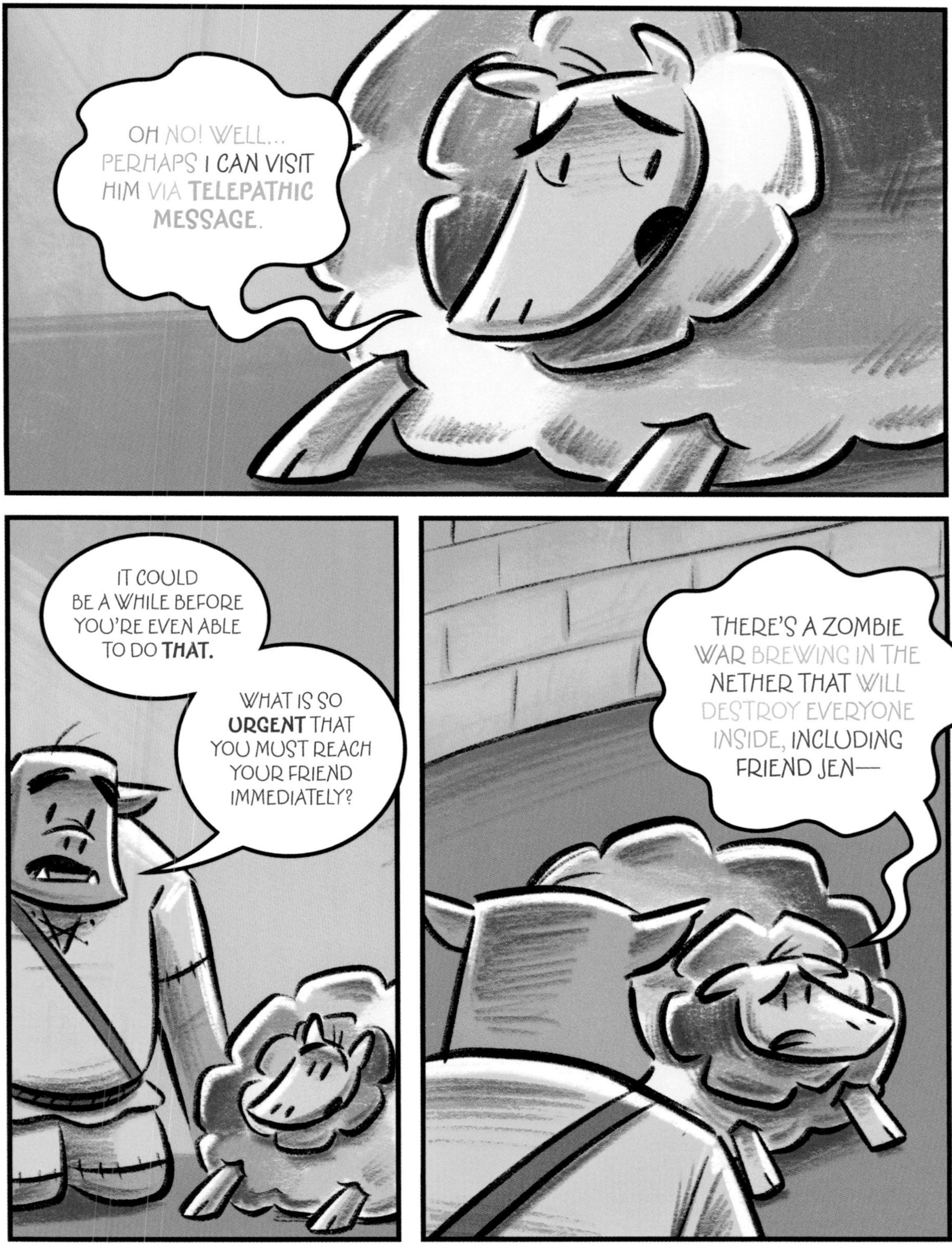
OH NO! WELL... PERHAPS I CAN VISIT HIM VIA TELEPATHIC MESSAGE.
IT COULD BE A WHILE BEFORE YOU'RE EVEN ABLE TO DO THAT.
WHAT IS SO URGENT THAT YOU MUST REACH YOUR FRIEND IMMEDIATELY?
THERE'S A ZOMBIE WAR BREWING IN THE NETHER THAT WILL DESTROY EVERYONE INSIDE, INCLUDING FRIEND JEN—

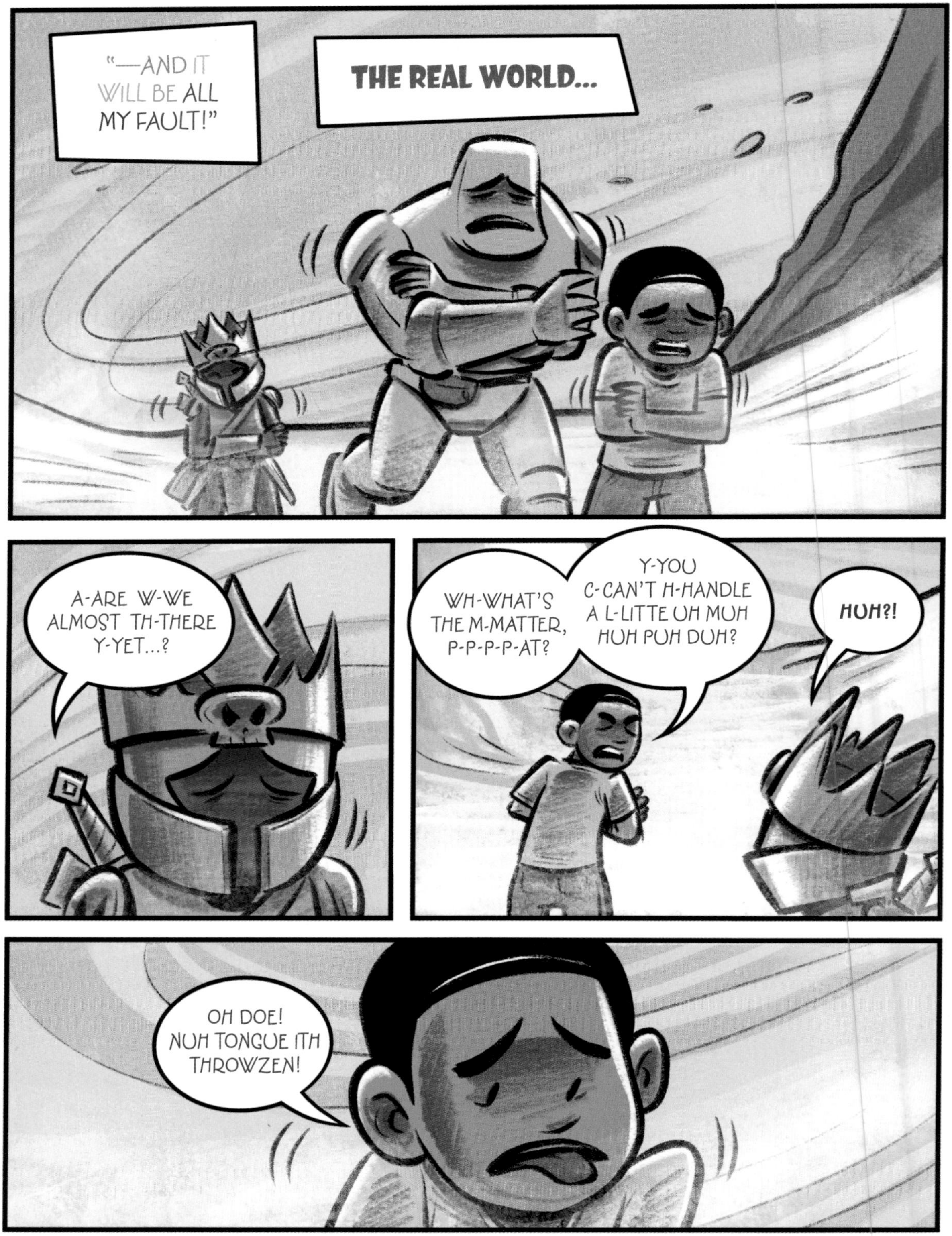
"—AND IT WILL BE ALL MY FAULT!"
THE REAL WORLD...
A-ARE W-WE ALMOST TH-THERE Y-YET...?
WH-WHAT'S THE M-MATTER, P-P-P-P-AT?
Y-YOU C-CAN'T H-HANDLE A L-LITTE UH MUH HUH PUH DUH?
HUH?!
OH DOE! NUH TONGUE ITH THROWZEN!

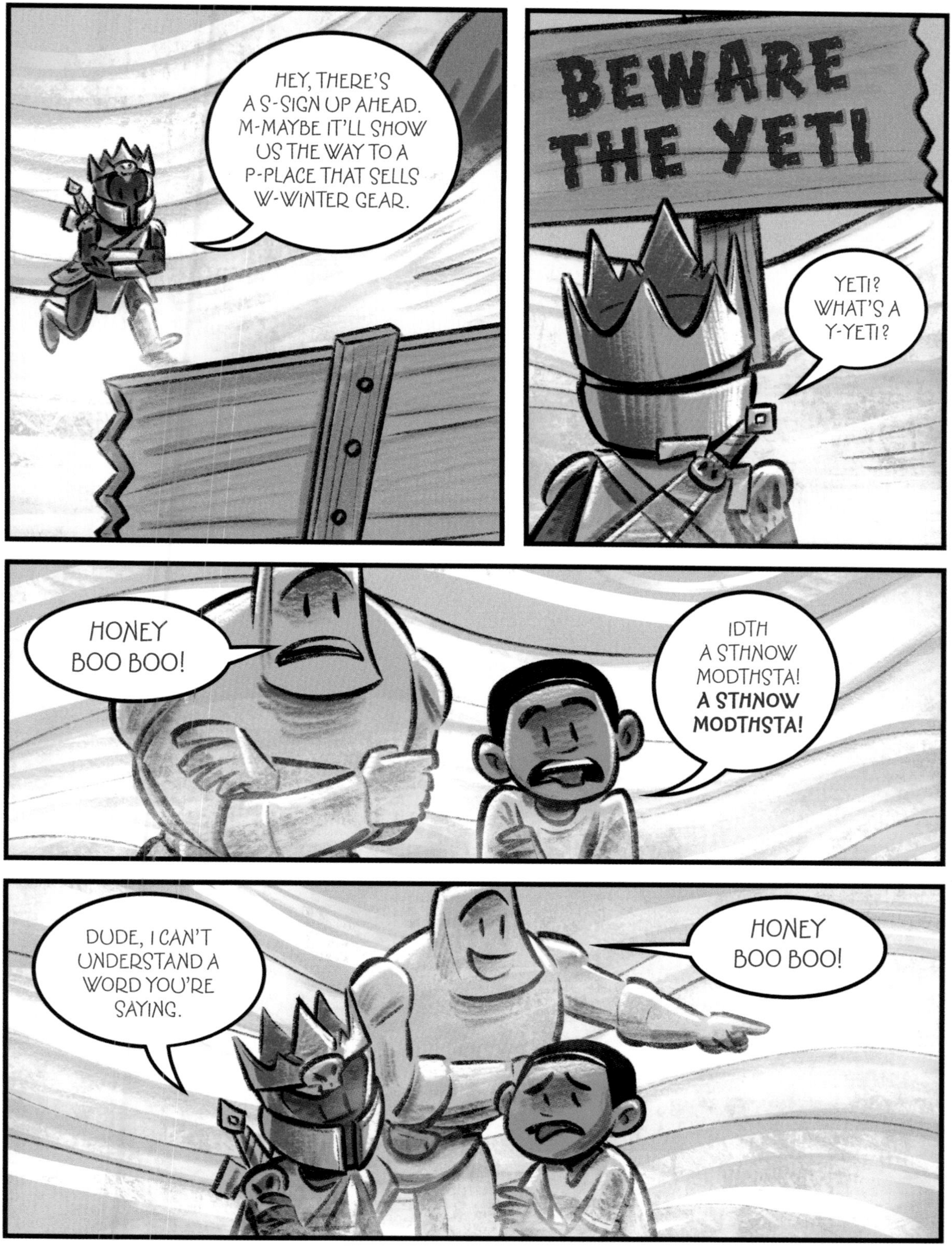
HEY, THERE'S A S-SIGN UP AHEAD. M-MAYBE IT'LL SHOW US THE WAY TO A P-PLACE THAT SELLS W-WINTER GEAR.
BEWARE THE YETI
YETI? WHAT'S A Y-YETI?
HONEY BOO BOO!
IDTH A STHNOW MODTHSTA! **A STHNOW MODTHSTA!**
DUDE, I CAN'T UNDERSTAND A WORD YOU'RE SAYING.
HONEY BOO BOO!

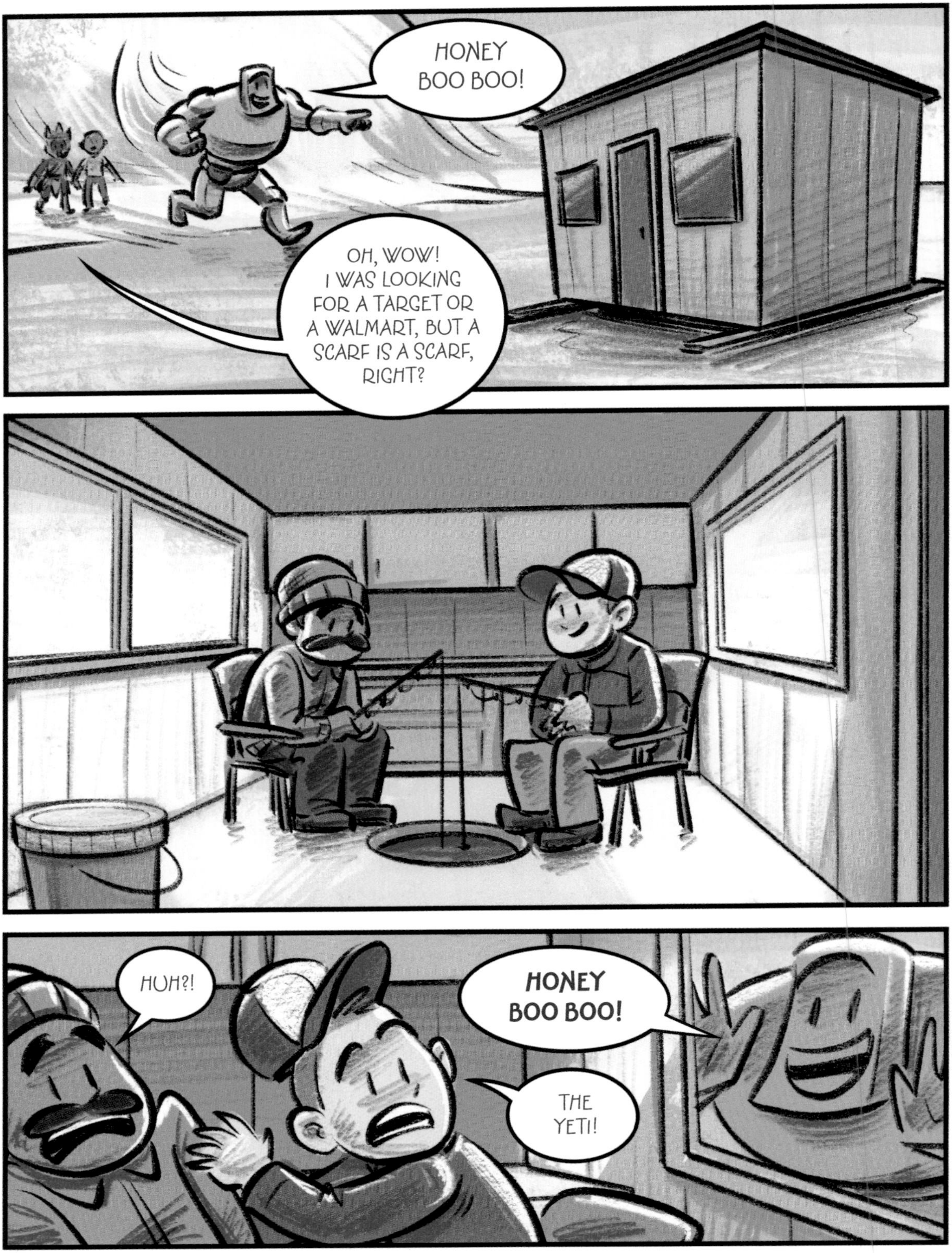
HONEY BOO BOO!
OH, WOW! I WAS LOOKING FOR A TARGET OR A WALMART, BUT A SCARF IS A SCARF, RIGHT?
HUH?!
HONEY BOO BOO!
THE YETI!

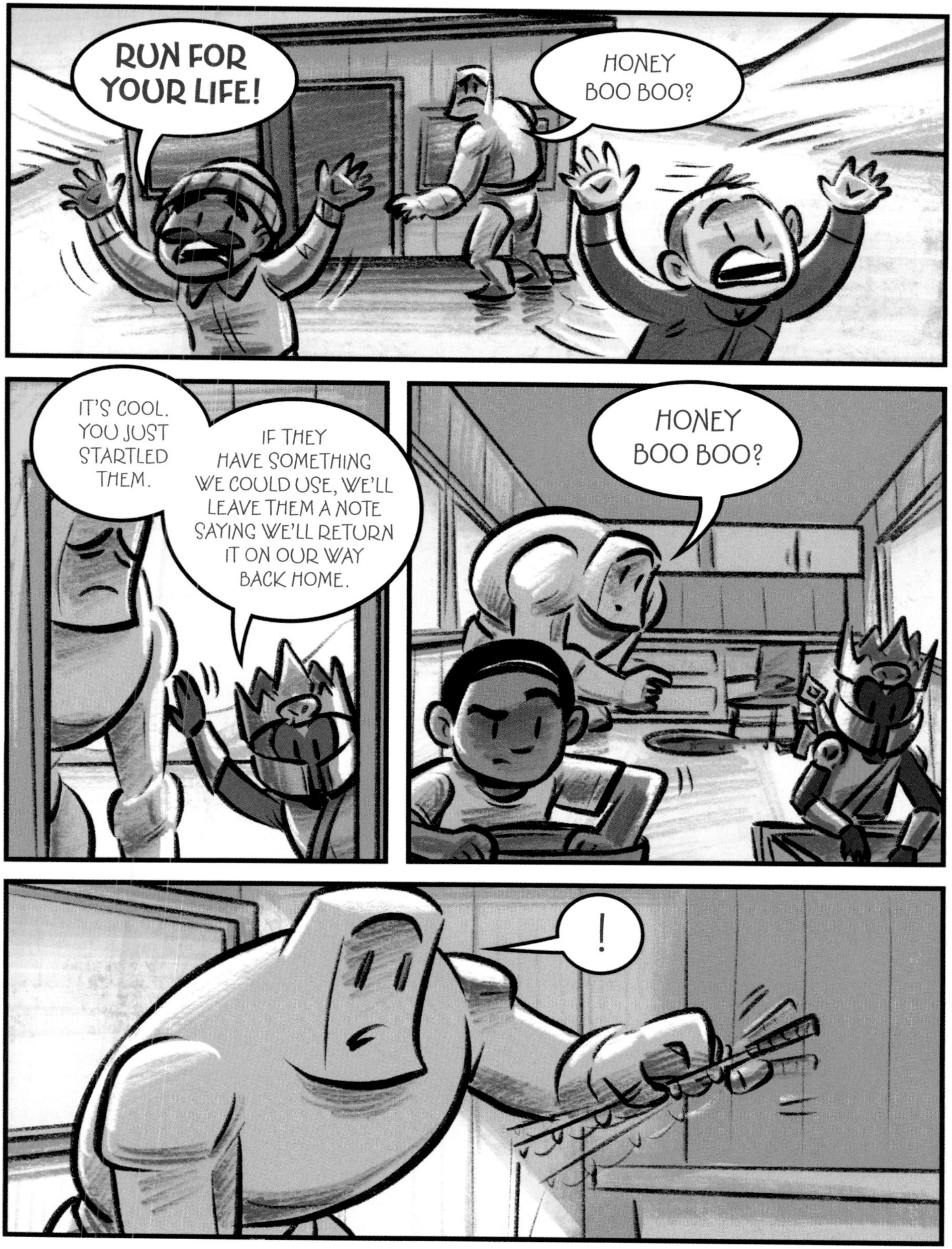
RUN FOR YOUR LIFE!
HONEY BOO BOO?
IT'S COOL. YOU JUST STARTLED THEM.
IF THEY HAVE SOMETHING WE COULD USE, WE'LL LEAVE THEM A NOTE SAYING WE'LL RETURN IT ON OUR WAY BACK HOME.
HONEY BOO BOO?
!

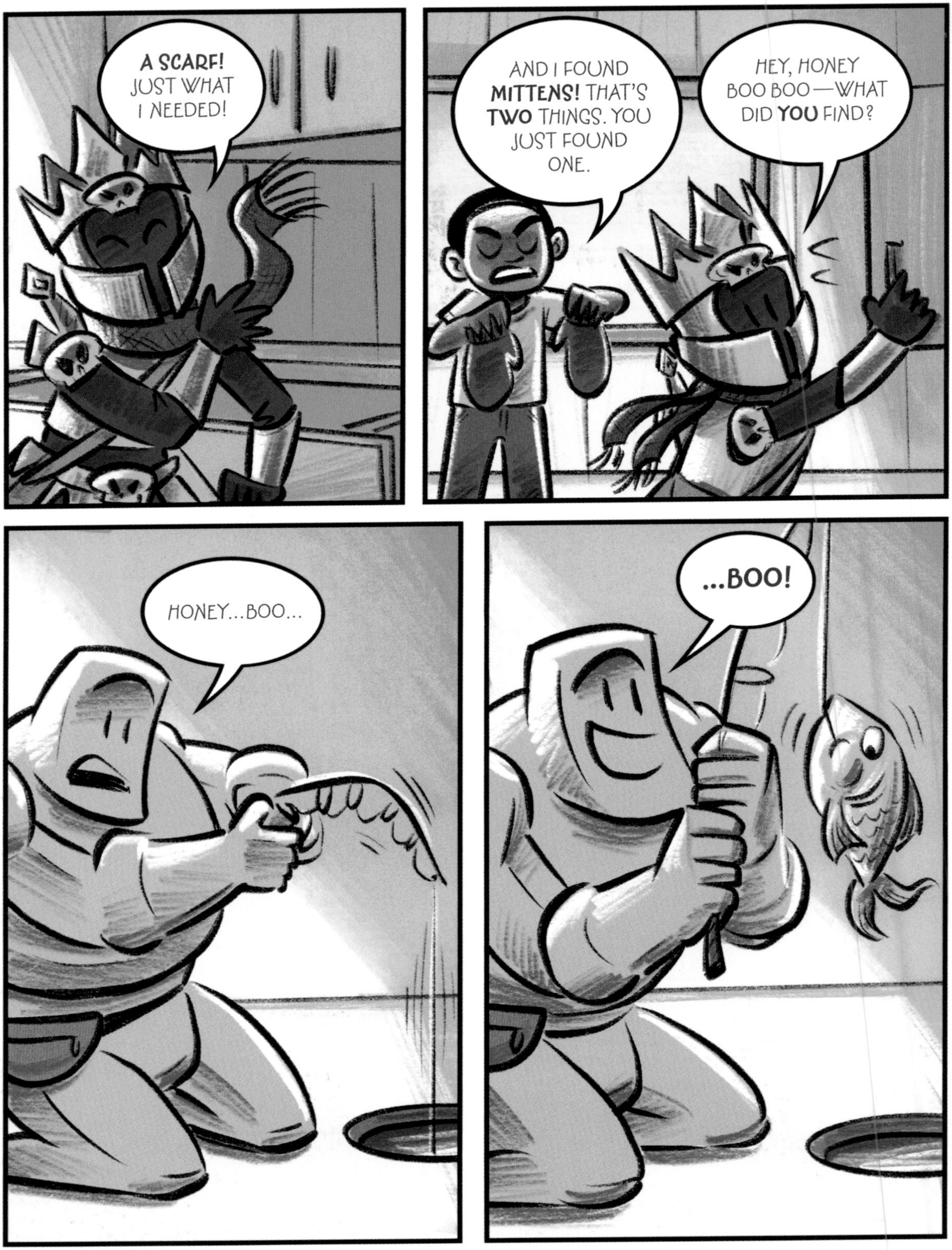
A SCARF! JUST WHAT I NEEDED!
AND I FOUND MITTENS! THAT'S TWO THINGS. YOU JUST FOUND ONE.
HEY, HONEY BOO BOO—WHAT DID YOU FIND?
HONEY...BOO...
...BOO!

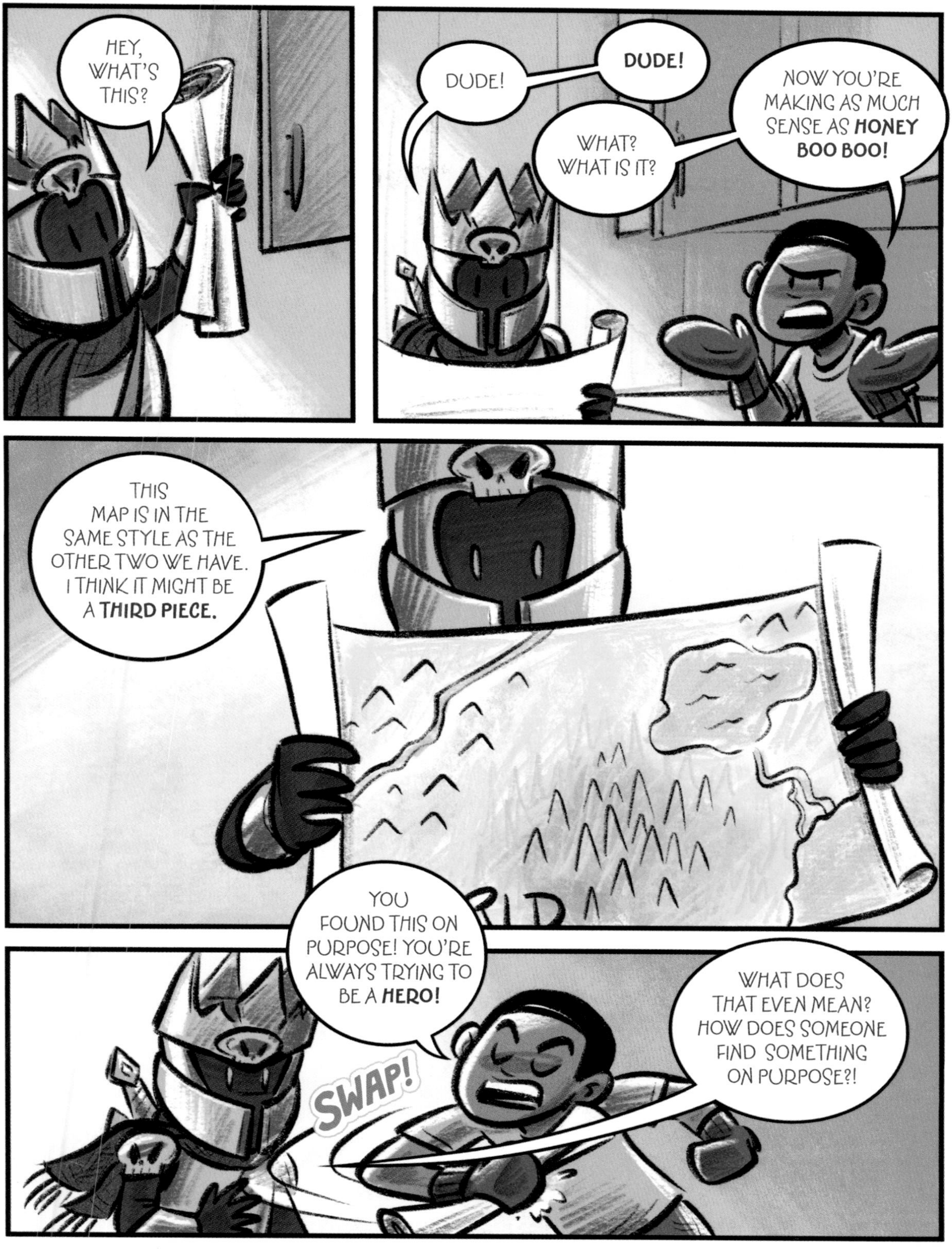
HEY, WHAT'S THIS?
DUDE!
DUDE!
WHAT? WHAT IS IT?
NOW YOU'RE MAKING AS MUCH SENSE AS HONEY BOO BOO!
THIS MAP IS IN THE SAME STYLE AS THE OTHER TWO WE HAVE. I THINK IT MIGHT BE A THIRD PIECE.
YOU FOUND THIS ON PURPOSE! YOU'RE ALWAYS TRYING TO BE A HERO!
SWAP!
WHAT DOES THAT EVEN MEAN? HOW DOES SOMEONE FIND SOMETHING ON PURPOSE?!

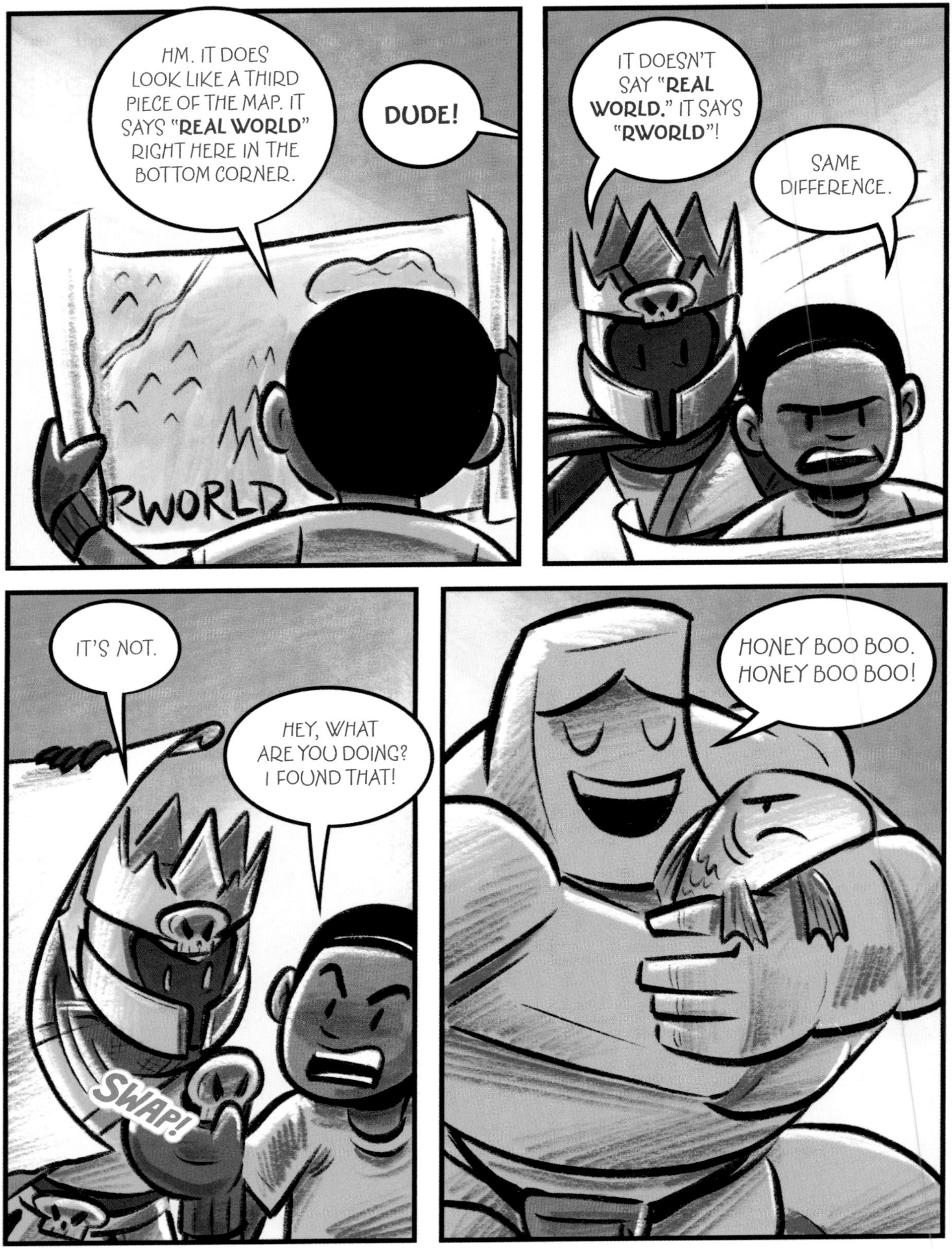
HM. IT DOES LOOK LIKE A THIRD PIECE OF THE MAP. IT SAYS "**REAL WORLD**" RIGHT HERE IN THE BOTTOM CORNER.
RWORLD
DUDE!
IT DOESN'T SAY "**REAL WORLD.**" IT SAYS "**RWORLD**"!
SAME DIFFERENCE.
IT'S NOT.
HEY, WHAT ARE YOU DOING? I FOUND THAT!
SWAP!
HONEY BOO BOO. HONEY BOO BOO!

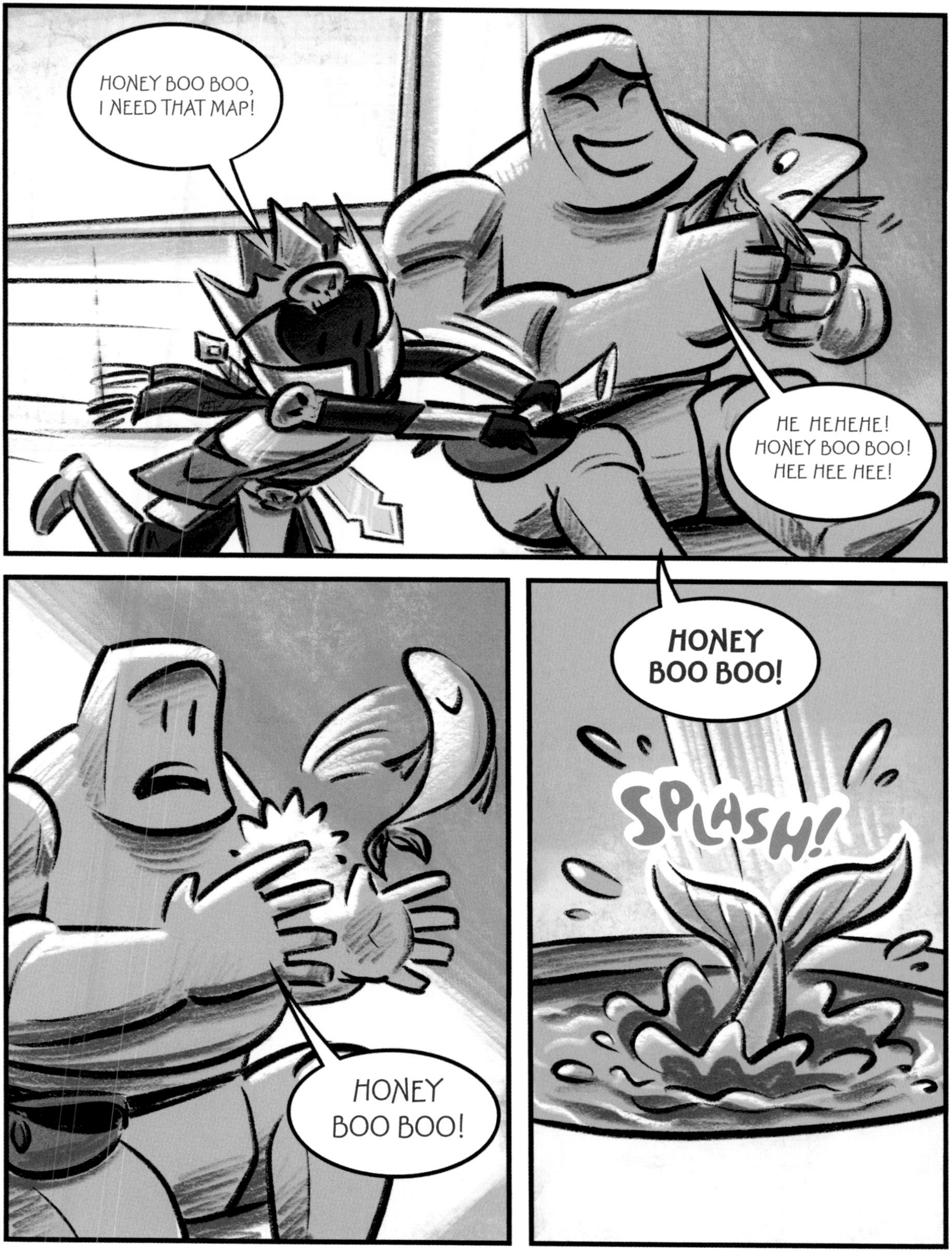
HONEY BOO BOO, I NEED THAT MAP!
HE HEHEHE! HONEY BOO BOO! HEE HEE HEE!
HONEY BOO BOO!
HONEY BOO BOO!
SPLASH!

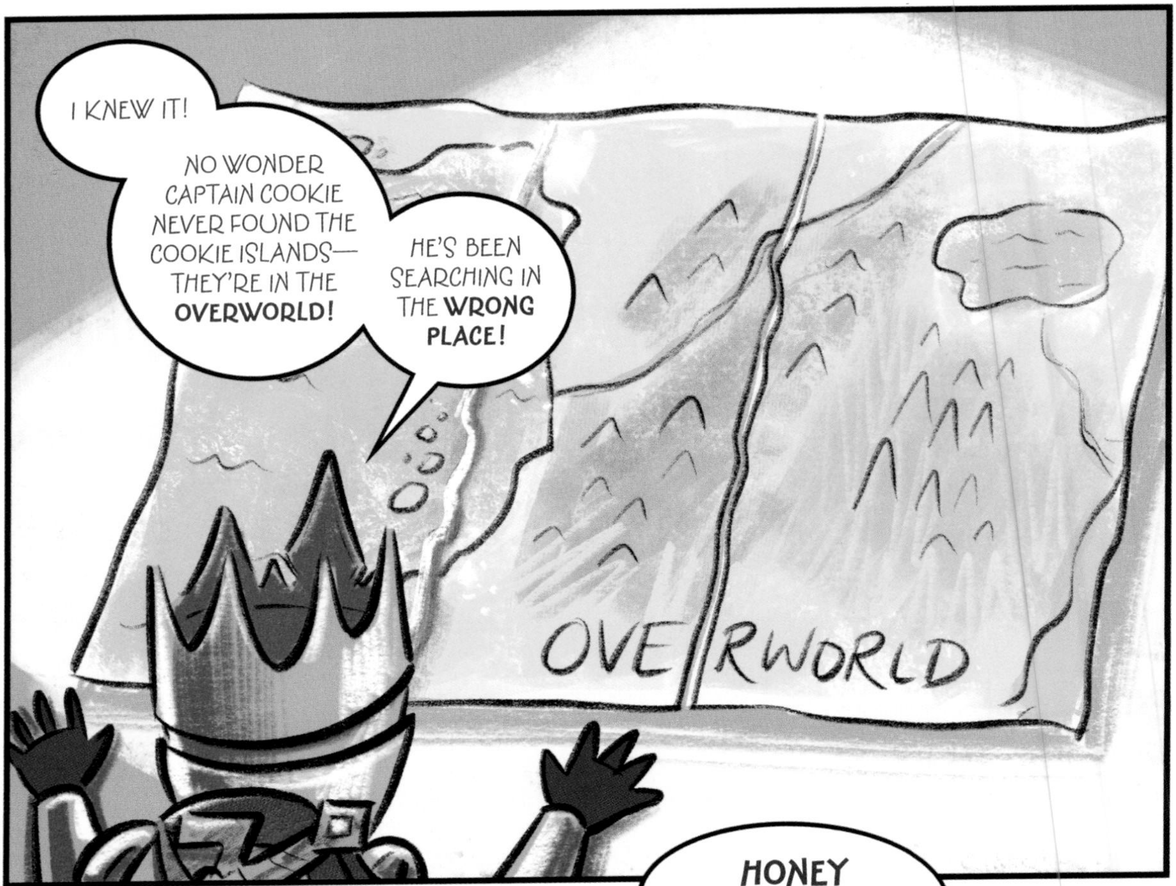
I KNEW IT!
NO WONDER CAPTAIN COOKIE NEVER FOUND THE COOKIE ISLANDS—THEY'RE IN THE OVERWORLD!
HE'S BEEN SEARCHING IN THE WRONG PLACE!
OVERWORLD

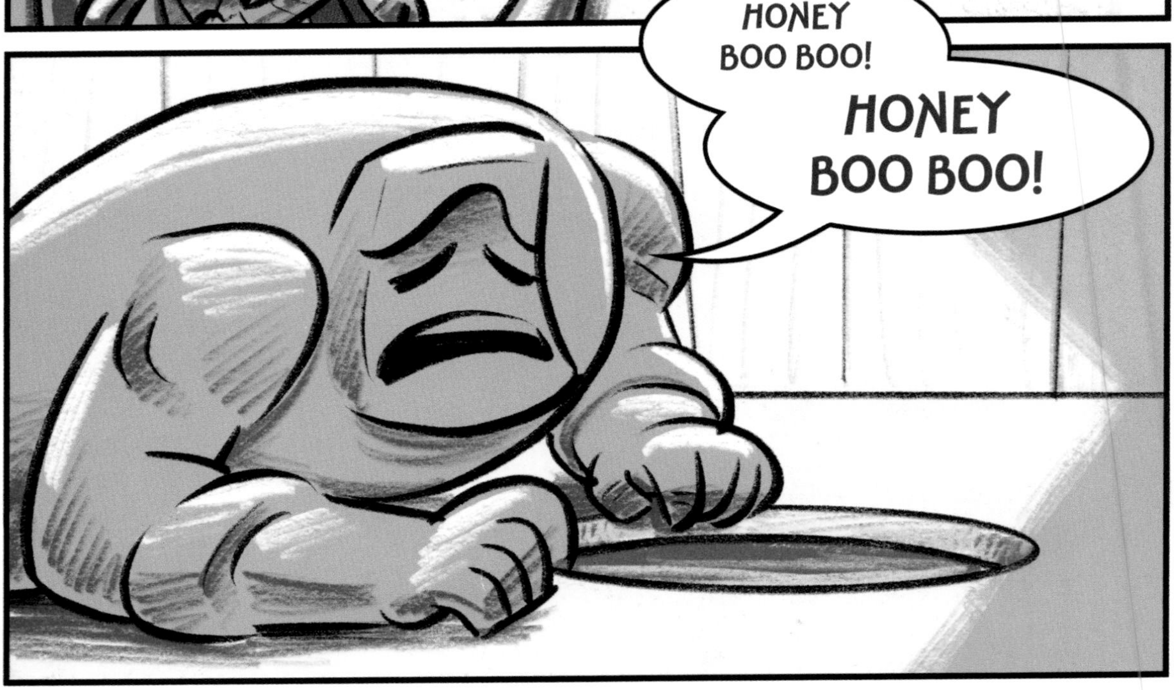
HONEY BOO BOO!
HONEY BOO BOO!

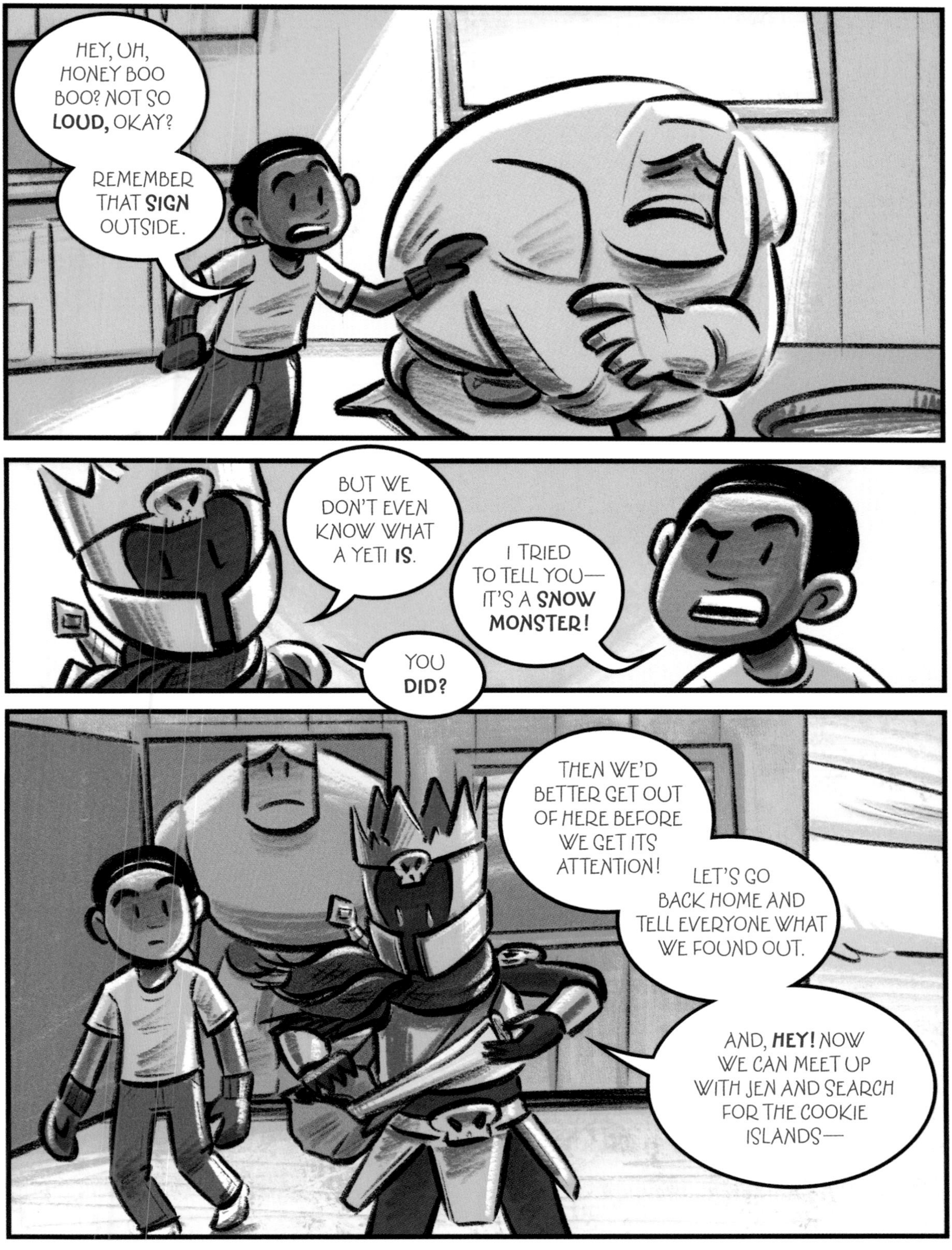
HEY, UH, HONEY BOO BOO? NOT SO **LOUD,** OKAY?
REMEMBER THAT **SIGN** OUTSIDE.
BUT WE DON'T EVEN KNOW WHAT A YETI **IS**.
I TRIED TO TELL YOU— IT'S A **SNOW MONSTER!**
YOU **DID?**
THEN WE'D BETTER GET OUT OF HERE BEFORE WE GET ITS ATTENTION!
LET'S GO BACK HOME AND TELL EVERYONE WHAT WE FOUND OUT.
AND, **HEY!** NOW WE CAN MEET UP WITH JEN AND SEARCH FOR THE COOKIE ISLANDS—

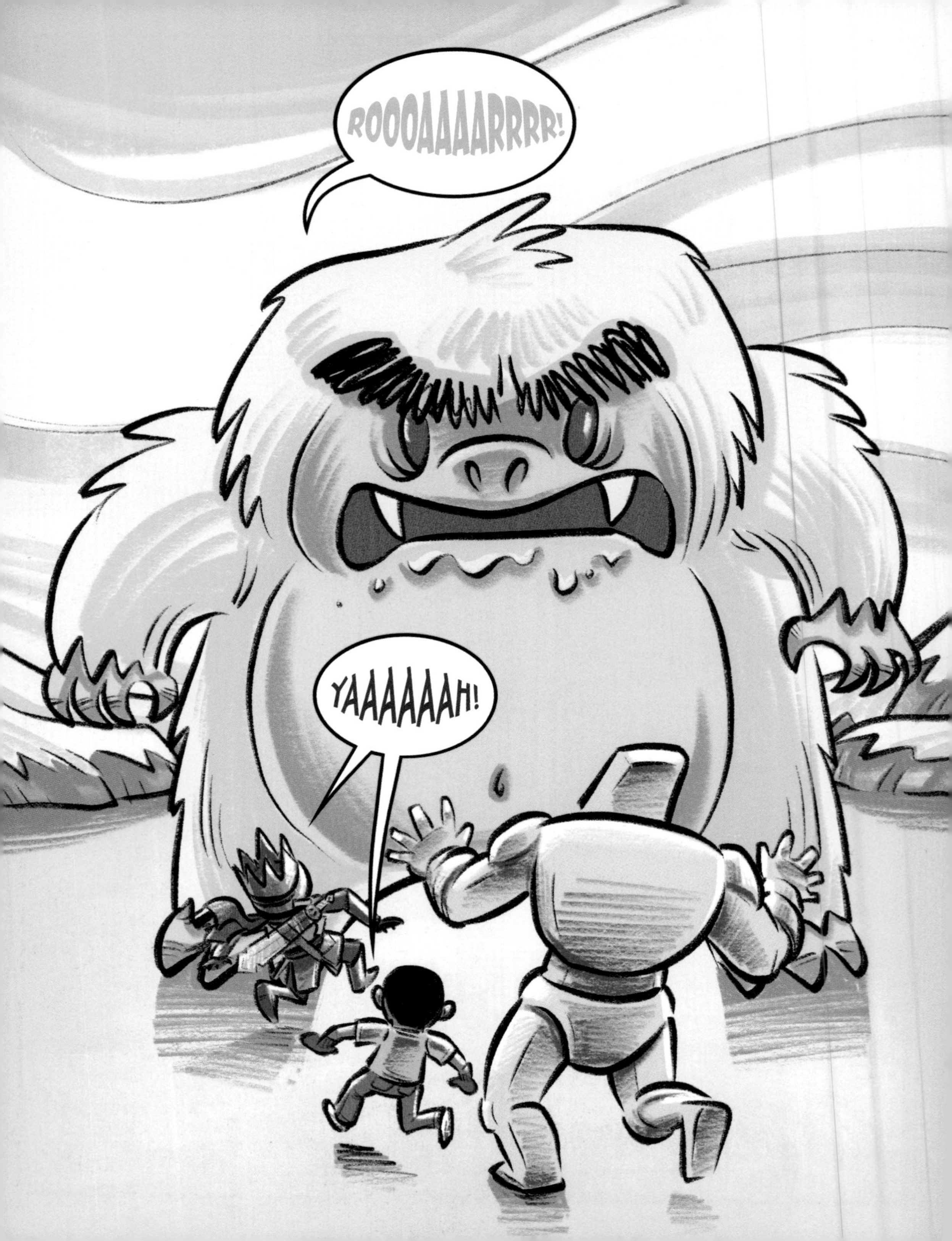
ROOOAAAARRRR!
YAAAAAAH!

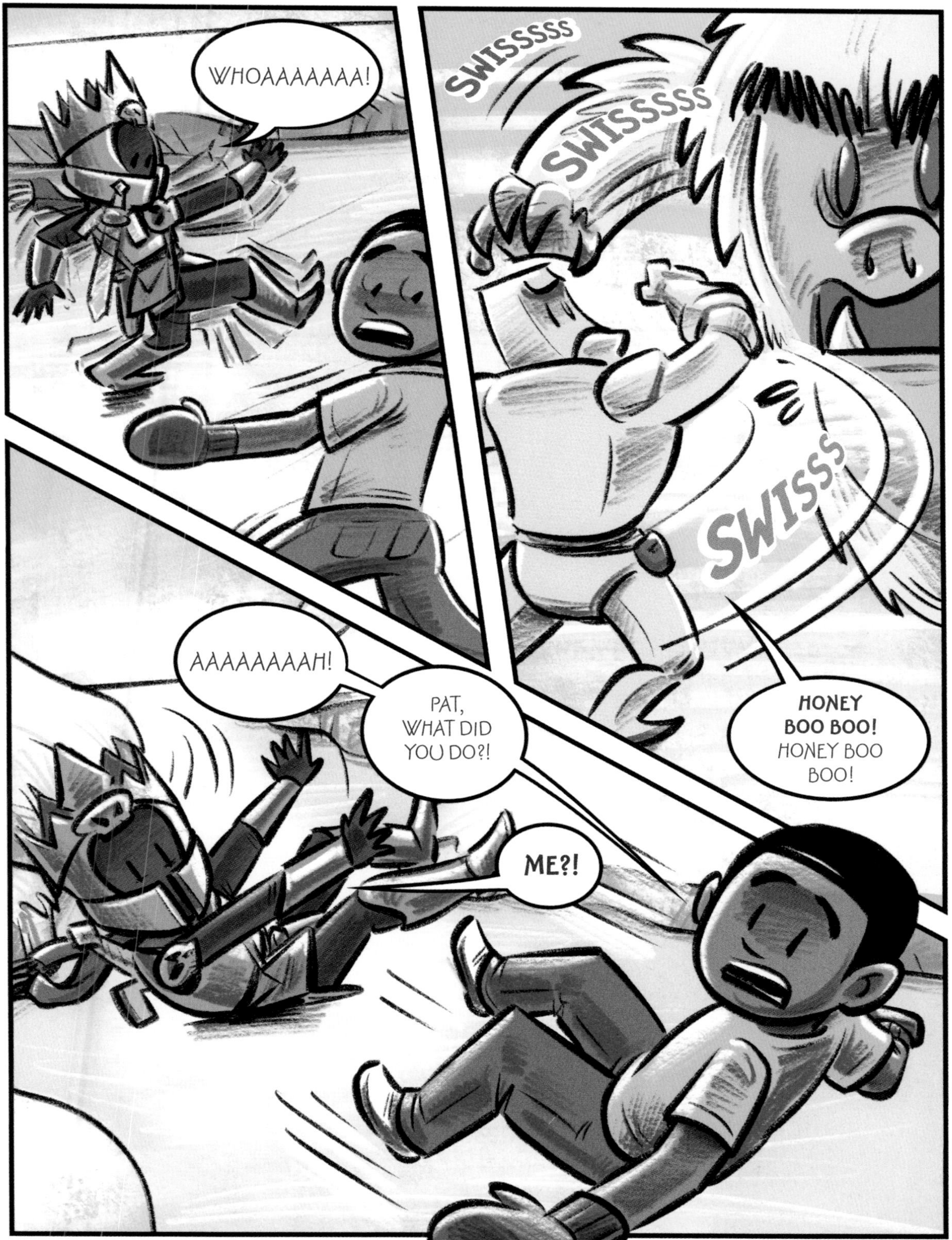
WHOAAAAAAA!
SWISSSSS
SWISSSSS
SWISSSSS
SWISSS
HONEY BOO BOO! HONEY BOO BOO!
AAAAAAAAAH!
PAT, WHAT DID YOU DO?!
ME?!

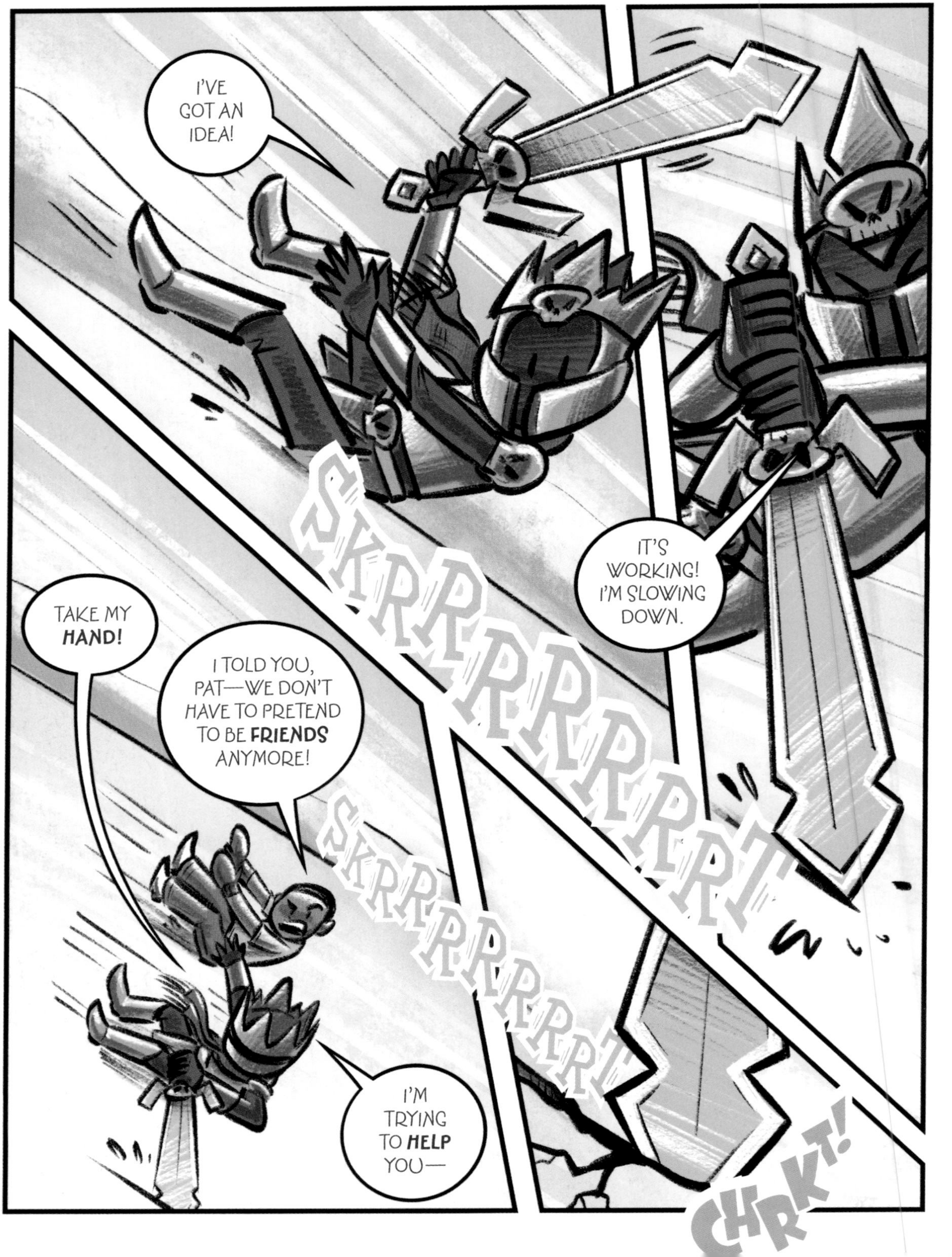
I'VE GOT AN IDEA!
IT'S WORKING! I'M SLOWING DOWN.
SKRRRRRRRRT
TAKE MY **HAND!**
I TOLD YOU, PAT—WE DON'T HAVE TO PRETEND TO BE **FRIENDS** ANYMORE!
SKRRRRRRRRRT
I'M TRYING TO **HELP** YOU—
CHRKT!

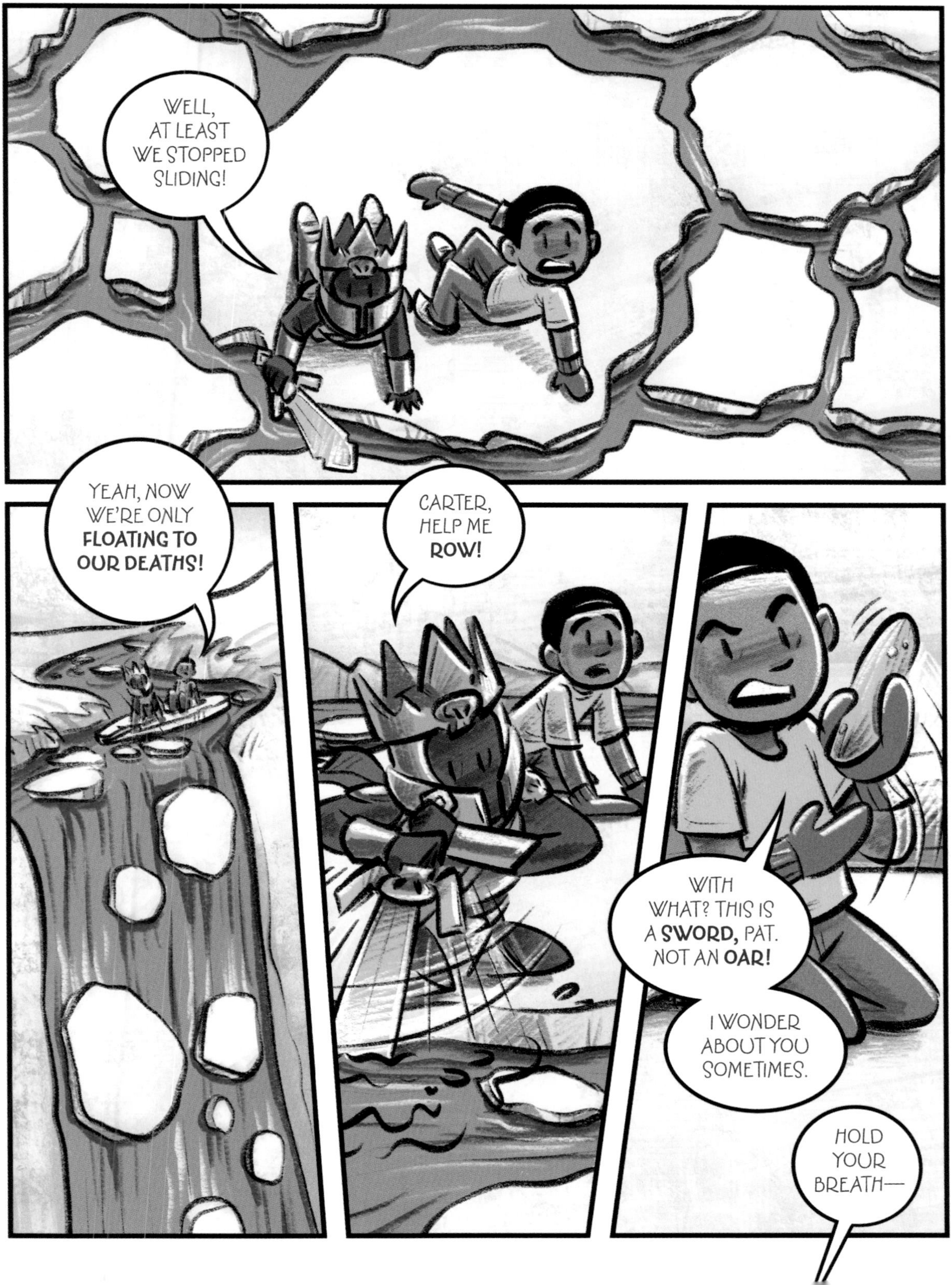
WELL, AT LEAST WE STOPPED SLIDING!
YEAH, NOW WE'RE ONLY **FLOATING TO OUR DEATHS!**
CARTER, HELP ME **ROW!**
WITH WHAT? THIS IS A **SWORD,** PAT. NOT AN **OAR!**
I WONDER ABOUT YOU SOMETIMES.
HOLD YOUR BREATH—

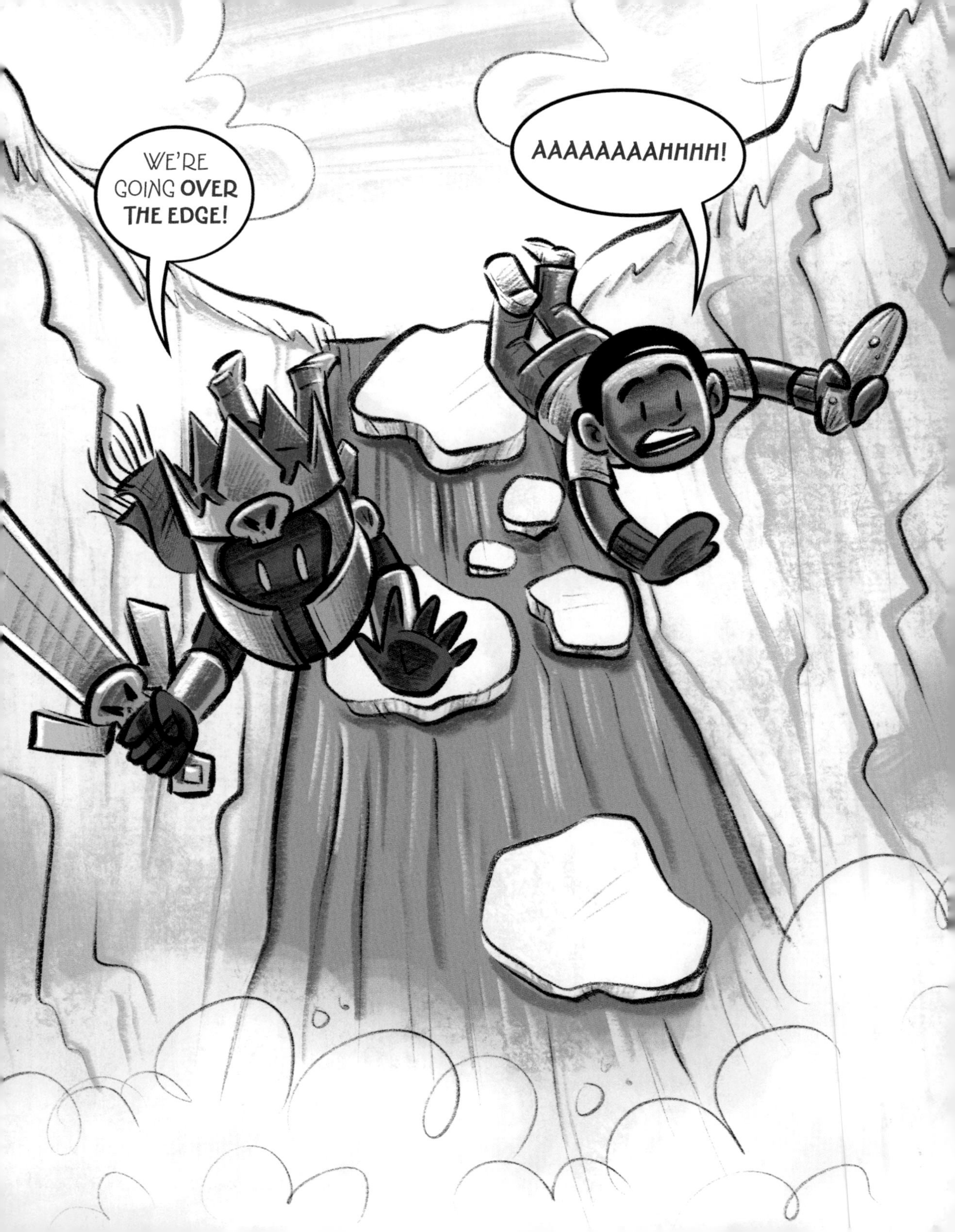
WE'RE GOING **OVER THE EDGE!**
AAAAAAAAHHHH!

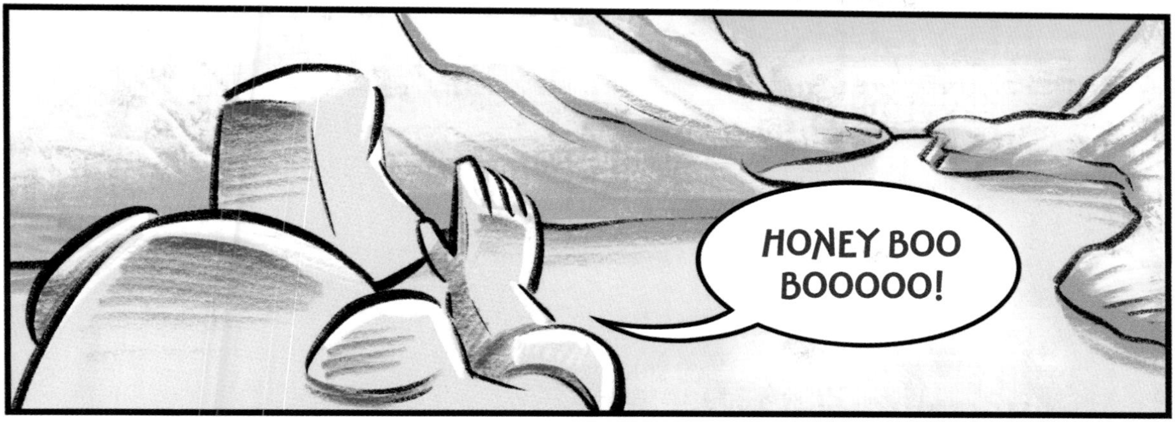
HONEY BOO BOOOOO!

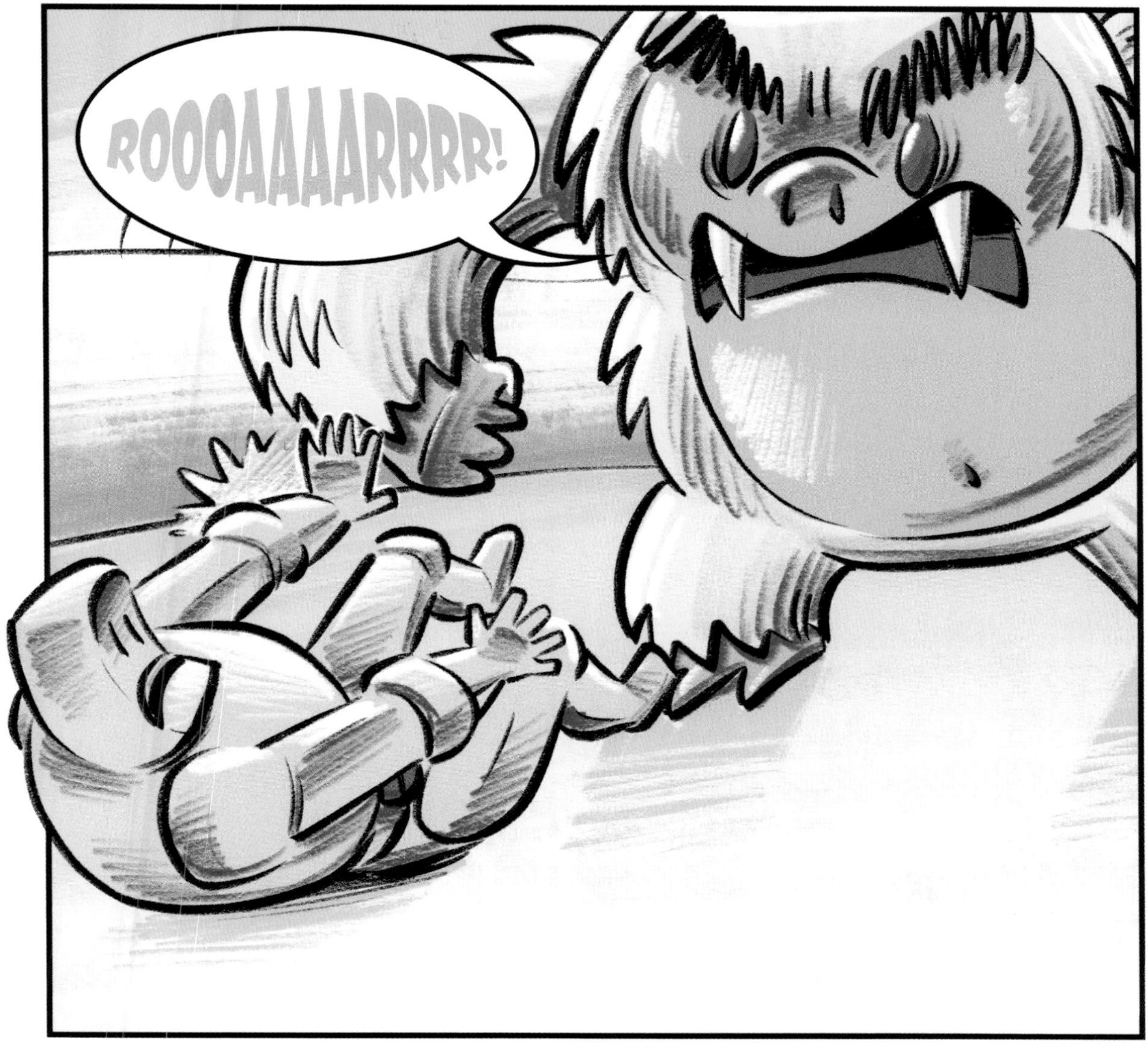
ROOOAAAARRRR!

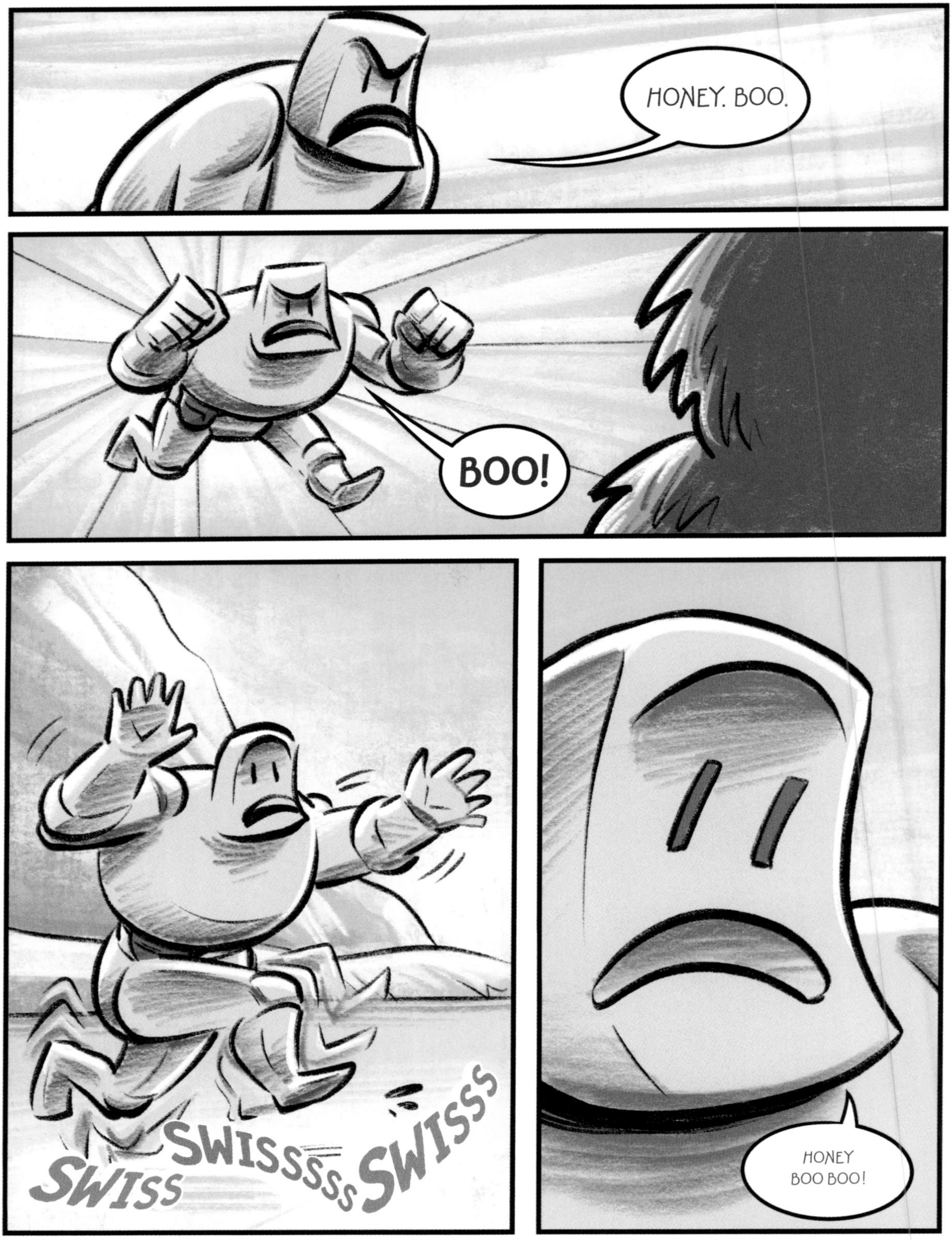
HONEY. BOO.
BOO!
SWISS SWISSSSSS SWISSS
HONEY BOO BOO!

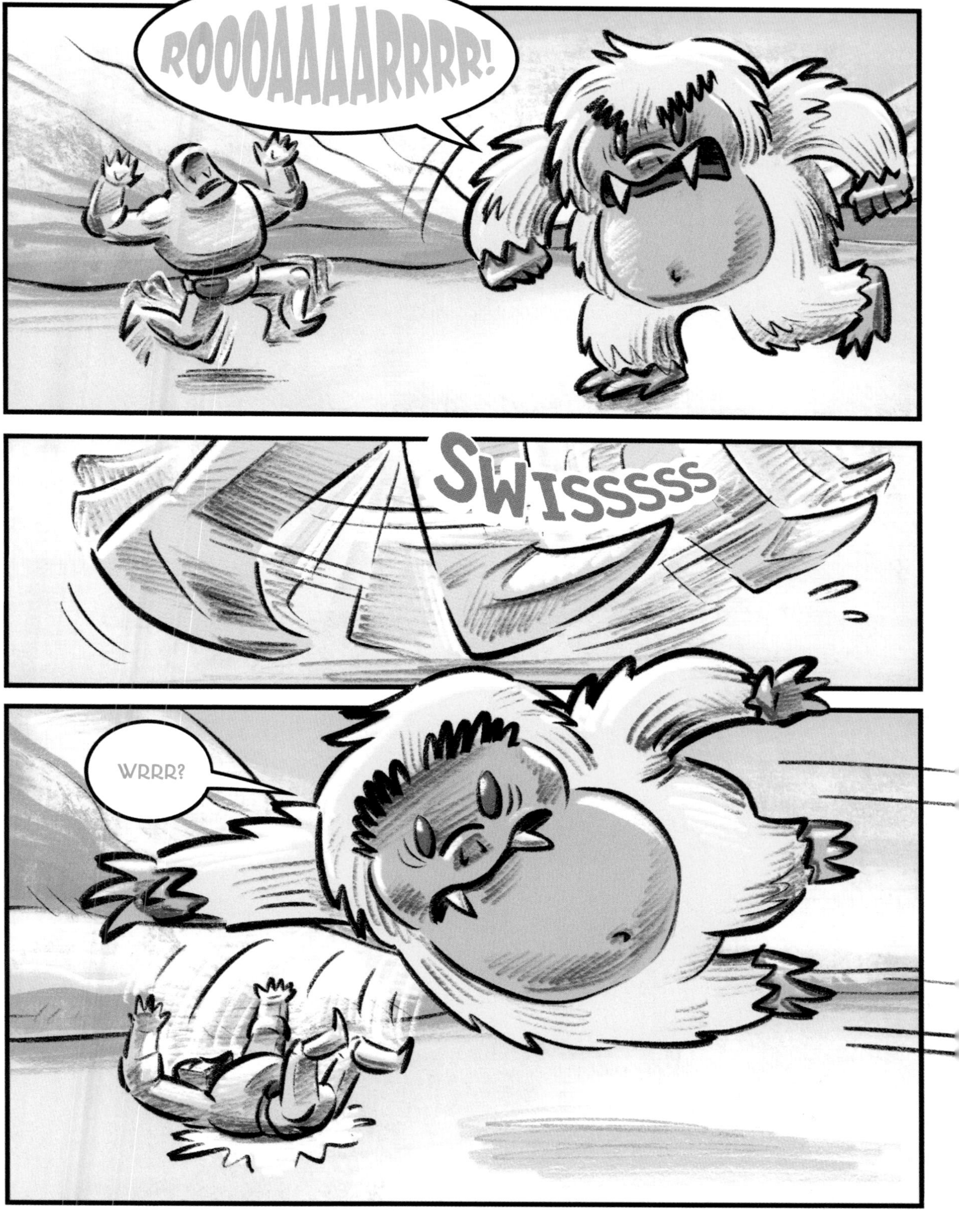
ROOOAAAARRRR!
SWISSSSS
WRRR?

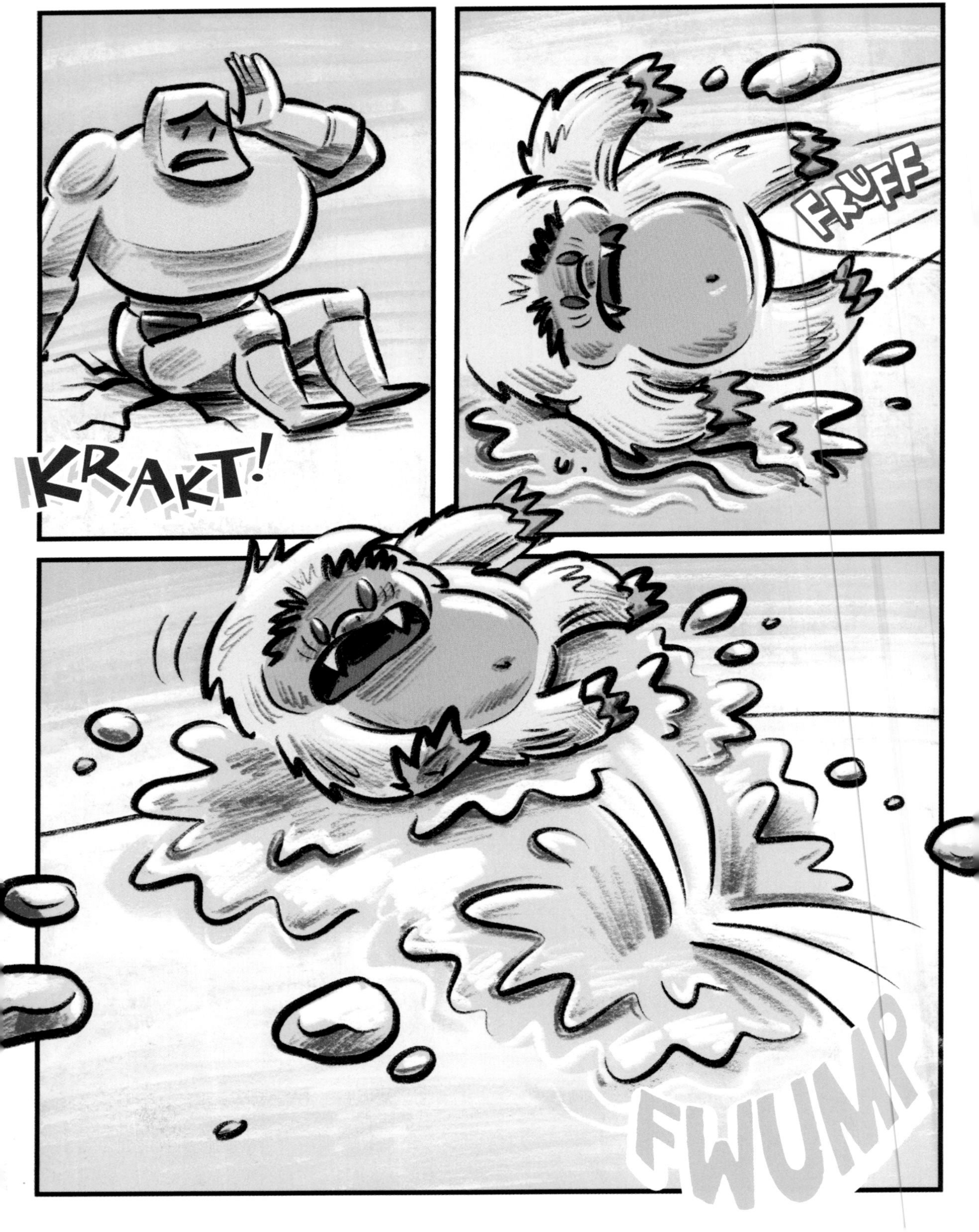
KRAKT!
FRUFF
FWUMP

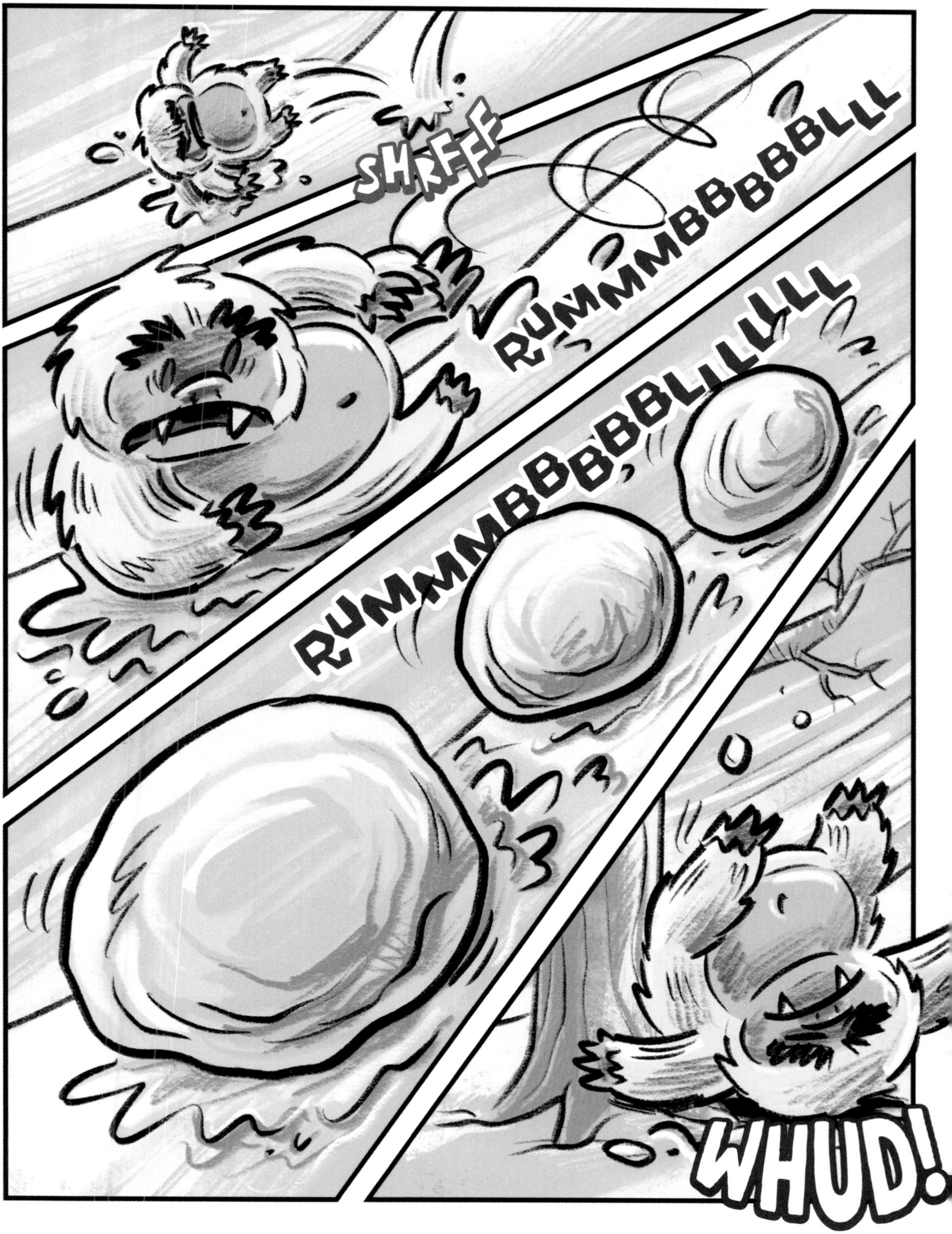
SHRFFF
RUMMMMBBBBBBLLL
RUMMMMBBBBBBLLLLLLL
WHUD!

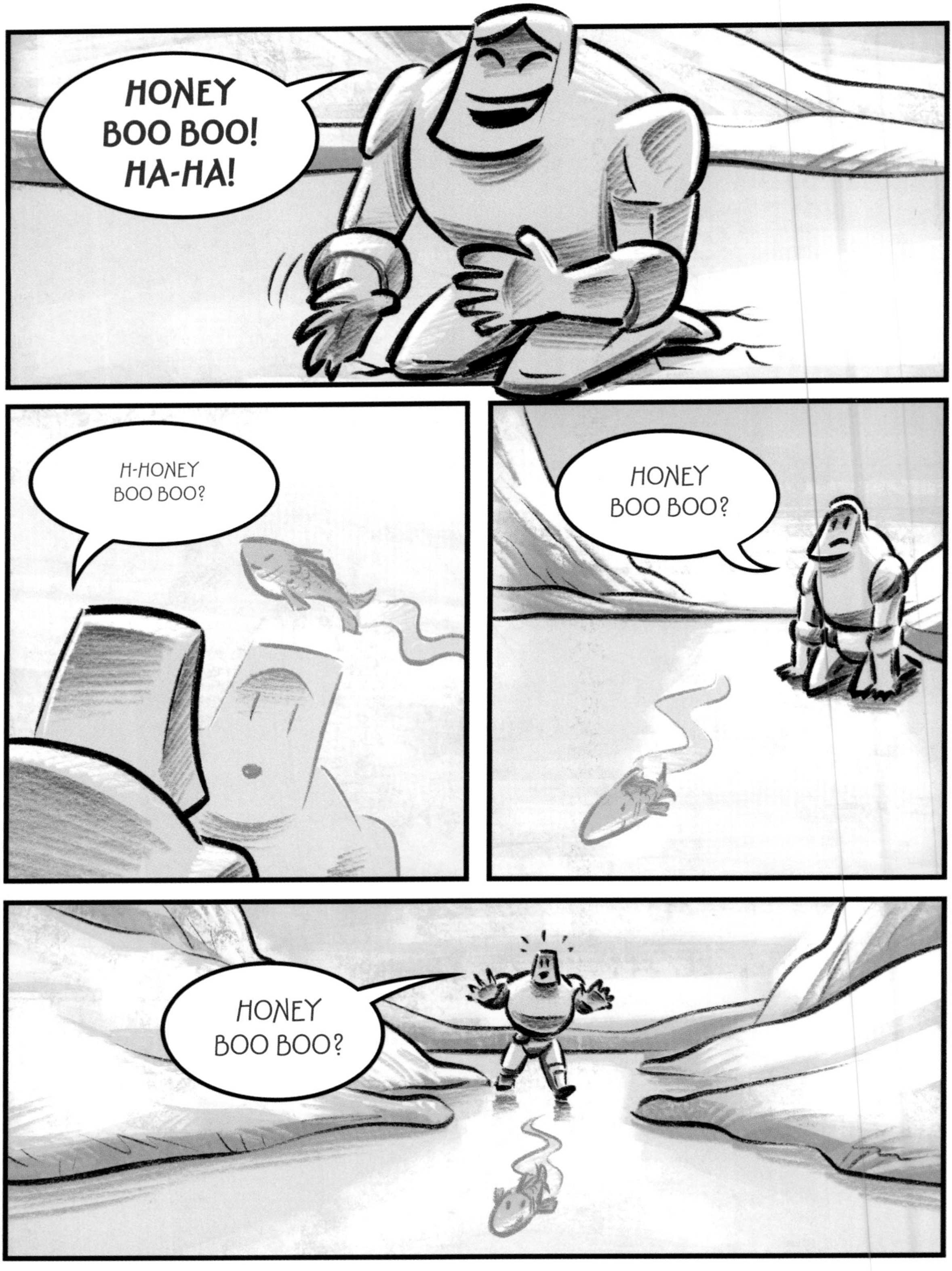
HONEY BOO BOO! HA-HA!
H-HONEY BOO BOO?
HONEY BOO BOO?
HONEY BOO BOO?

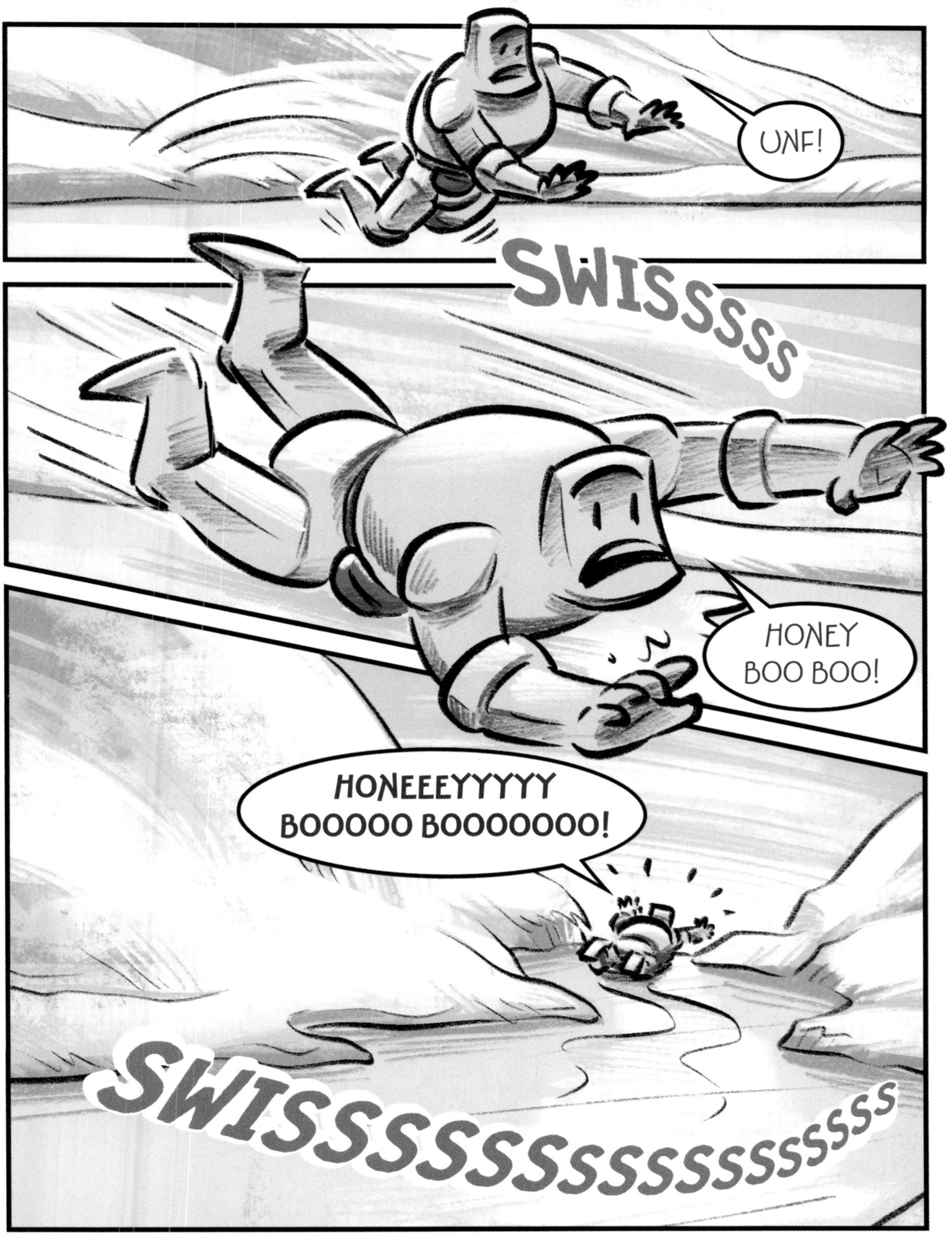
UNF!
SWISSSSS
HONEY BOO BOO!
HONEEEYYYYY BOOOOO BOOOOOOO!
SWISSSSSSSSSSSSSSS

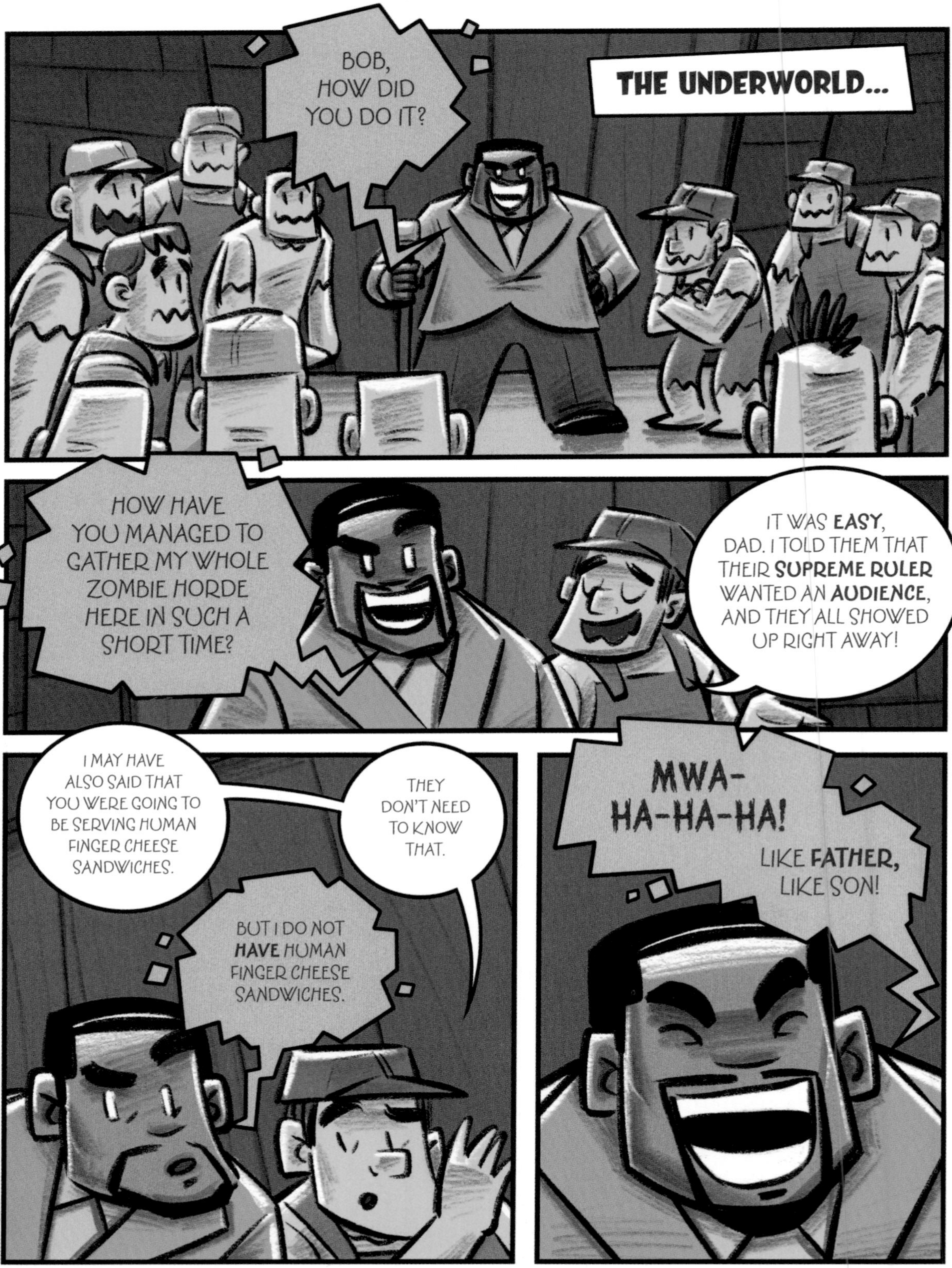
THE UNDERWORLD...
BOB, HOW DID YOU DO IT?
HOW HAVE YOU MANAGED TO GATHER MY WHOLE ZOMBIE HORDE HERE IN SUCH A SHORT TIME?
IT WAS EASY, DAD. I TOLD THEM THAT THEIR SUPREME RULER WANTED AN AUDIENCE, AND THEY ALL SHOWED UP RIGHT AWAY!
I MAY HAVE ALSO SAID THAT YOU WERE GOING TO BE SERVING HUMAN FINGER CHEESE SANDWICHES.
BUT I DO NOT HAVE HUMAN FINGER CHEESE SANDWICHES.
THEY DON'T NEED TO KNOW THAT.
MWA-HA-HA-HA!
LIKE FATHER, LIKE SON!

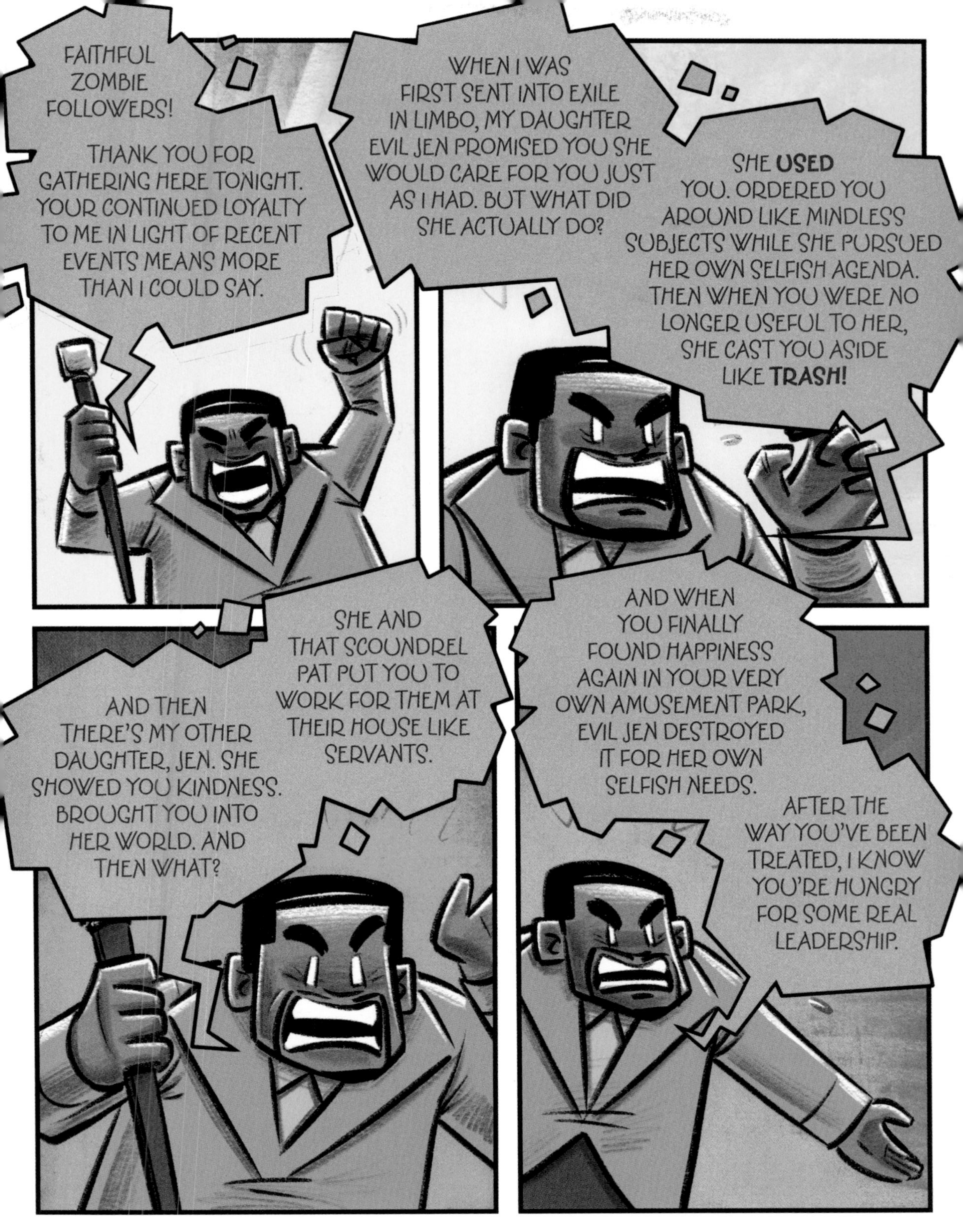
FAITHFUL ZOMBIE FOLLOWERS!
THANK YOU FOR GATHERING HERE TONIGHT. YOUR CONTINUED LOYALTY TO ME IN LIGHT OF RECENT EVENTS MEANS MORE THAN I COULD SAY.
WHEN I WAS FIRST SENT INTO EXILE IN LIMBO, MY DAUGHTER EVIL JEN PROMISED YOU SHE WOULD CARE FOR YOU JUST AS I HAD. BUT WHAT DID SHE ACTUALLY DO?
SHE **USED** YOU. ORDERED YOU AROUND LIKE MINDLESS SUBJECTS WHILE SHE PURSUED HER OWN SELFISH AGENDA. THEN WHEN YOU WERE NO LONGER USEFUL TO HER, SHE CAST YOU ASIDE LIKE **TRASH!**
AND THEN THERE'S MY OTHER DAUGHTER, JEN. SHE SHOWED YOU KINDNESS. BROUGHT YOU INTO HER WORLD. AND THEN WHAT?
SHE AND THAT SCOUNDREL PAT PUT YOU TO WORK FOR THEM AT THEIR HOUSE LIKE SERVANTS.
AND WHEN YOU FINALLY FOUND HAPPINESS AGAIN IN YOUR VERY OWN AMUSEMENT PARK, EVIL JEN DESTROYED IT FOR HER OWN SELFISH NEEDS.
AFTER THE WAY YOU'VE BEEN TREATED, I KNOW YOU'RE HUNGRY FOR SOME REAL LEADERSHIP.

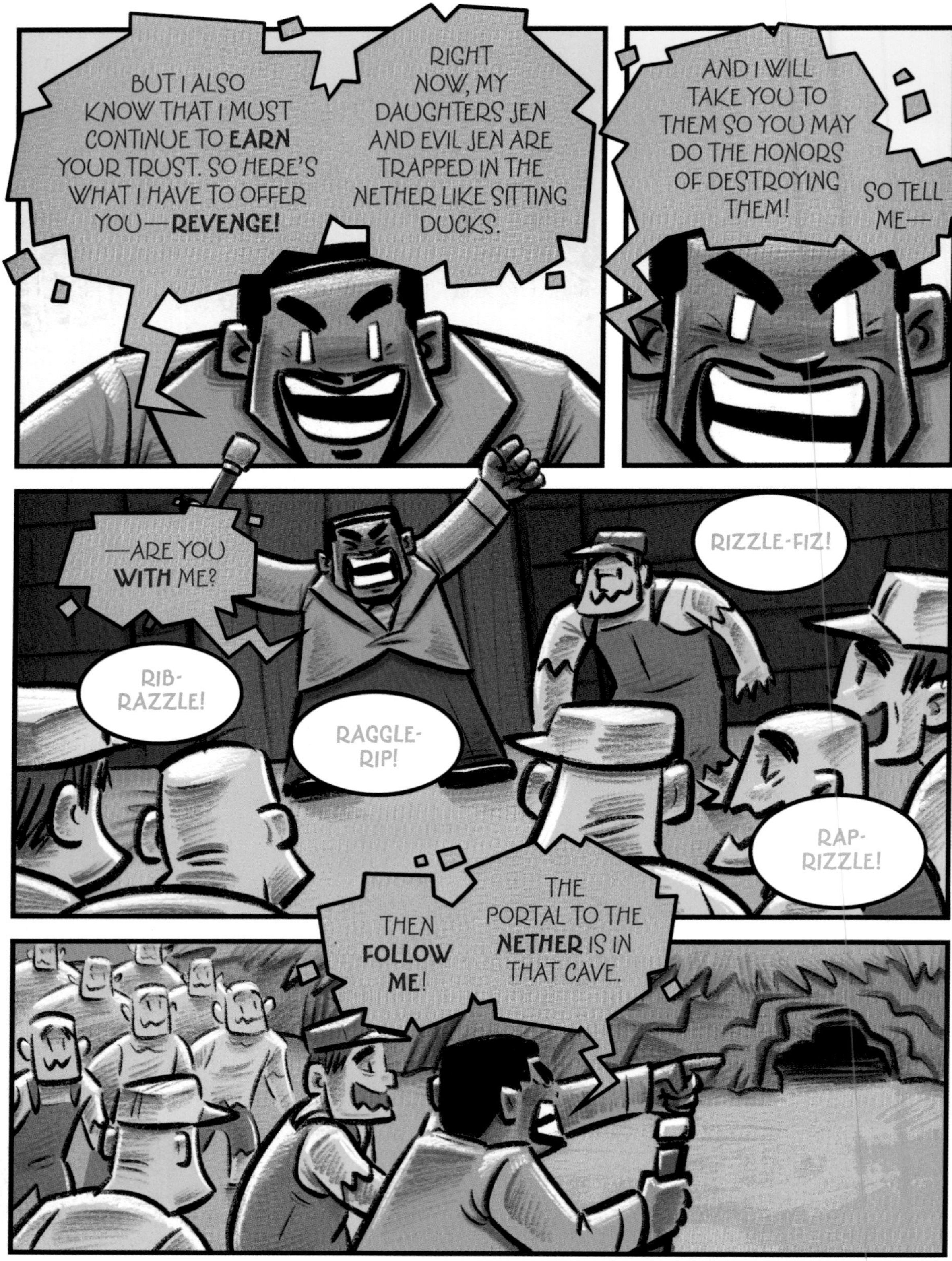
BUT I ALSO KNOW THAT I MUST CONTINUE TO **EARN** YOUR TRUST. SO HERE'S WHAT I HAVE TO OFFER YOU—**REVENGE!**
RIGHT NOW, MY DAUGHTERS JEN AND EVIL JEN ARE TRAPPED IN THE NETHER LIKE SITTING DUCKS.
AND I WILL TAKE YOU TO THEM SO YOU MAY DO THE HONORS OF DESTROYING THEM!
SO TELL ME—
—ARE YOU **WITH** ME?
RIZZLE-FIZ!
RIB-RAZZLE!
RAGGLE-RIP!
RAP-RIZZLE!
THE PORTAL TO THE **NETHER** IS IN THAT CAVE.
THEN **FOLLOW ME**!

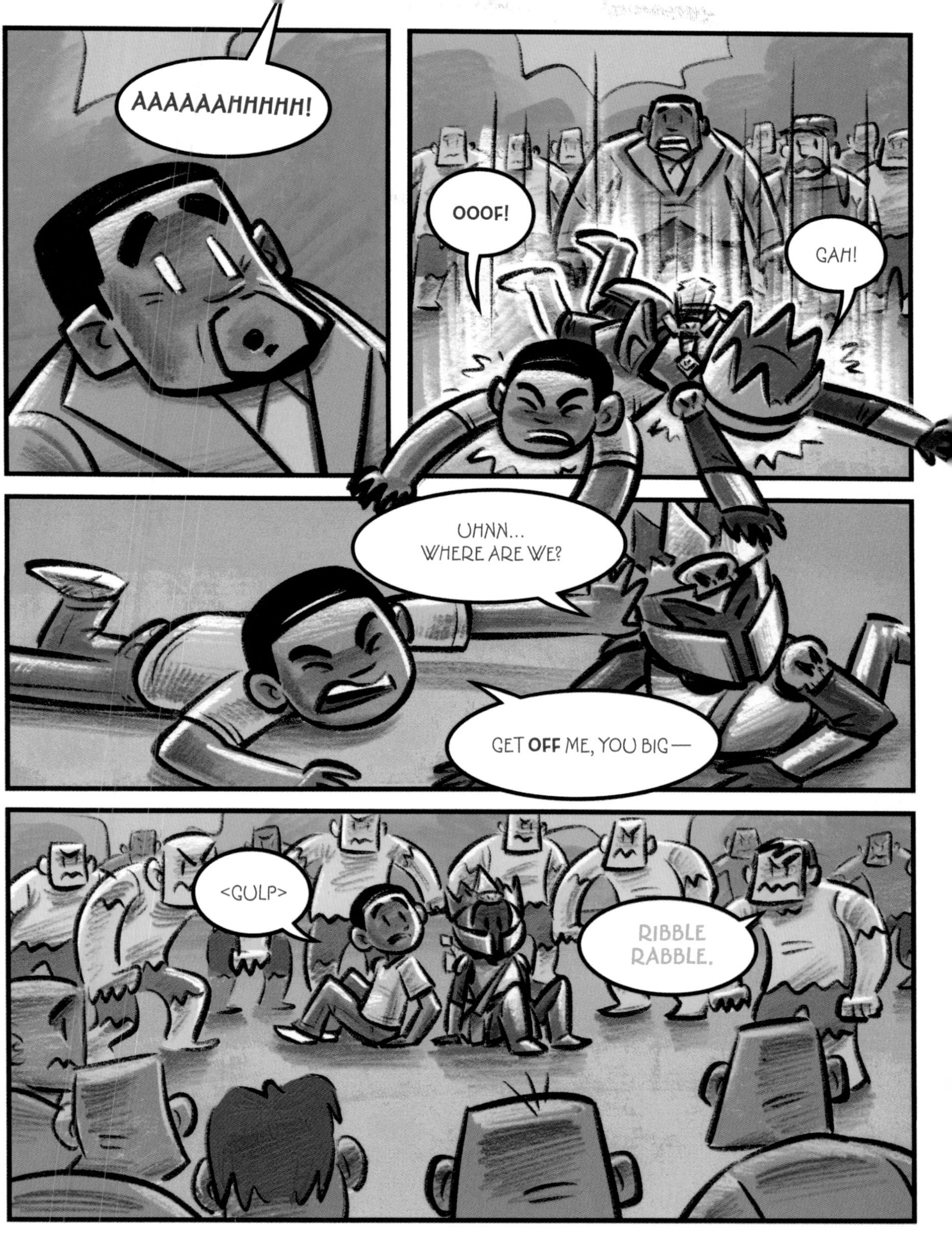
AAAAAAHHHHH!
OOOF!
GAH!
UHNN...
WHERE ARE WE?
GET **OFF** ME, YOU BIG—
<GULP>
RIBBLE
RABBLE.

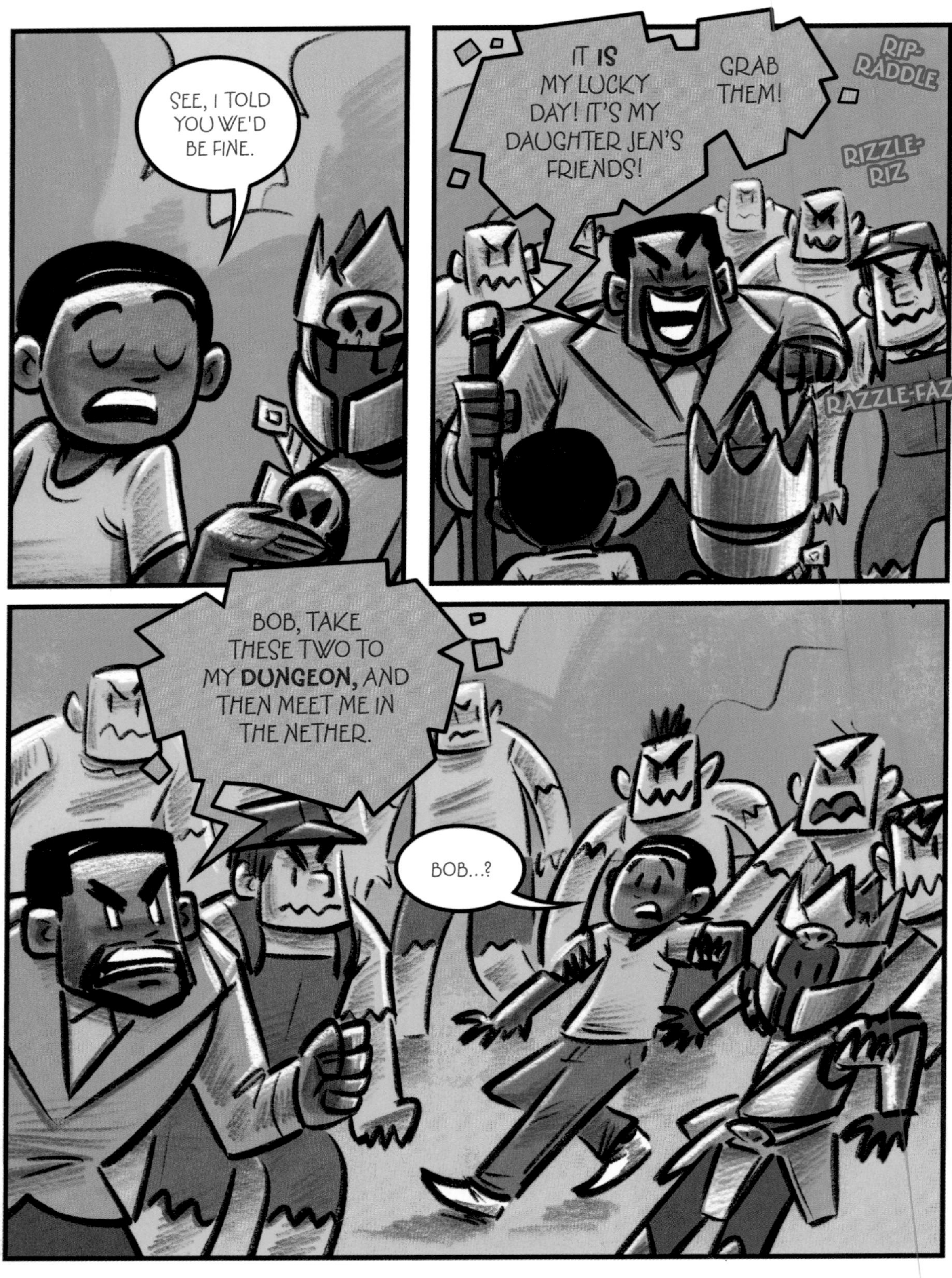
SEE, I TOLD YOU WE'D BE FINE.
IT IS MY LUCKY DAY! IT'S MY DAUGHTER JEN'S FRIENDS!
GRAB THEM!
RIP-RADDLE
RIZZLE-RIZ
RAZZLE-FAZ!
BOB, TAKE THESE TWO TO MY DUNGEON, AND THEN MEET ME IN THE NETHER.
BOB...?

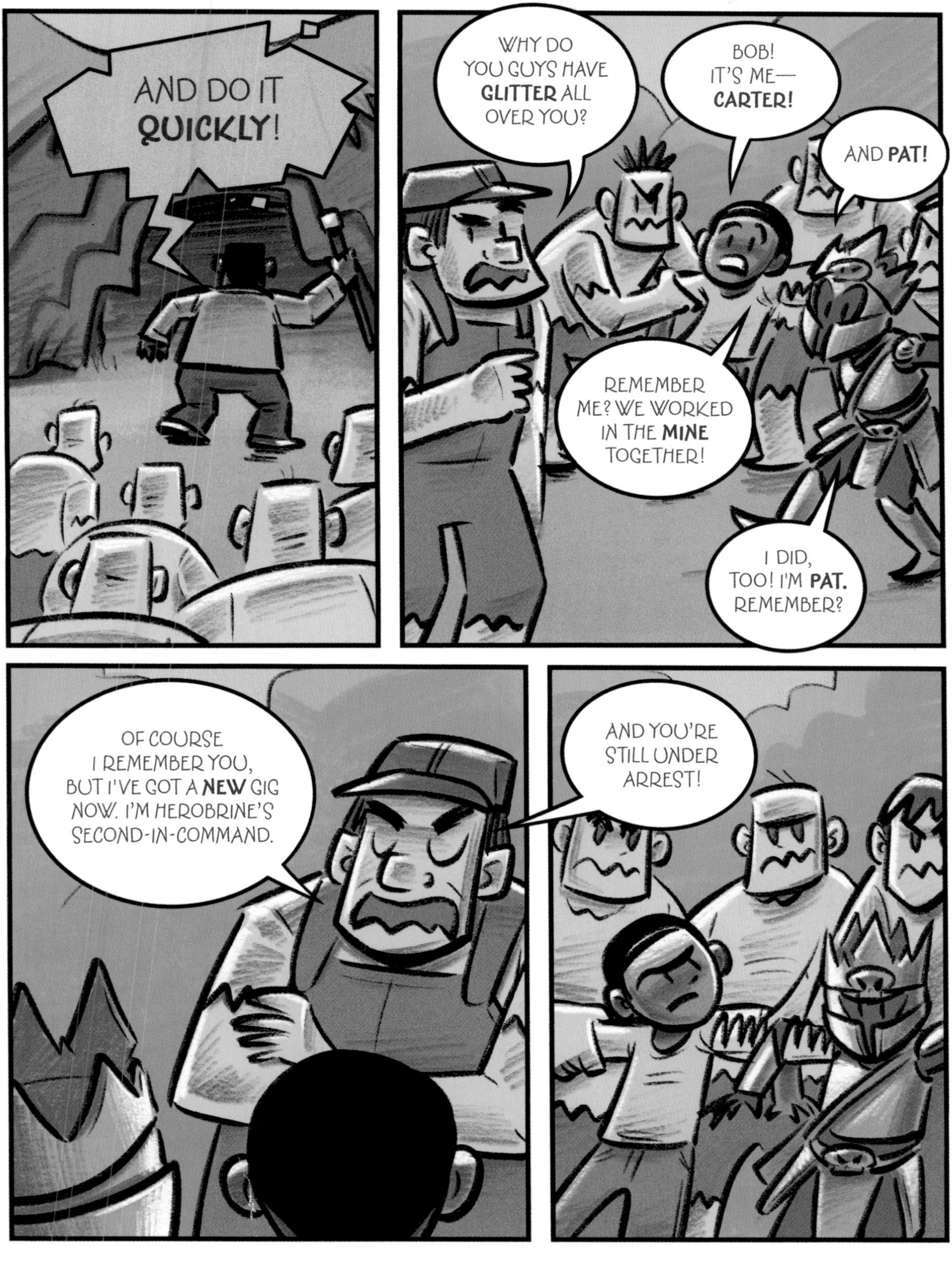
AND DO IT QUICKLY!
WHY DO YOU GUYS HAVE GLITTER ALL OVER YOU?
BOB! IT'S ME— CARTER!
AND PAT!
REMEMBER ME? WE WORKED IN THE MINE TOGETHER!
I DID, TOO! I'M PAT. REMEMBER?
OF COURSE I REMEMBER YOU, BUT I'VE GOT A NEW GIG NOW. I'M HEROBRINE'S SECOND-IN-COMMAND.
AND YOU'RE STILL UNDER ARREST!

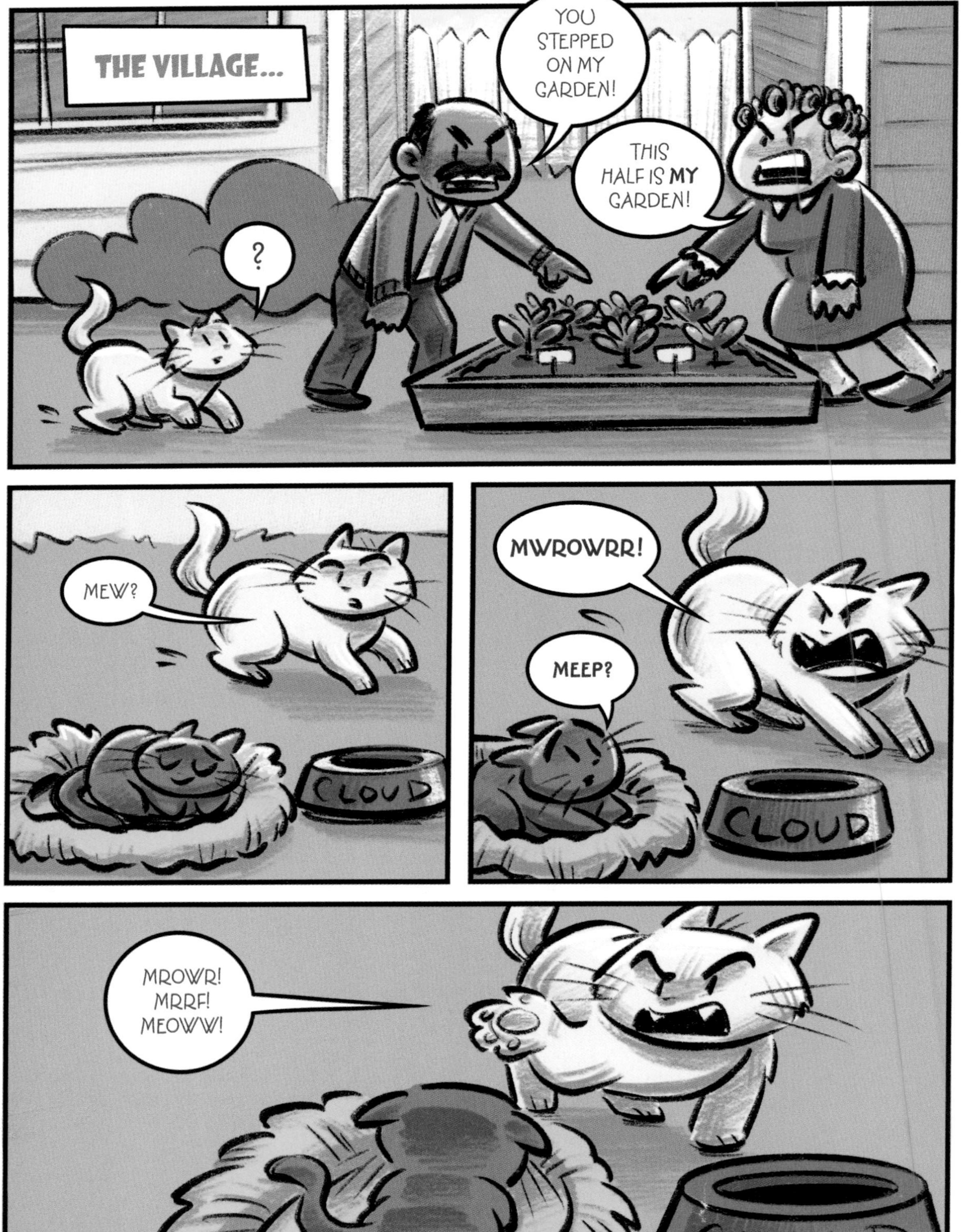
THE VILLAGE...
YOU STEPPED ON MY GARDEN!
THIS HALF IS **MY** GARDEN!
?
MEW?
MWROWRR!
MEEP?
CLOUD
CLOUD
MROWR! MRRF! MEOWW!

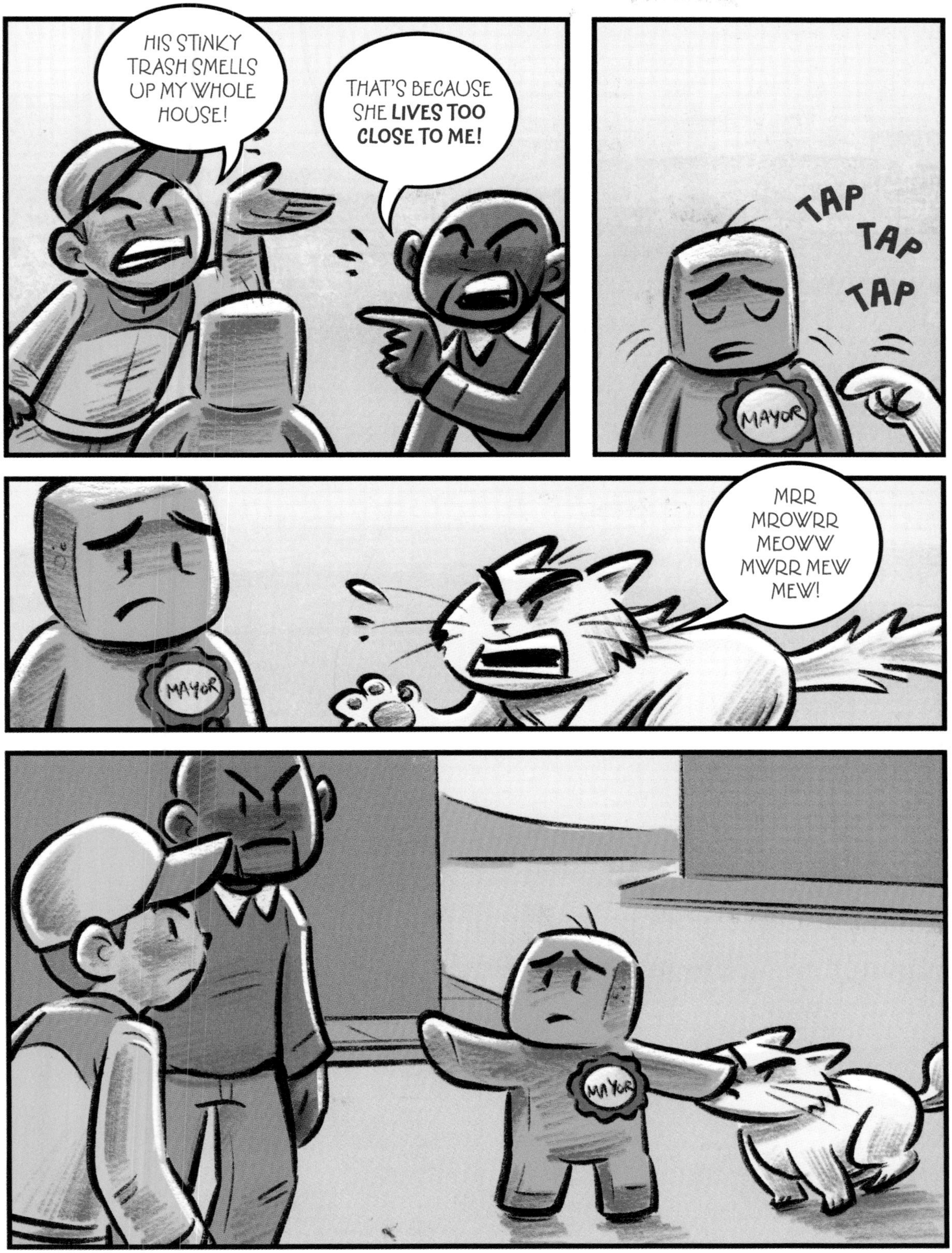
HIS STINKY TRASH SMELLS UP MY WHOLE HOUSE!
THAT'S BECAUSE SHE **LIVES TOO CLOSE TO ME!**
TAP TAP TAP
MAYOR
MAYOR
MRR MROWRR MEOWW MWRR MEW MEW!
MAYOR

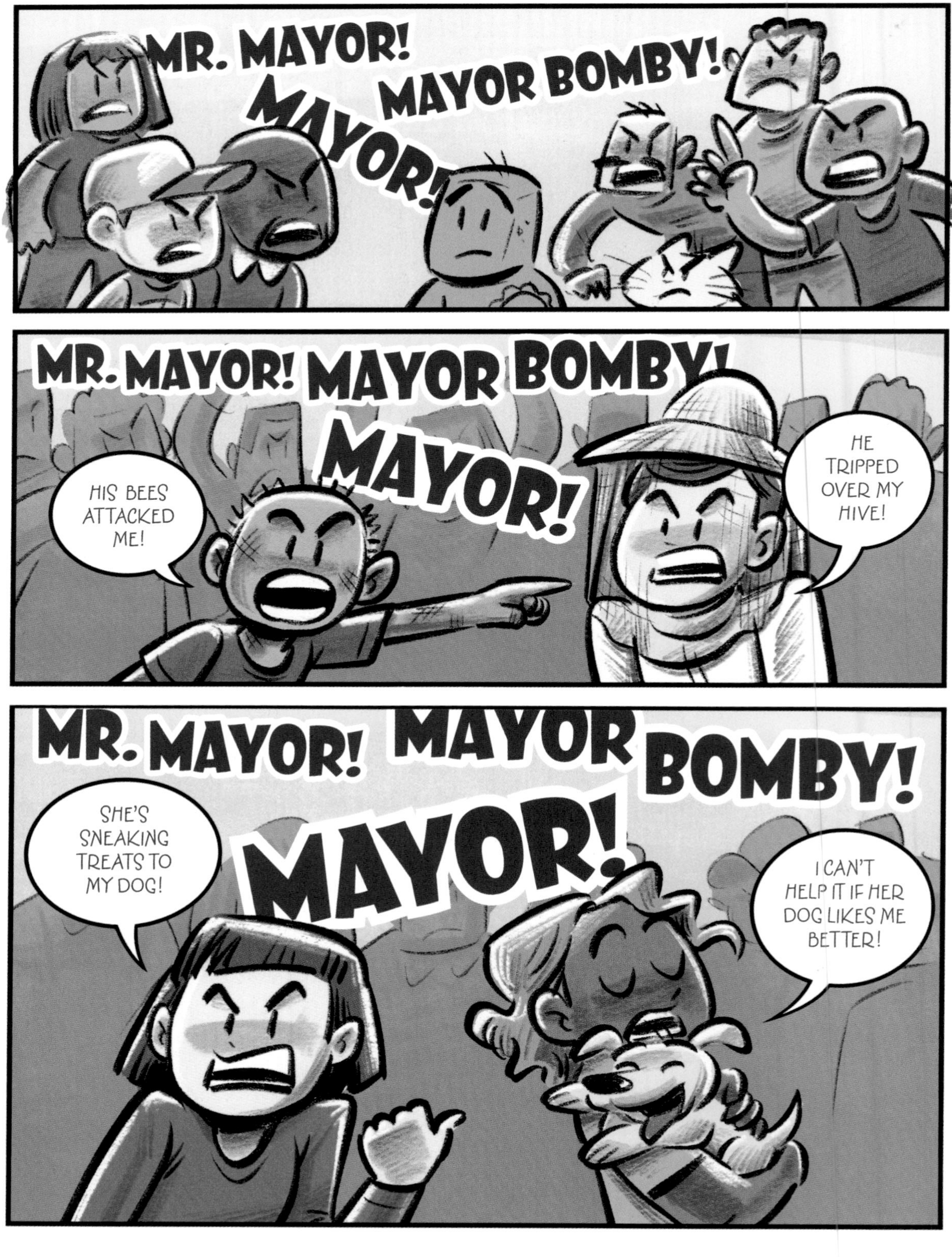
MR. MAYOR!
MAYOR BOMBY!
MAYOR!
MR. MAYOR!
MAYOR BOMBY!
MAYOR!
HIS BEES ATTACKED ME!
HE TRIPPED OVER MY HIVE!
MR. MAYOR!
MAYOR BOMBY!
MAYOR!
SHE'S SNEAKING TREATS TO MY DOG!
I CAN'T HELP IT IF HER DOG LIKES ME BETTER!

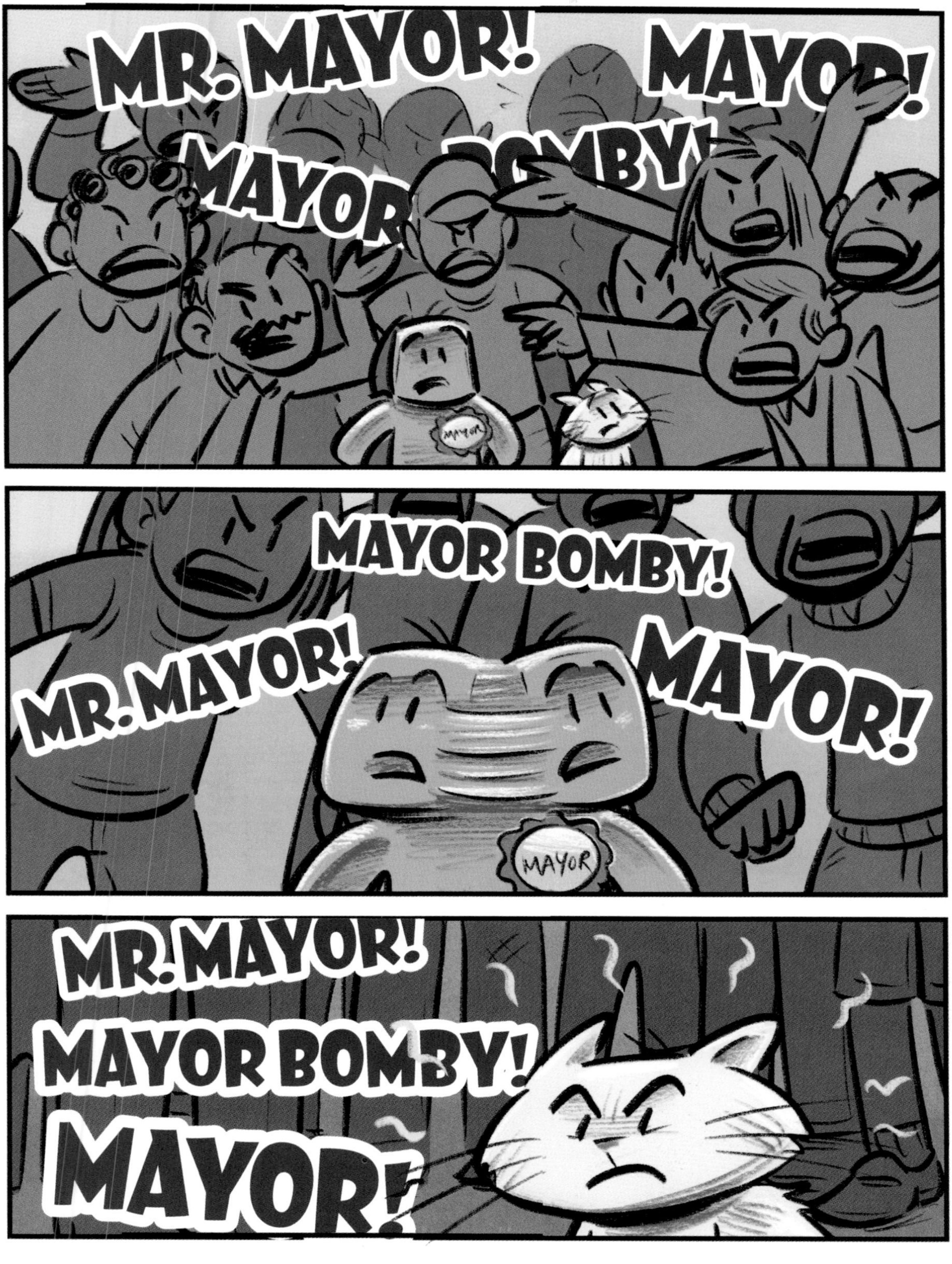
MR. MAYOR!
MAYOR
MAYOR
MAYOR BOMBY!
MR. MAYOR!
MAYOR!
MAYOR
MR. MAYOR!
MAYOR BOMBY!
MAYOR!

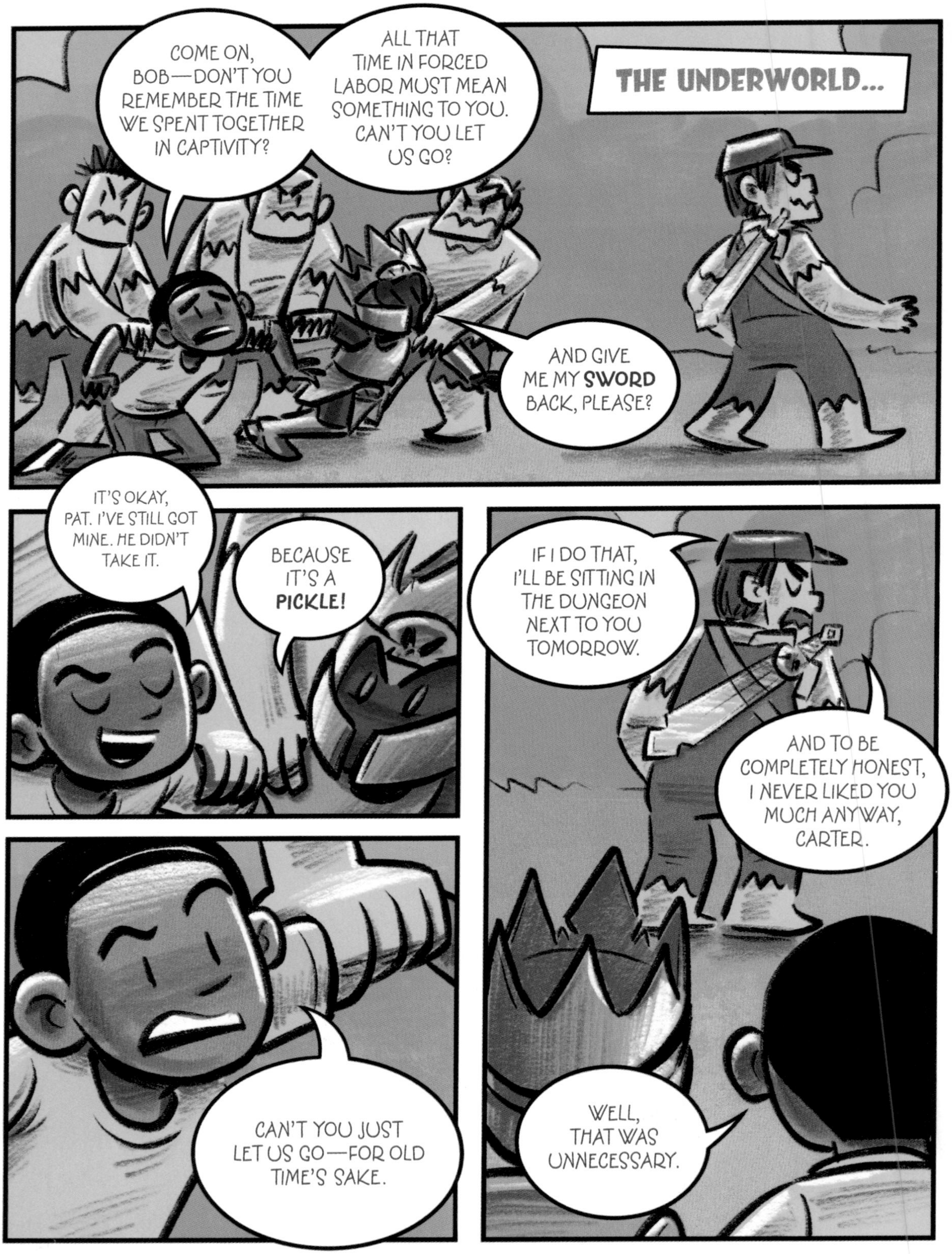
THE UNDERWORLD...
COME ON, BOB—DON'T YOU REMEMBER THE TIME WE SPENT TOGETHER IN CAPTIVITY?
ALL THAT TIME IN FORCED LABOR MUST MEAN SOMETHING TO YOU. CAN'T YOU LET US GO?
AND GIVE ME MY **SWORD** BACK, PLEASE?
IT'S OKAY, PAT. I'VE STILL GOT MINE. HE DIDN'T TAKE IT.
BECAUSE IT'S A **PICKLE!**
CAN'T YOU JUST LET US GO—FOR OLD TIME'S SAKE.
IF I DO THAT, I'LL BE SITTING IN THE DUNGEON NEXT TO YOU TOMORROW.
AND TO BE COMPLETELY HONEST, I NEVER LIKED YOU MUCH ANYWAY, CARTER.
WELL, THAT WAS UNNECESSARY.

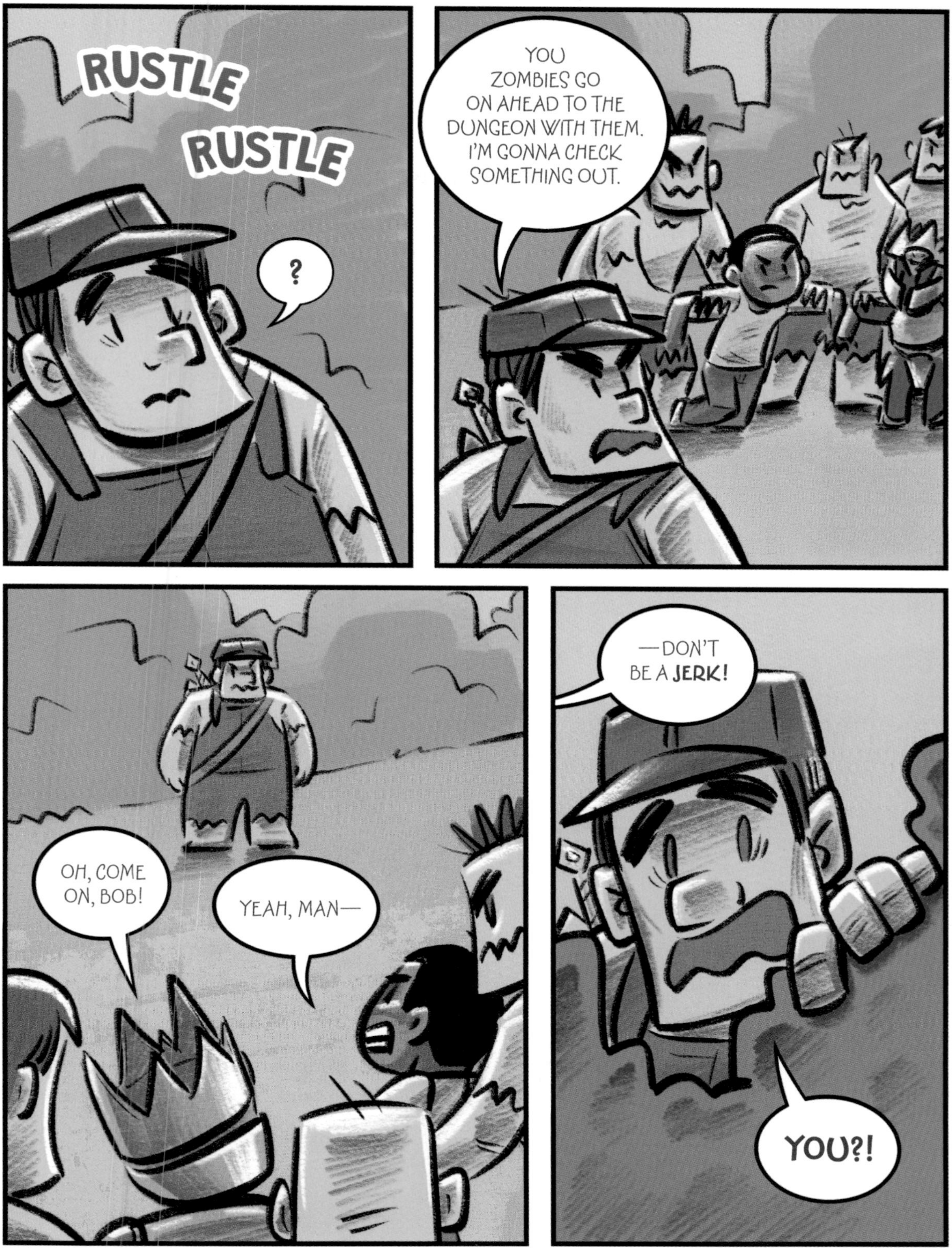
RUSTLE
RUSTLE
?
YOU ZOMBIES GO ON AHEAD TO THE DUNGEON WITH THEM. I'M GONNA CHECK SOMETHING OUT.
OH, COME ON, BOB!
YEAH, MAN—
—DON'T BE A JERK!
YOU?!

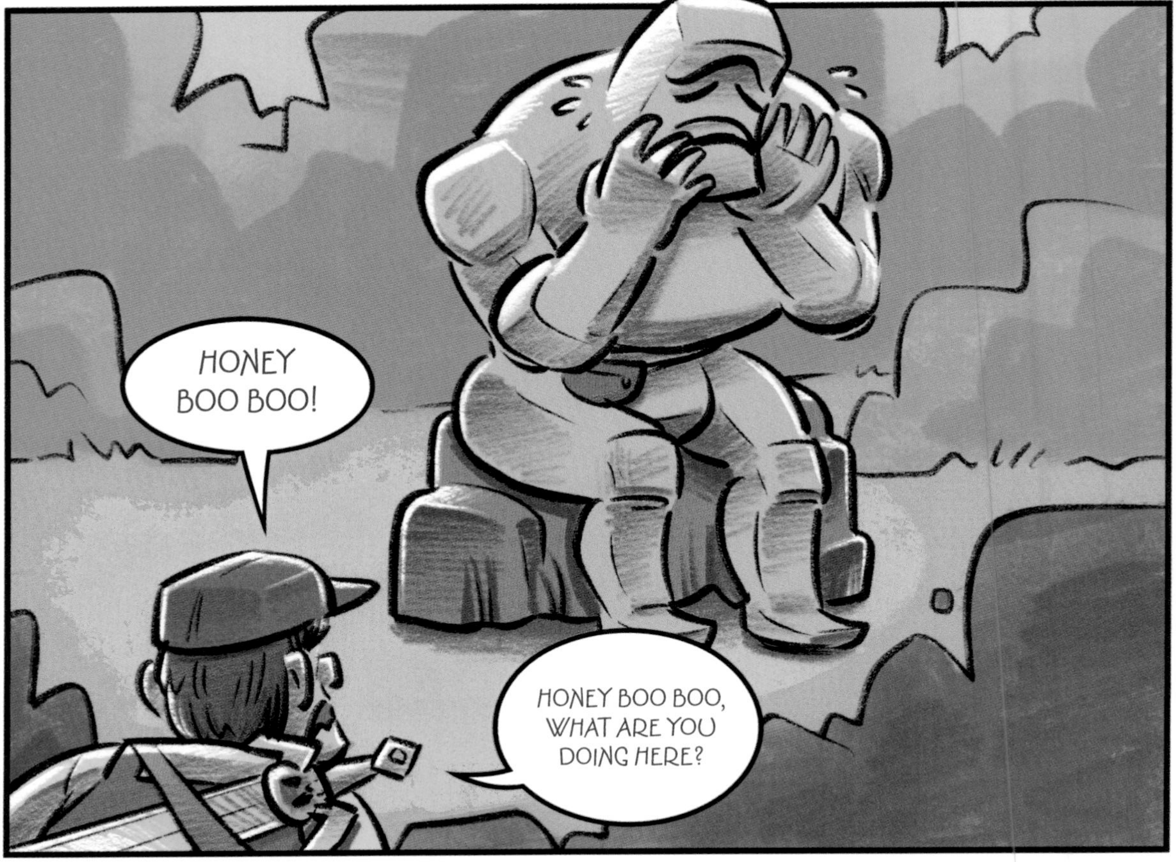
HONEY BOO BOO!
HONEY BOO BOO, WHAT ARE YOU DOING HERE?

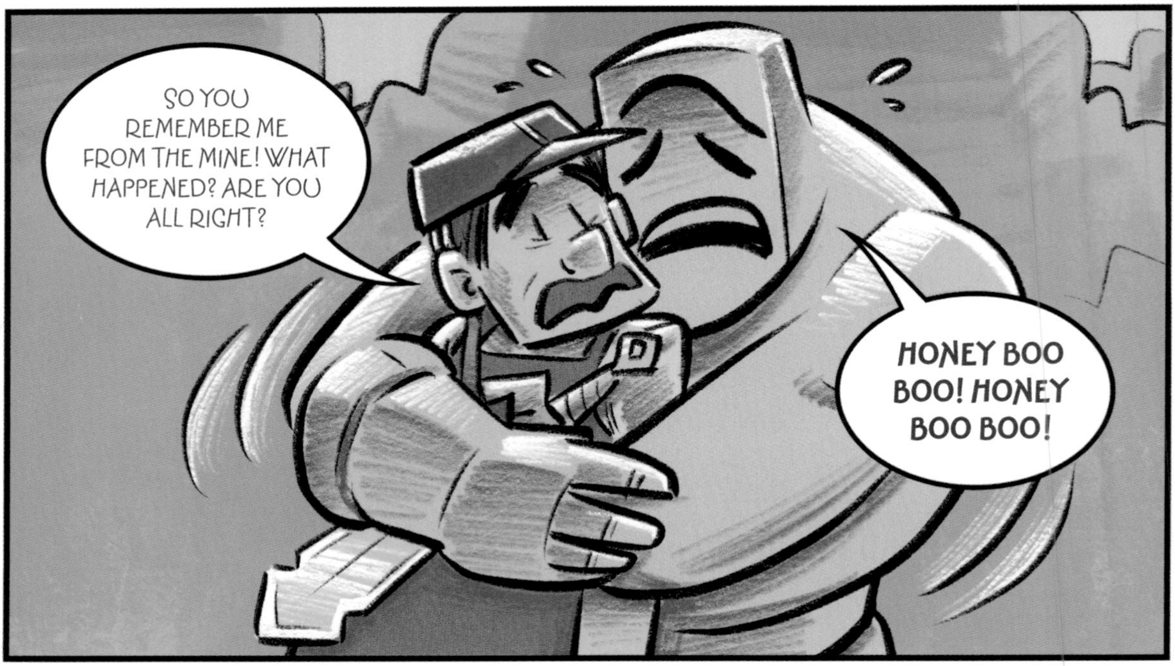
SO YOU REMEMBER ME FROM THE MINE! WHAT HAPPENED? ARE YOU ALL RIGHT?
HONEY BOO BOO! HONEY BOO BOO!

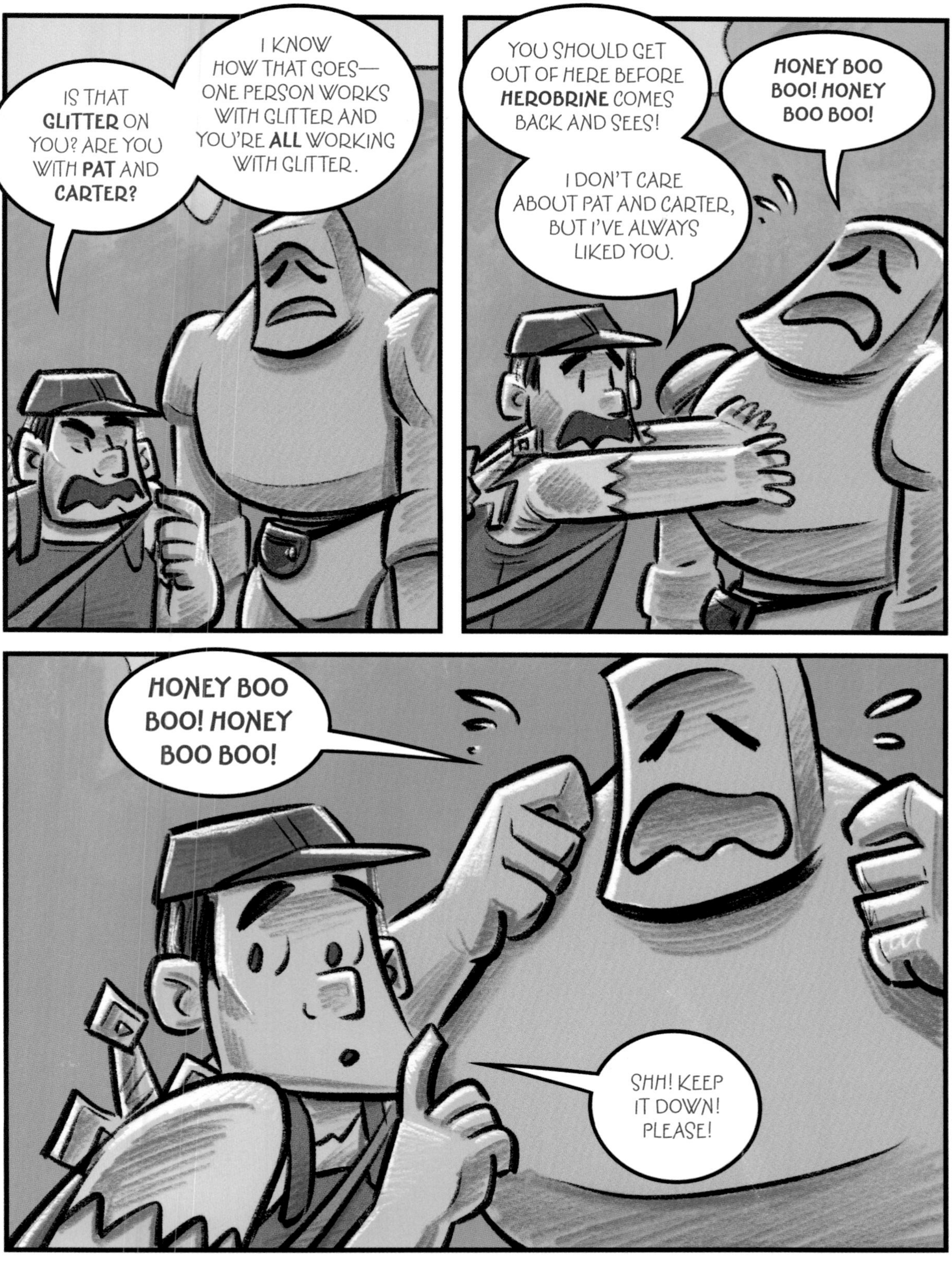
IS THAT **GLITTER** ON YOU? ARE YOU WITH **PAT** AND **CARTER?**
I KNOW HOW THAT GOES— ONE PERSON WORKS WITH GLITTER AND YOU'RE **ALL** WORKING WITH GLITTER.
YOU SHOULD GET OUT OF HERE BEFORE **HEROBRINE** COMES BACK AND SEES!
I DON'T CARE ABOUT PAT AND CARTER, BUT I'VE ALWAYS LIKED YOU.
HONEY BOO BOO! HONEY BOO BOO!
HONEY BOO BOO! HONEY BOO BOO!
SHH! KEEP IT DOWN! PLEASE!

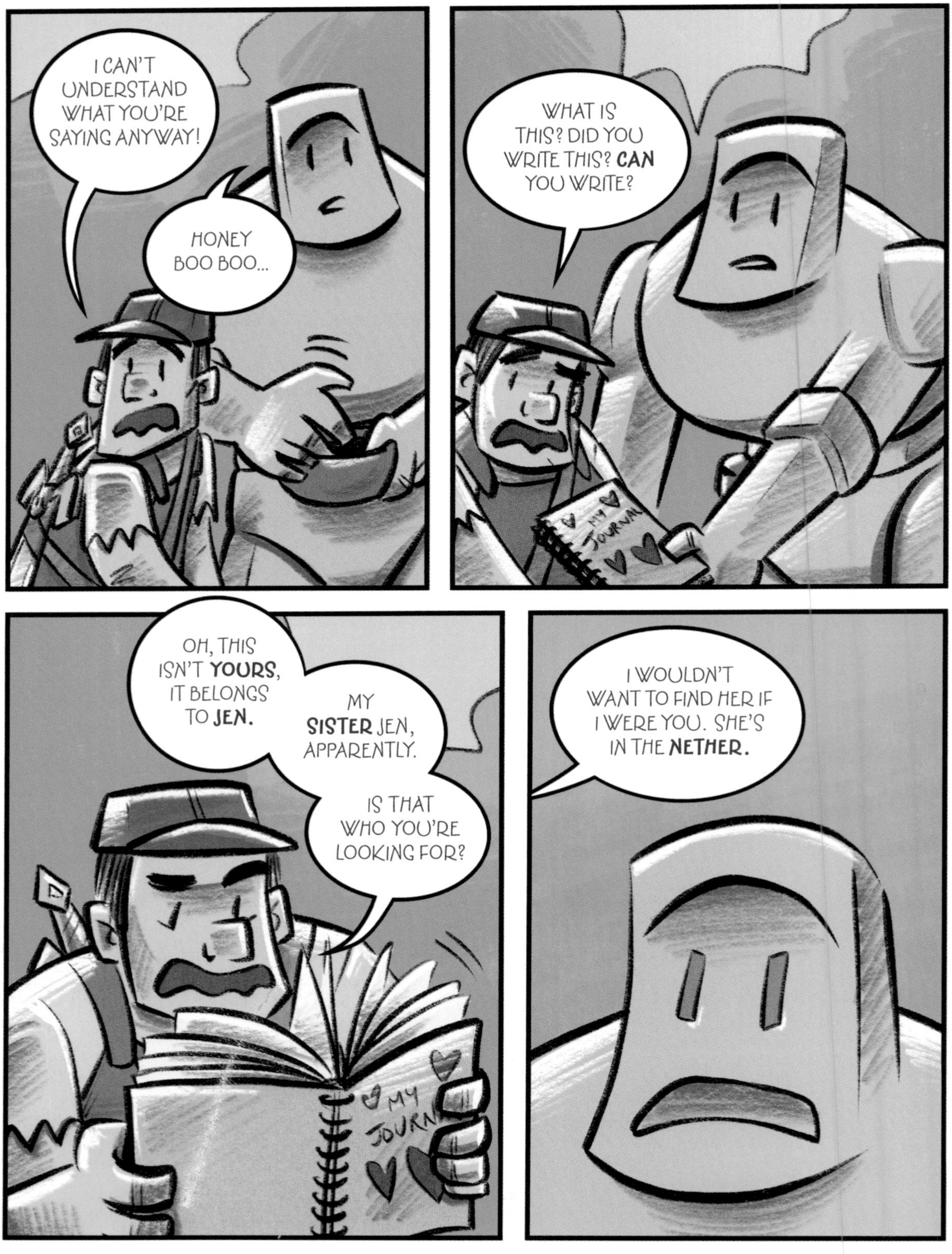
I CAN'T UNDERSTAND WHAT YOU'RE SAYING ANYWAY!
HONEY BOO BOO...
WHAT IS THIS? DID YOU WRITE THIS? **CAN** YOU WRITE?
MY JOURNAL
OH, THIS ISN'T **YOURS**, IT BELONGS TO **JEN.**
MY **SISTER** JEN, APPARENTLY.
IS THAT WHO YOU'RE LOOKING FOR?
I WOULDN'T WANT TO FIND HER IF I WERE YOU. SHE'S IN THE **NETHER.**

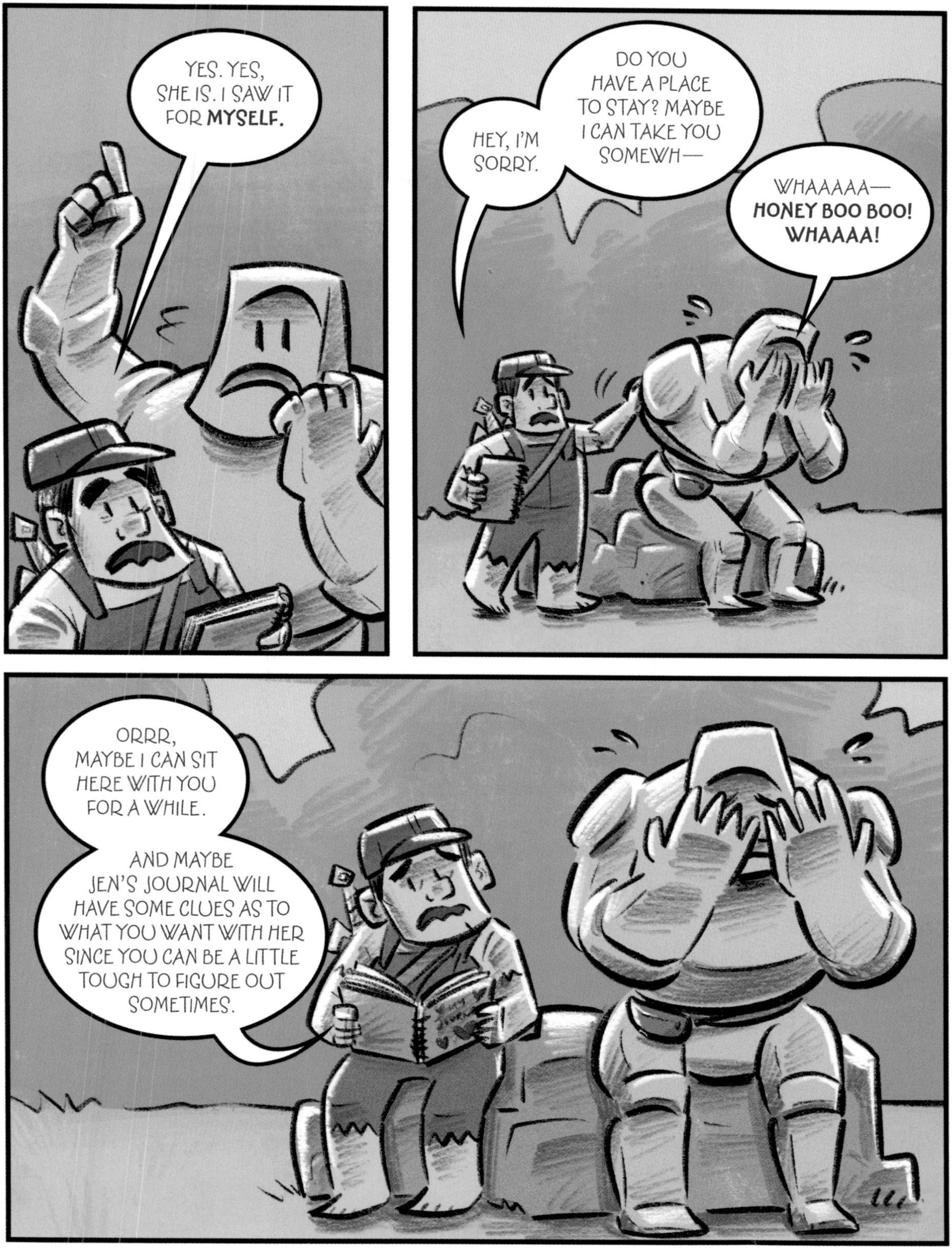
YES. YES, SHE IS. I SAW IT FOR **MYSELF.**
HEY, I'M SORRY.
DO YOU HAVE A PLACE TO STAY? MAYBE I CAN TAKE YOU SOMEWH—
WHAAAAA— **HONEY BOO BOO! WHAAAA!**
ORRR, MAYBE I CAN SIT HERE WITH YOU FOR A WHILE.
AND MAYBE JEN'S JOURNAL WILL HAVE SOME CLUES AS TO WHAT YOU WANT WITH HER SINCE YOU CAN BE A LITTLE TOUGH TO FIGURE OUT SOMETIMES.

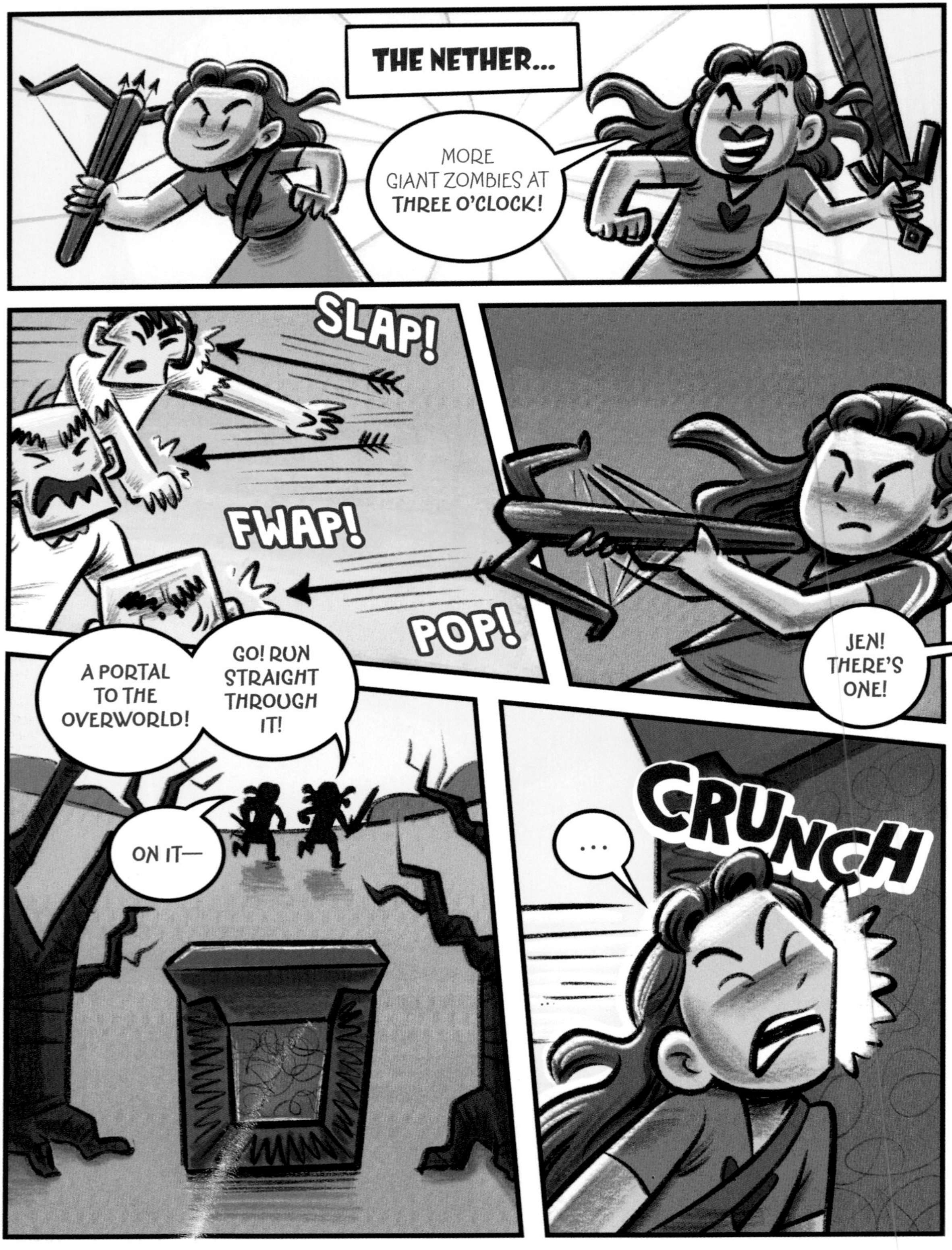
THE NETHER...
MORE GIANT ZOMBIES AT THREE O'CLOCK!
SLAP!
FWAP!
POP!
JEN! THERE'S ONE!
A PORTAL TO THE OVERWORLD!
GO! RUN STRAIGHT THROUGH IT!
ON IT—
CRUNCH
...

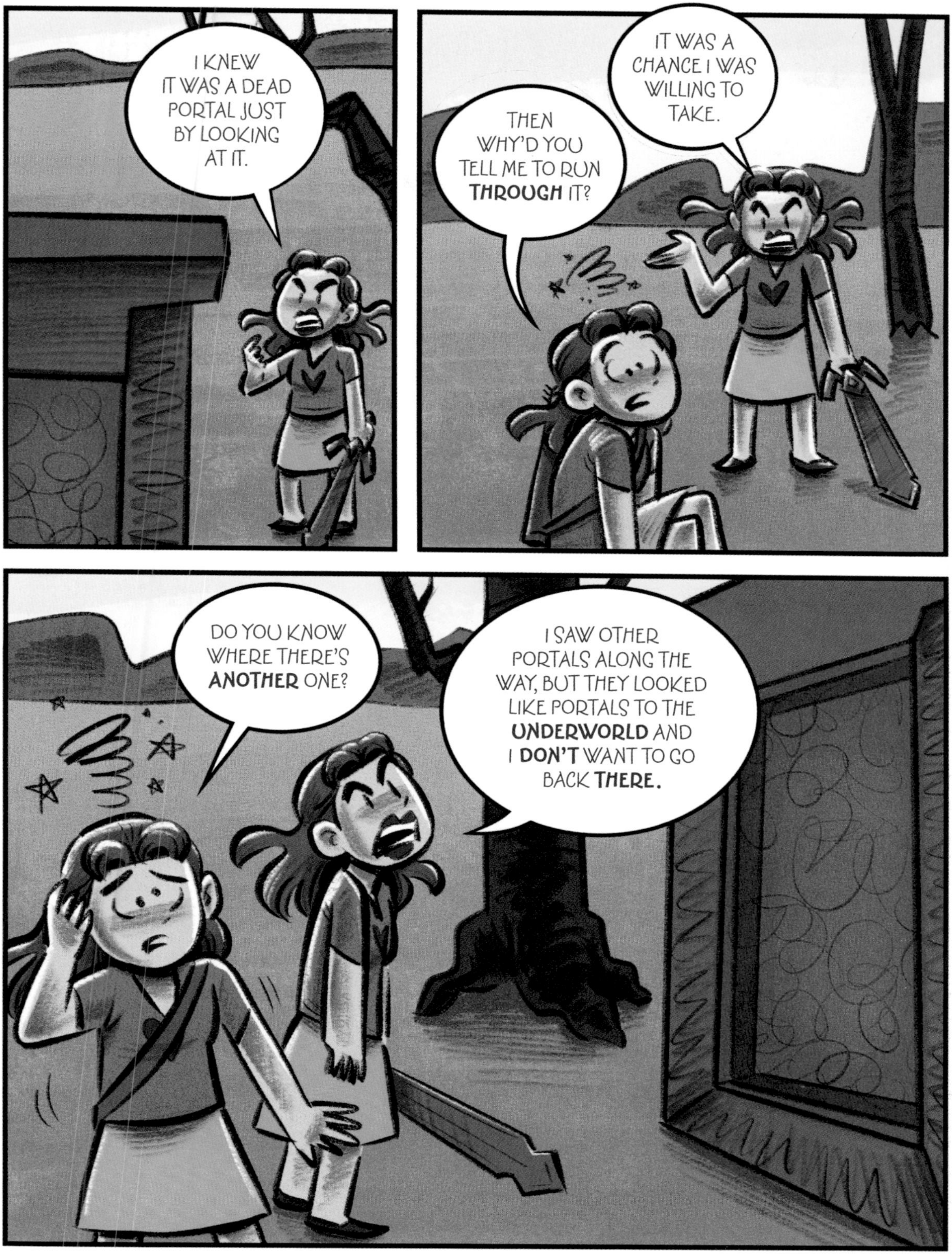
I KNEW IT WAS A DEAD PORTAL JUST BY LOOKING AT IT.
THEN WHY'D YOU TELL ME TO RUN **THROUGH** IT?
IT WAS A CHANCE I WAS WILLING TO TAKE.
DO YOU KNOW WHERE THERE'S **ANOTHER** ONE?
I SAW OTHER PORTALS ALONG THE WAY, BUT THEY LOOKED LIKE PORTALS TO THE **UNDERWORLD** AND I **DON'T** WANT TO GO BACK **THERE.**

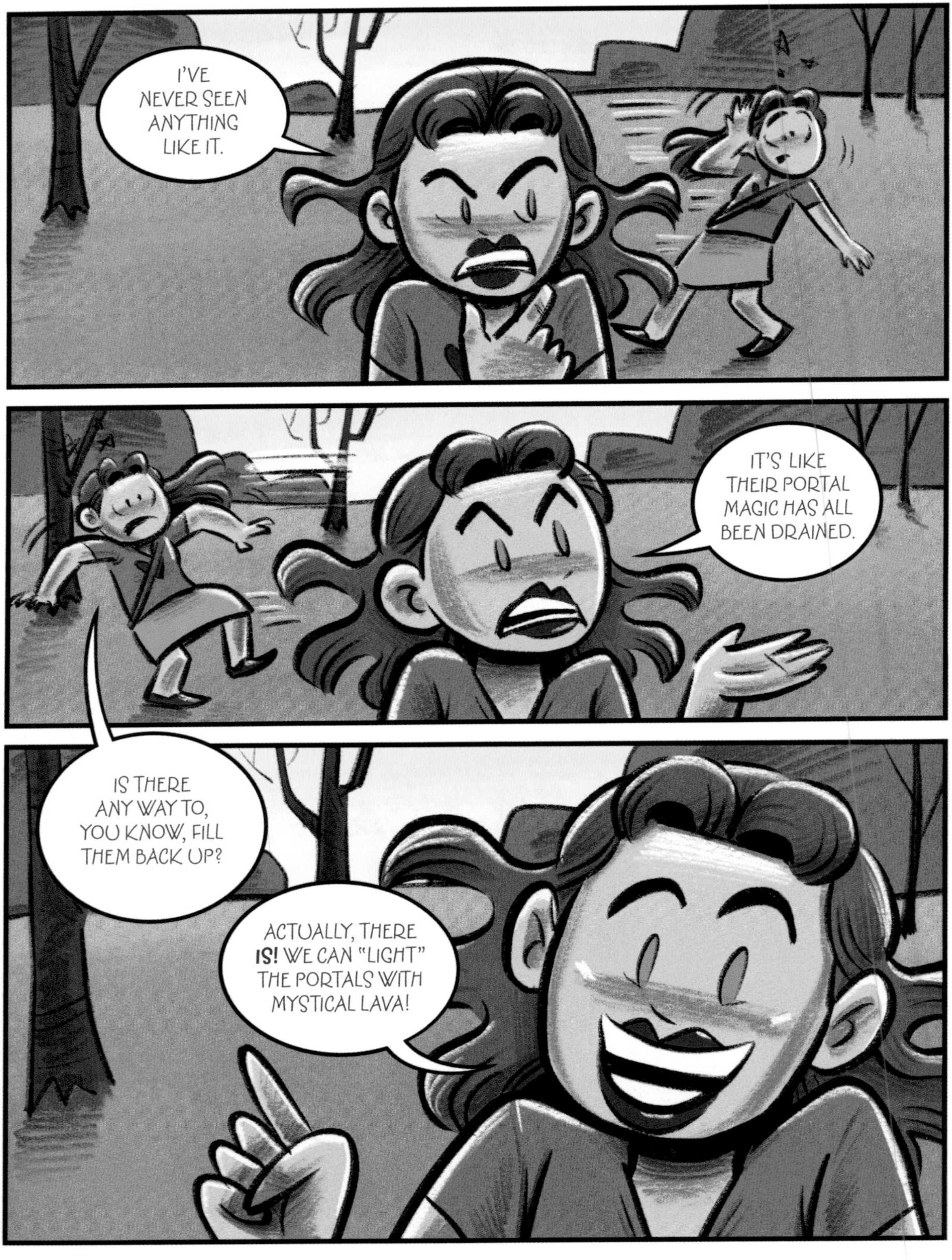
I'VE NEVER SEEN ANYTHING LIKE IT.
IT'S LIKE THEIR PORTAL MAGIC HAS ALL BEEN DRAINED.
IS THERE ANY WAY TO, YOU KNOW, FILL THEM BACK UP?
ACTUALLY, THERE **IS!** WE CAN "LIGHT" THE PORTALS WITH MYSTICAL LAVA!

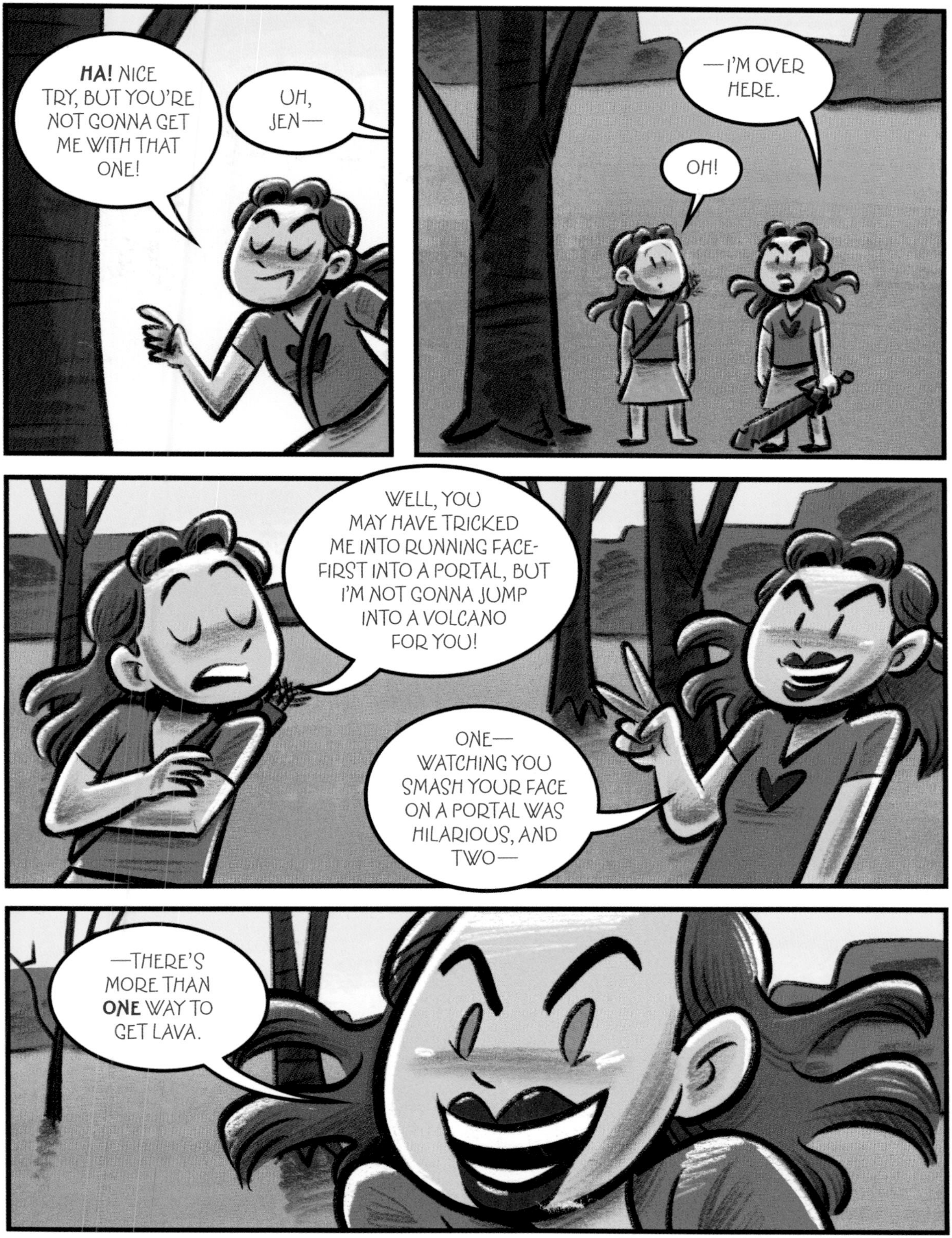

HA! NICE TRY, BUT YOU'RE NOT GONNA GET ME WITH THAT ONE!
UH, JEN—
—I'M OVER HERE.
OH!
WELL, YOU MAY HAVE TRICKED ME INTO RUNNING FACE-FIRST INTO A PORTAL, BUT I'M NOT GONNA JUMP INTO A VOLCANO FOR YOU!
ONE—WATCHING YOU SMASH YOUR FACE ON A PORTAL WAS HILARIOUS, AND TWO—
—THERE'S MORE THAN **ONE** WAY TO GET LAVA.

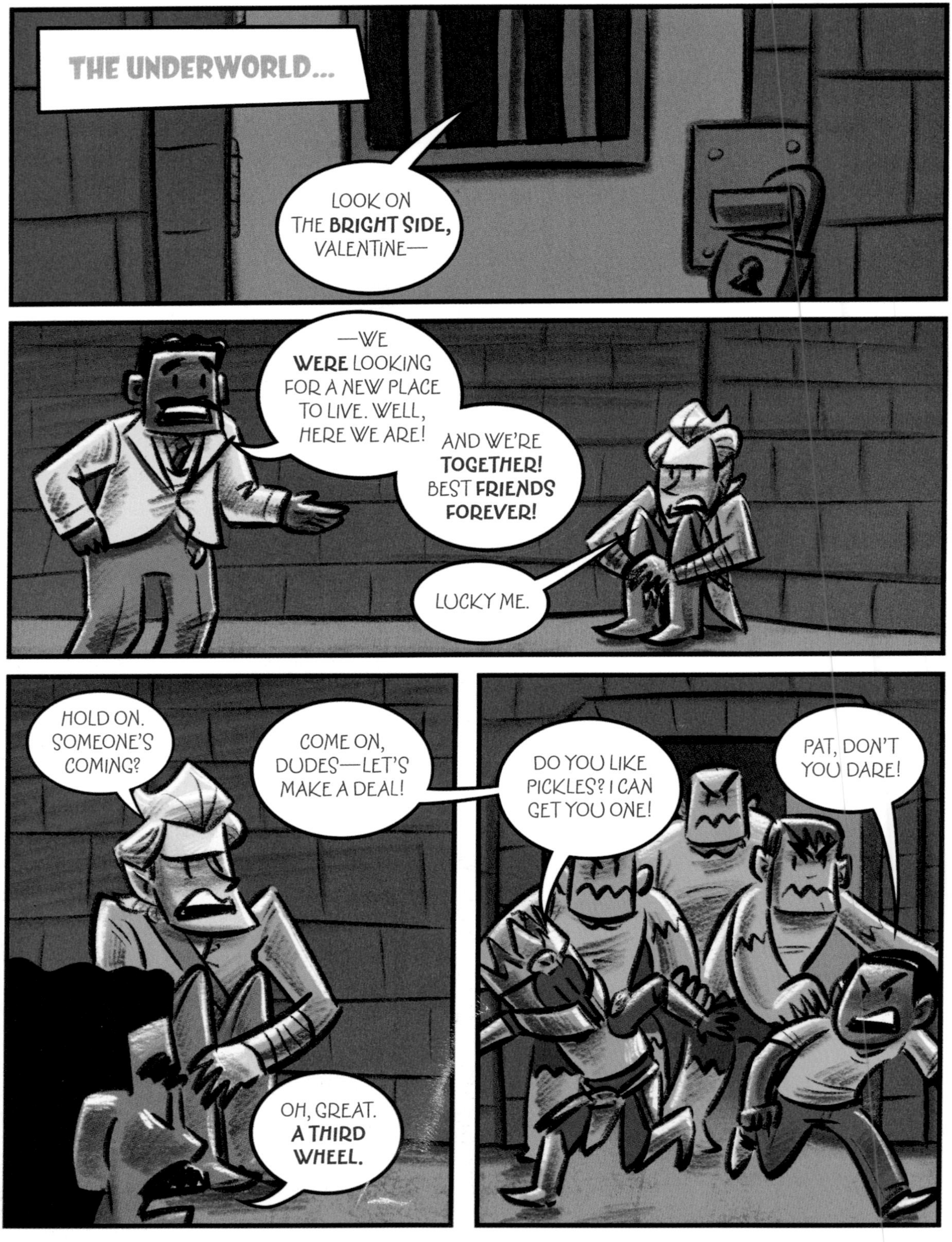
THE UNDERWORLD...
LOOK ON THE BRIGHT SIDE, VALENTINE—
—WE WERE LOOKING FOR A NEW PLACE TO LIVE. WELL, HERE WE ARE!
AND WE'RE TOGETHER! BEST FRIENDS FOREVER!
LUCKY ME.
HOLD ON. SOMEONE'S COMING?
OH, GREAT. A THIRD WHEEL.
COME ON, DUDES—LET'S MAKE A DEAL!
DO YOU LIKE PICKLES? I CAN GET YOU ONE!
PAT, DON'T YOU DARE!

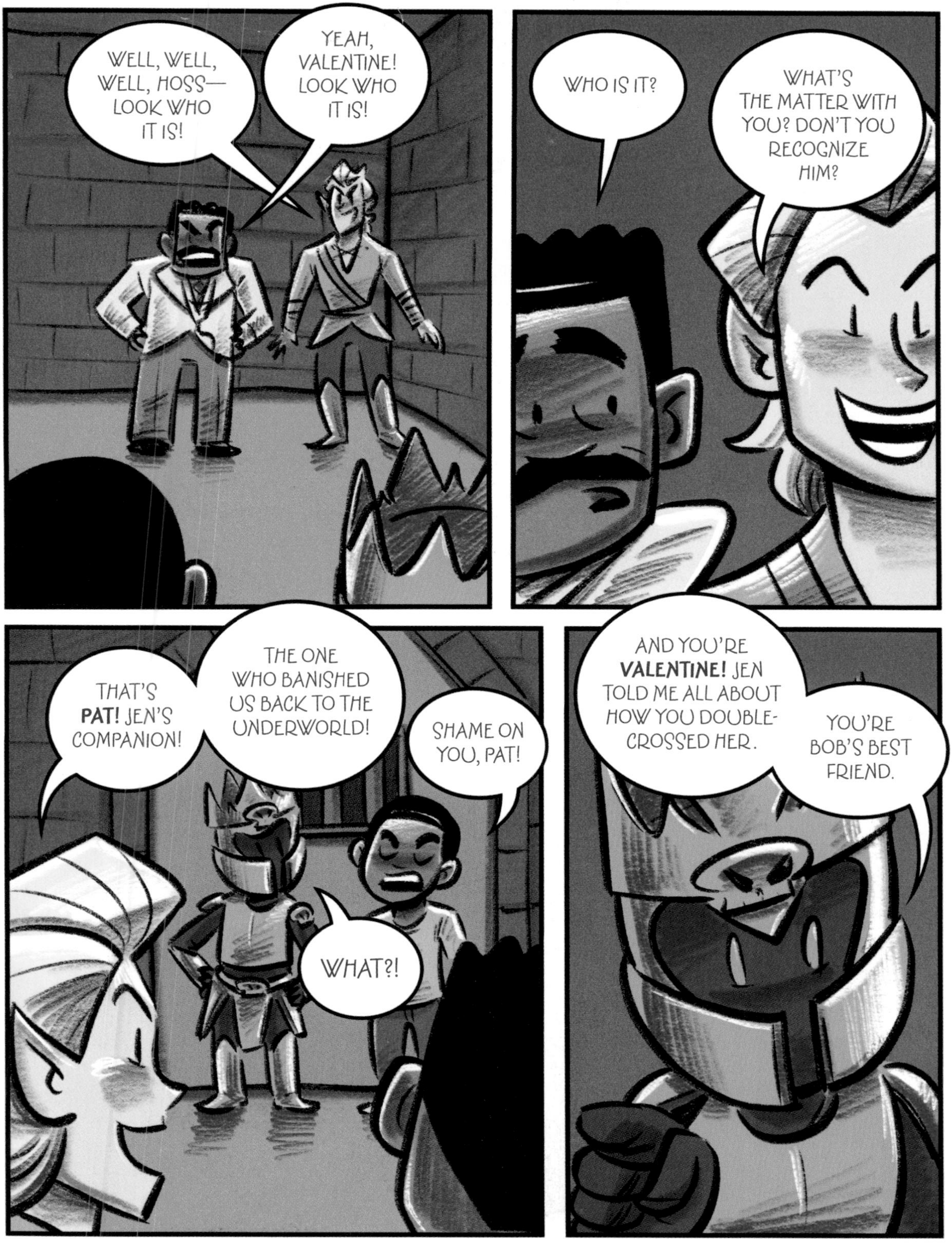
WELL, WELL, WELL, HOSS—LOOK WHO IT IS!
YEAH, VALENTINE! LOOK WHO IT IS!
WHO IS IT?
WHAT'S THE MATTER WITH YOU? DON'T YOU RECOGNIZE HIM?
THAT'S **PAT!** JEN'S COMPANION!
THE ONE WHO BANISHED US BACK TO THE UNDERWORLD!
SHAME ON YOU, PAT!
WHAT?!
AND YOU'RE **VALENTINE!** JEN TOLD ME ALL ABOUT HOW YOU DOUBLE-CROSSED HER.
YOU'RE BOB'S BEST FRIEND.

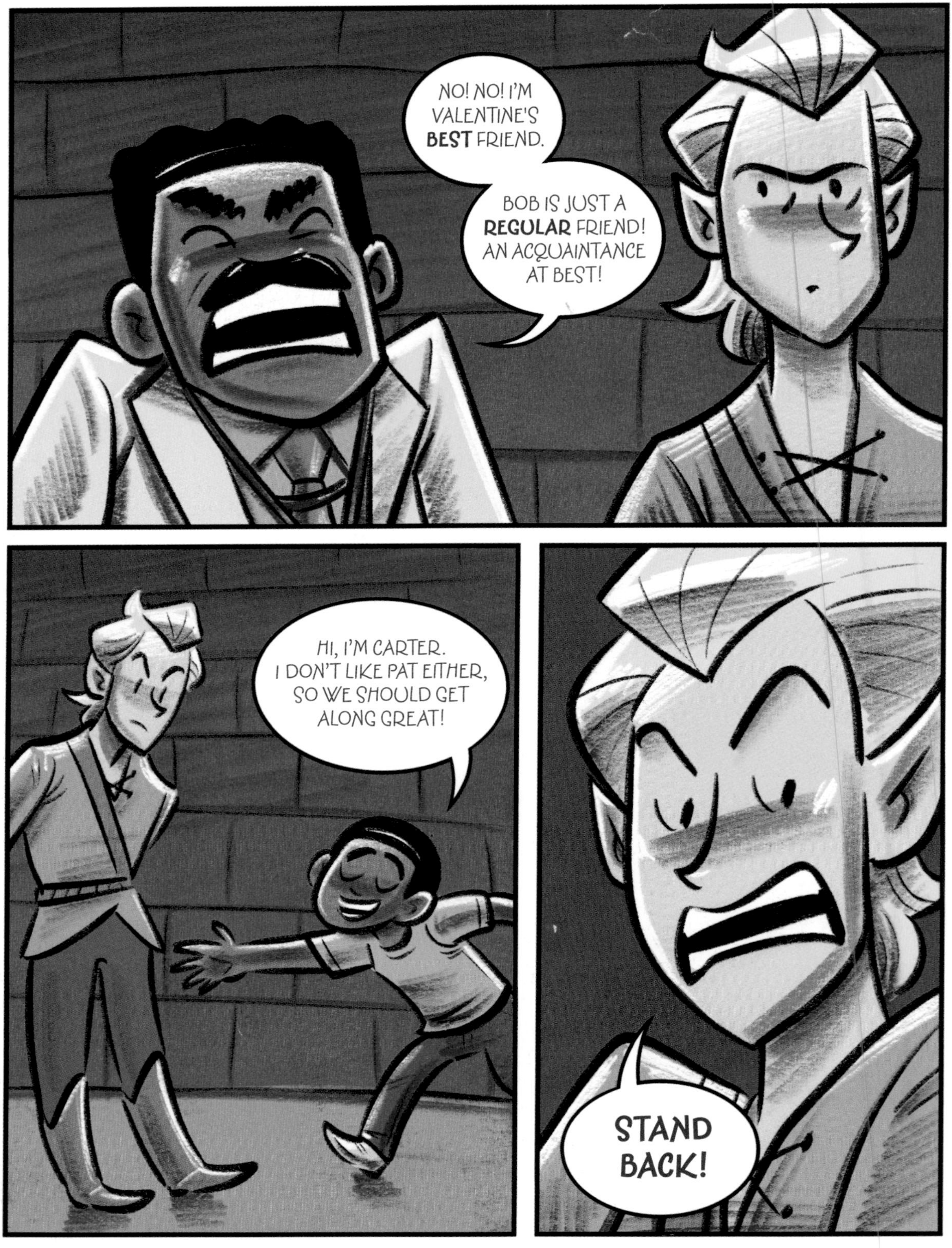
NO! NO! I'M VALENTINE'S **BEST** FRIEND.
BOB IS JUST A **REGULAR** FRIEND! AN ACQUAINTANCE AT BEST!
HI, I'M CARTER. I DON'T LIKE PAT EITHER, SO WE SHOULD GET ALONG GREAT!
STAND BACK!

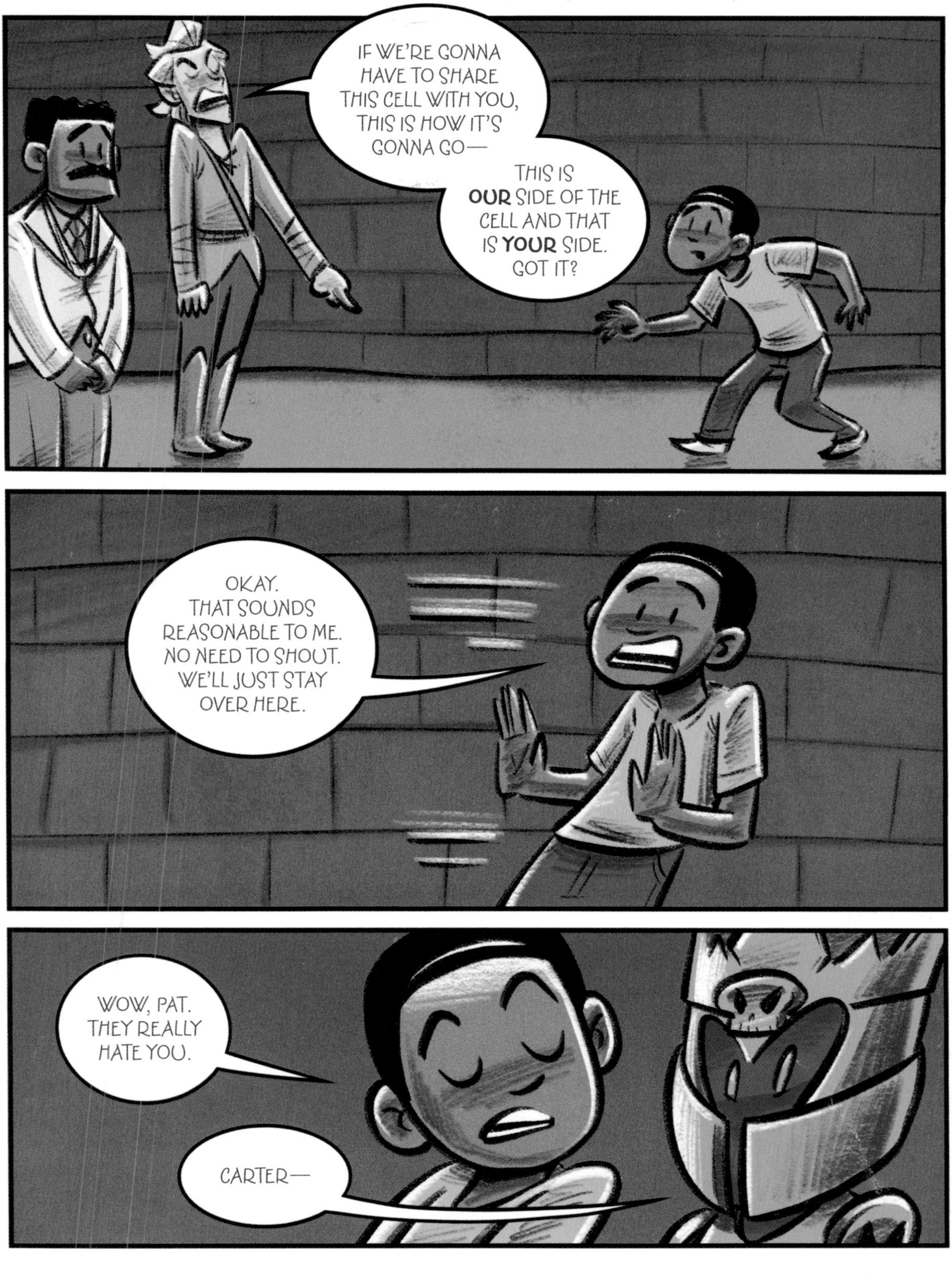
IF WE'RE GONNA HAVE TO SHARE THIS CELL WITH YOU, THIS IS HOW IT'S GONNA GO—
THIS IS **OUR** SIDE OF THE CELL AND THAT IS **YOUR** SIDE. GOT IT?
OKAY. THAT SOUNDS REASONABLE TO ME. NO NEED TO SHOUT. WE'LL JUST STAY OVER HERE.
WOW, PAT. THEY REALLY HATE YOU.
CARTER—

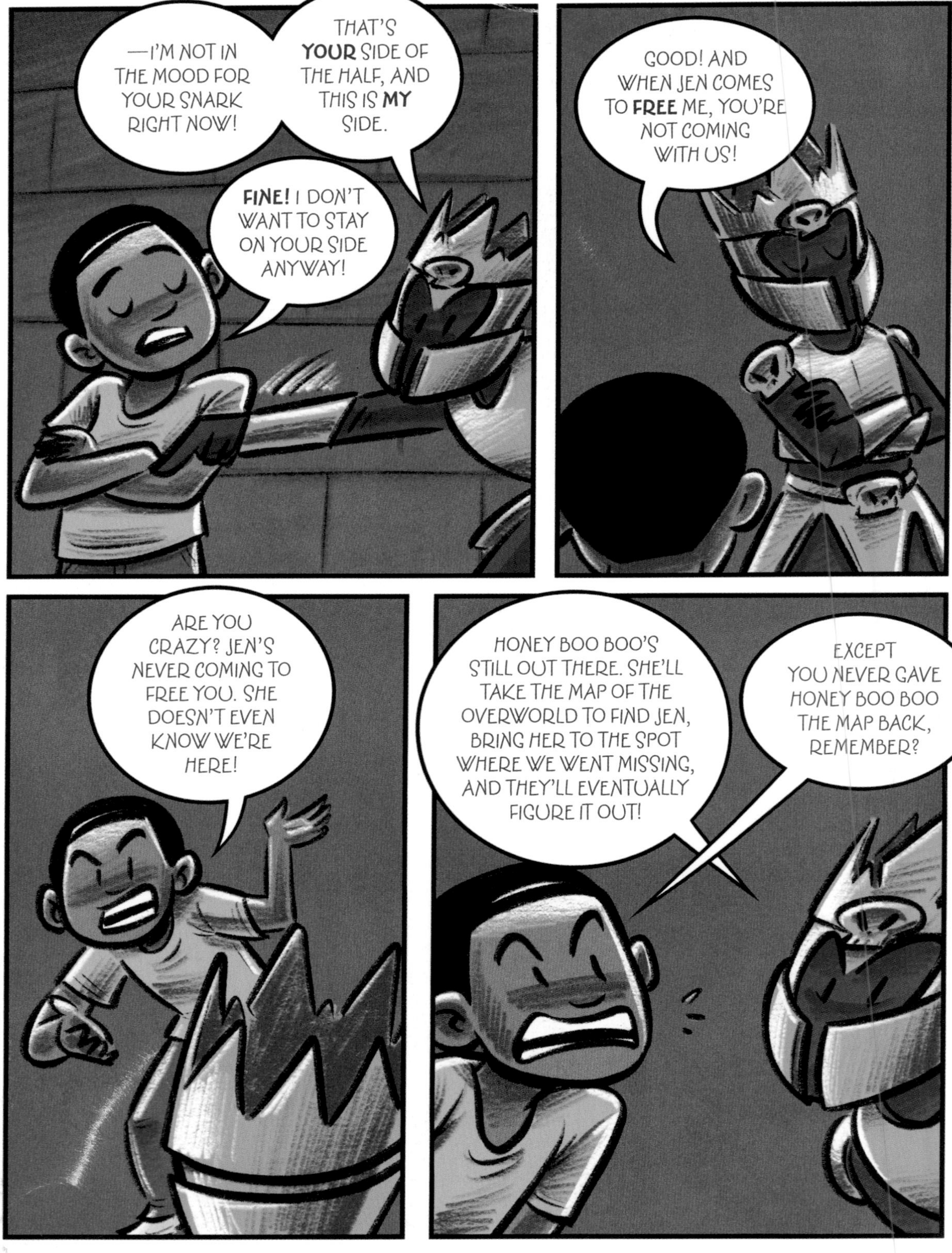
—I'M NOT IN THE MOOD FOR YOUR SNARK RIGHT NOW!
THAT'S **YOUR** SIDE OF THE HALF, AND THIS IS **MY** SIDE.
FINE! I DON'T WANT TO STAY ON YOUR SIDE ANYWAY!
GOOD! AND WHEN JEN COMES TO **FREE** ME, YOU'RE NOT COMING WITH US!
ARE YOU CRAZY? JEN'S NEVER COMING TO FREE YOU. SHE DOESN'T EVEN KNOW WE'RE HERE!
HONEY BOO BOO'S STILL OUT THERE. SHE'LL TAKE THE MAP OF THE OVERWORLD TO FIND JEN, BRING HER TO THE SPOT WHERE WE WENT MISSING, AND THEY'LL EVENTUALLY FIGURE IT OUT!
EXCEPT YOU NEVER GAVE HONEY BOO BOO THE MAP BACK, REMEMBER?

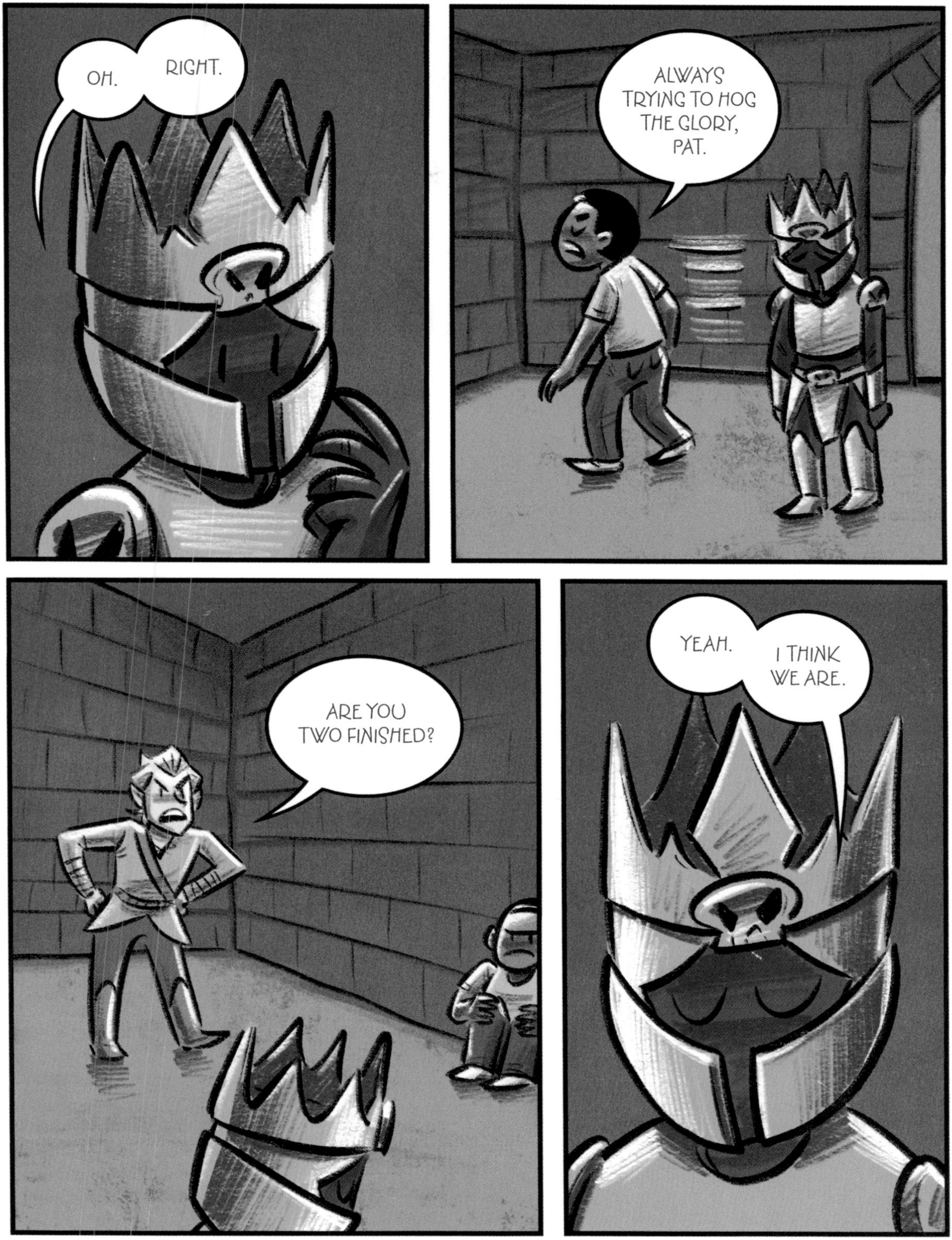
OH.
RIGHT.
ALWAYS TRYING TO HOG THE GLORY, PAT.
ARE YOU TWO FINISHED?
YEAH.
I THINK WE ARE.

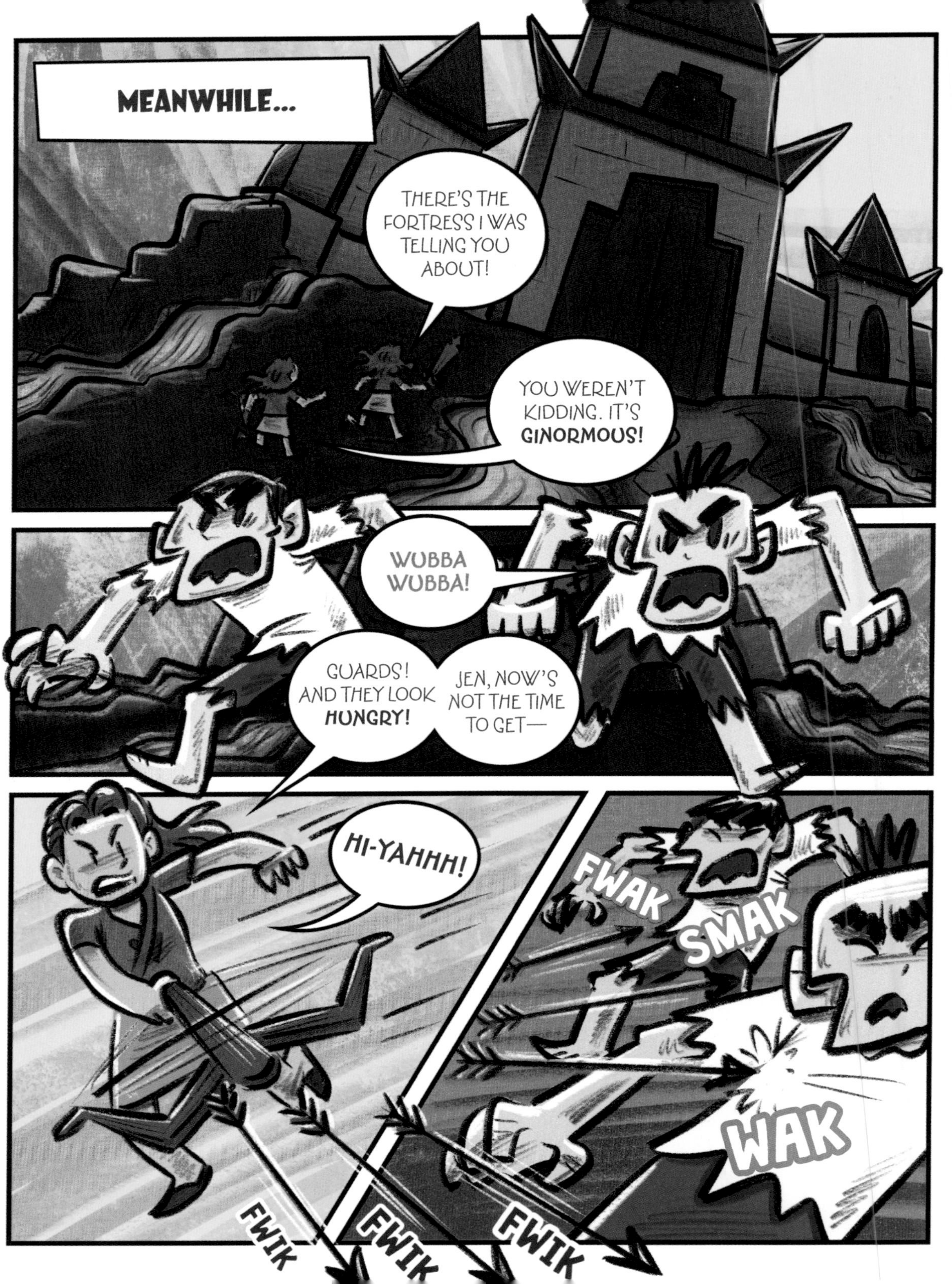
MEANWHILE...
THERE'S THE FORTRESS I WAS TELLING YOU ABOUT!
YOU WEREN'T KIDDING. IT'S GINORMOUS!
WUBBA WUBBA!
GUARDS! AND THEY LOOK HUNGRY!
JEN, NOW'S NOT THE TIME TO GET—
HI-YAHHH!
FWAK
SMAK
WAK
FWIK
FWIK
FWIK

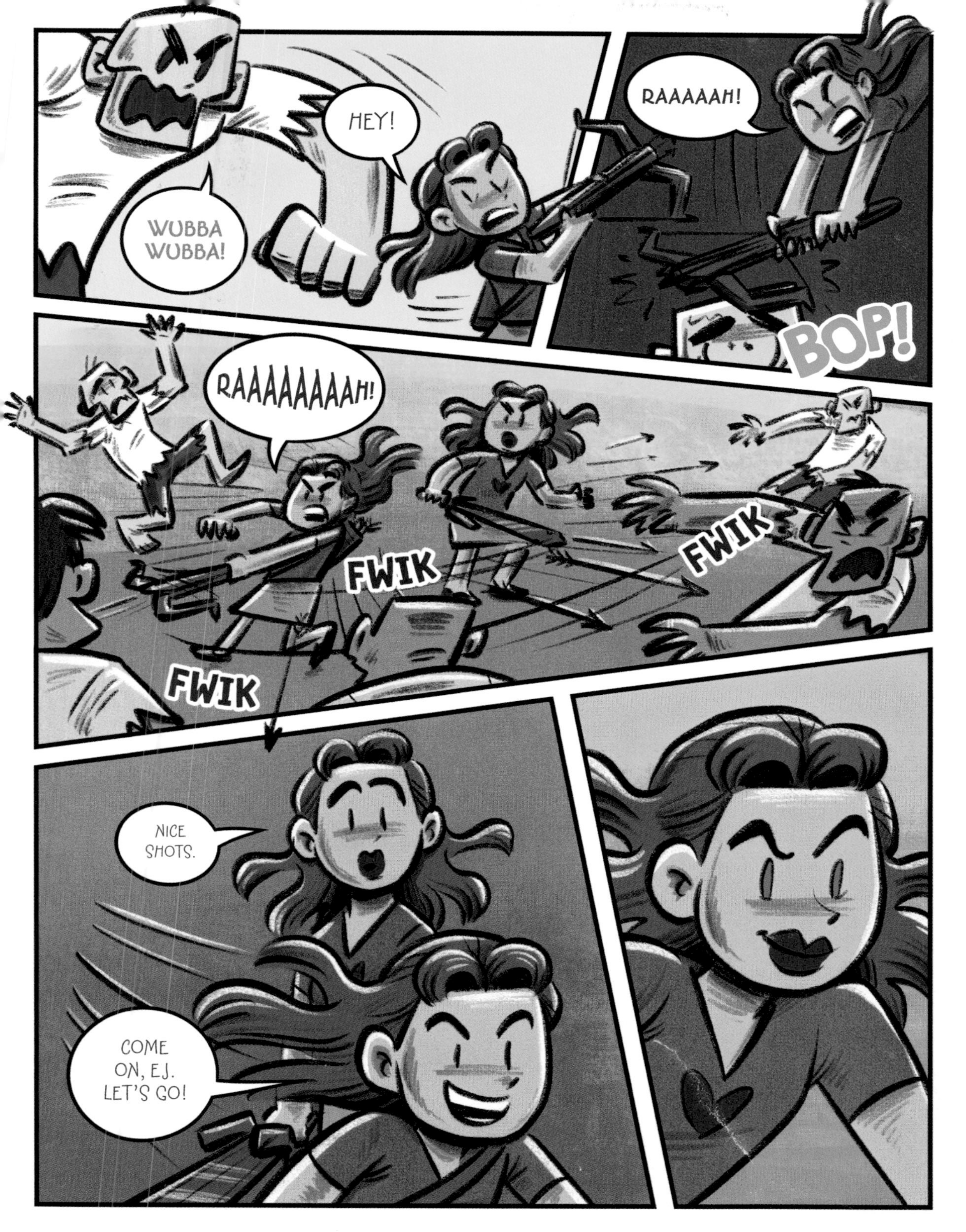
HEY!
WUBBA WUBBA!
RAAAAAH!
BOP!
RAAAAAAAAH!
FWIK
FWIK
FWIK
NICE SHOTS.
COME ON, E.J. LET'S GO!

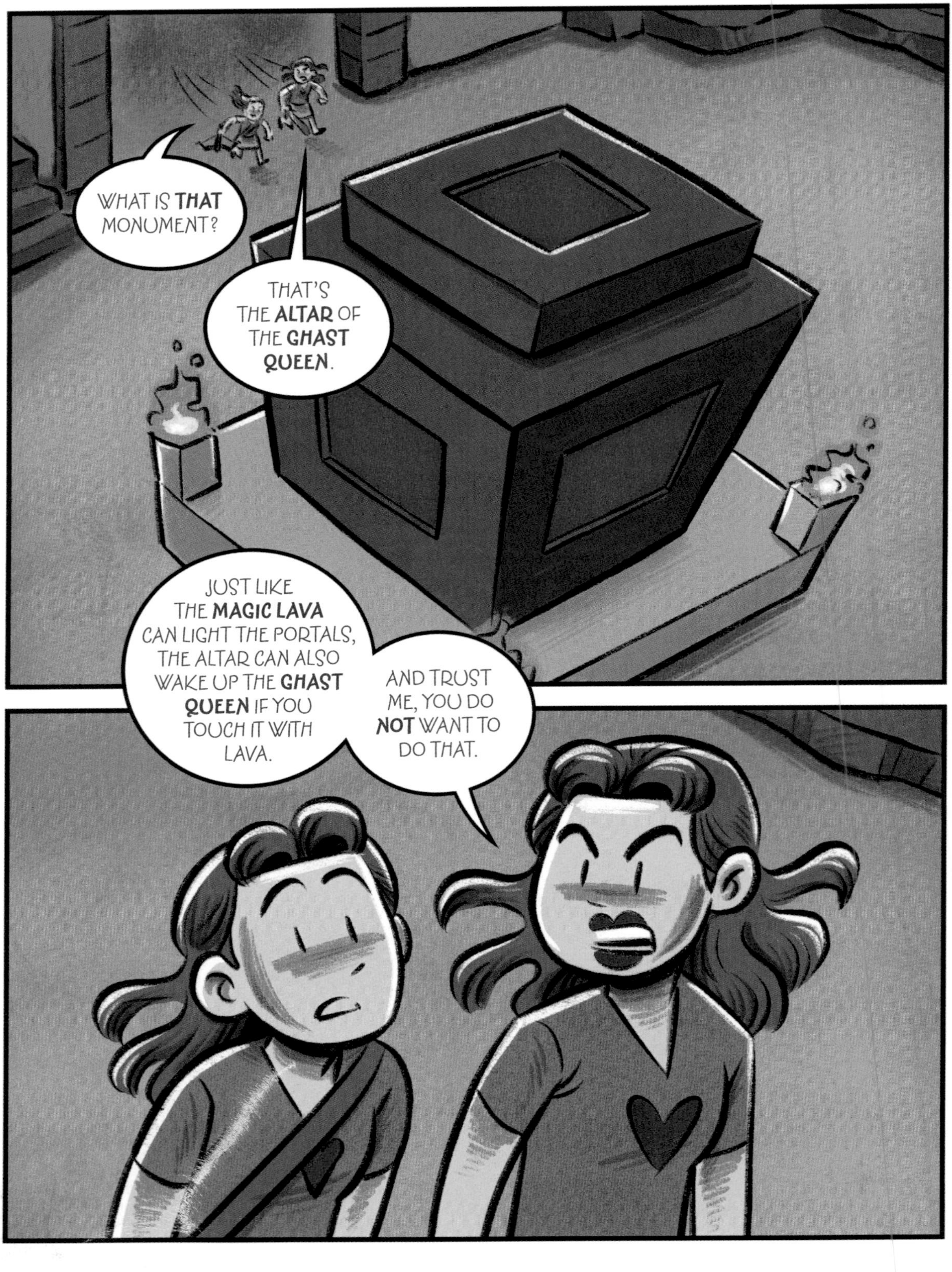

WHAT IS **THAT** MONUMENT?
THAT'S THE **ALTAR** OF THE **GHAST QUEEN**.
JUST LIKE THE **MAGIC LAVA** CAN LIGHT THE PORTALS, THE ALTAR CAN ALSO WAKE UP THE **GHAST QUEEN** IF YOU TOUCH IT WITH LAVA.
AND TRUST ME, YOU DO **NOT** WANT TO DO THAT.

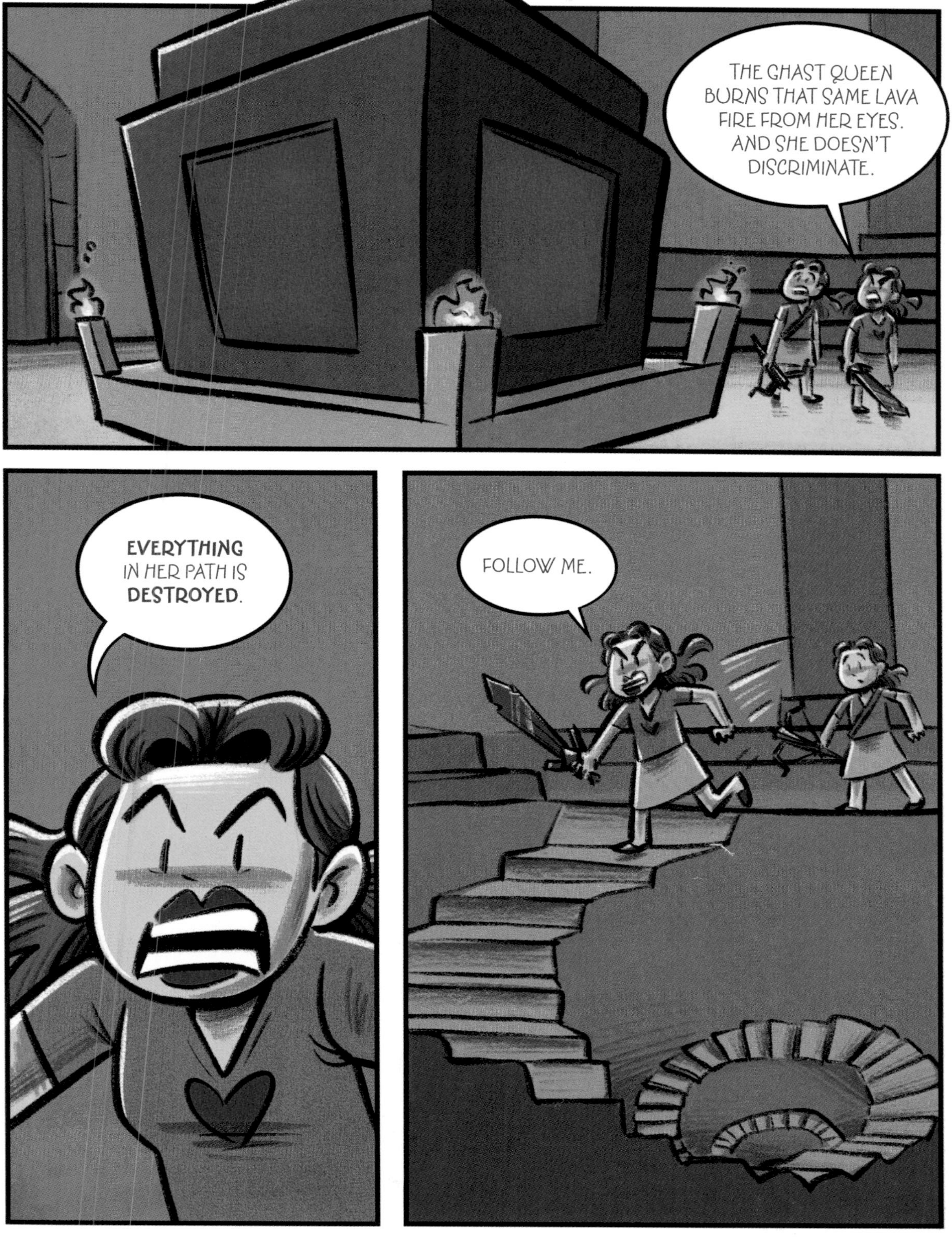
THE GHAST QUEEN BURNS THAT SAME LAVA FIRE FROM HER EYES. AND SHE DOESN'T DISCRIMINATE.
EVERYTHING IN HER PATH IS **DESTROYED**.
FOLLOW ME.

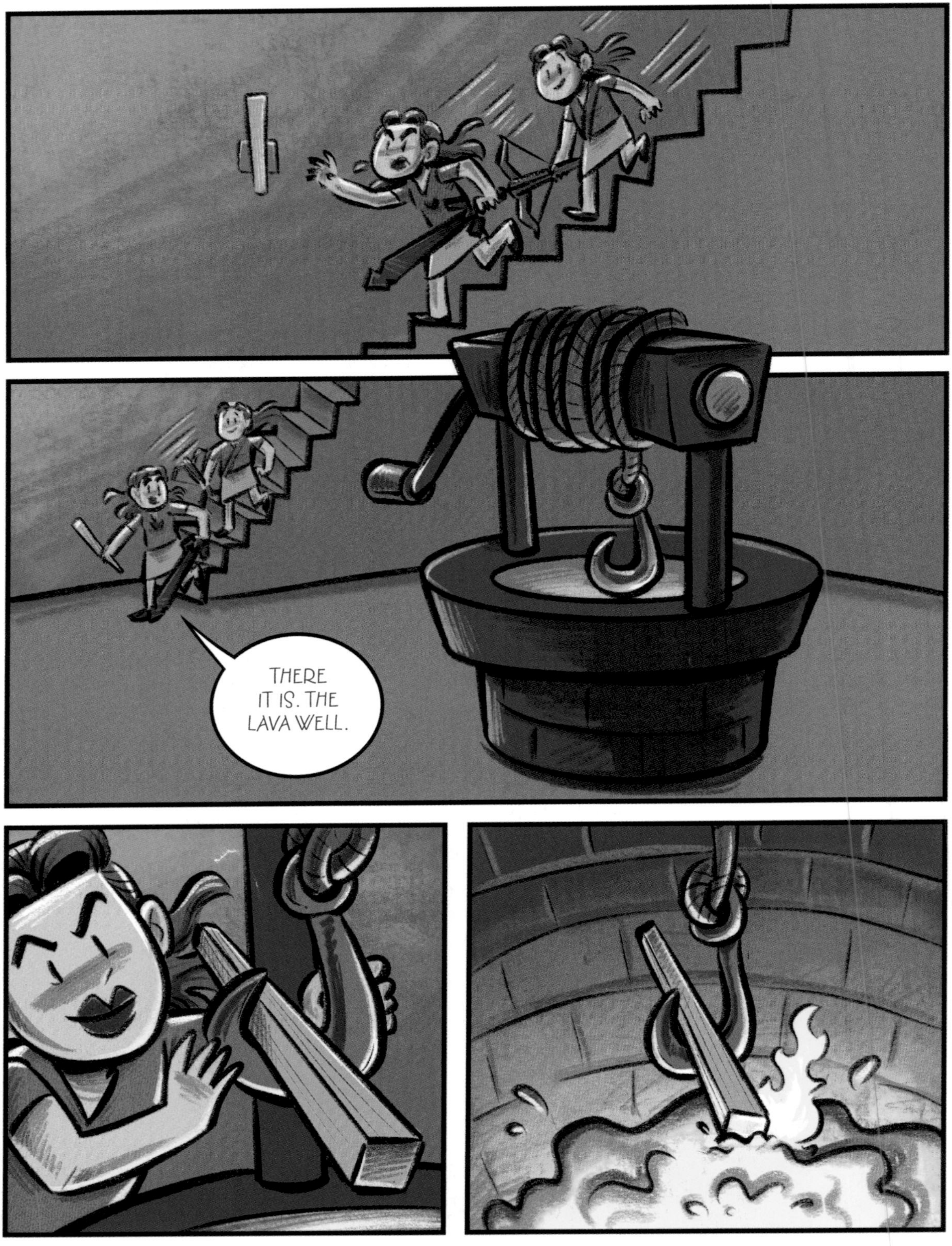
THERE IT IS. THE LAVA WELL.

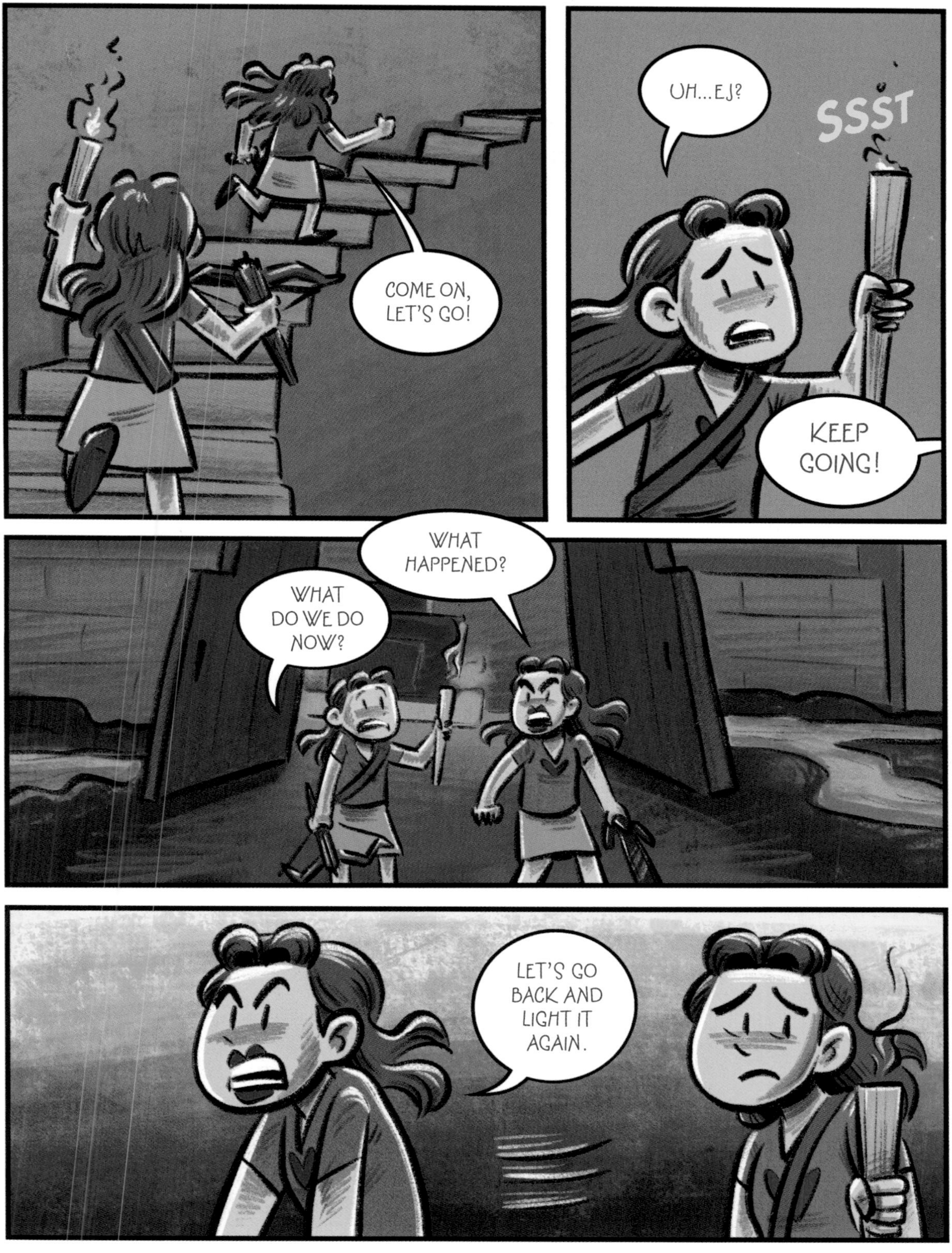
COME ON, LET'S GO!
UH...EJ?
SSST
KEEP GOING!
WHAT HAPPENED?
WHAT DO WE DO NOW?
LET'S GO BACK AND LIGHT IT AGAIN.

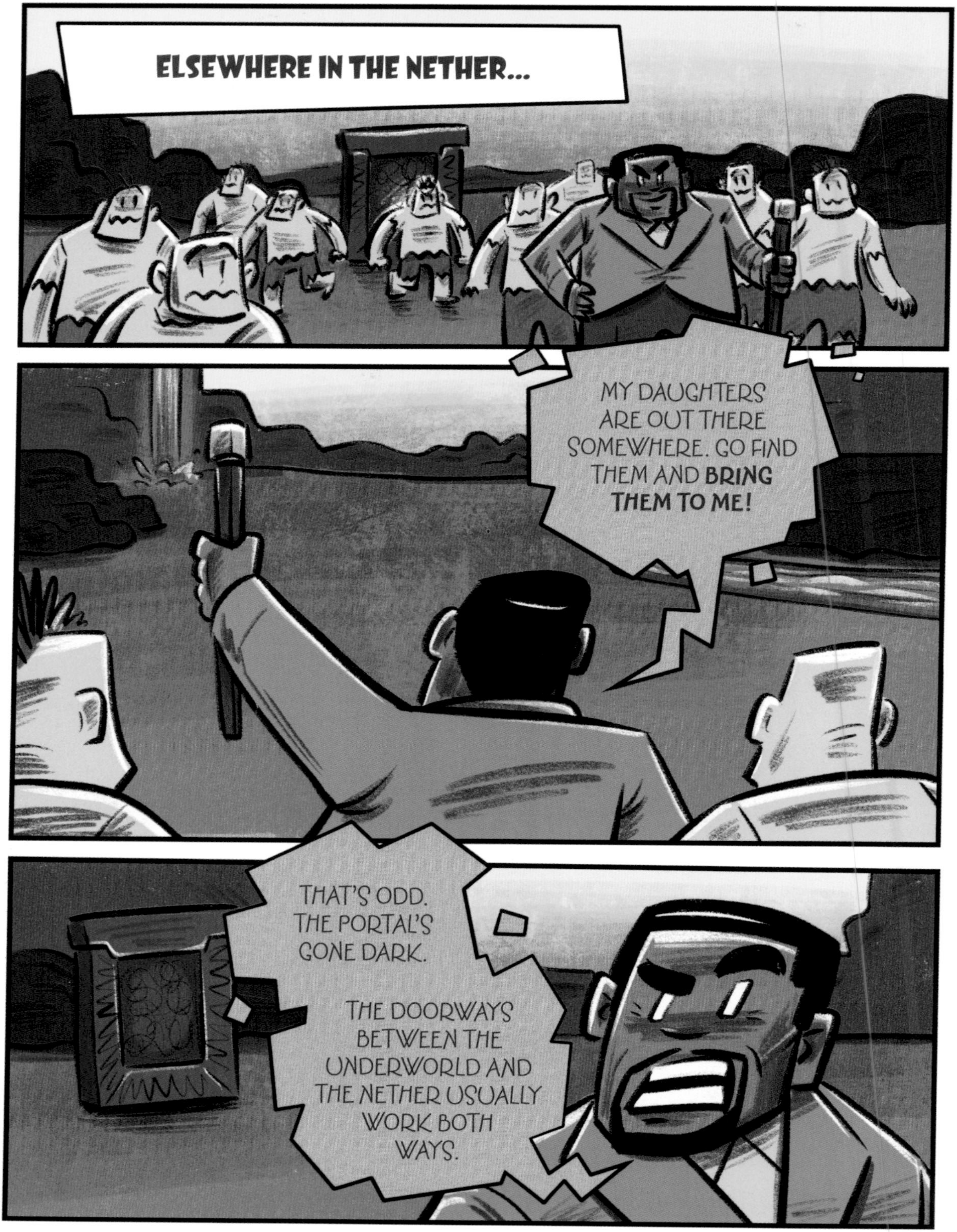
ELSEWHERE IN THE NETHER...
MY DAUGHTERS ARE OUT THERE SOMEWHERE. GO FIND THEM AND BRING THEM TO ME!
THAT'S ODD. THE PORTAL'S GONE DARK.
THE DOORWAYS BETWEEN THE UNDERWORLD AND THE NETHER USUALLY WORK BOTH WAYS.

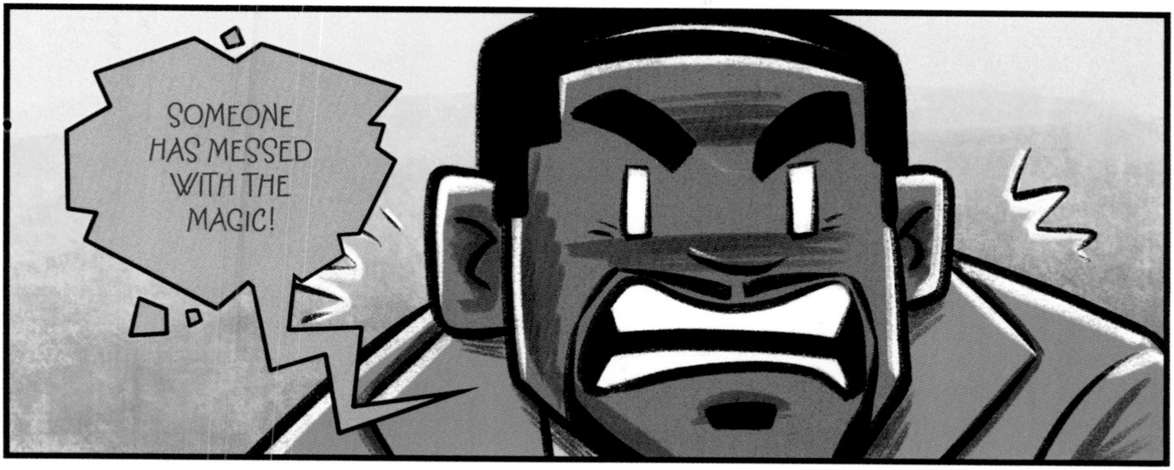
SOMEONE HAS MESSED WITH THE MAGIC!
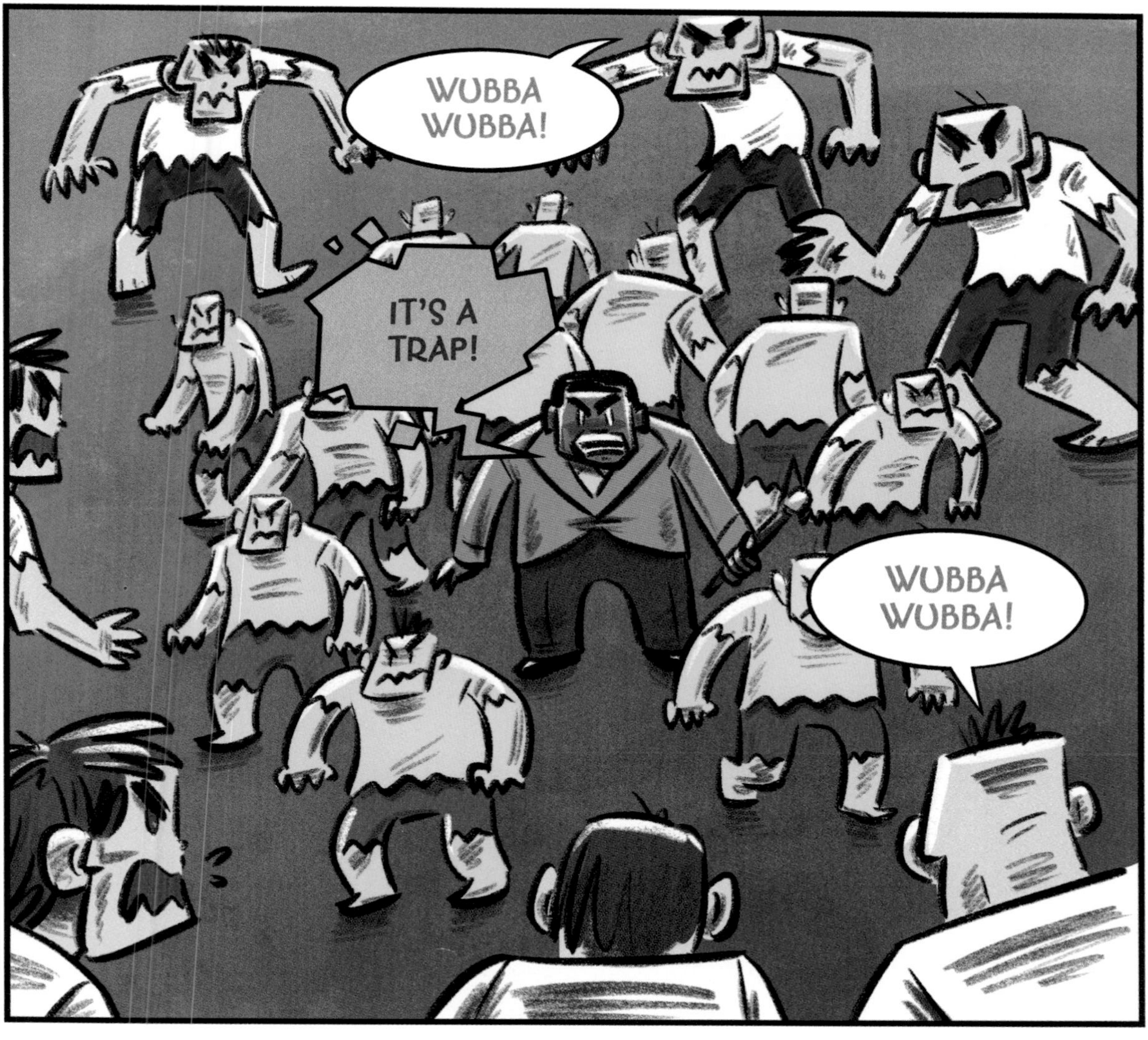
WUBBA WUBBA!
IT'S A TRAP!
WUBBA WUBBA!

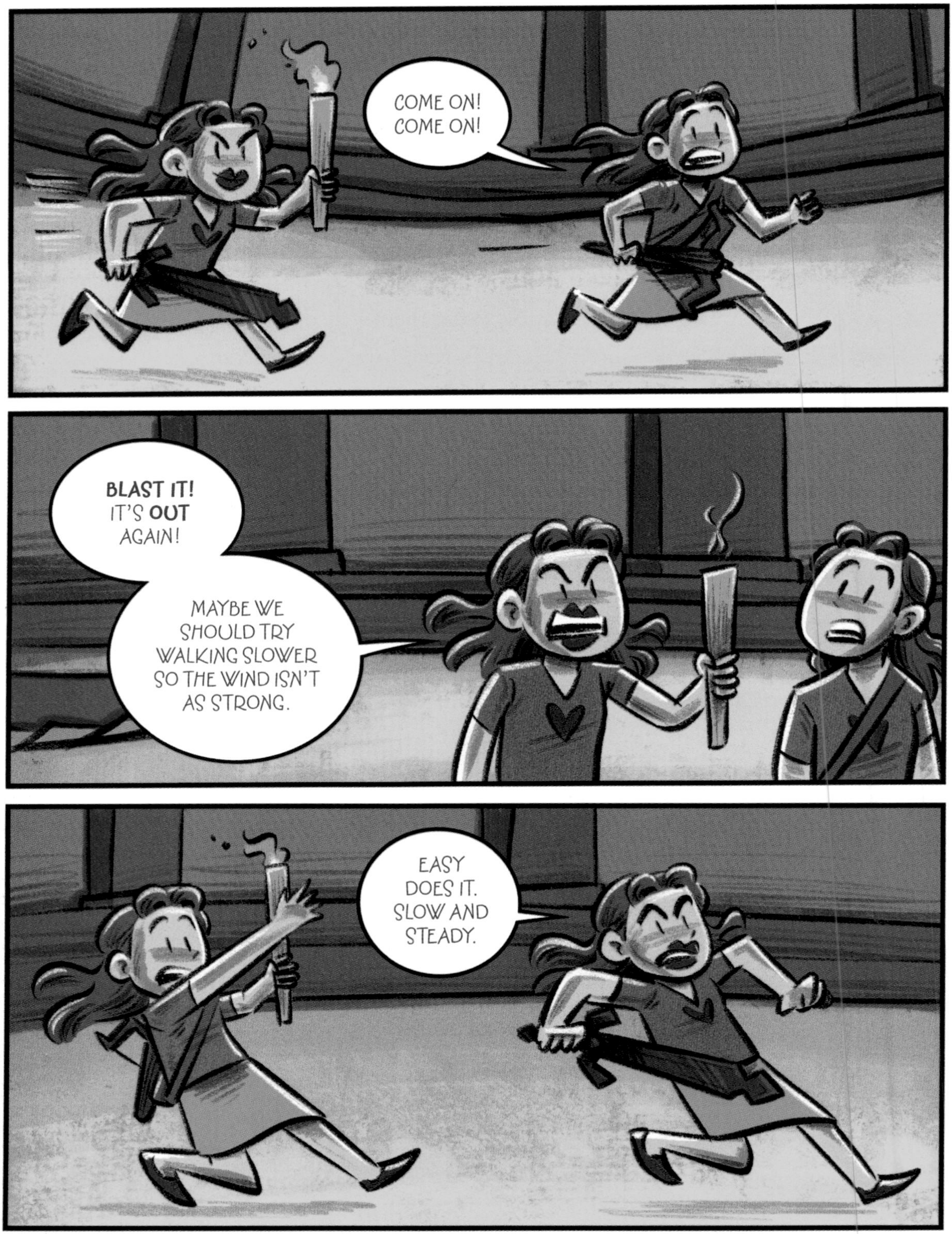
COME ON! COME ON!
BLAST IT! IT'S OUT AGAIN!
MAYBE WE SHOULD TRY WALKING SLOWER SO THE WIND ISN'T AS STRONG.
EASY DOES IT. SLOW AND STEADY.

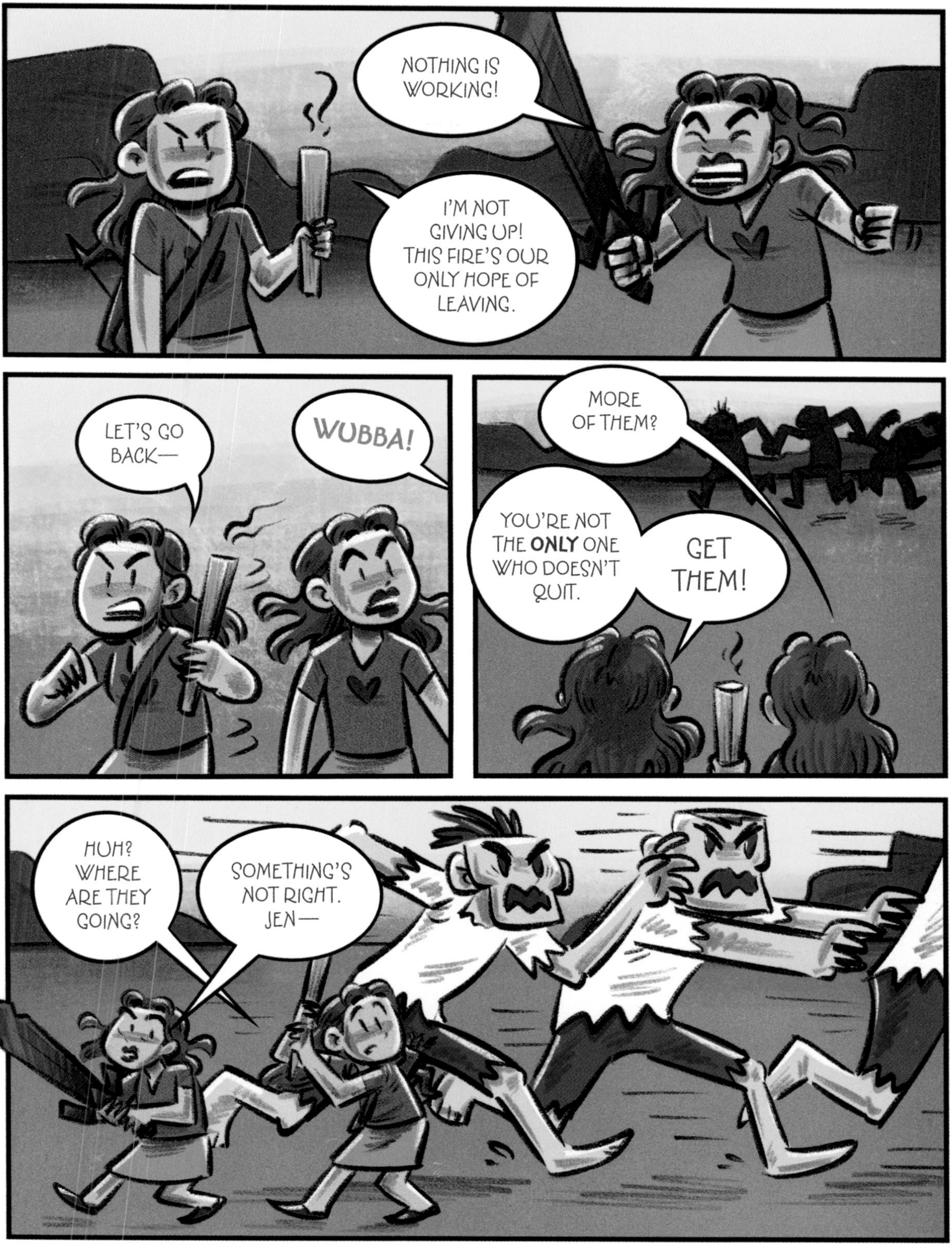
NOTHING IS WORKING!
I'M NOT GIVING UP! THIS FIRE'S OUR ONLY HOPE OF LEAVING.
LET'S GO BACK—
WUBBA!
MORE OF THEM?
YOU'RE NOT THE **ONLY** ONE WHO DOESN'T QUIT.
GET THEM!
HUH? WHERE ARE THEY GOING?
SOMETHING'S NOT RIGHT. JEN—

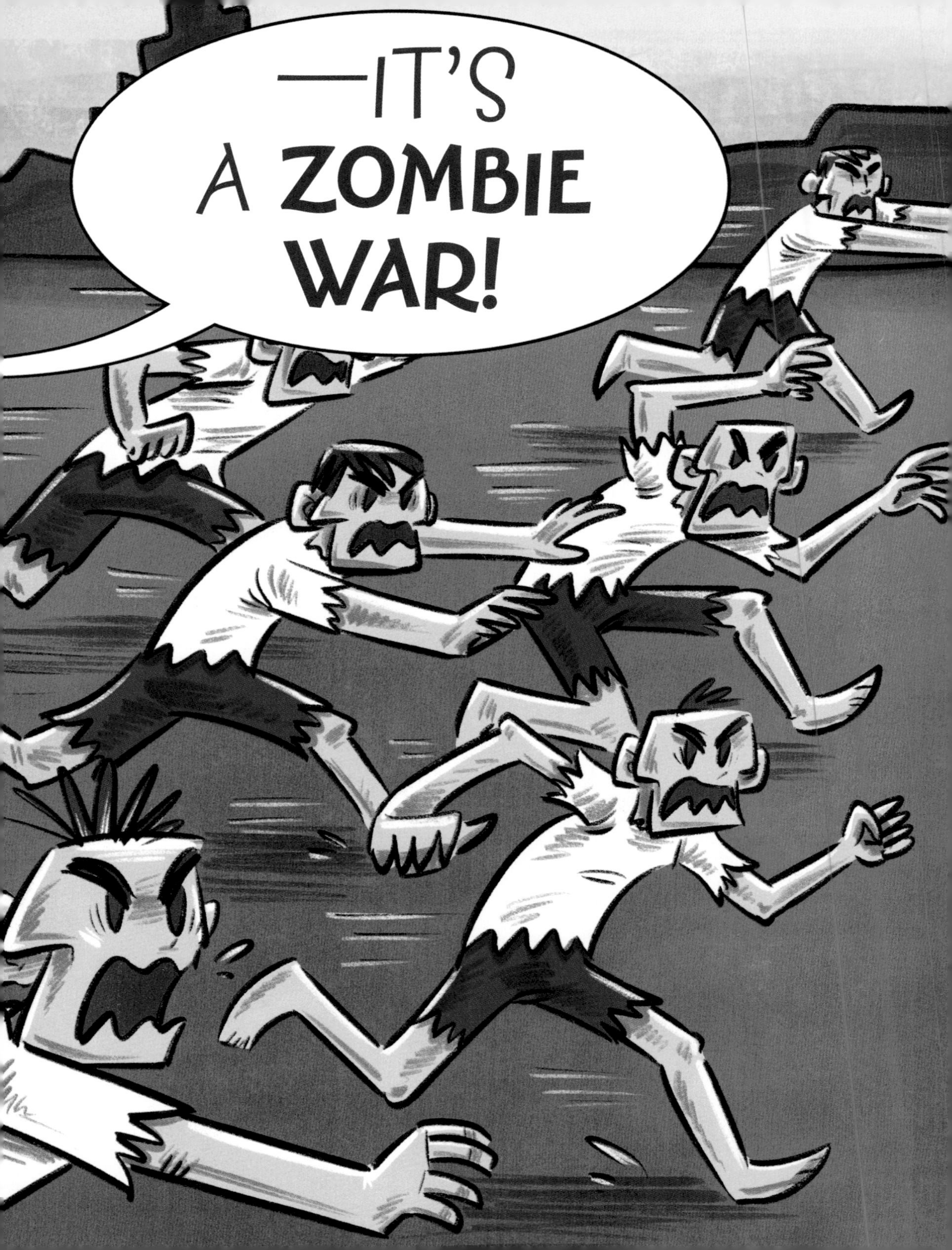
—IT'S A ZOMBIE WAR!

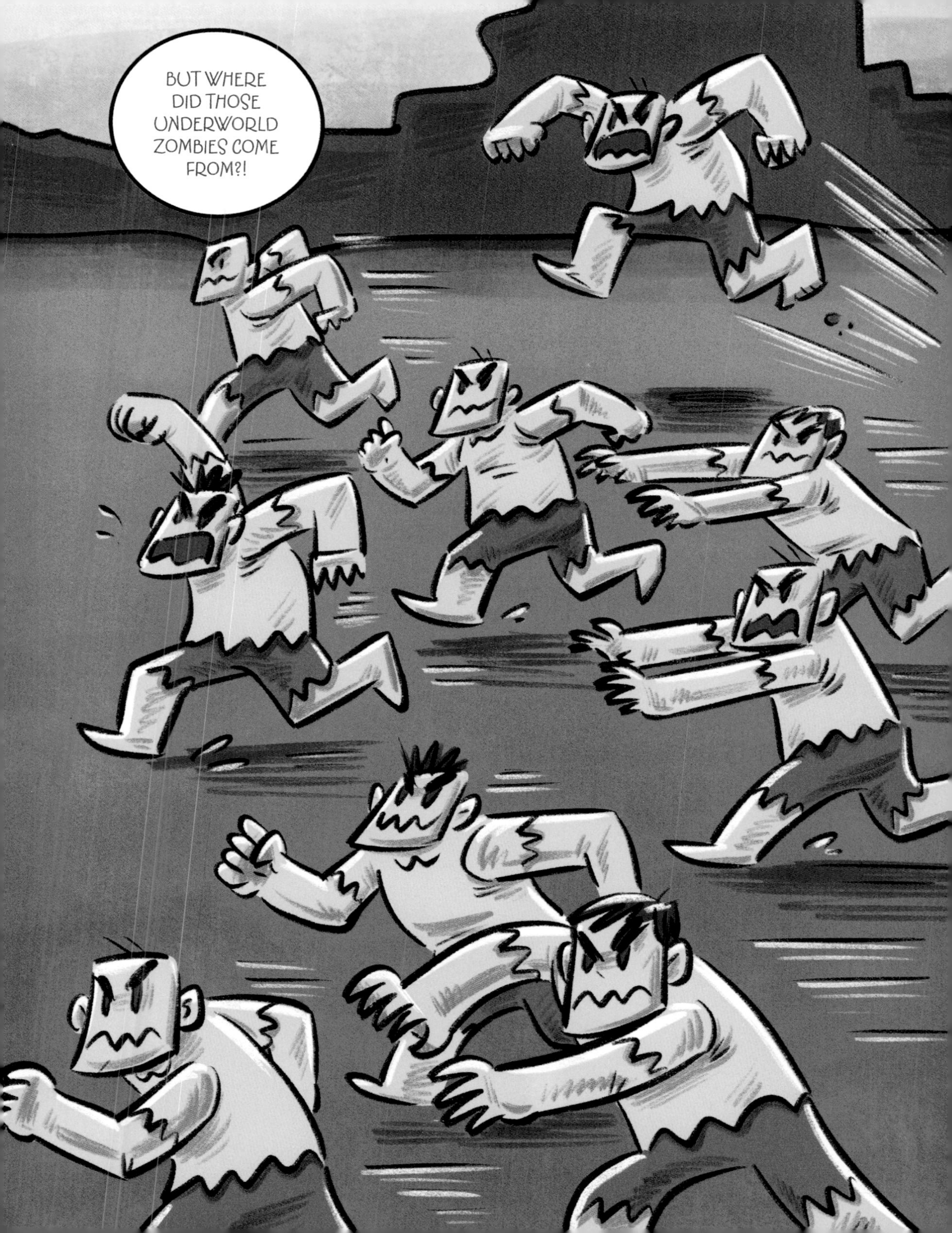
BUT WHERE DID THOSE UNDERWORLD ZOMBIES COME FROM?!

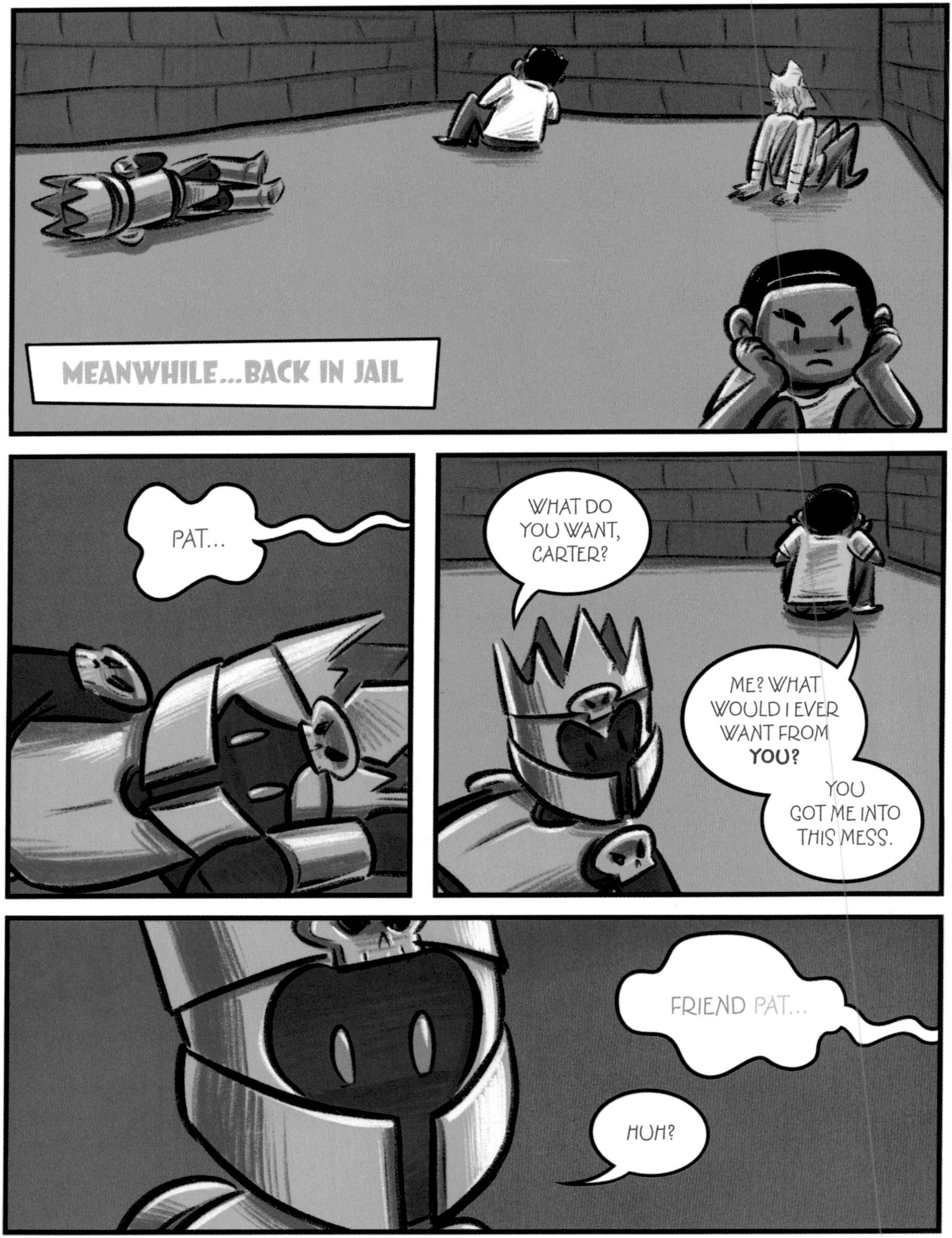
MEANWHILE...BACK IN JAIL
PAT...
WHAT DO YOU WANT, CARTER?
ME? WHAT WOULD I EVER WANT FROM **YOU?**
YOU GOT ME INTO THIS MESS.
FRIEND PAT...
HUH?

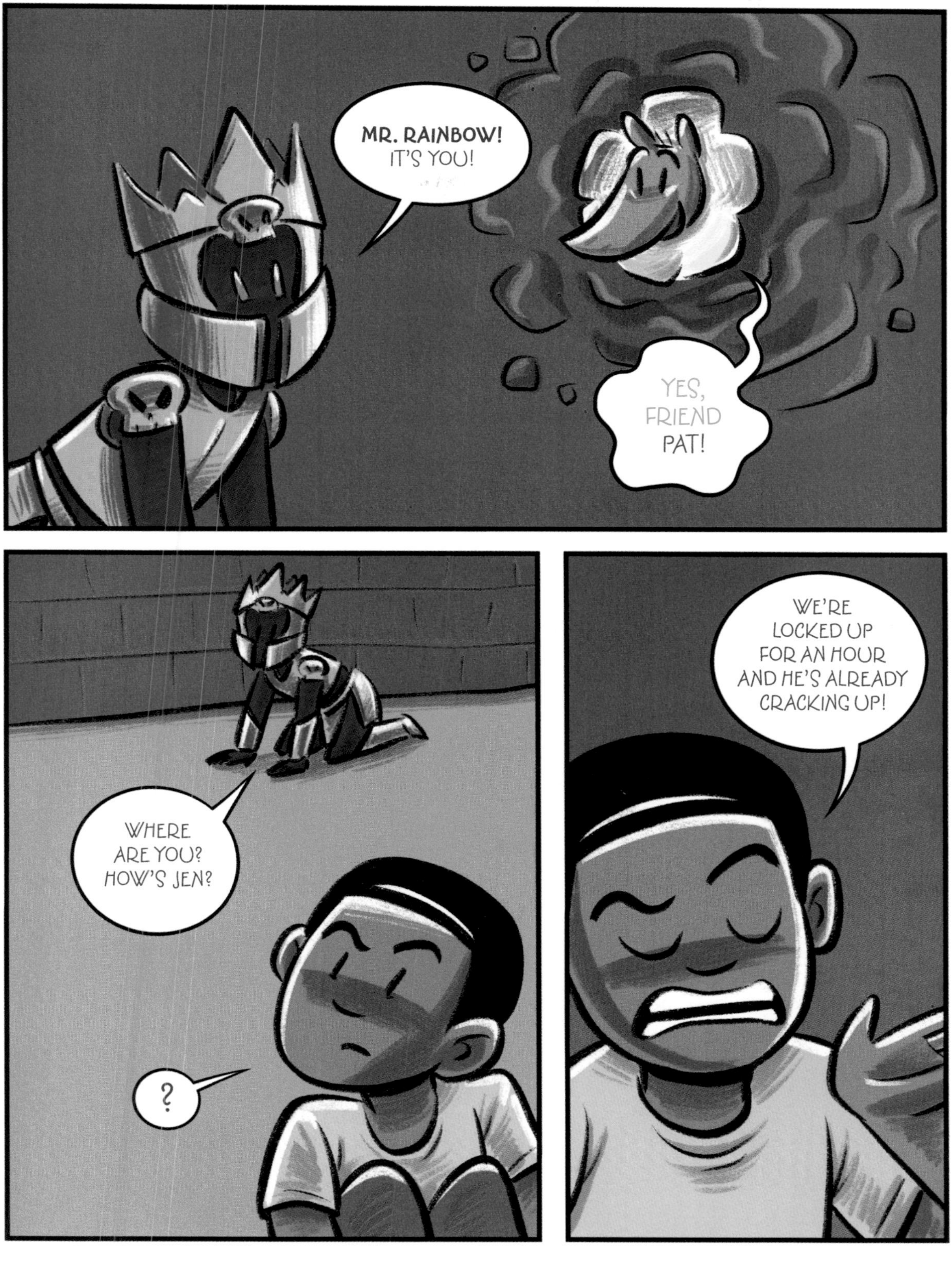
MR. RAINBOW! IT'S YOU!
YES, FRIEND PAT!
WHERE ARE YOU? HOW'S JEN?
?
WE'RE LOCKED UP FOR AN HOUR AND HE'S ALREADY CRACKING UP!

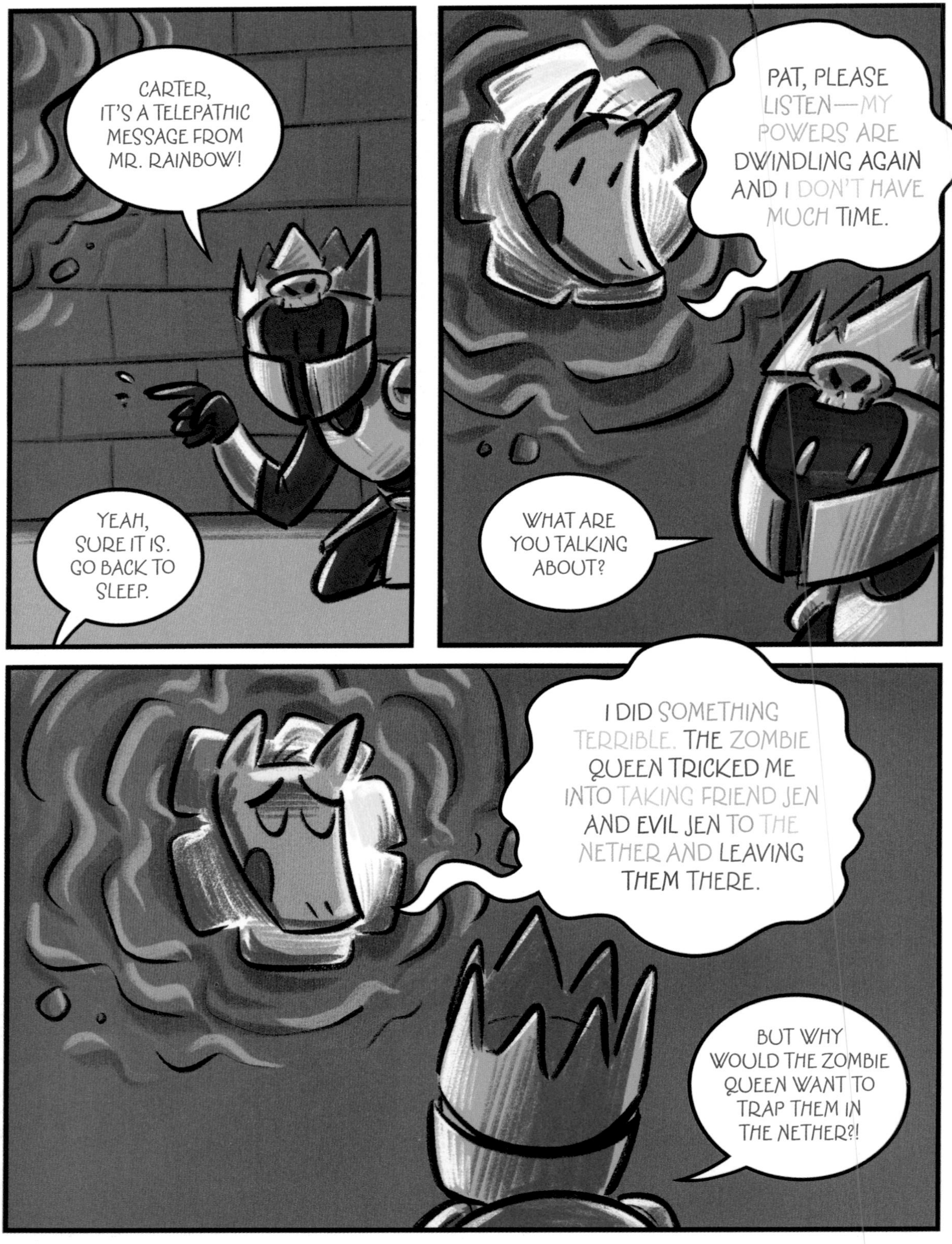
CARTER, IT'S A TELEPATHIC MESSAGE FROM MR. RAINBOW!
YEAH, SURE IT IS. GO BACK TO SLEEP.
PAT, PLEASE LISTEN—MY POWERS ARE DWINDLING AGAIN AND I DON'T HAVE MUCH TIME.
WHAT ARE YOU TALKING ABOUT?
I DID SOMETHING TERRIBLE. THE ZOMBIE QUEEN TRICKED ME INTO TAKING FRIEND JEN AND EVIL JEN TO THE NETHER AND LEAVING THEM THERE.
BUT WHY WOULD THE ZOMBIE QUEEN WANT TO TRAP THEM IN THE NETHER?!

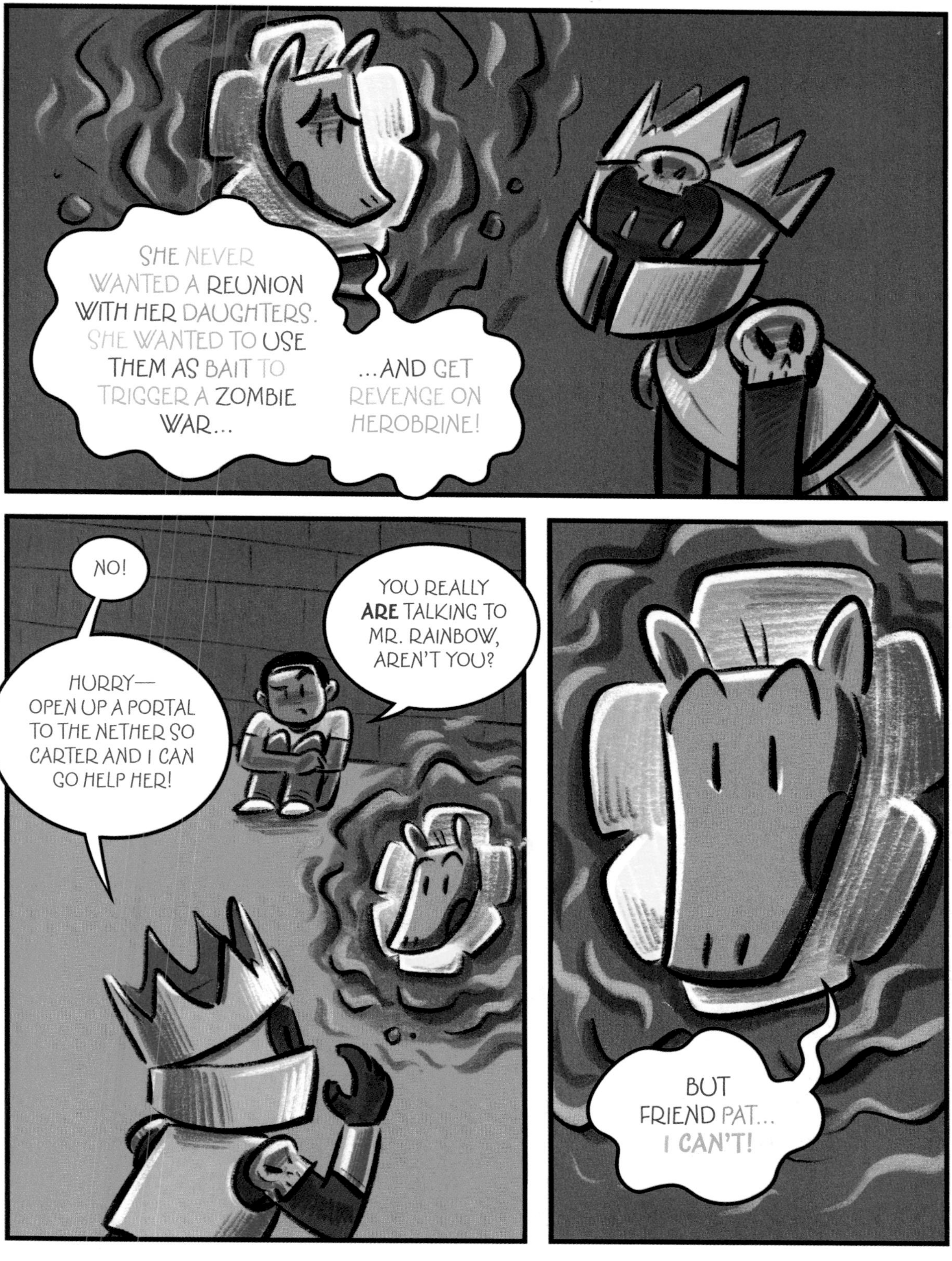
SHE NEVER WANTED A REUNION WITH HER DAUGHTERS. SHE WANTED TO USE THEM AS BAIT TO TRIGGER A ZOMBIE WAR...
...AND GET REVENGE ON HEROBRINE!
NO!
HURRY— OPEN UP A PORTAL TO THE NETHER SO CARTER AND I CAN GO HELP HER!
YOU REALLY ARE TALKING TO MR. RAINBOW, AREN'T YOU?
BUT FRIEND PAT... I CAN'T!

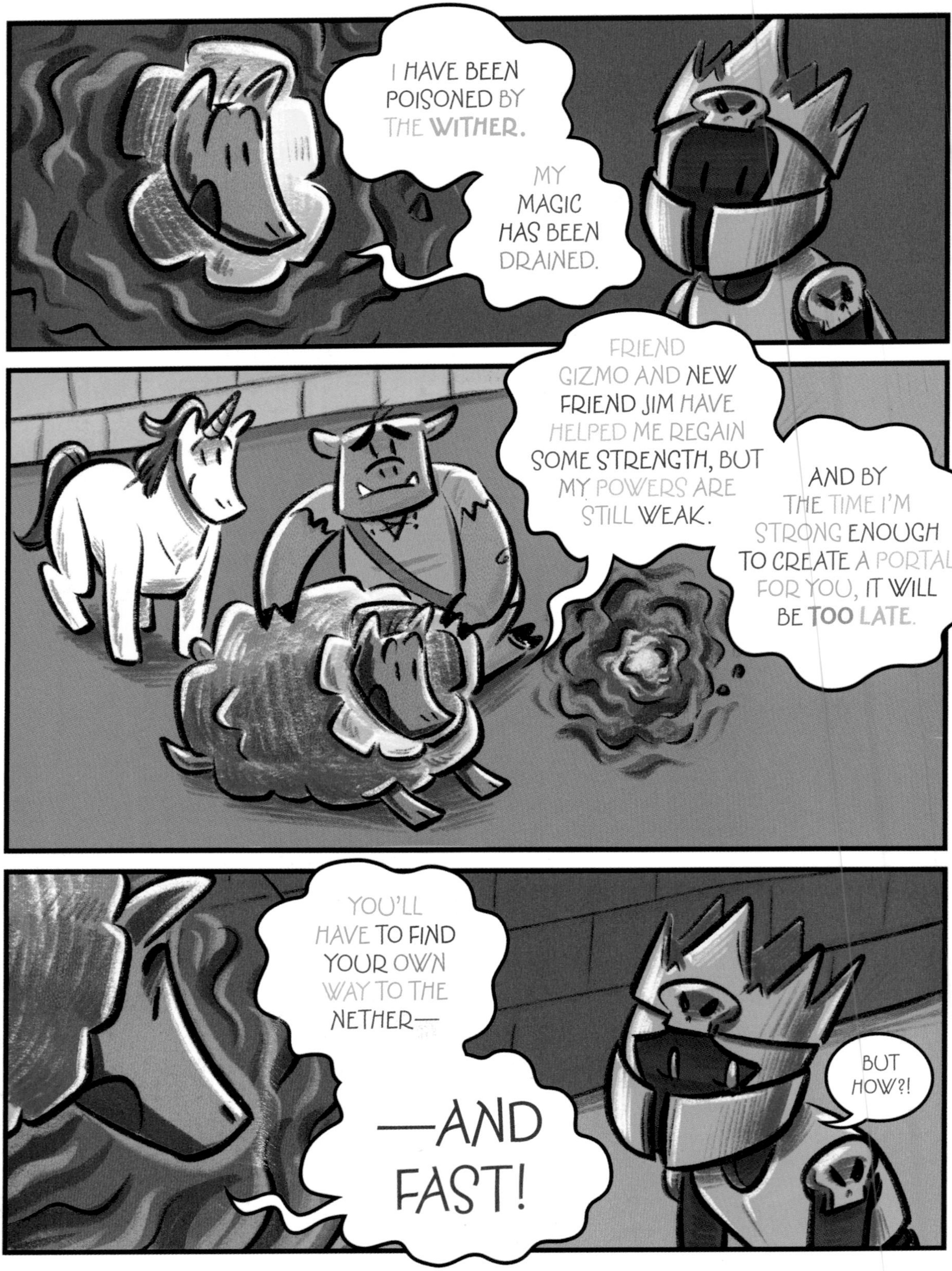
I HAVE BEEN POISONED BY THE WITHER.
MY MAGIC HAS BEEN DRAINED.
FRIEND GIZMO AND NEW FRIEND JIM HAVE HELPED ME REGAIN SOME STRENGTH, BUT MY POWERS ARE STILL WEAK.
AND BY THE TIME I'M STRONG ENOUGH TO CREATE A PORTAL FOR YOU, IT WILL BE TOO LATE.
YOU'LL HAVE TO FIND YOUR OWN WAY TO THE NETHER—
—AND FAST!
BUT HOW?!

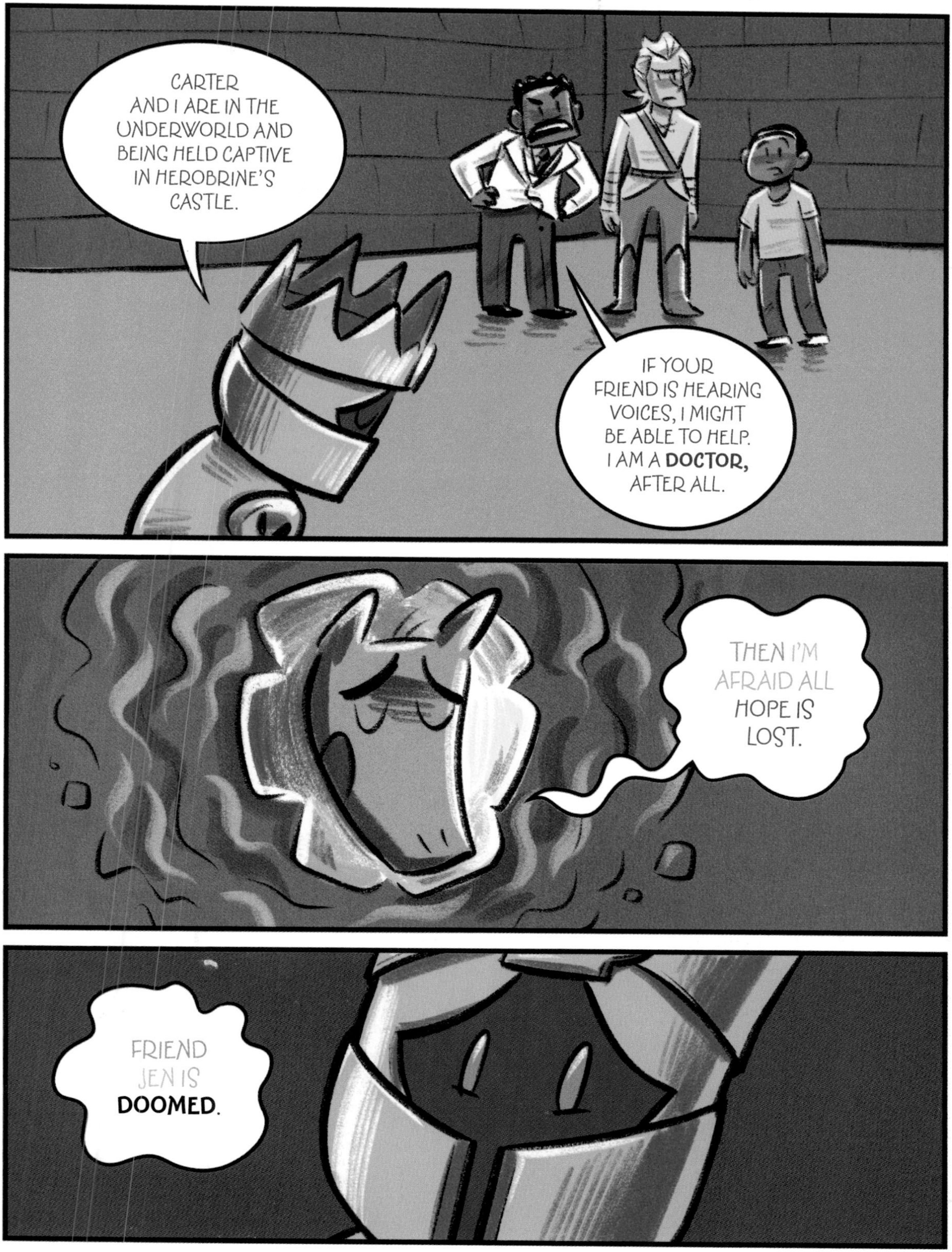
CARTER AND I ARE IN THE UNDERWORLD AND BEING HELD CAPTIVE IN HEROBRINE'S CASTLE.
IF YOUR FRIEND IS HEARING VOICES, I MIGHT BE ABLE TO HELP. I AM A **DOCTOR,** AFTER ALL.
THEN I'M AFRAID ALL HOPE IS LOST.
FRIEND JEN IS **DOOMED**.

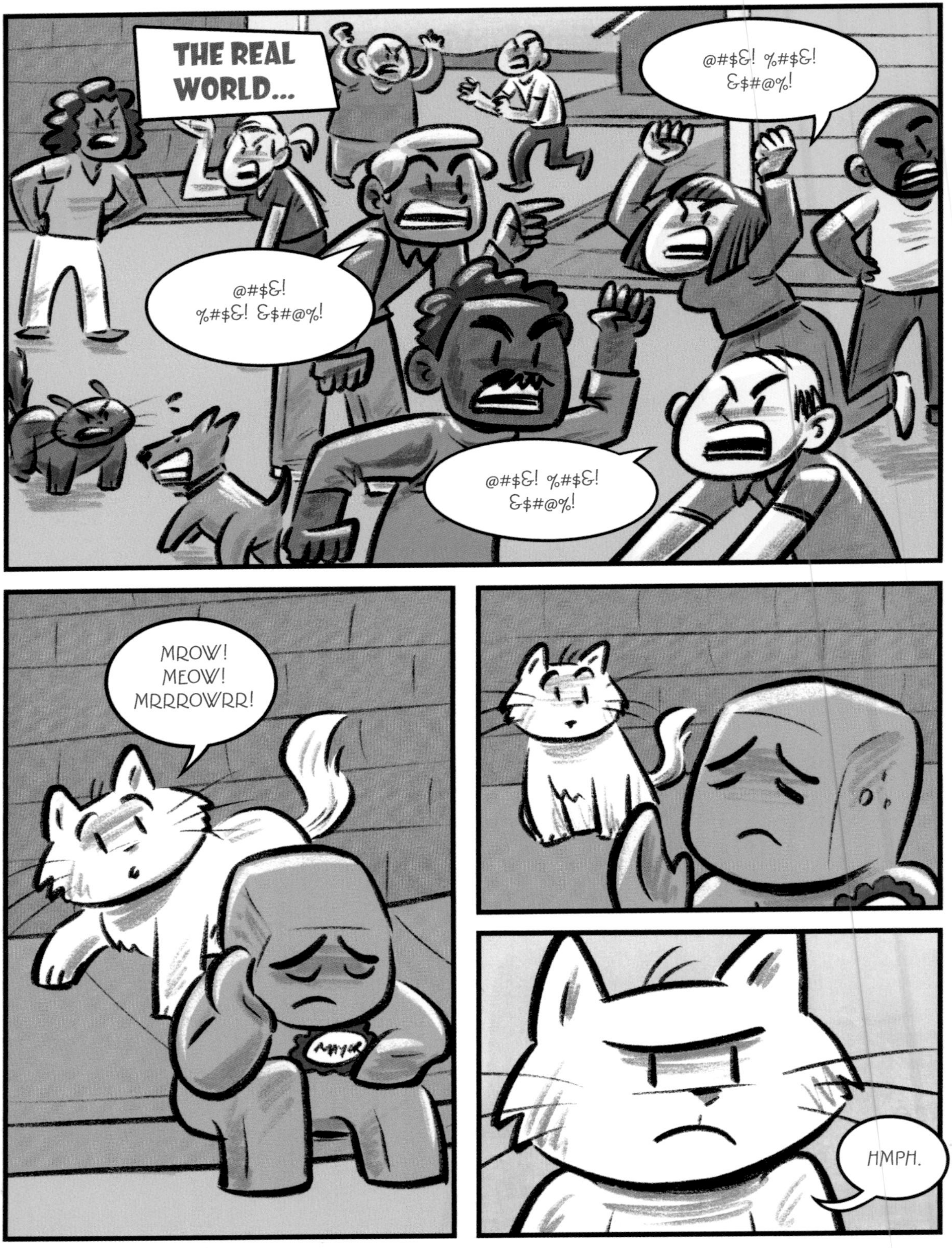
THE REAL WORLD...
@#$&! %#$&! &$#@%!
@#$&! %#$&! &$#@%!
@#$&! %#$&! &$#@%!
MROW! MEOW! MRRROWRR!
HMPH.

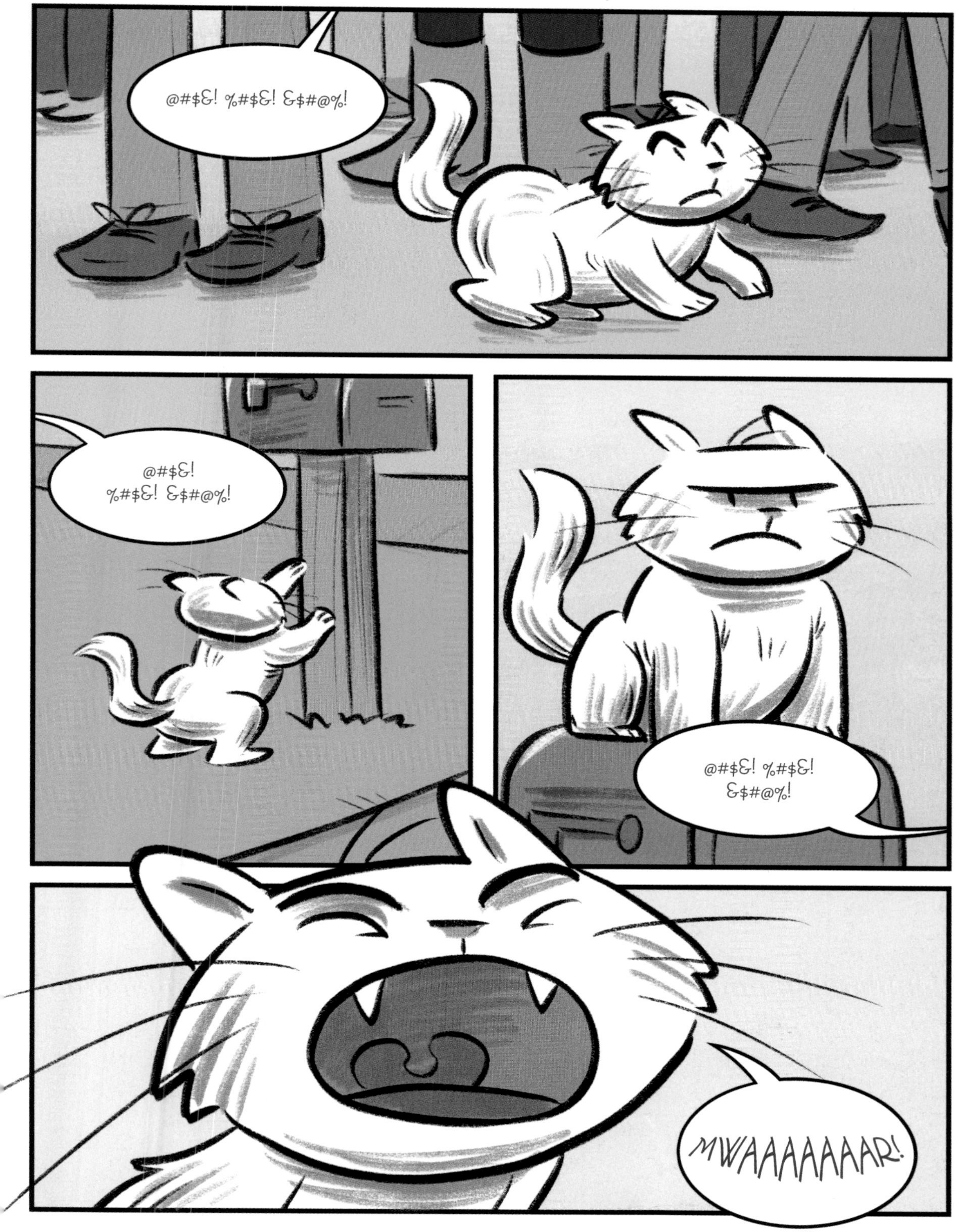
@#$&! %#$&! &$#@%!
@#$&!
%#$&! &$#@%!
@#$&! %#$&!
&$#@%!
MWAAAAAAAR!

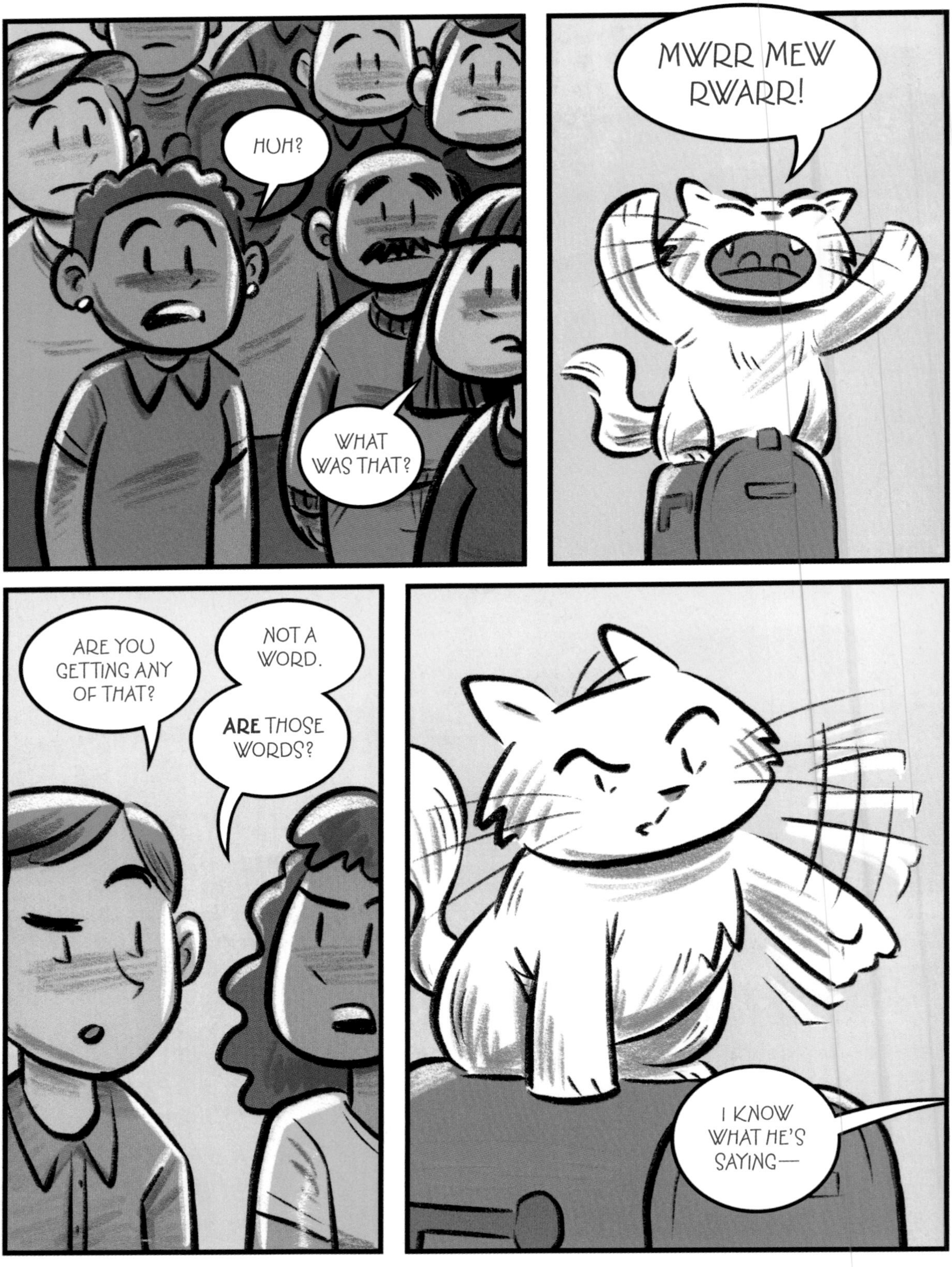
HUH?
WHAT WAS THAT?
MWRR MEW RWARR!
ARE YOU GETTING ANY OF THAT?
NOT A WORD.
ARE THOSE WORDS?
I KNOW WHAT HE'S SAYING—

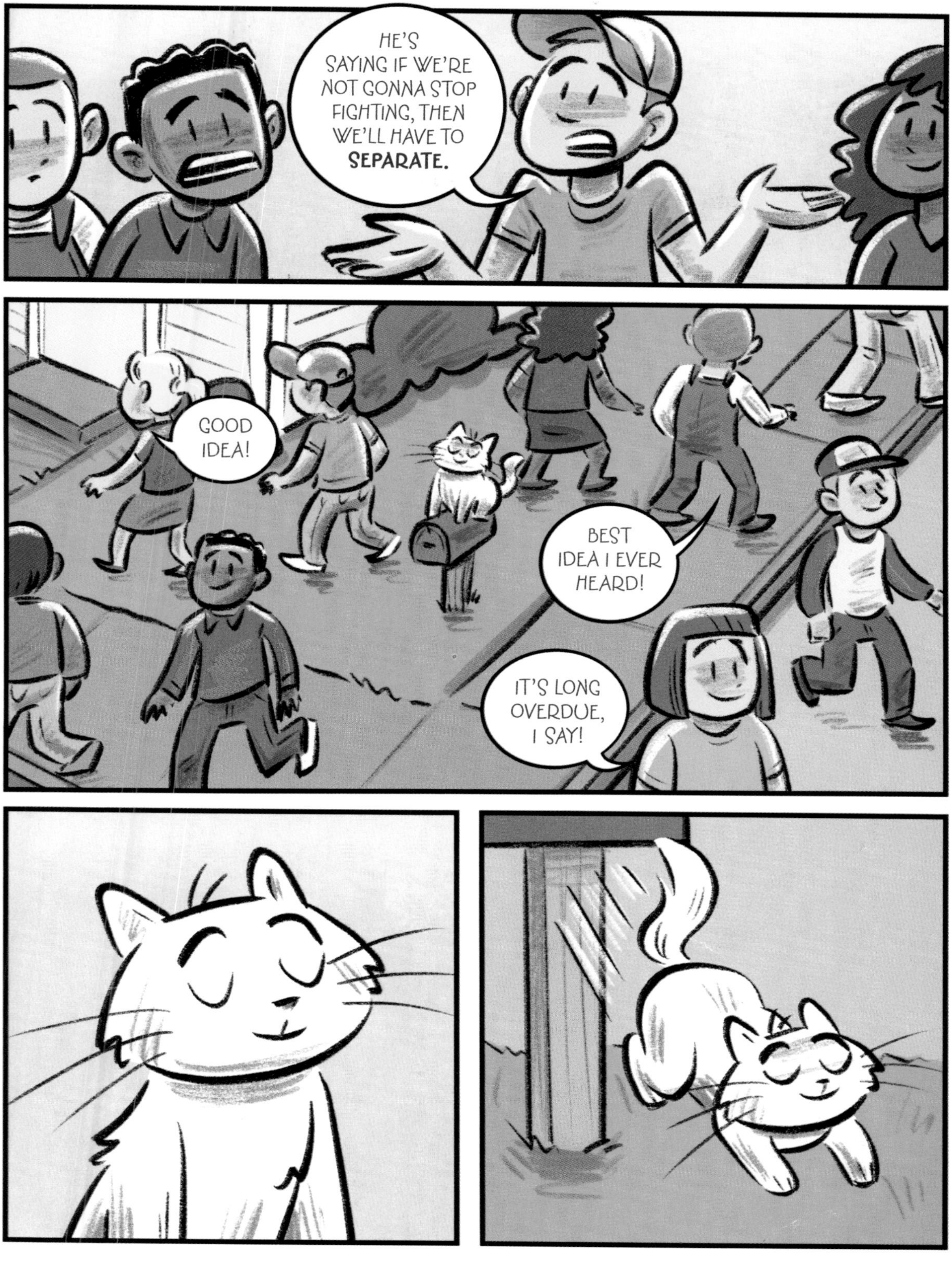
HE'S SAYING IF WE'RE NOT GONNA STOP FIGHTING, THEN WE'LL HAVE TO **SEPARATE.**
GOOD IDEA!
BEST IDEA I EVER HEARD!
IT'S LONG OVERDUE, I SAY!

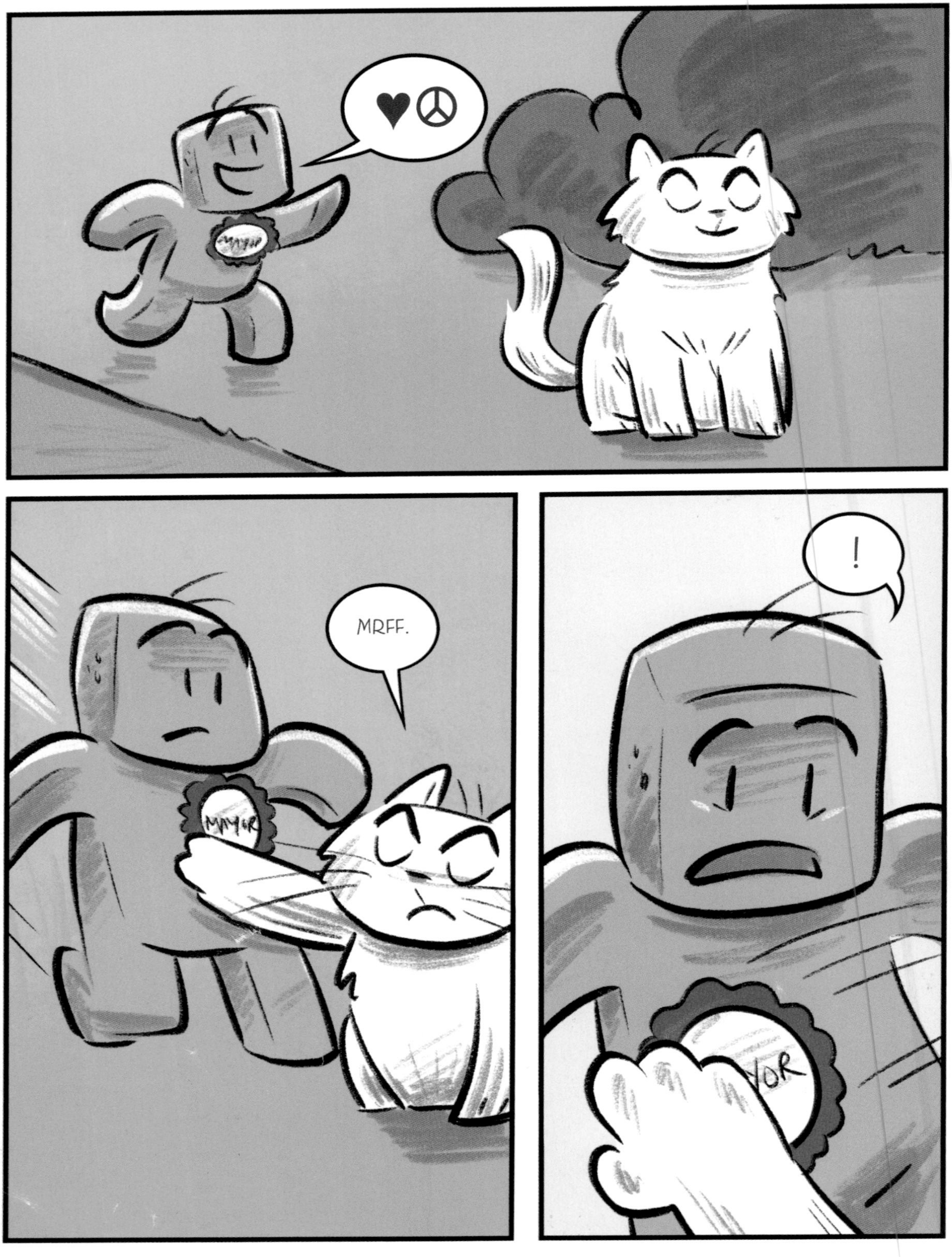
♥☮
MRFF.
MAYOR
!
YOR

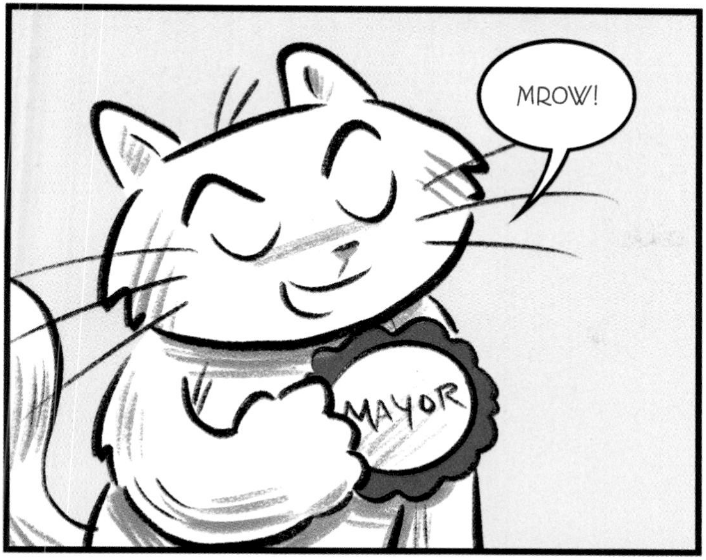
MROW!
MAYOR
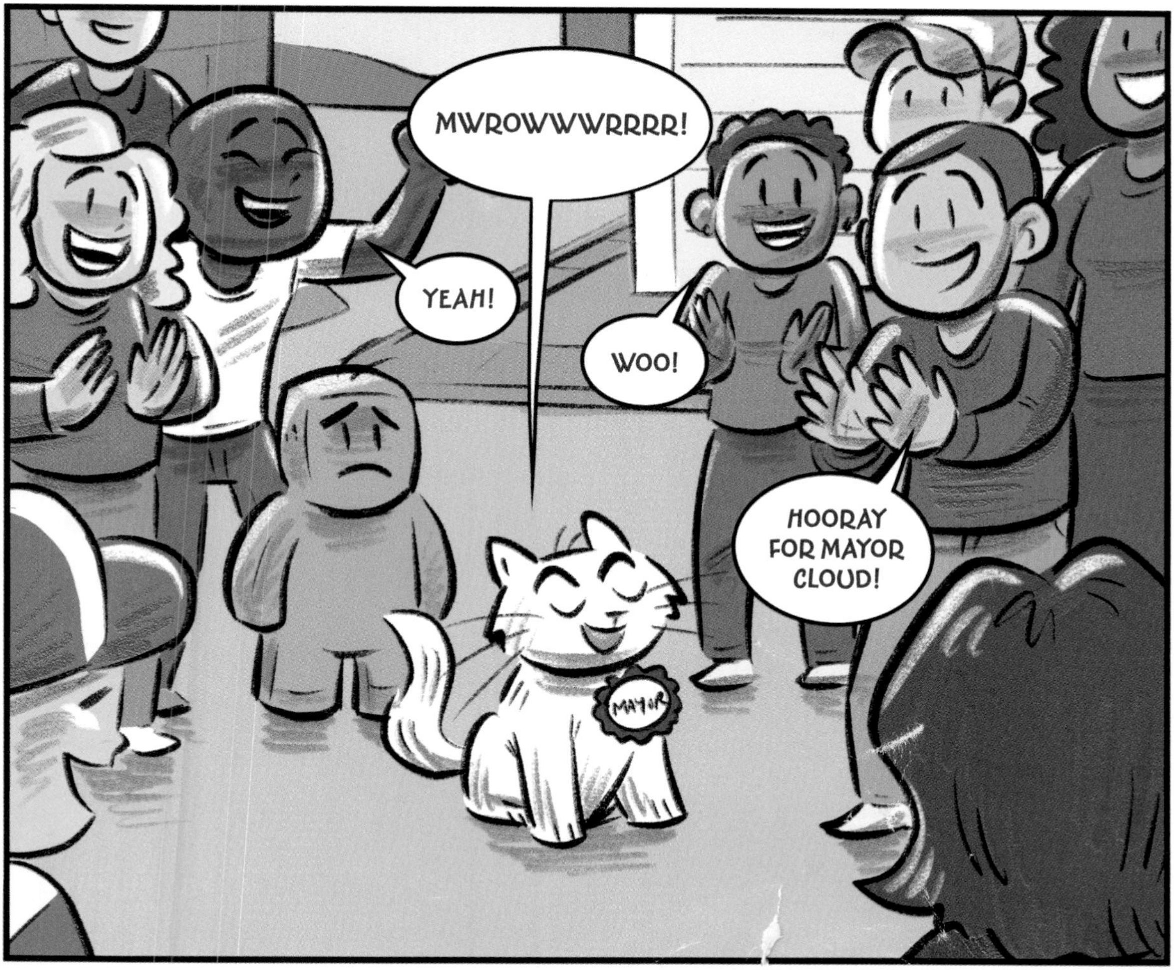
MWROWWWRRRR!
YEAH!
WOO!
HOORAY FOR MAYOR CLOUD!
MAYOR

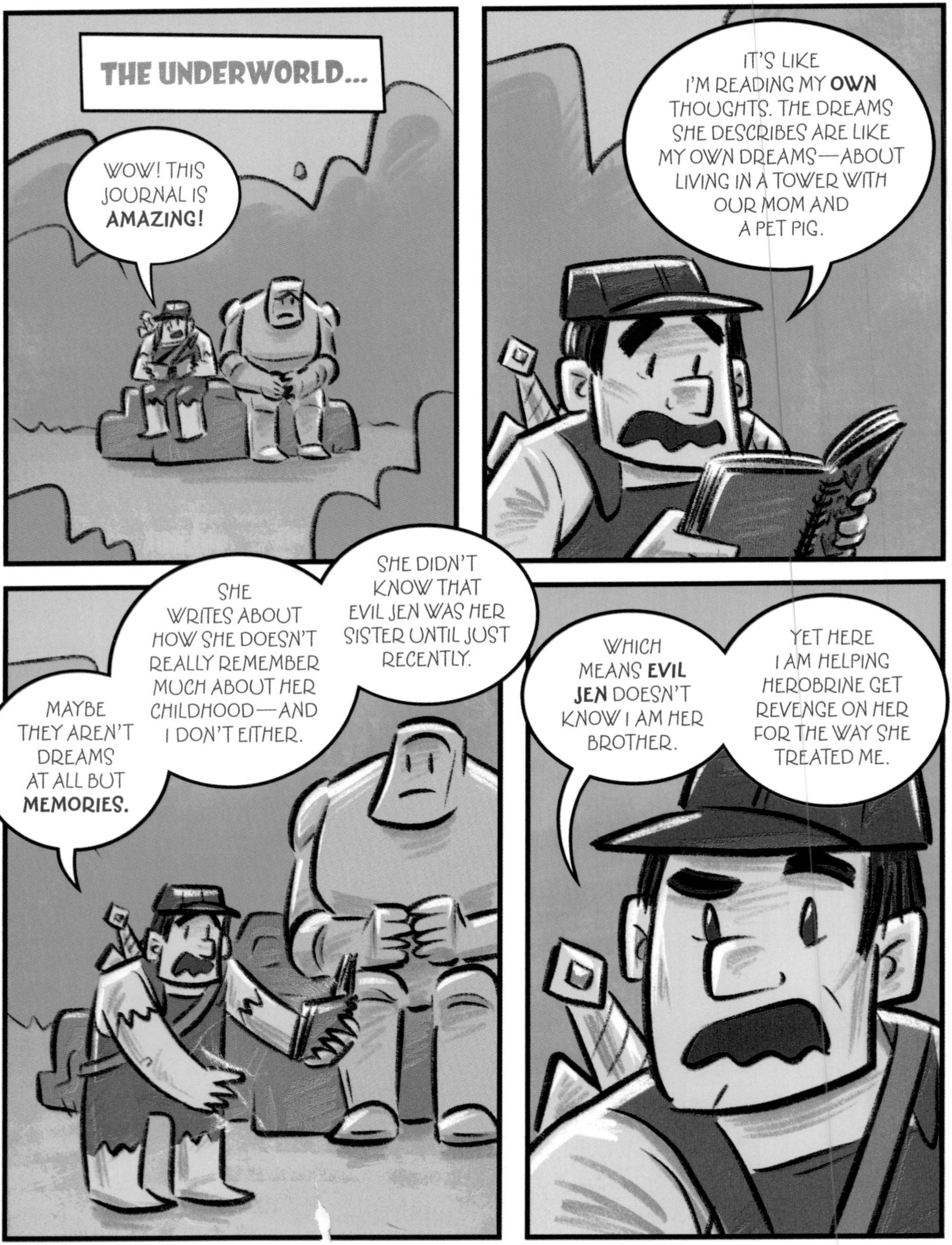
THE UNDERWORLD...
WOW! THIS JOURNAL IS AMAZING!
IT'S LIKE I'M READING MY OWN THOUGHTS. THE DREAMS SHE DESCRIBES ARE LIKE MY OWN DREAMS—ABOUT LIVING IN A TOWER WITH OUR MOM AND A PET PIG.
SHE WRITES ABOUT HOW SHE DOESN'T REALLY REMEMBER MUCH ABOUT HER CHILDHOOD—AND I DON'T EITHER.
SHE DIDN'T KNOW THAT EVIL JEN WAS HER SISTER UNTIL JUST RECENTLY.
MAYBE THEY AREN'T DREAMS AT ALL BUT MEMORIES.
WHICH MEANS EVIL JEN DOESN'T KNOW I AM HER BROTHER.
YET HERE I AM HELPING HEROBRINE GET REVENGE ON HER FOR THE WAY SHE TREATED ME.

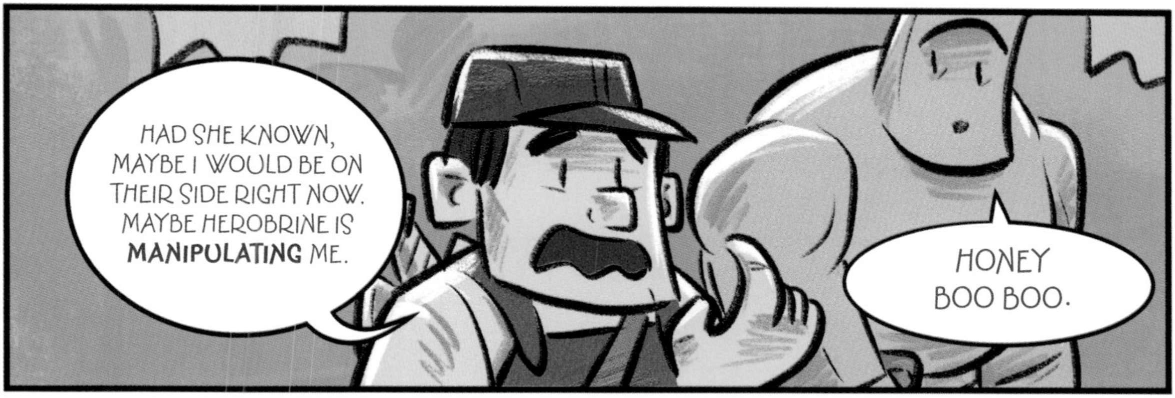
HAD SHE KNOWN, MAYBE I WOULD BE ON THEIR SIDE RIGHT NOW. MAYBE HEROBRINE IS **MANIPULATING** ME.
HONEY BOO BOO.

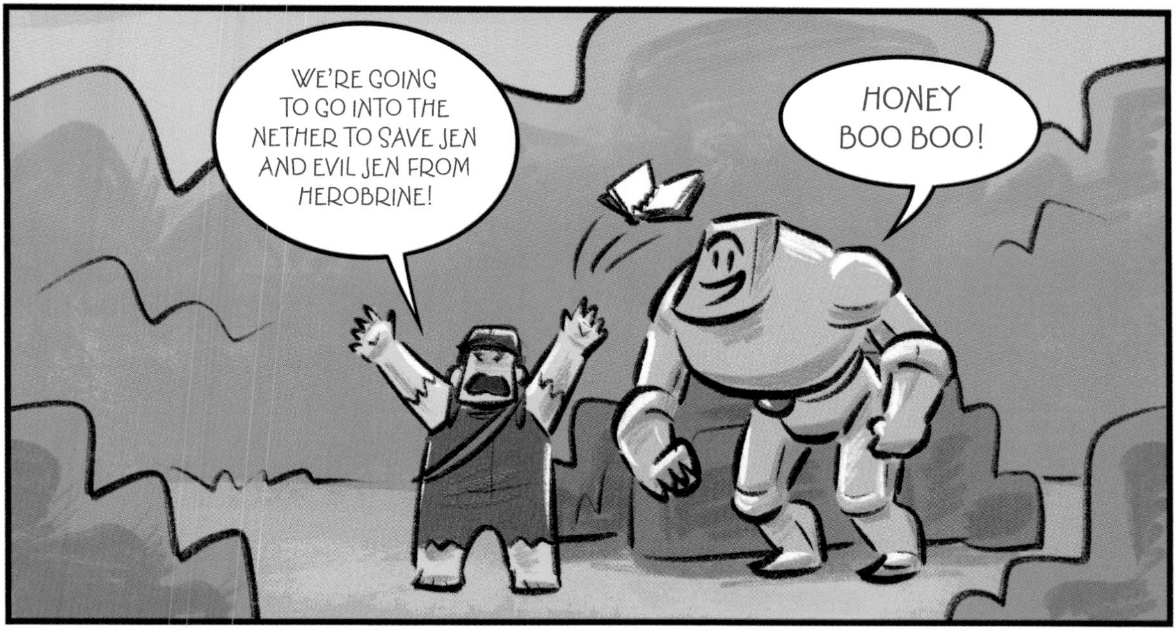
WE'RE GOING TO GO INTO THE NETHER TO SAVE JEN AND EVIL JEN FROM HEROBRINE!
HONEY BOO BOO!

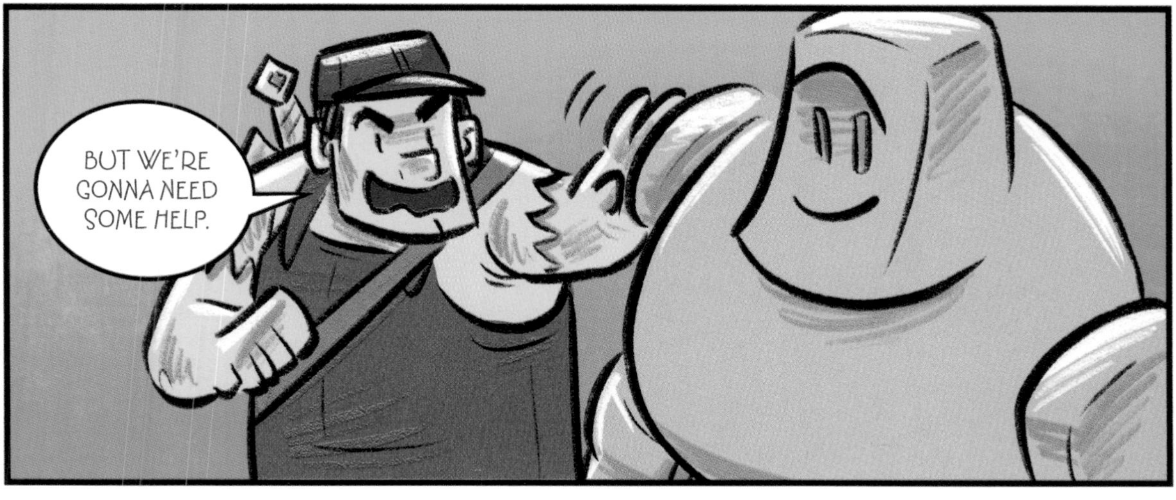
BUT WE'RE GONNA NEED SOME HELP.

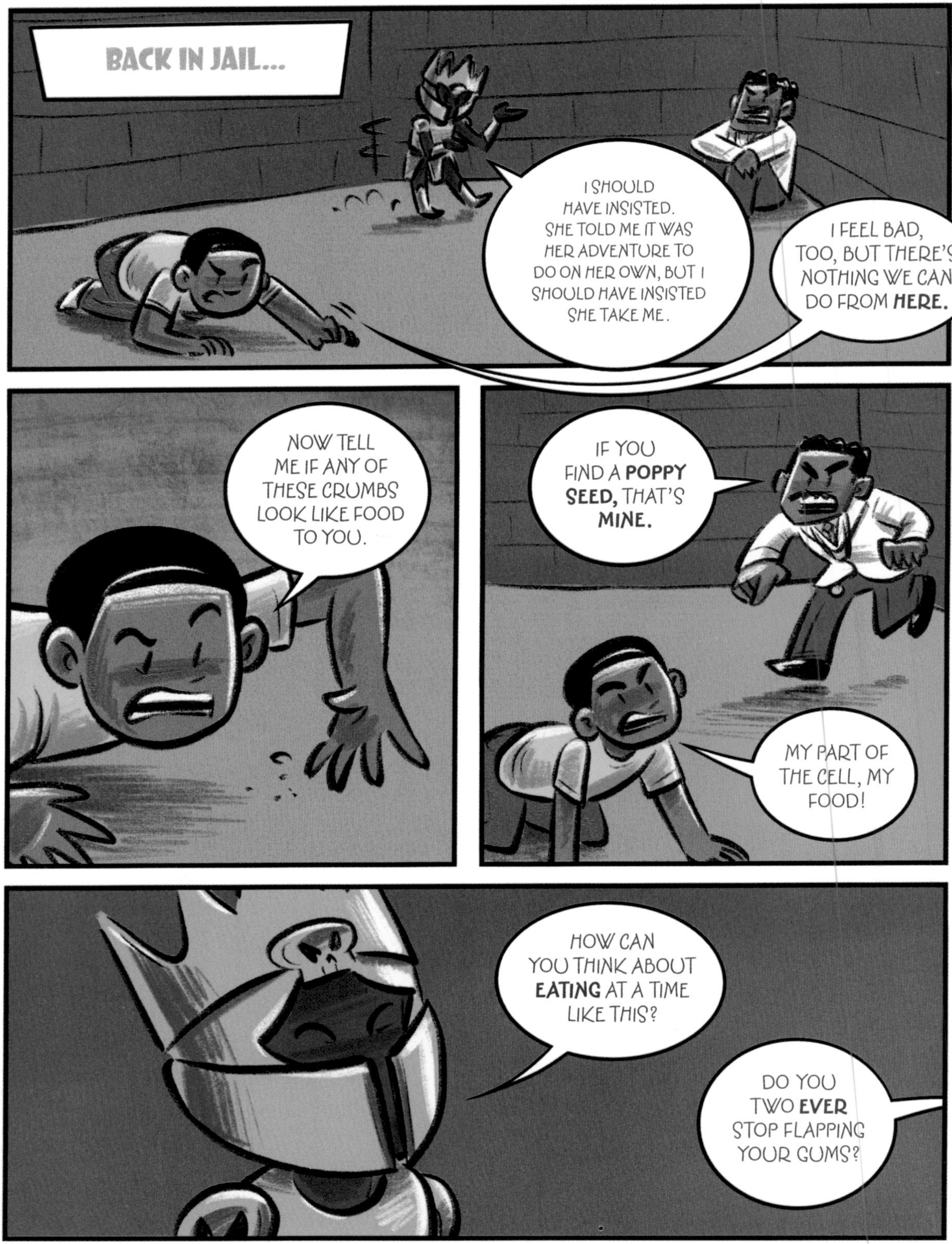
BACK IN JAIL...
I SHOULD HAVE INSISTED. SHE TOLD ME IT WAS HER ADVENTURE TO DO ON HER OWN, BUT I SHOULD HAVE INSISTED SHE TAKE ME.
I FEEL BAD, TOO, BUT THERE'S NOTHING WE CAN DO FROM **HERE.**
NOW TELL ME IF ANY OF THESE CRUMBS LOOK LIKE FOOD TO YOU.
IF YOU FIND A **POPPY SEED,** THAT'S **MINE.**
MY PART OF THE CELL, MY FOOD!
HOW CAN YOU THINK ABOUT **EATING** AT A TIME LIKE THIS?
DO YOU TWO **EVER** STOP FLAPPING YOUR GUMS?

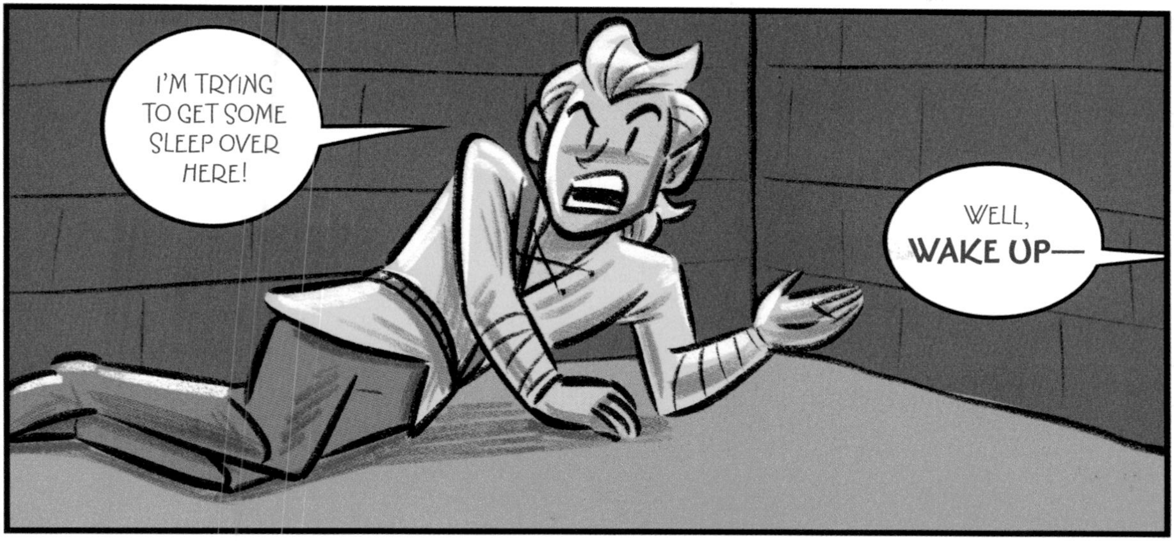
I'M TRYING TO GET SOME SLEEP OVER HERE!
WELL, WAKE UP—

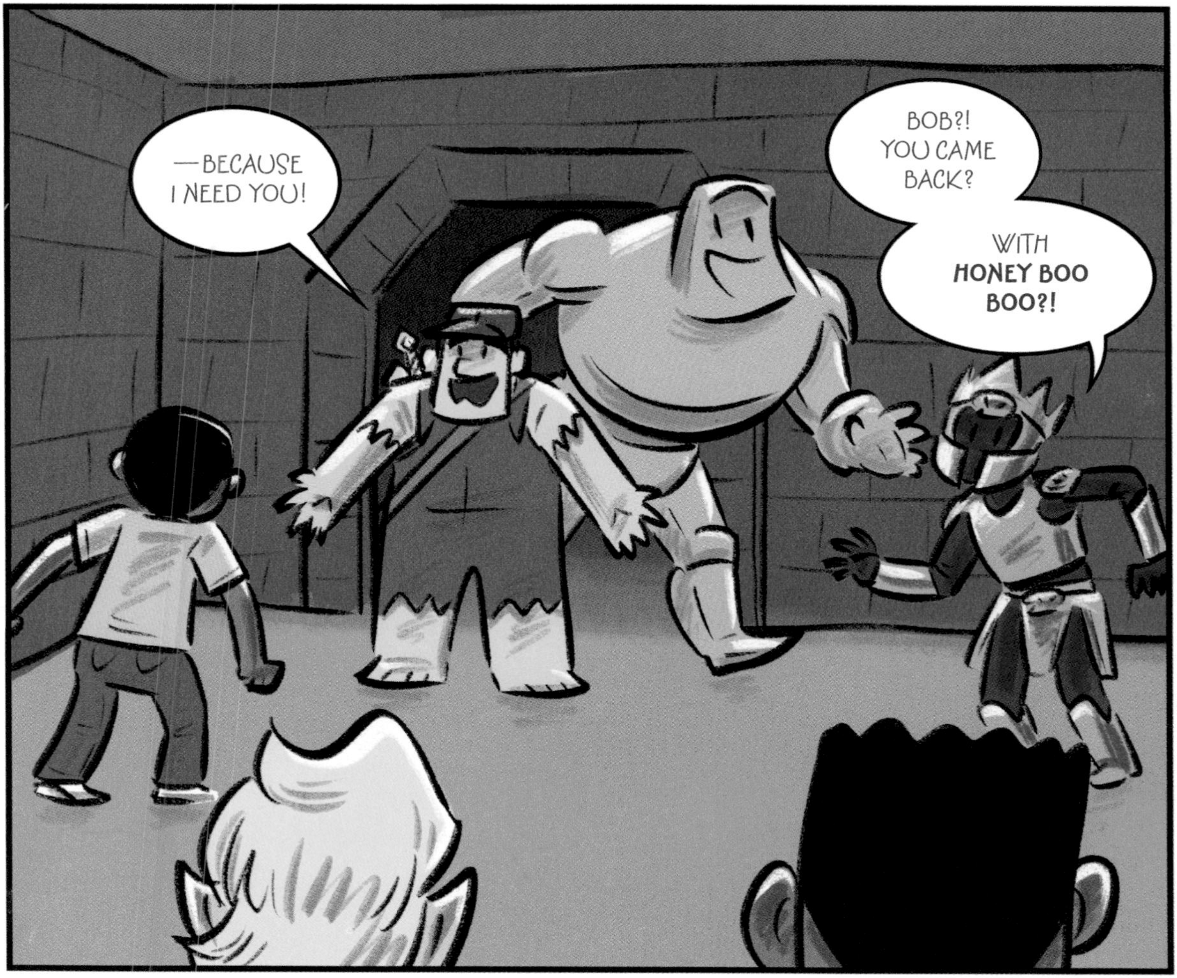
—BECAUSE I NEED YOU!
BOB?! YOU CAME BACK?
WITH HONEY BOO BOO?!

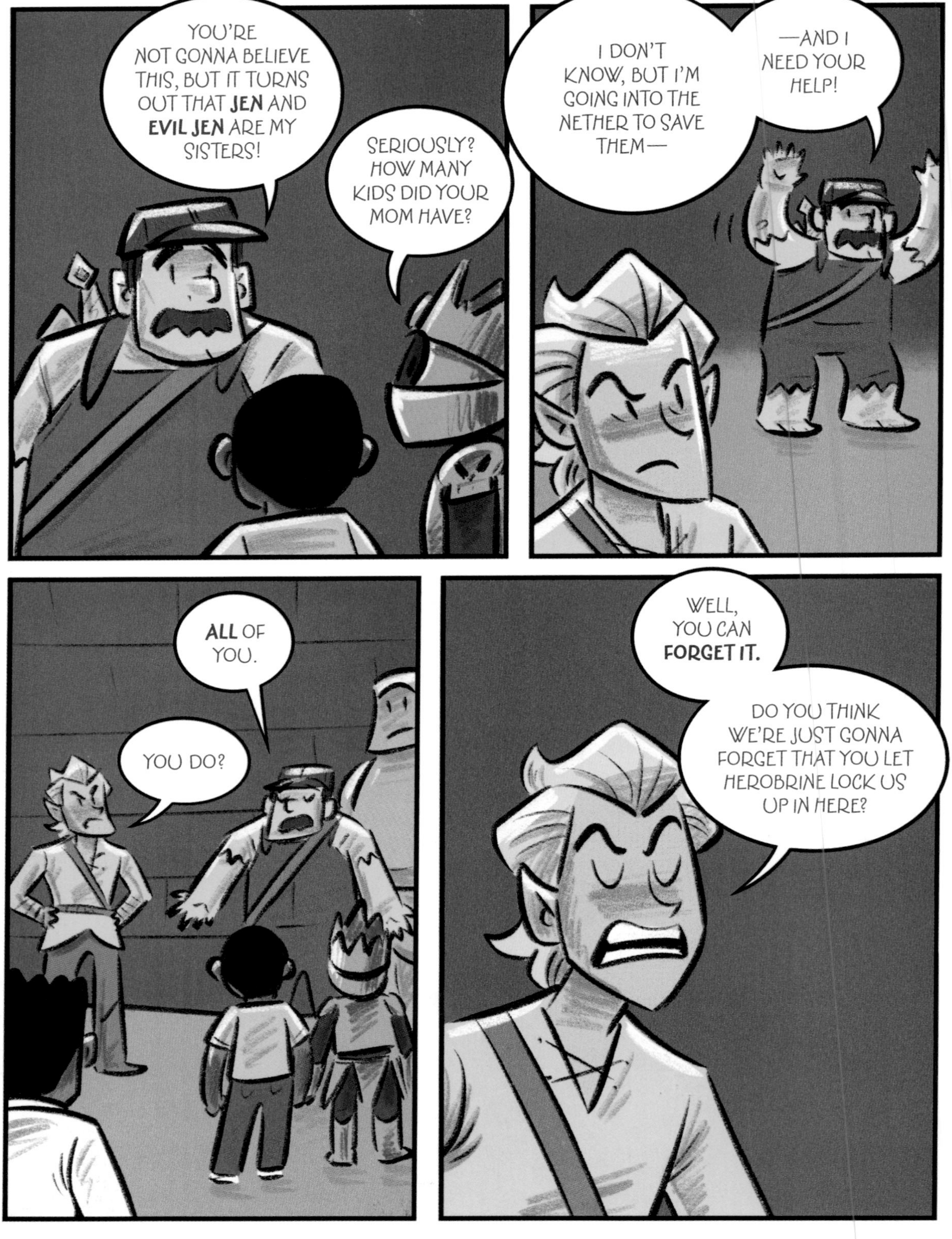
YOU'RE NOT GONNA BELIEVE THIS, BUT IT TURNS OUT THAT **JEN** AND **EVIL JEN** ARE MY SISTERS!
SERIOUSLY? HOW MANY KIDS DID YOUR MOM HAVE?
I DON'T KNOW, BUT I'M GOING INTO THE NETHER TO SAVE THEM—
—AND I NEED YOUR HELP!
ALL OF YOU.
YOU DO?
WELL, YOU CAN **FORGET IT.**
DO YOU THINK WE'RE JUST GONNA FORGET THAT YOU LET HEROBRINE LOCK US UP IN HERE?

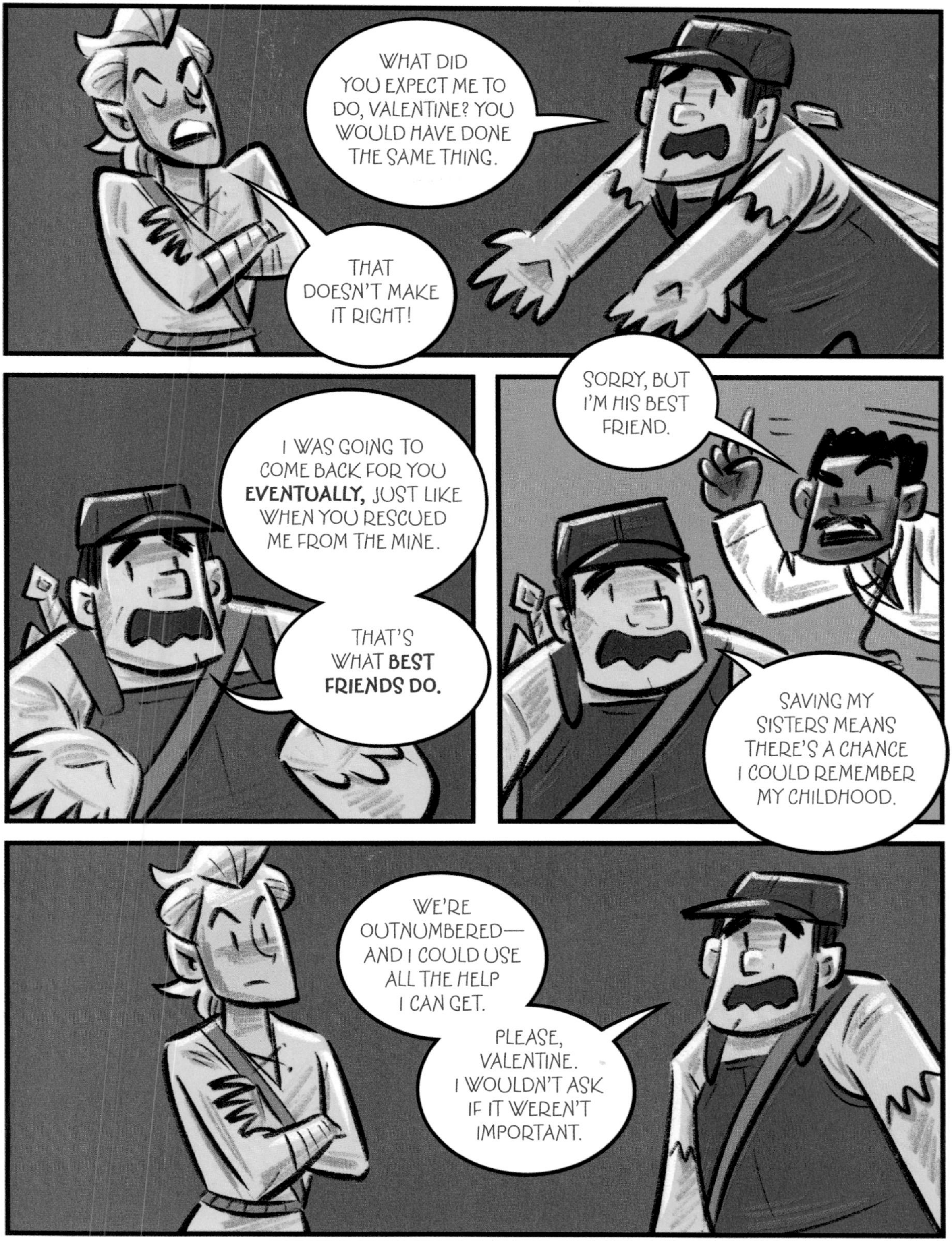
WHAT DID YOU EXPECT ME TO DO, VALENTINE? YOU WOULD HAVE DONE THE SAME THING.
THAT DOESN'T MAKE IT RIGHT!
I WAS GOING TO COME BACK FOR YOU **EVENTUALLY,** JUST LIKE WHEN YOU RESCUED ME FROM THE MINE.
THAT'S WHAT **BEST FRIENDS DO.**
SORRY, BUT I'M HIS BEST FRIEND.
SAVING MY SISTERS MEANS THERE'S A CHANCE I COULD REMEMBER MY CHILDHOOD.
WE'RE OUTNUMBERED—AND I COULD USE ALL THE HELP I CAN GET.
PLEASE, VALENTINE. I WOULDN'T ASK IF IT WEREN'T IMPORTANT.

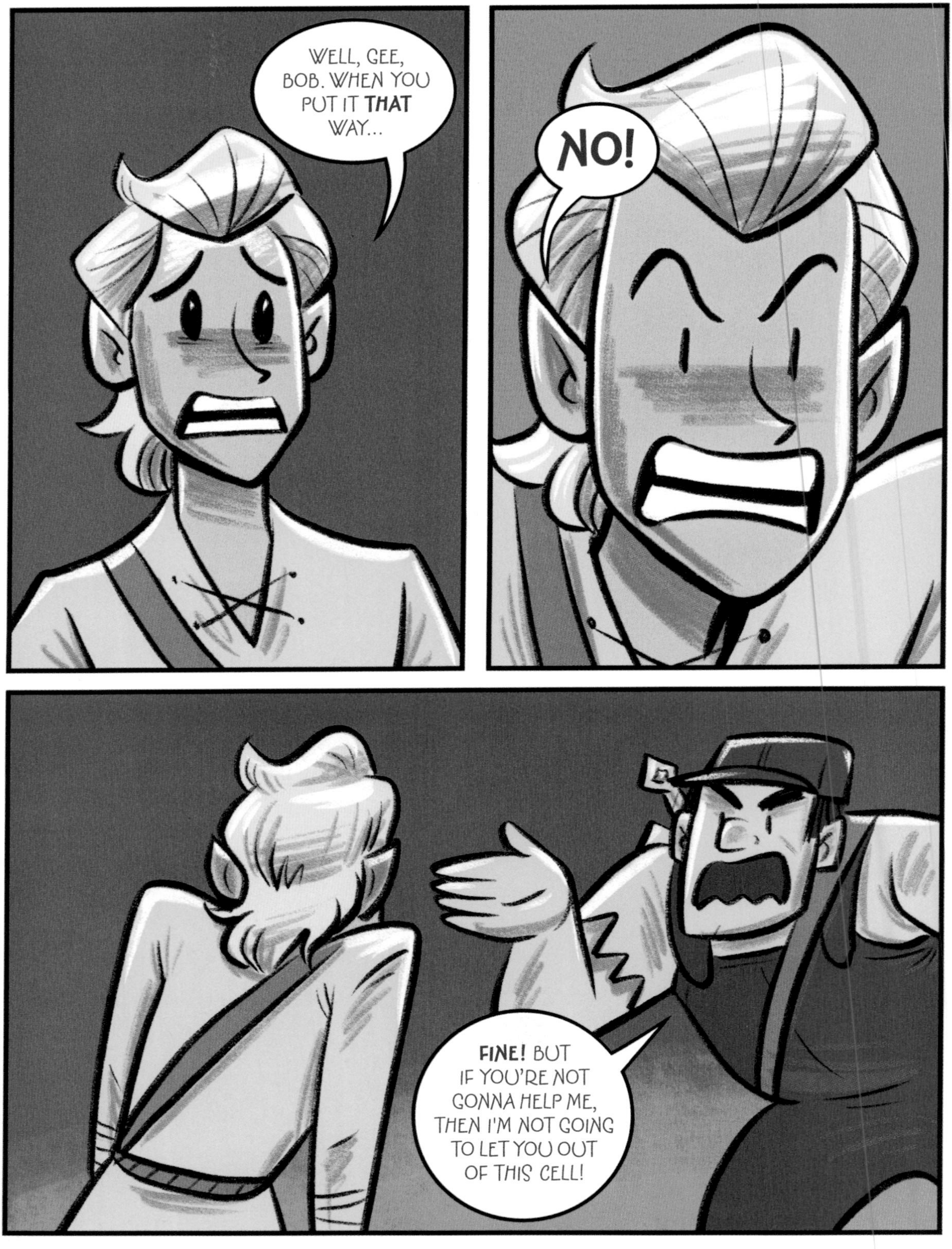
WELL, GEE, BOB. WHEN YOU PUT IT **THAT** WAY...
NO!
FINE! BUT IF YOU'RE NOT GONNA HELP ME, THEN I'M NOT GOING TO LET YOU OUT OF THIS CELL!

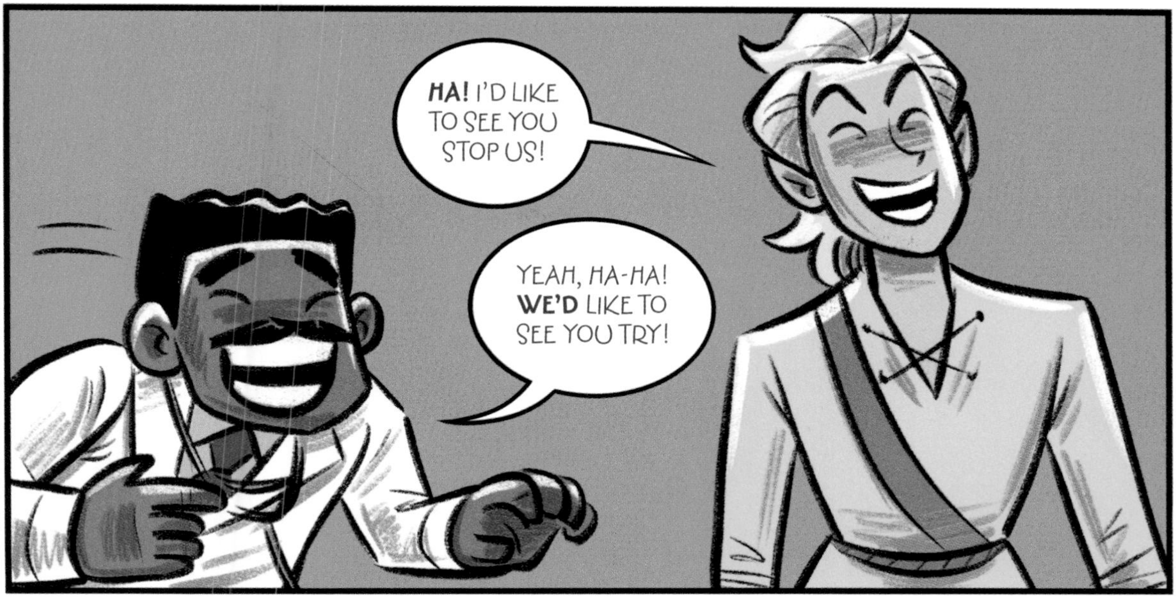
HA! I'D LIKE TO SEE YOU STOP US!
YEAH, HA-HA! **WE'D** LIKE TO SEE YOU TRY!

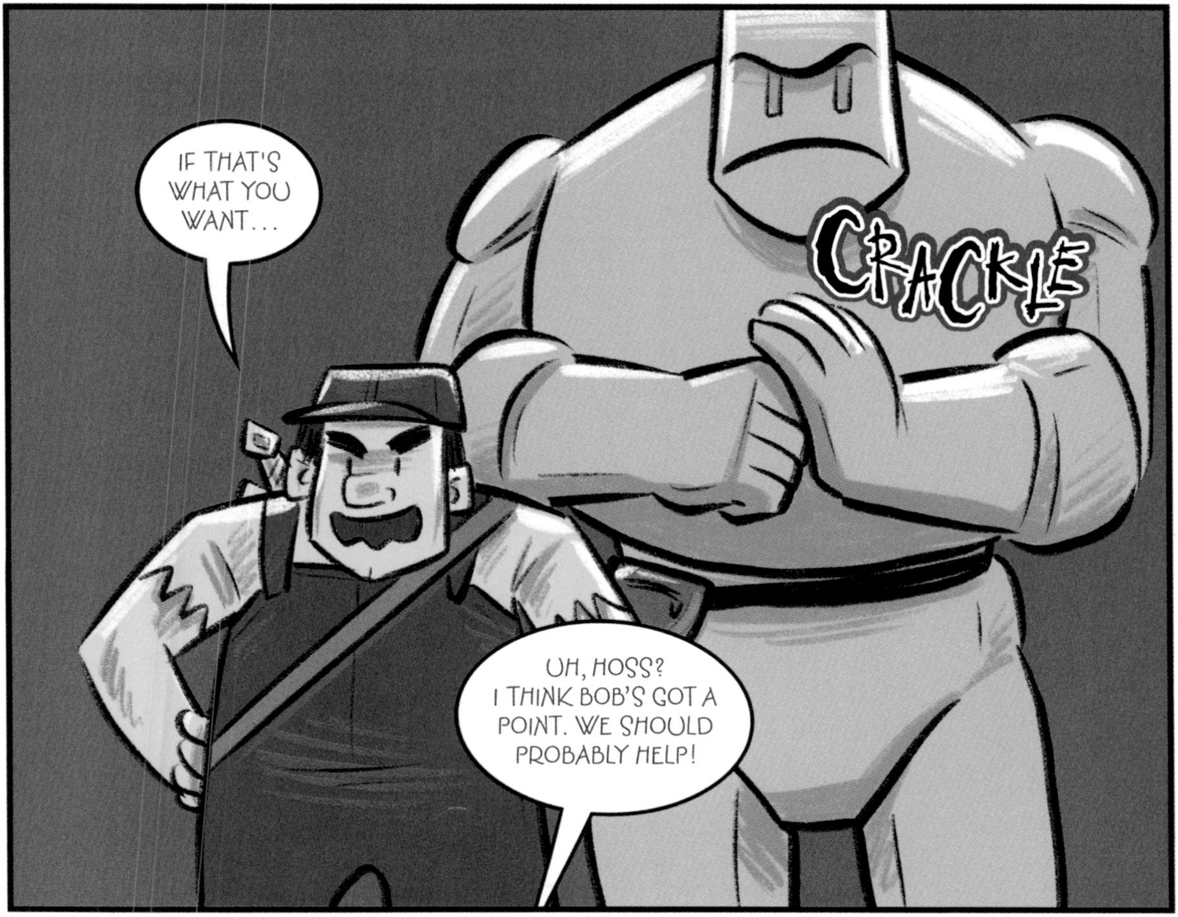
IF THAT'S WHAT YOU WANT...
CRACKLE
UH, HOSS? I THINK BOB'S GOT A POINT. WE SHOULD PROBABLY HELP!

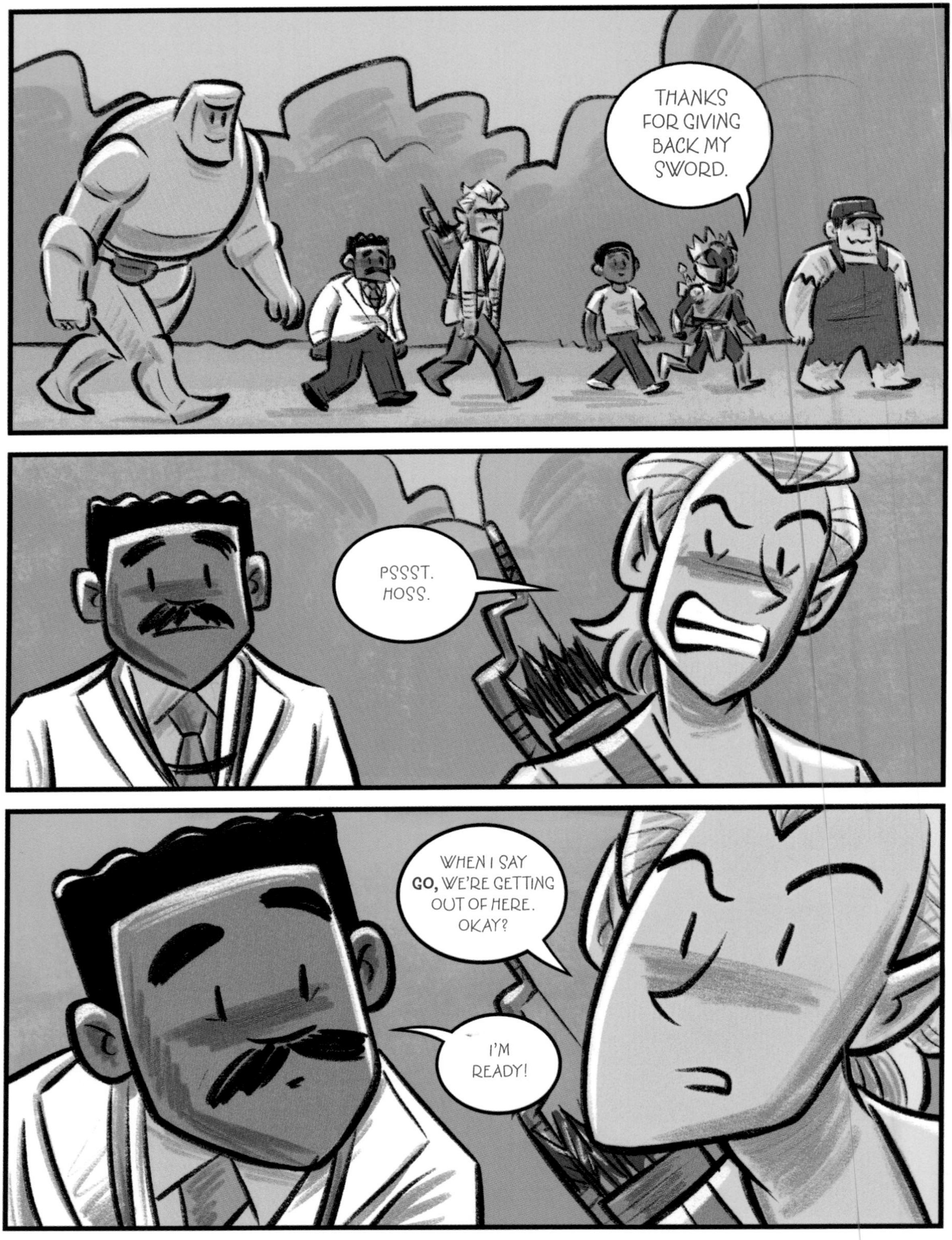
THANKS FOR GIVING BACK MY SWORD.
PSSST. HOSS.
WHEN I SAY **GO,** WE'RE GETTING OUT OF HERE. OKAY?
I'M READY!

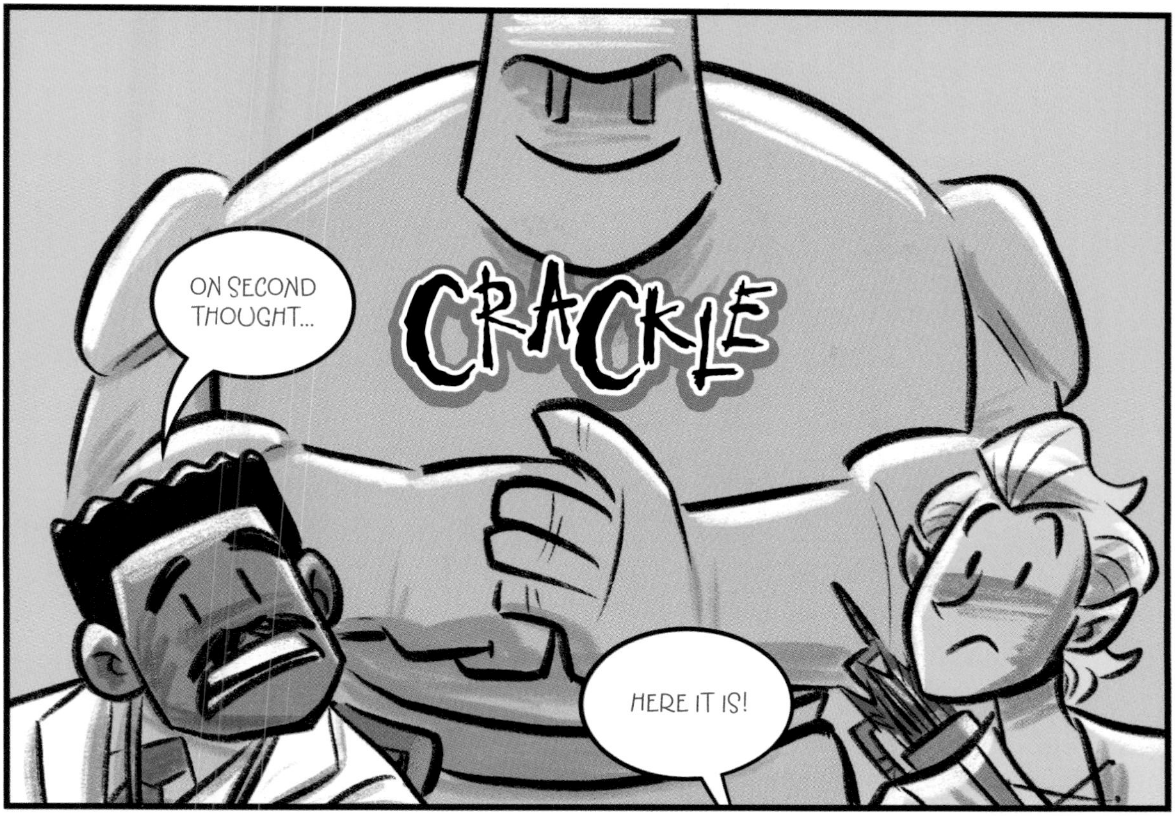
ON SECOND THOUGHT...
CRACKLE
HERE IT IS!

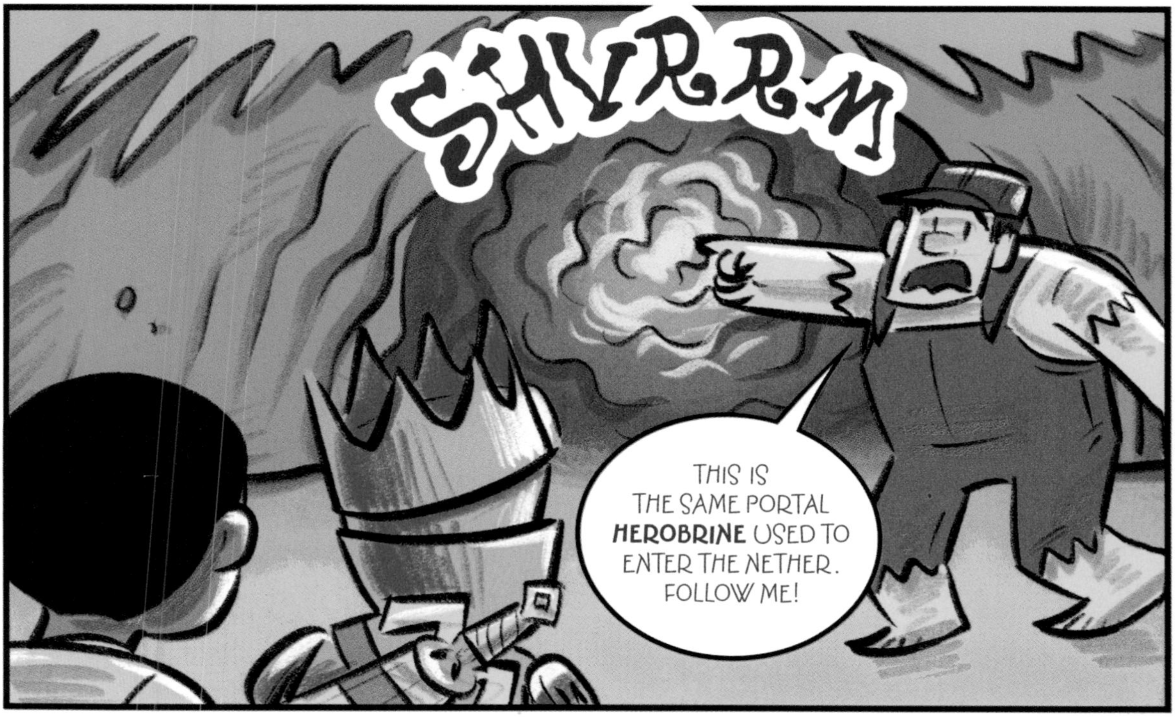
SHVRRM
THIS IS THE SAME PORTAL **HEROBRINE** USED TO ENTER THE NETHER. FOLLOW ME!

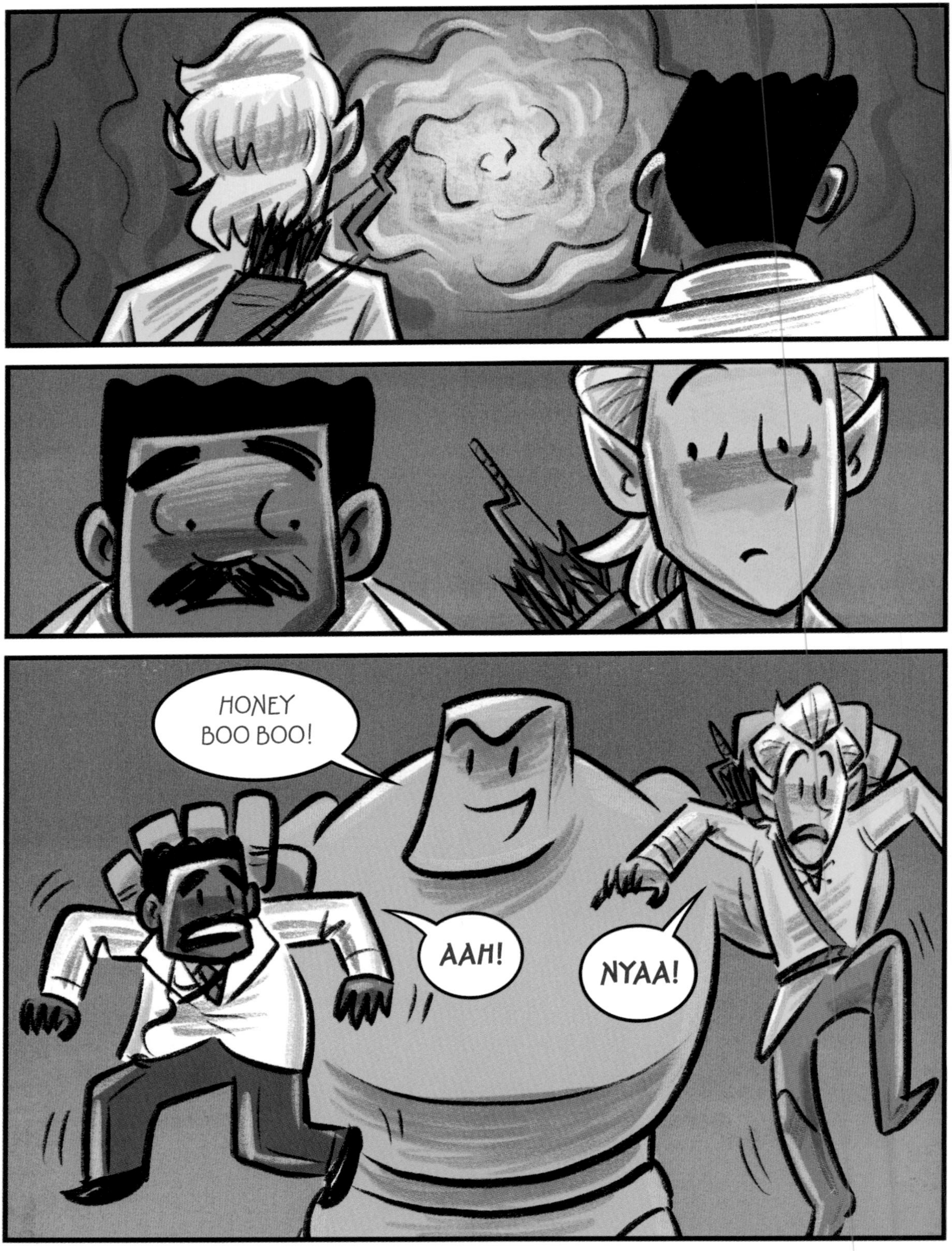
HONEY BOO BOO!
AAH!
NYAA!

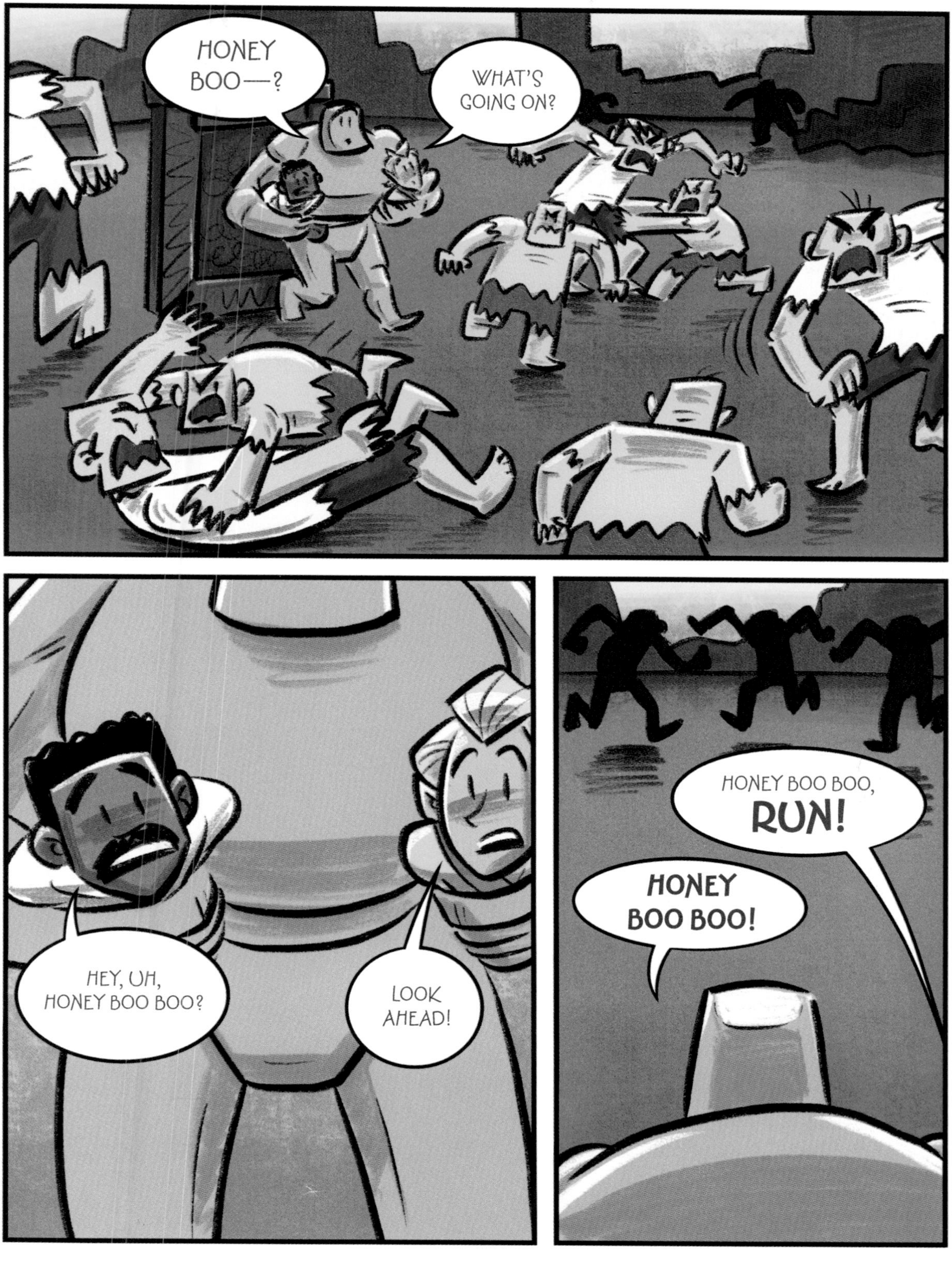
HONEY BOO—?
WHAT'S GOING ON?
HEY, UH, HONEY BOO BOO?
LOOK AHEAD!
HONEY BOO BOO, RUN!
HONEY BOO BOO!

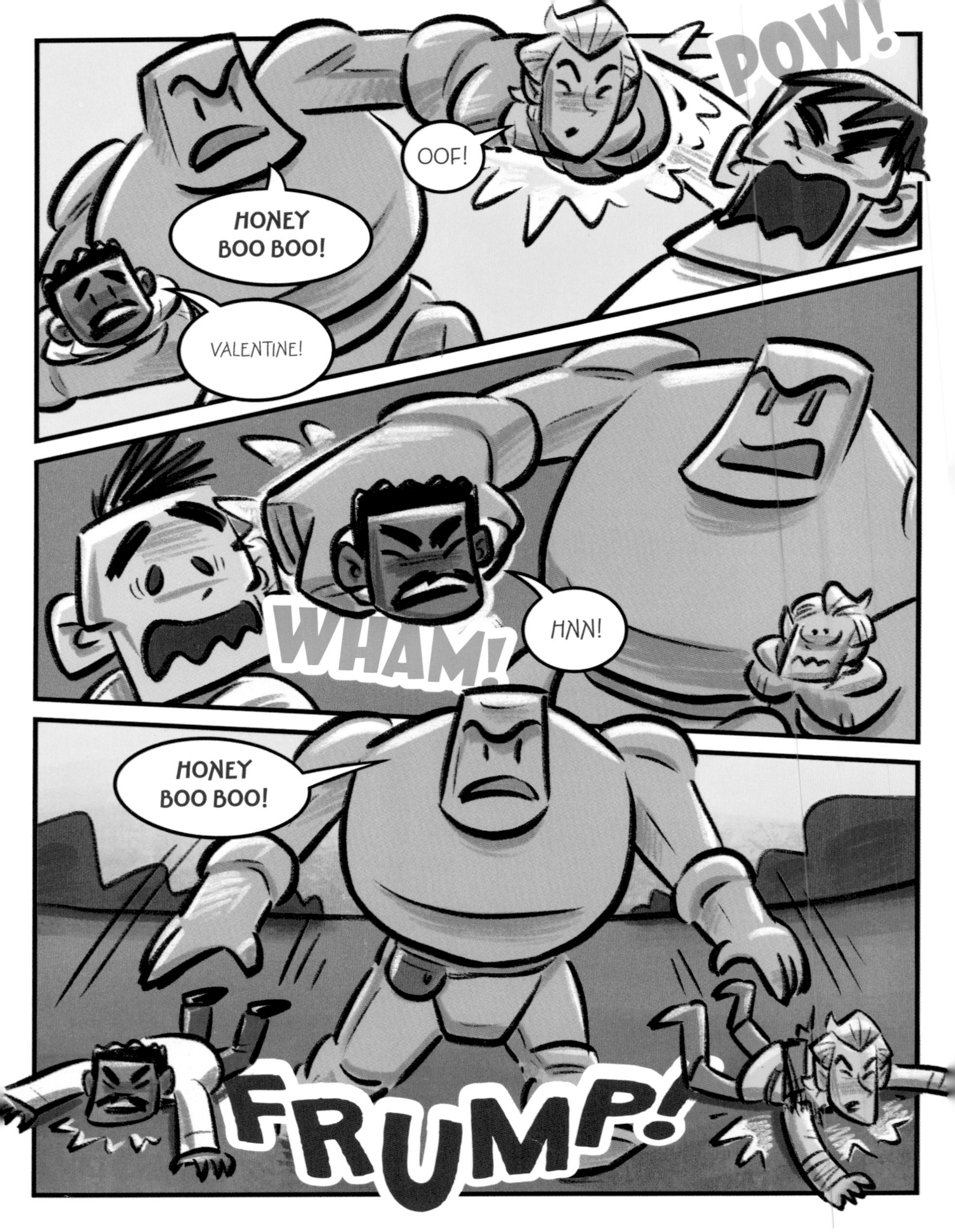
POW!
OOF!
HONEY BOO BOO!
VALENTINE!
WHAM!
HNN!
HONEY BOO BOO!
FRUMP!

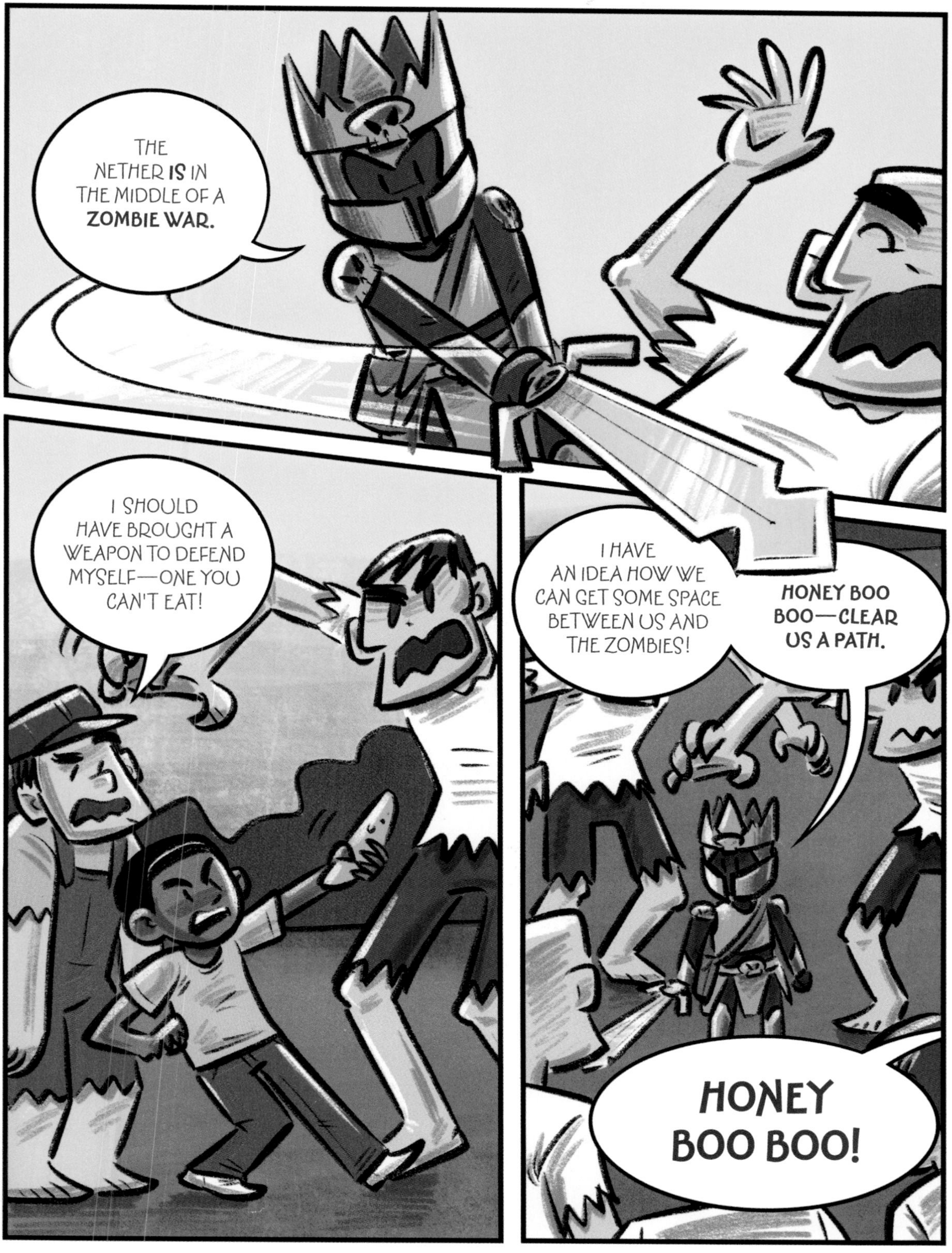
THE NETHER **IS** IN THE MIDDLE OF A **ZOMBIE WAR.**
I SHOULD HAVE BROUGHT A WEAPON TO DEFEND MYSELF—ONE YOU CAN'T EAT!
I HAVE AN IDEA HOW WE CAN GET SOME SPACE BETWEEN US AND THE ZOMBIES!
HONEY BOO BOO—CLEAR US A PATH.
HONEY BOO BOO!

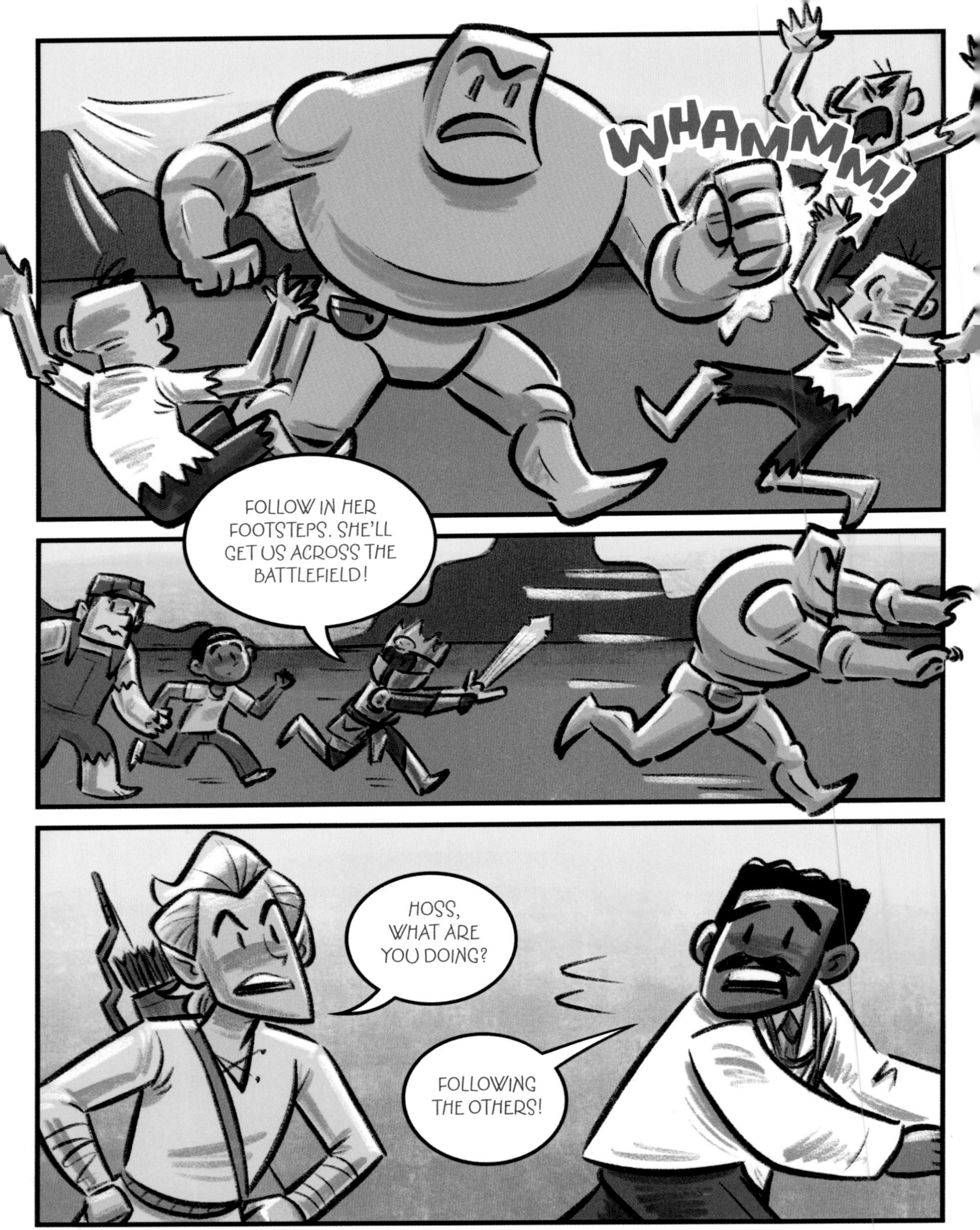
WHAMMM!
FOLLOW IN HER FOOTSTEPS. SHE'LL GET US ACROSS THE BATTLEFIELD!
HOSS, WHAT ARE YOU DOING?
FOLLOWING THE OTHERS!

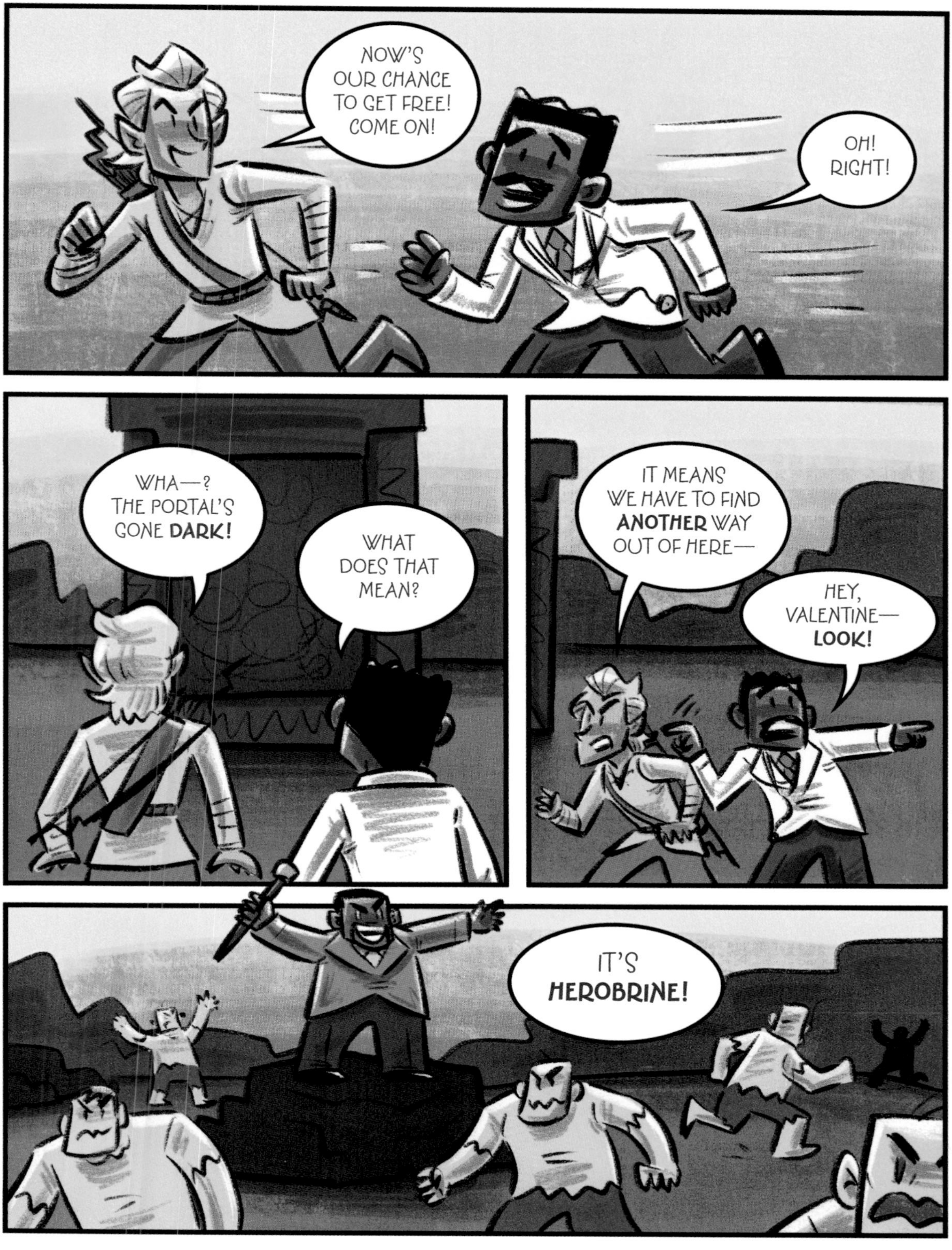
NOW'S OUR CHANCE TO GET FREE! COME ON!
OH! RIGHT!
WHA—? THE PORTAL'S GONE **DARK!**
WHAT DOES THAT MEAN?
IT MEANS WE HAVE TO FIND **ANOTHER** WAY OUT OF HERE—
HEY, VALENTINE— **LOOK!**
IT'S **HEROBRINE!**

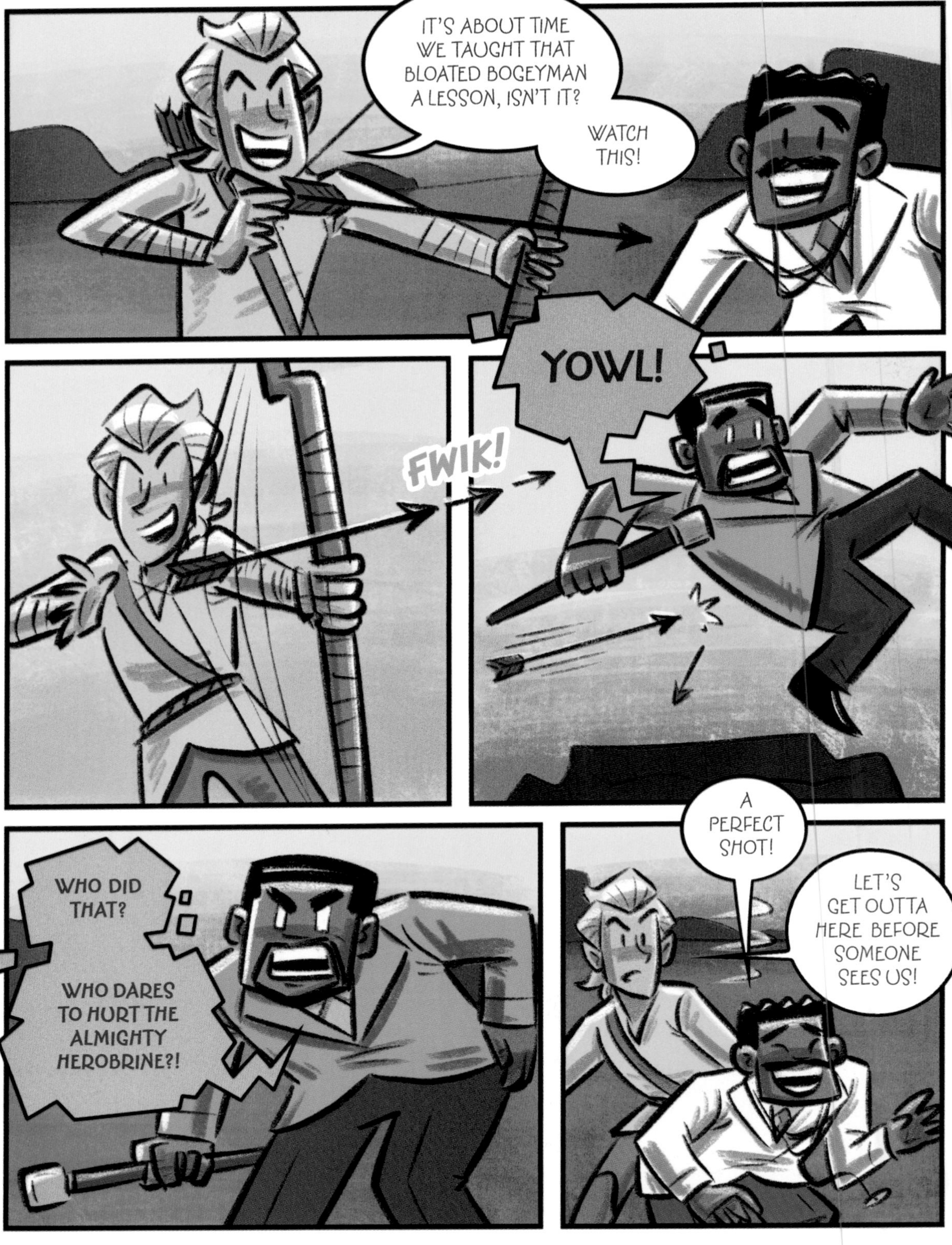

IT'S ABOUT TIME WE TAUGHT THAT BLOATED BOGEYMAN A LESSON, ISN'T IT?
WATCH THIS!
YOWL!
FWIK!
WHO DID THAT?
WHO DARES TO HURT THE ALMIGHTY HEROBRINE?!
A PERFECT SHOT!
LET'S GET OUTTA HERE BEFORE SOMEONE SEES US!

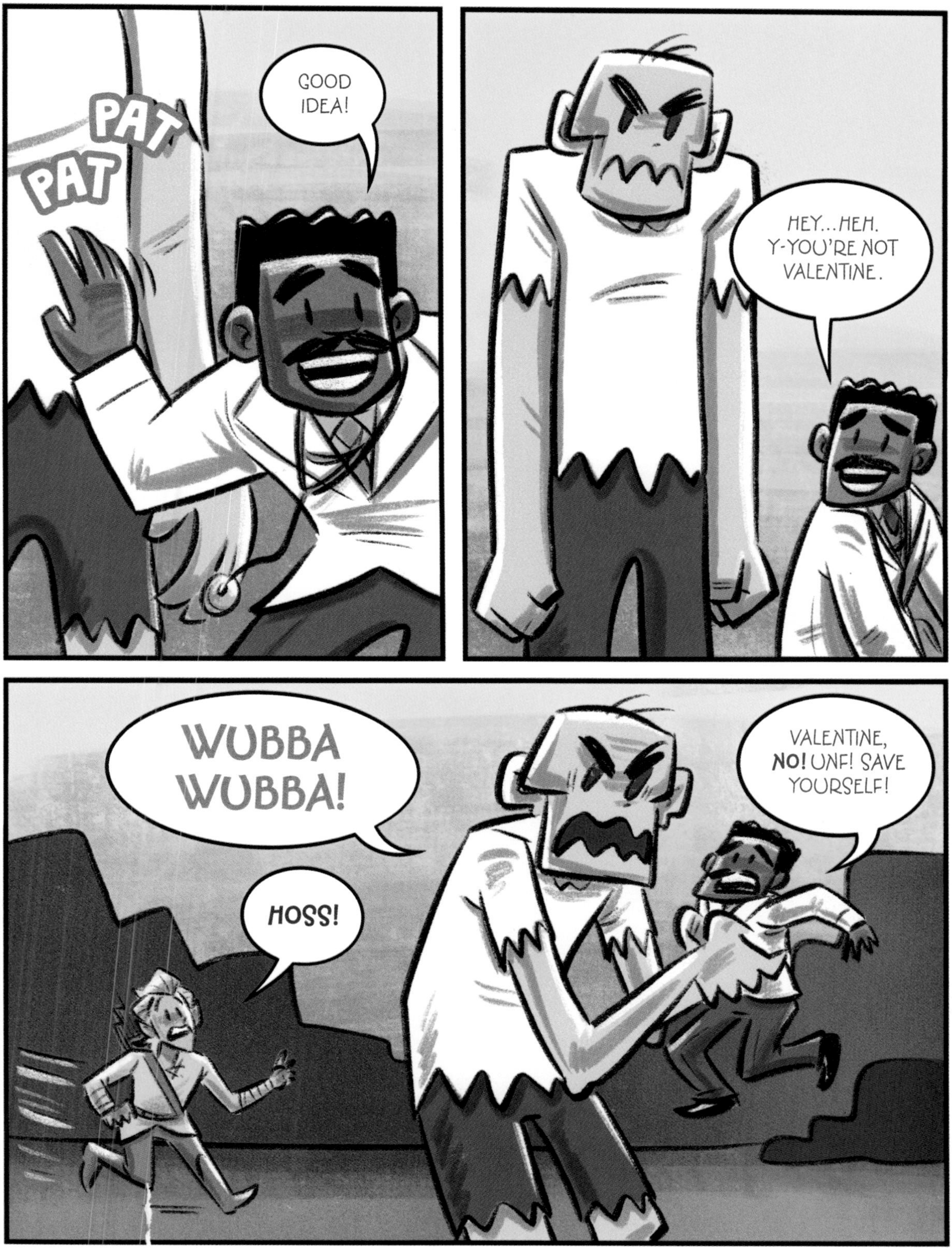
PAT
PAT
GOOD IDEA!
HEY...HEH. Y-YOU'RE NOT VALENTINE.
WUBBA WUBBA!
VALENTINE, NO! UNF! SAVE YOURSELF!
HOSS!

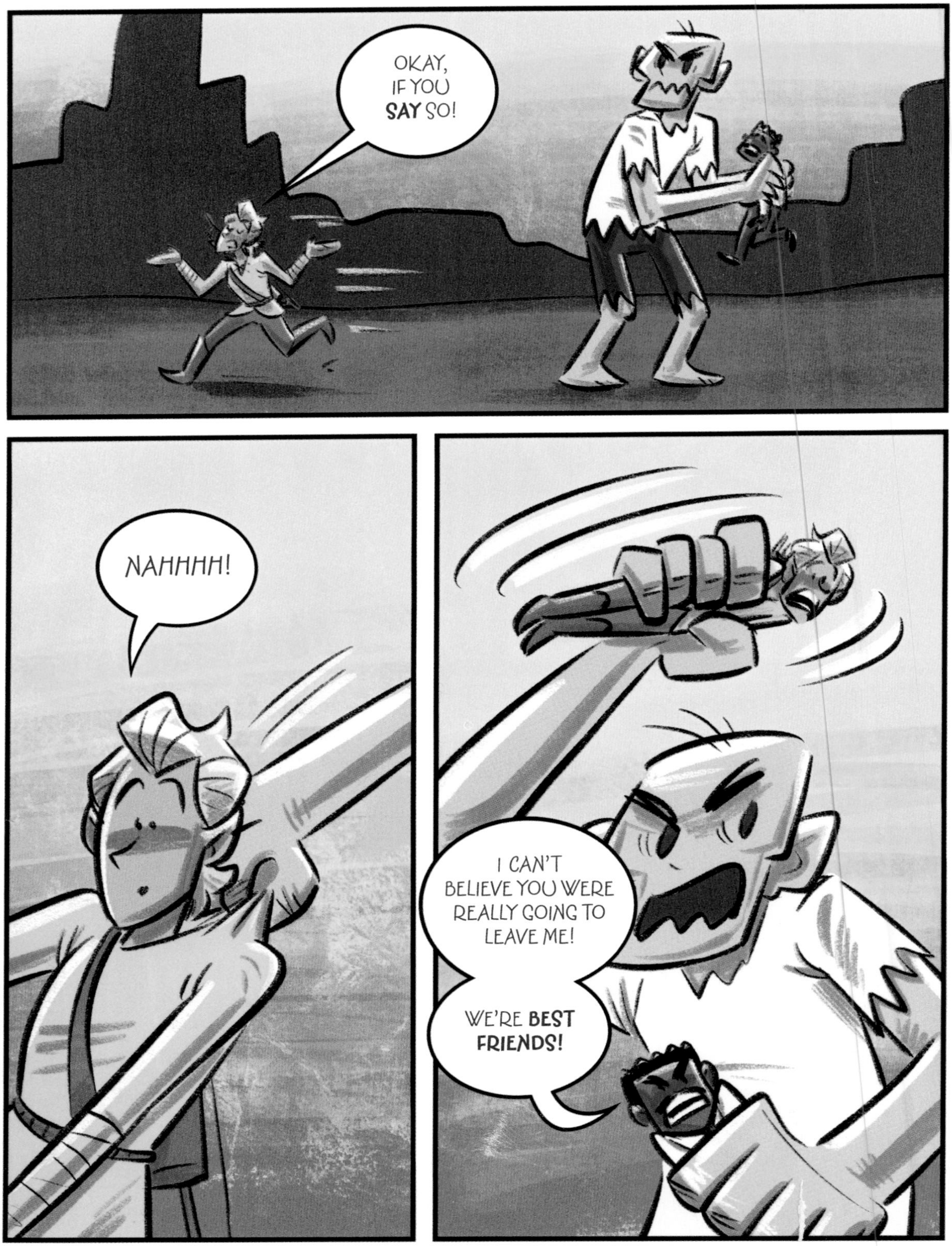
OKAY, IF YOU **SAY** SO!
NAHHHH!
I CAN'T BELIEVE YOU WERE REALLY GOING TO LEAVE ME!
WE'RE **BEST FRIENDS!**

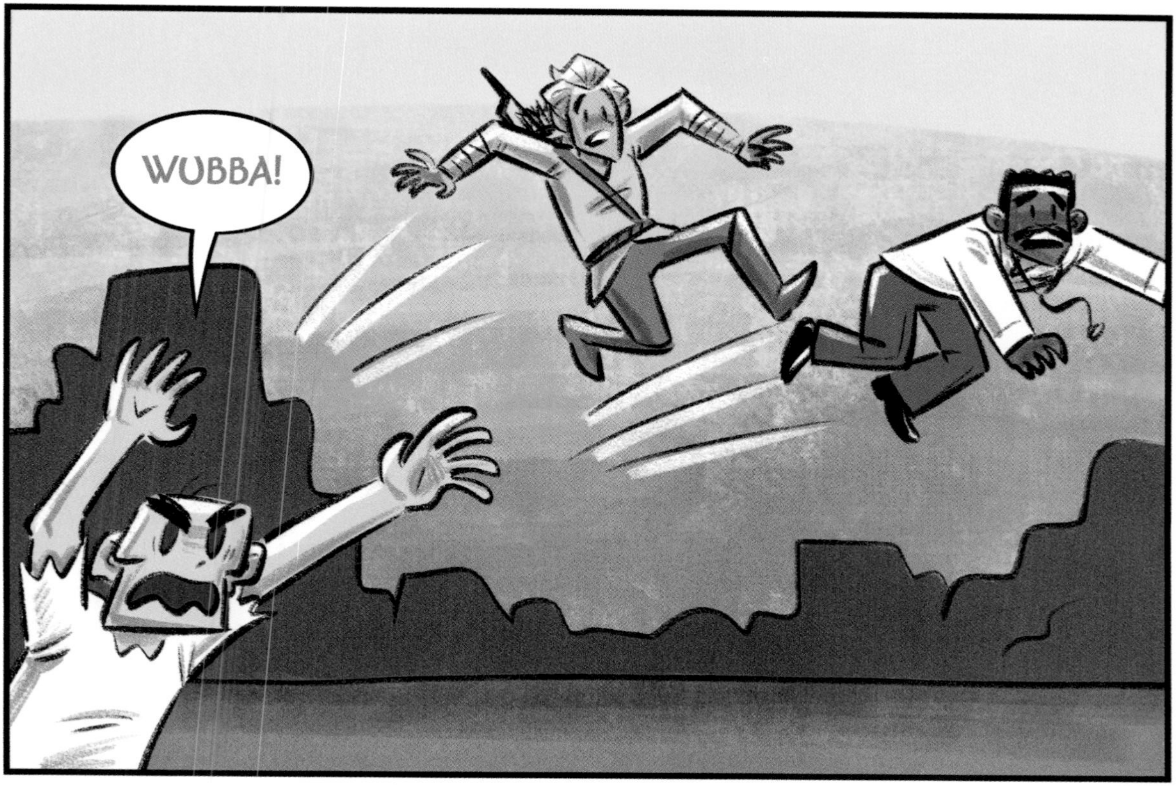
WUBBA!

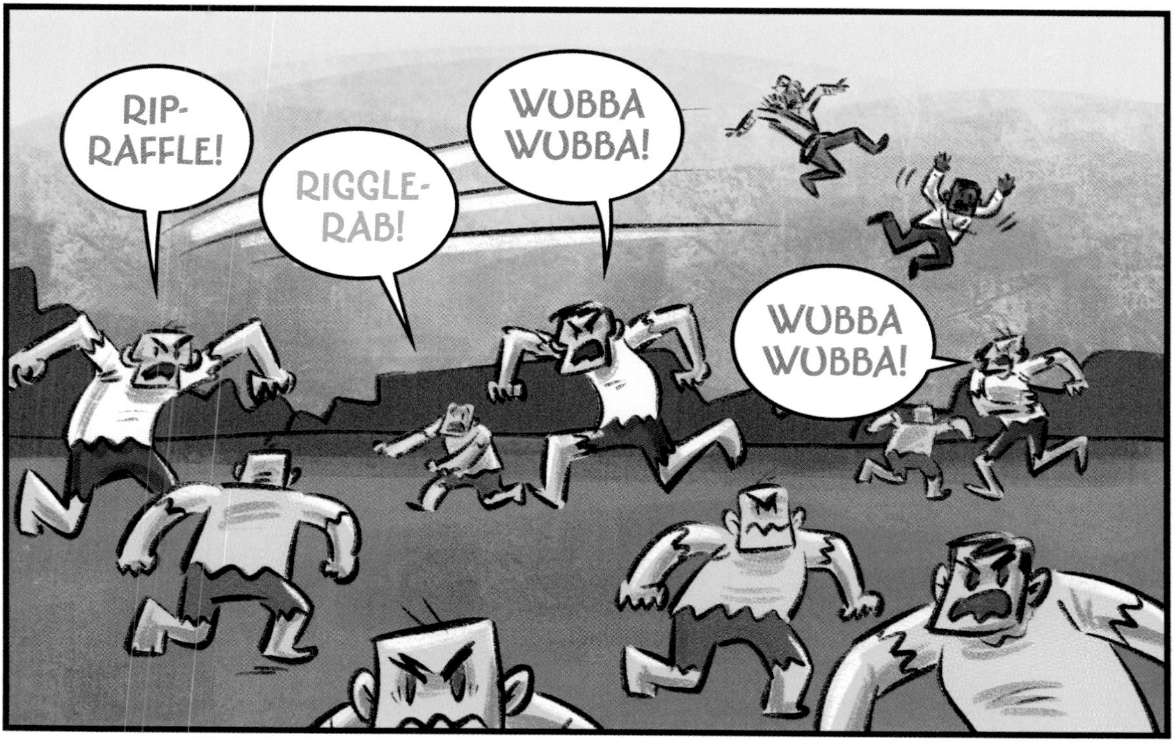
RIP-RAFFLE!
RIGGLE-RAB!
WUBBA WUBBA!
WUBBA WUBBA!

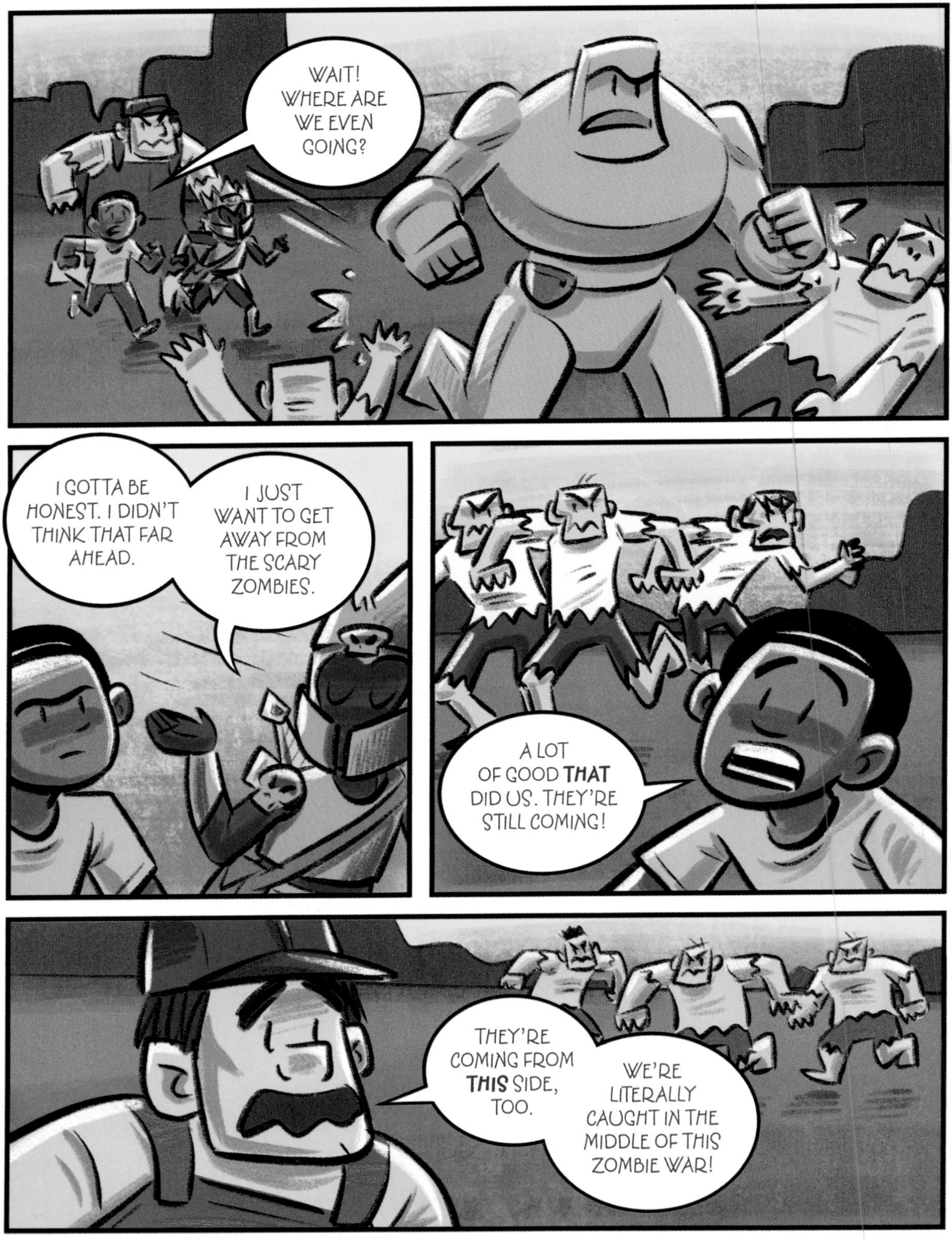
WAIT! WHERE ARE WE EVEN GOING?
I GOTTA BE HONEST. I DIDN'T THINK THAT FAR AHEAD.
I JUST WANT TO GET AWAY FROM THE SCARY ZOMBIES.
A LOT OF GOOD **THAT** DID US. THEY'RE STILL COMING!
THEY'RE COMING FROM **THIS** SIDE, TOO.
WE'RE LITERALLY CAUGHT IN THE MIDDLE OF THIS ZOMBIE WAR!

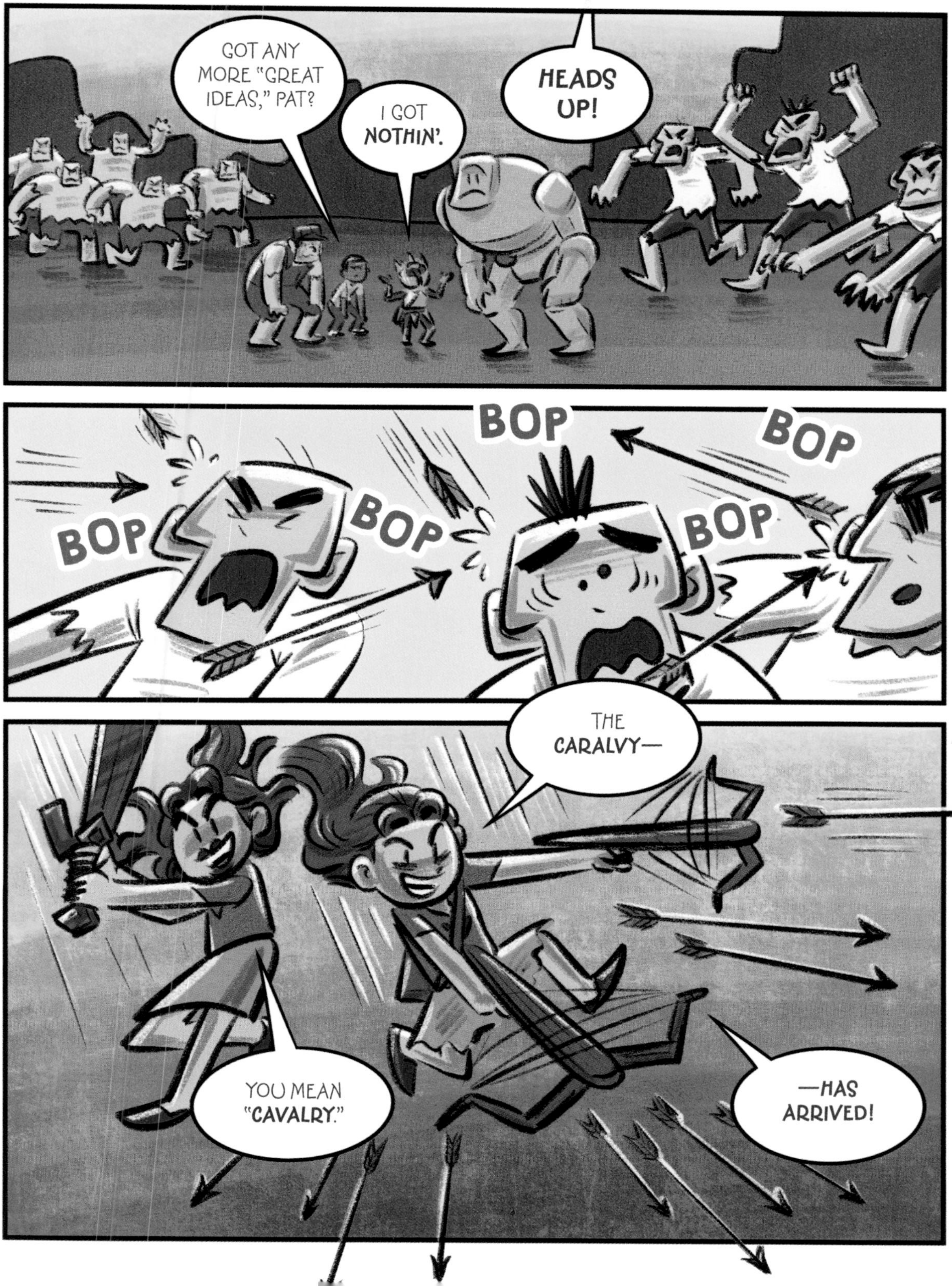
GOT ANY MORE "GREAT IDEAS," PAT?
I GOT NOTHIN'.
HEADS UP!
BOP
BOP
BOP
BOP
BOP
THE CARALVY—
YOU MEAN "CAVALRY."
—HAS ARRIVED!

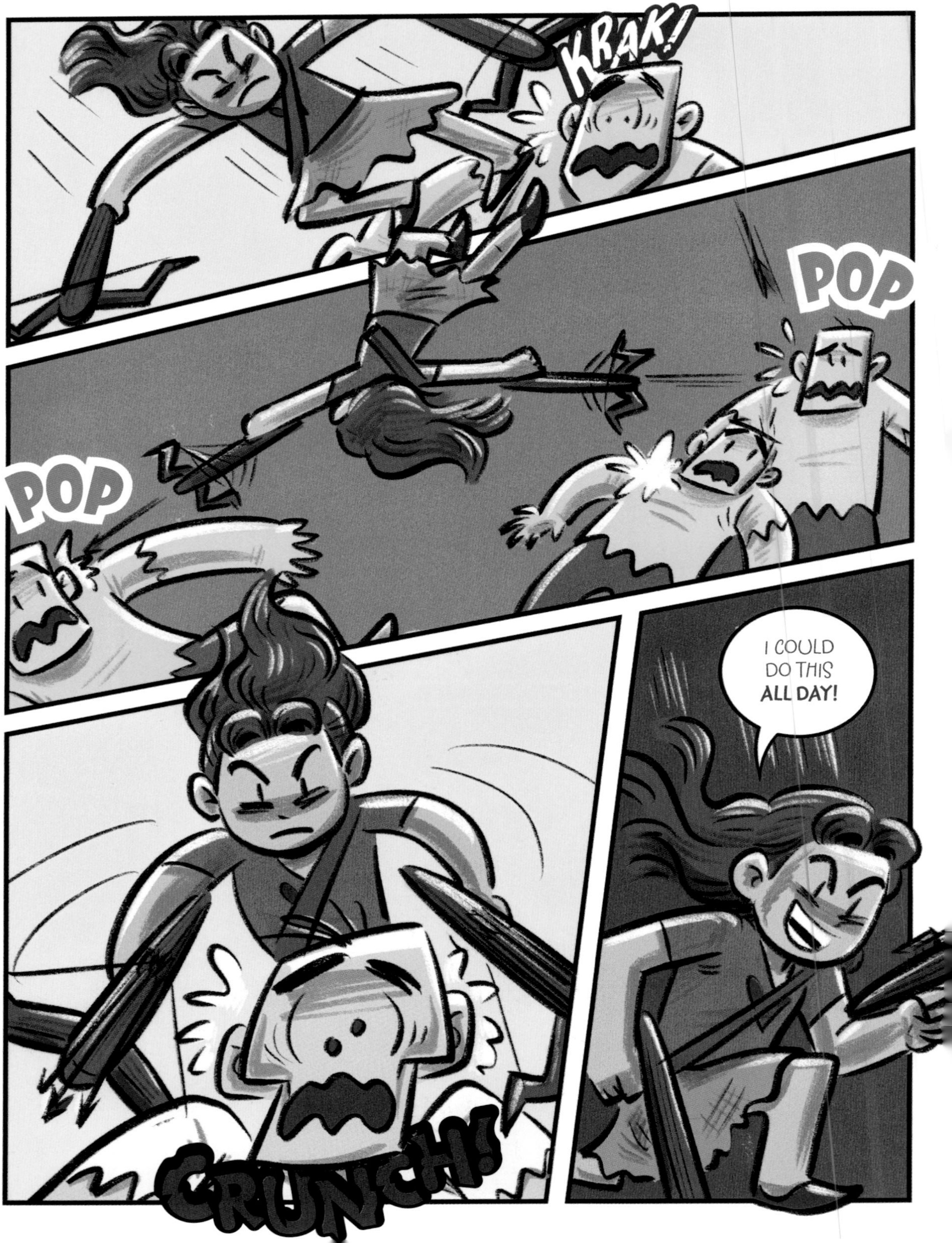
KRAK!
POP
POP
I COULD DO THIS ALL DAY!
CRUNCH!

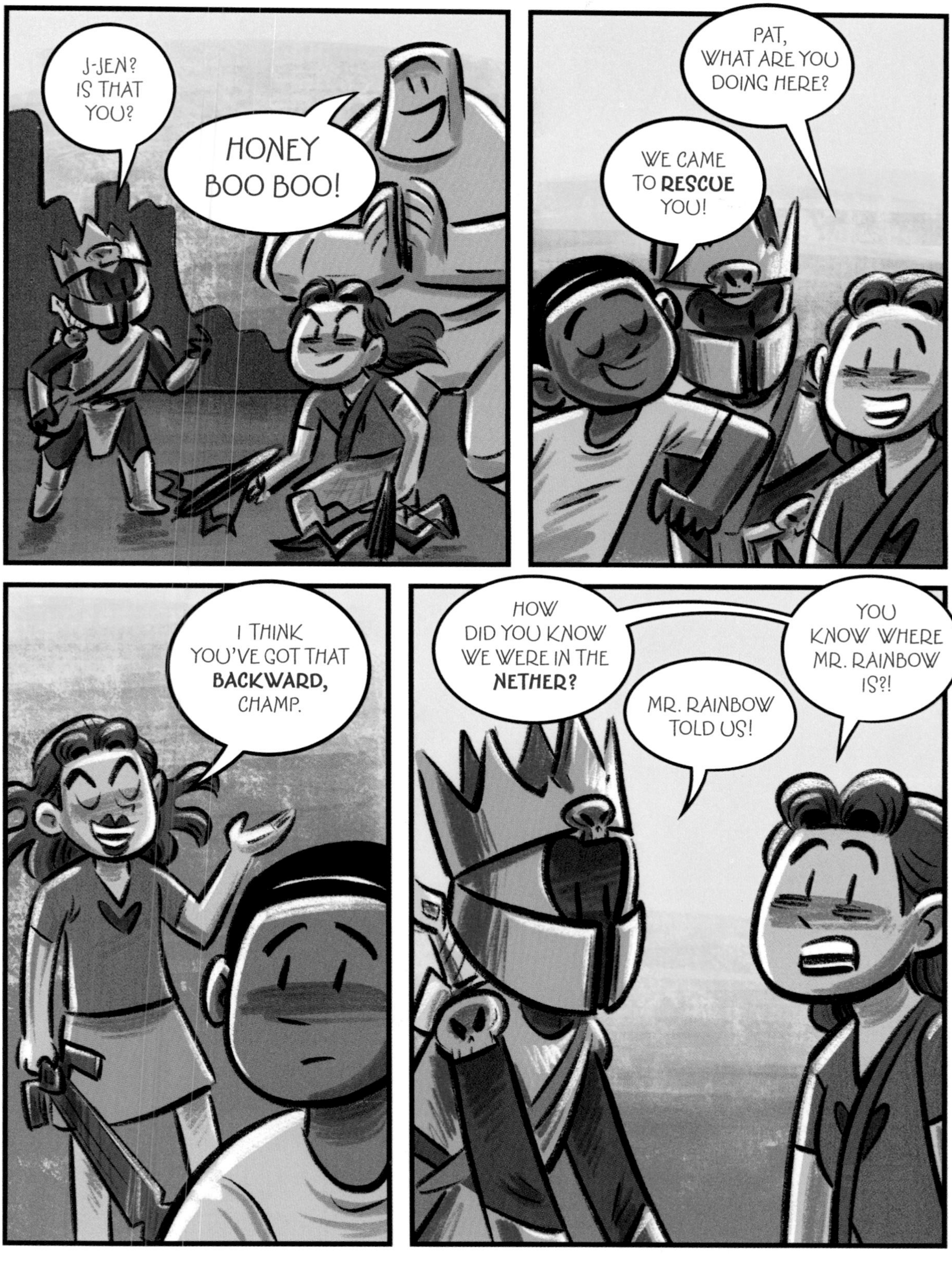
J-JEN? IS THAT YOU?
HONEY BOO BOO!
PAT, WHAT ARE YOU DOING HERE?
WE CAME TO **RESCUE** YOU!
I THINK YOU'VE GOT THAT **BACKWARD,** CHAMP.
HOW DID YOU KNOW WE WERE IN THE **NETHER?**
MR. RAINBOW TOLD US!
YOU KNOW WHERE MR. RAINBOW IS?!

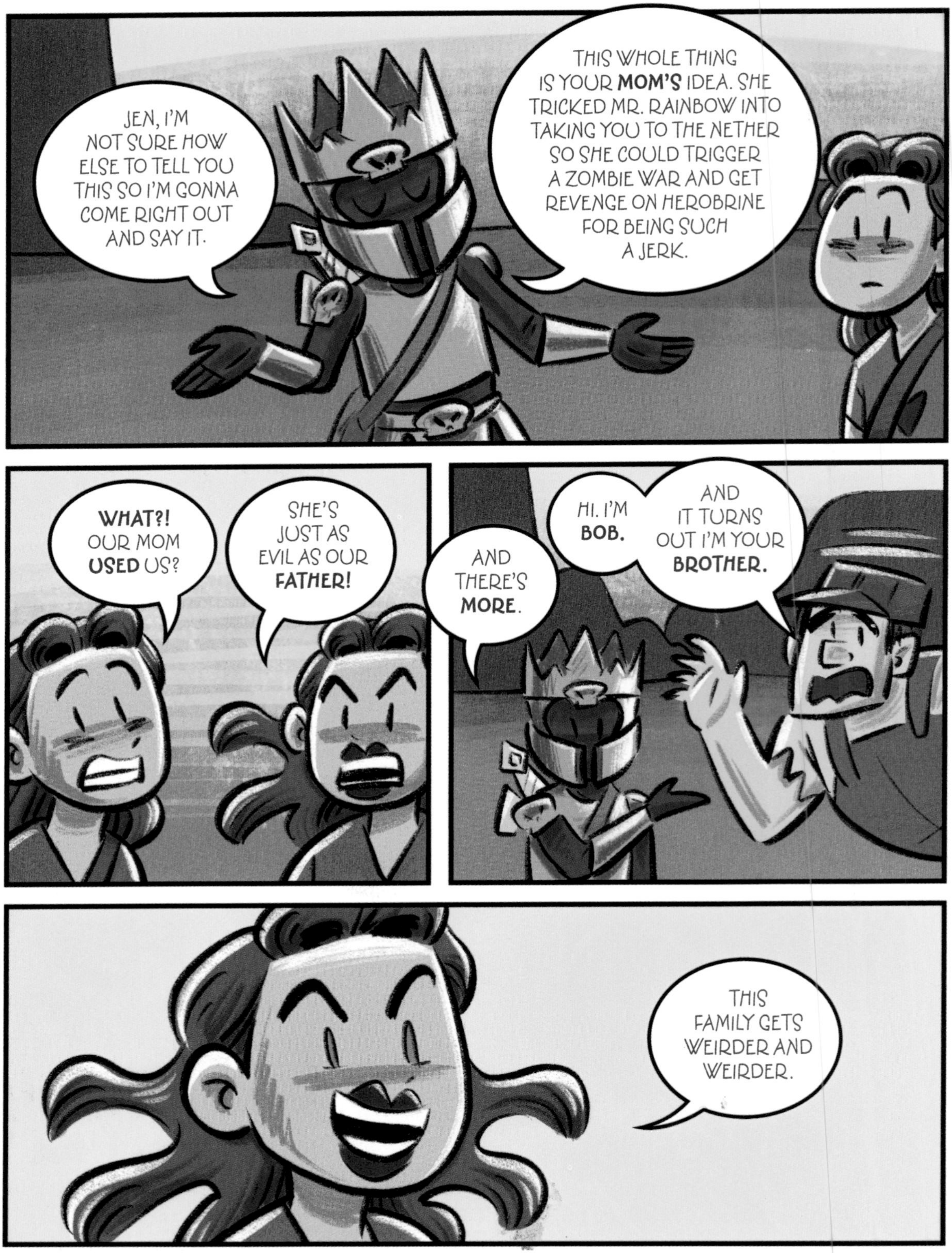
JEN, I'M NOT SURE HOW ELSE TO TELL YOU THIS SO I'M GONNA COME RIGHT OUT AND SAY IT.
THIS WHOLE THING IS YOUR **MOM'S** IDEA. SHE TRICKED MR. RAINBOW INTO TAKING YOU TO THE NETHER SO SHE COULD TRIGGER A ZOMBIE WAR AND GET REVENGE ON HEROBRINE FOR BEING SUCH A JERK.
WHAT?! OUR MOM **USED** US?
SHE'S JUST AS EVIL AS OUR **FATHER!**
AND THERE'S **MORE**.
HI. I'M **BOB.**
AND IT TURNS OUT I'M YOUR **BROTHER.**
THIS FAMILY GETS WEIRDER AND WEIRDER.

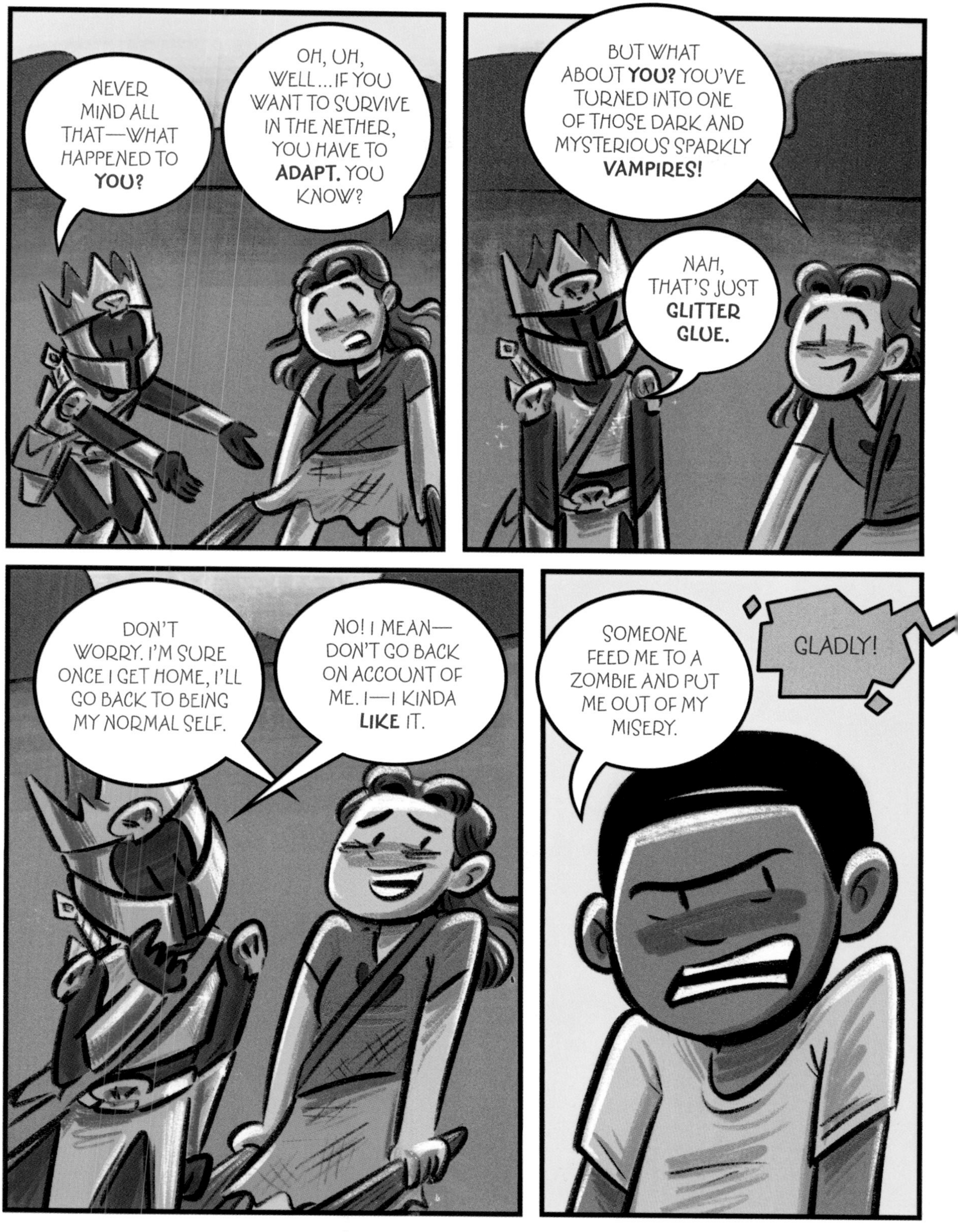
NEVER MIND ALL THAT—WHAT HAPPENED TO **YOU?**
OH, UH, WELL... IF YOU WANT TO SURVIVE IN THE NETHER, YOU HAVE TO **ADAPT.** YOU KNOW?
BUT WHAT ABOUT **YOU?** YOU'VE TURNED INTO ONE OF THOSE DARK AND MYSTERIOUS SPARKLY **VAMPIRES!**
NAH, THAT'S JUST **GLITTER GLUE.**
DON'T WORRY. I'M SURE ONCE I GET HOME, I'LL GO BACK TO BEING MY NORMAL SELF.
NO! I MEAN—DON'T GO BACK ON ACCOUNT OF ME. I—I KINDA **LIKE** IT.
SOMEONE FEED ME TO A ZOMBIE AND PUT ME OUT OF MY MISERY.
GLADLY!

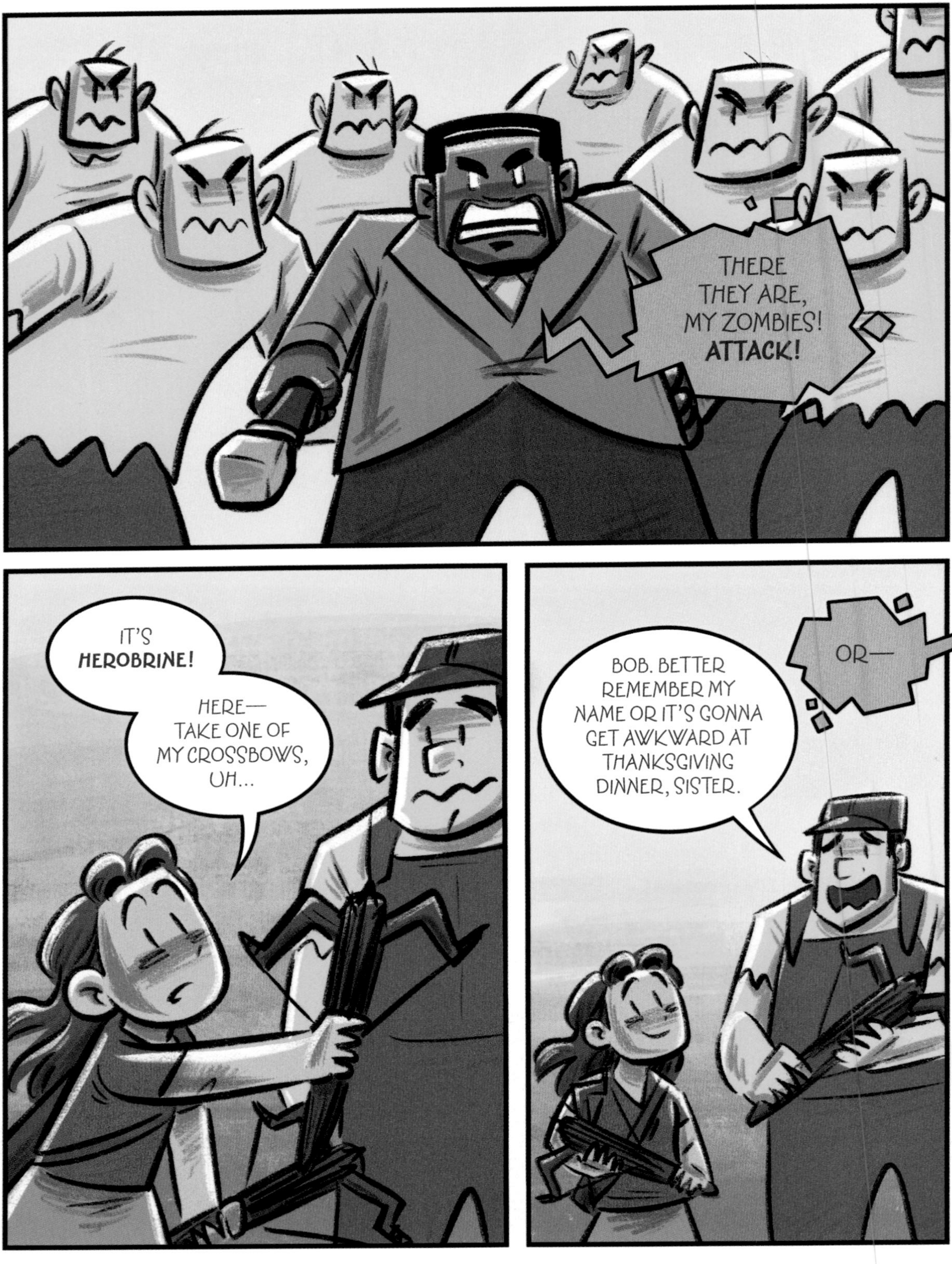
THERE THEY ARE, MY ZOMBIES! **ATTACK!**
IT'S **HEROBRINE!**
HERE— TAKE ONE OF MY CROSSBOWS, UH...
BOB. BETTER REMEMBER MY NAME OR IT'S GONNA GET AWKWARD AT THANKSGIVING DINNER, SISTER.
OR—

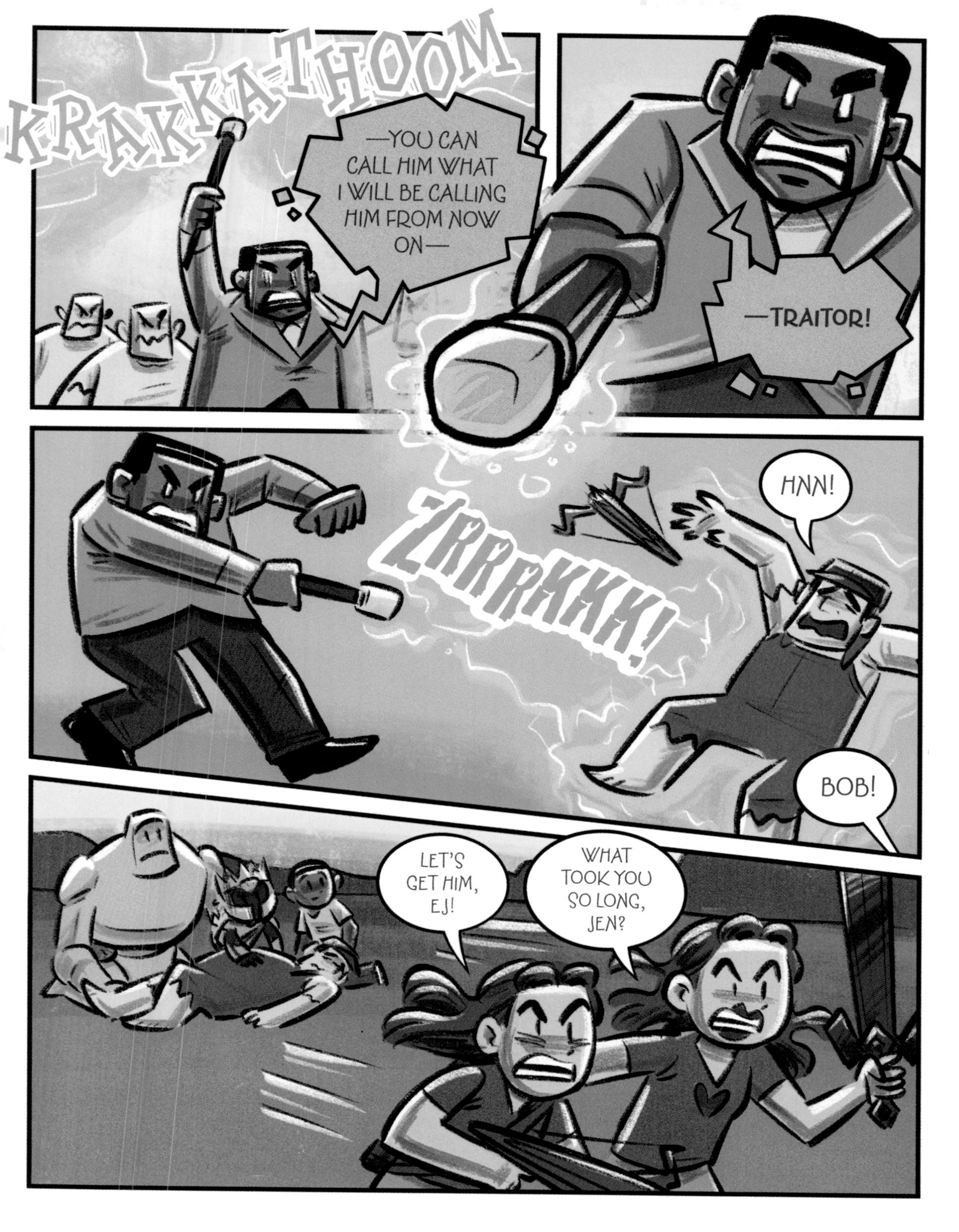
KRAKKA-THOOM
—YOU CAN CALL HIM WHAT I WILL BE CALLING HIM FROM NOW ON—
—TRAITOR!
ZRRRKKKK!
HNN!
BOB!
LET'S GET HIM, EJ!
WHAT TOOK YOU SO LONG, JEN?

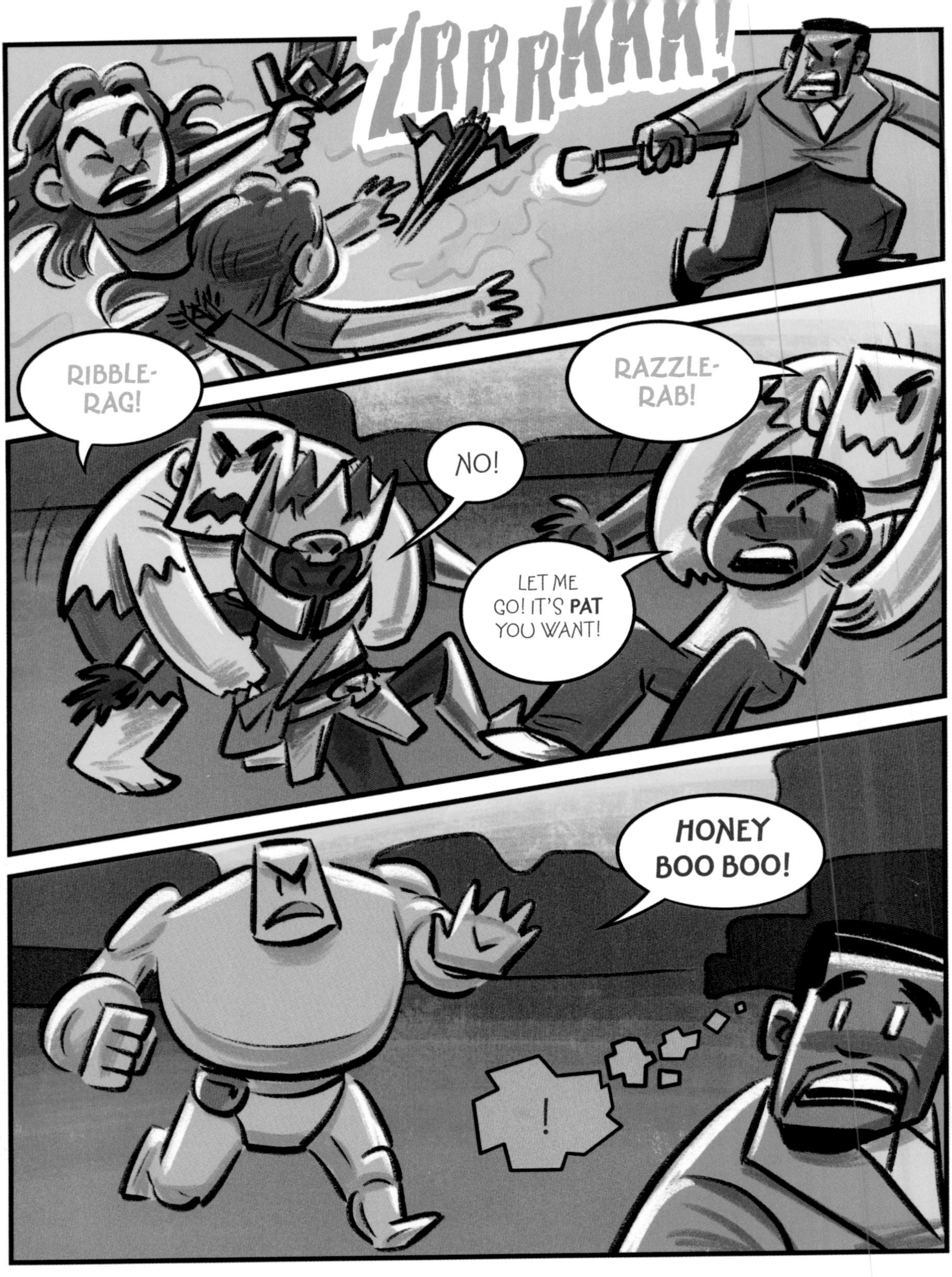
ZRRRKKK!
RIBBLE-RAG!
RAZZLE-RAB!
NO!
LET ME GO! IT'S **PAT** YOU WANT!
HONEY BOO BOO!
!

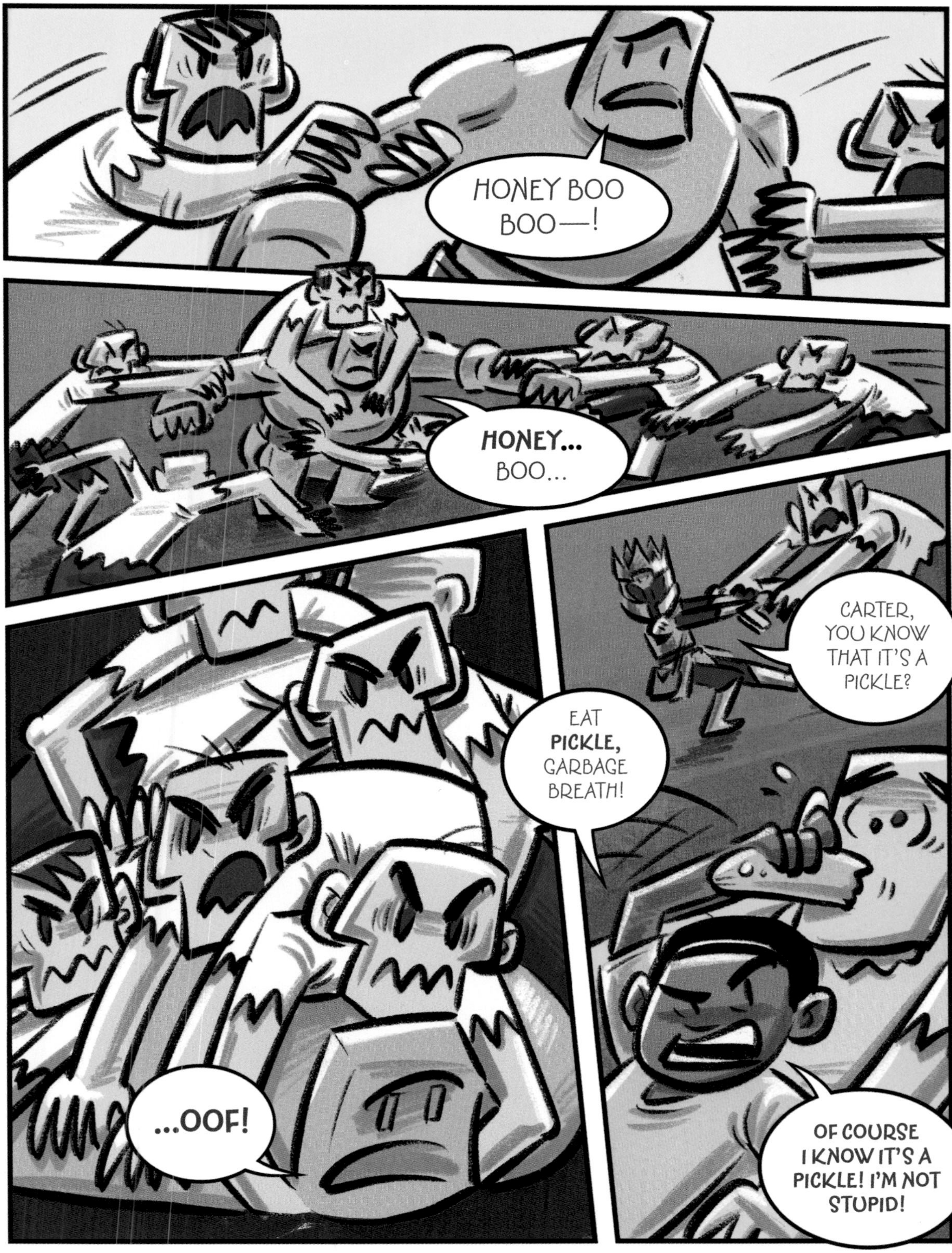
HONEY BOO BOO—!
HONEY... BOO...
CARTER, YOU KNOW THAT IT'S A PICKLE?
EAT PICKLE, GARBAGE BREATH!
...OOF!
OF COURSE I KNOW IT'S A PICKLE! I'M NOT STUPID!

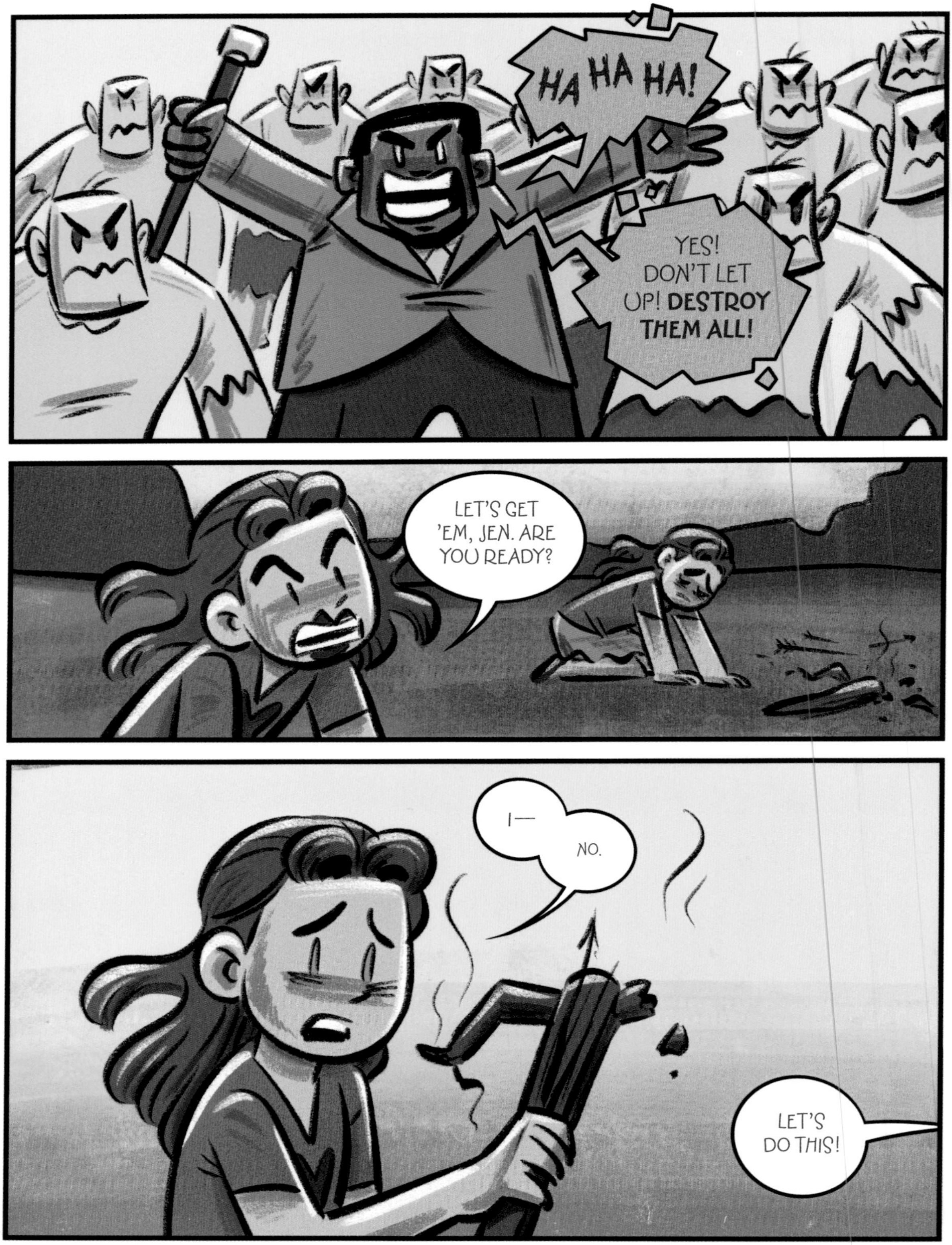
HA HA HA!
YES! DON'T LET UP! **DESTROY THEM ALL!**
LET'S GET 'EM, JEN. ARE YOU READY?
I—
NO.
LET'S DO THIS!

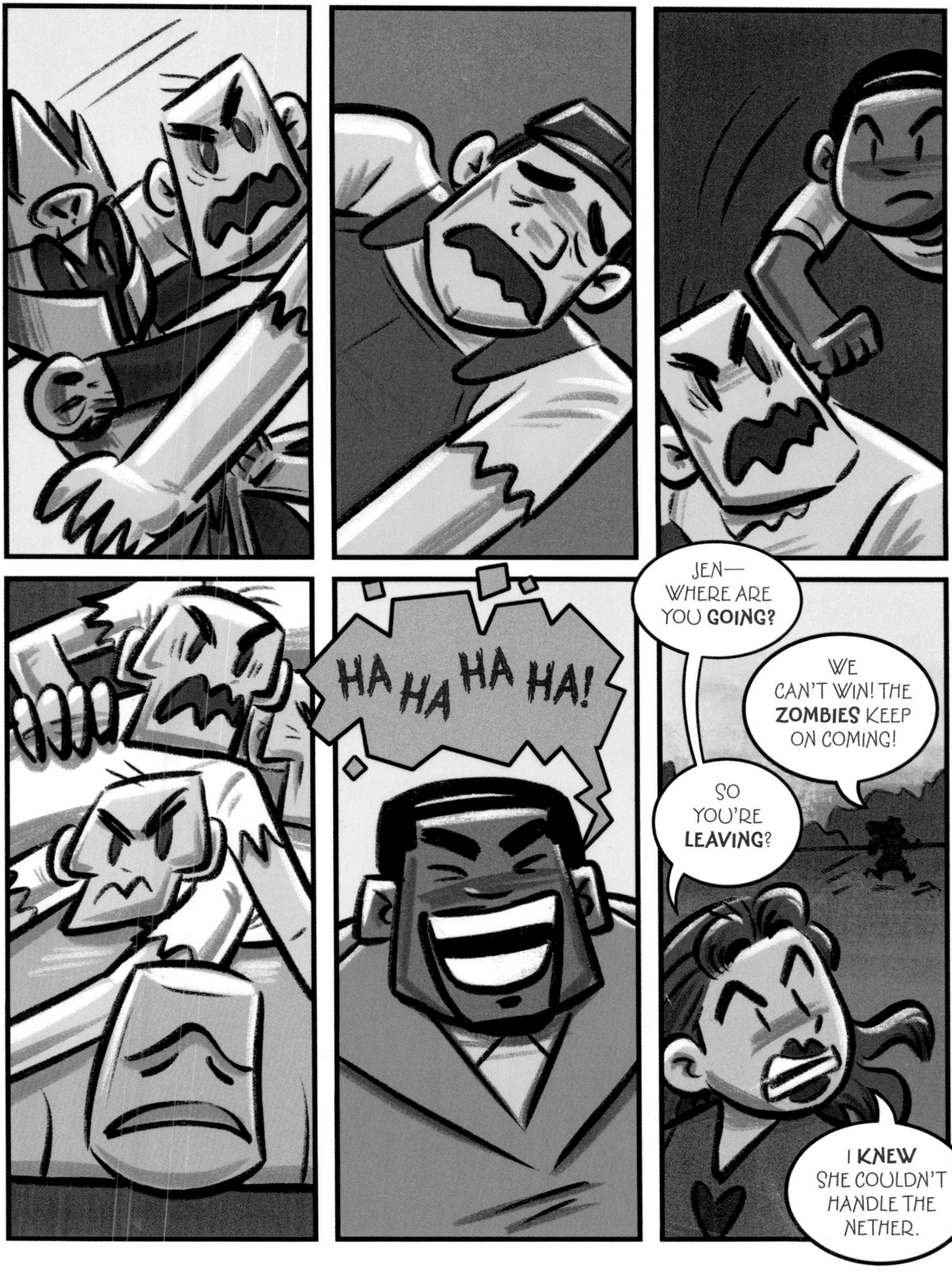
HA HA HA HA!
JEN—WHERE ARE YOU GOING?
WE CAN'T WIN! THE ZOMBIES KEEP ON COMING!
SO YOU'RE LEAVING?
I KNEW SHE COULDN'T HANDLE THE NETHER.

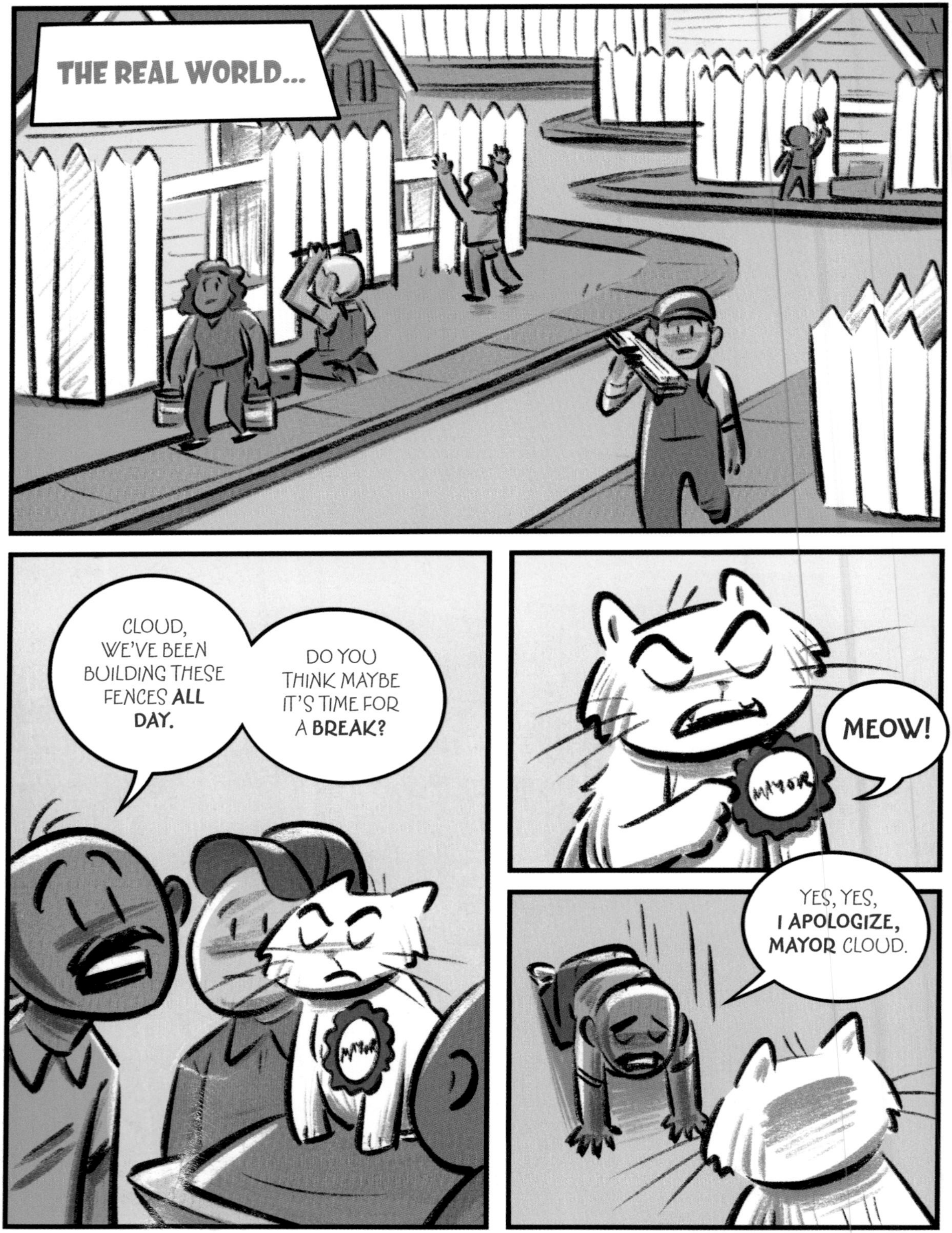
THE REAL WORLD...
CLOUD, WE'VE BEEN BUILDING THESE FENCES ALL DAY.
DO YOU THINK MAYBE IT'S TIME FOR A BREAK?
MEOW!
MAYOR
YES, YES, I APOLOGIZE, MAYOR CLOUD.

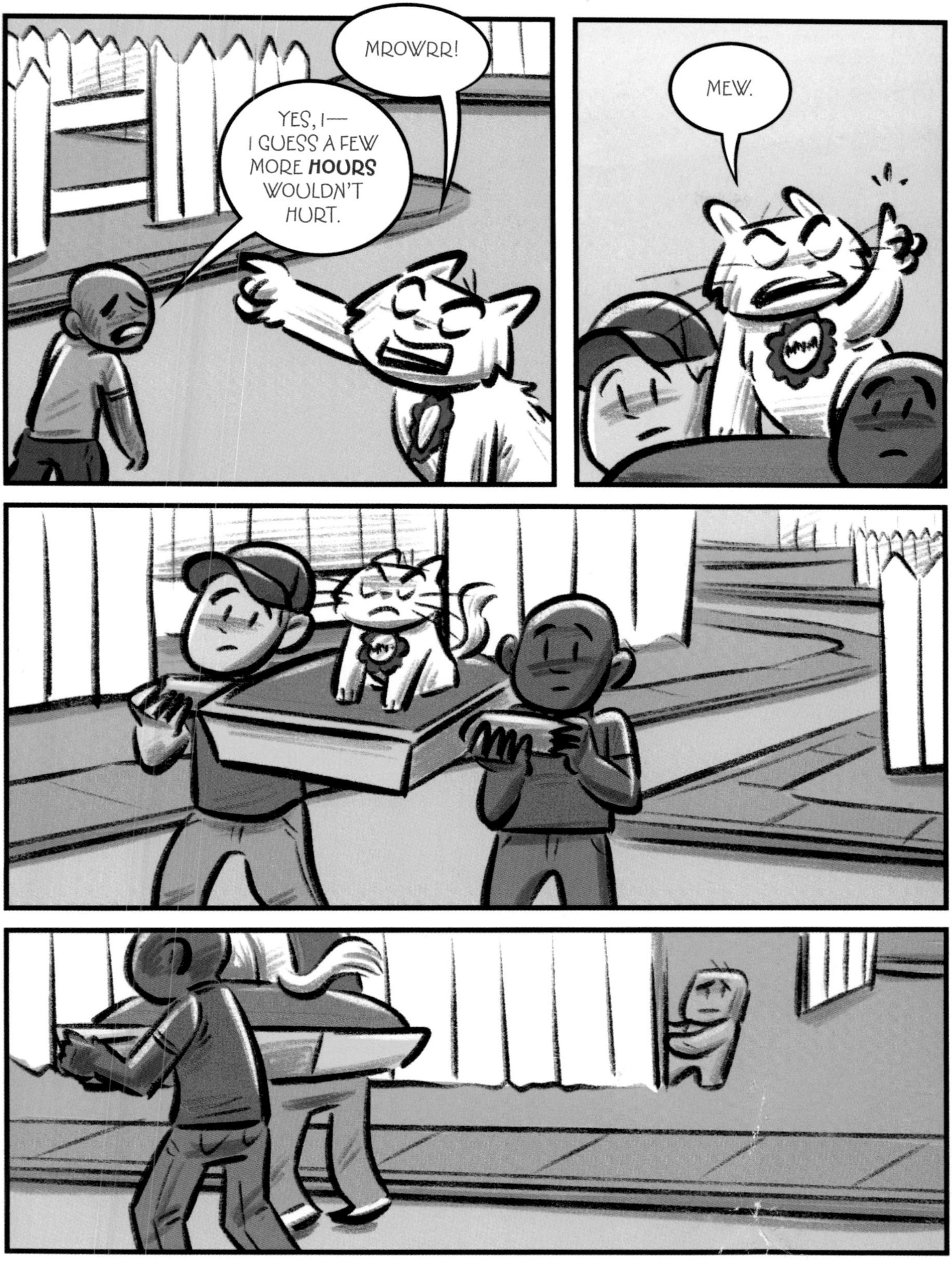
MROWRR!
YES, I— I GUESS A FEW MORE **HOURS** WOULDN'T HURT.
MEW.

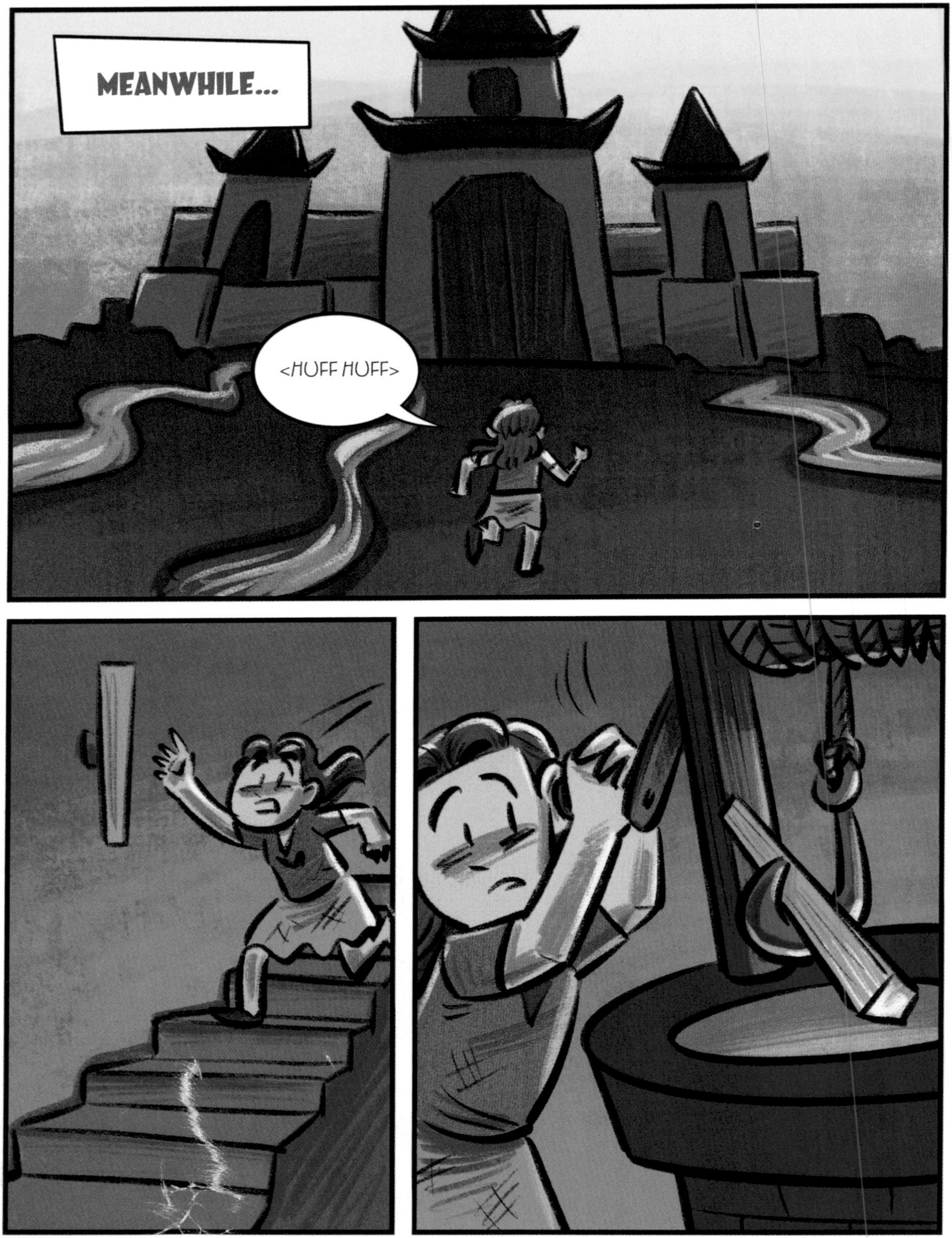
MEANWHILE...
<HUFF HUFF>

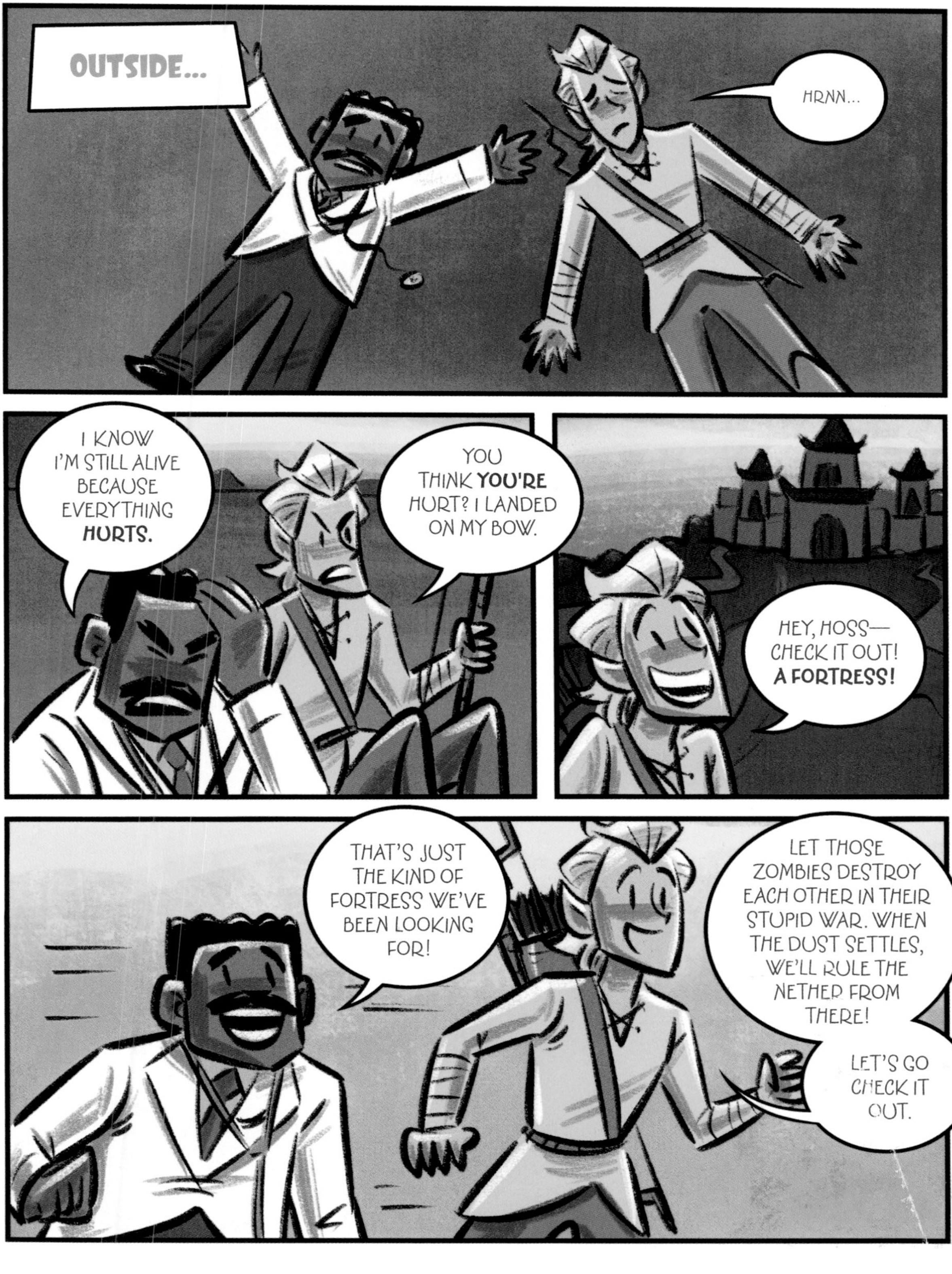
OUTSIDE...
HRNN...
I KNOW I'M STILL ALIVE BECAUSE EVERYTHING **HURTS.**
YOU THINK **YOU'RE** HURT? I LANDED ON MY BOW.
HEY, HOSS— CHECK IT OUT! **A FORTRESS!**
THAT'S JUST THE KIND OF FORTRESS WE'VE BEEN LOOKING FOR!
LET THOSE ZOMBIES DESTROY EACH OTHER IN THEIR STUPID WAR. WHEN THE DUST SETTLES, WE'LL RULE THE NETHER FROM THERE!
LET'S GO CHECK IT OUT.

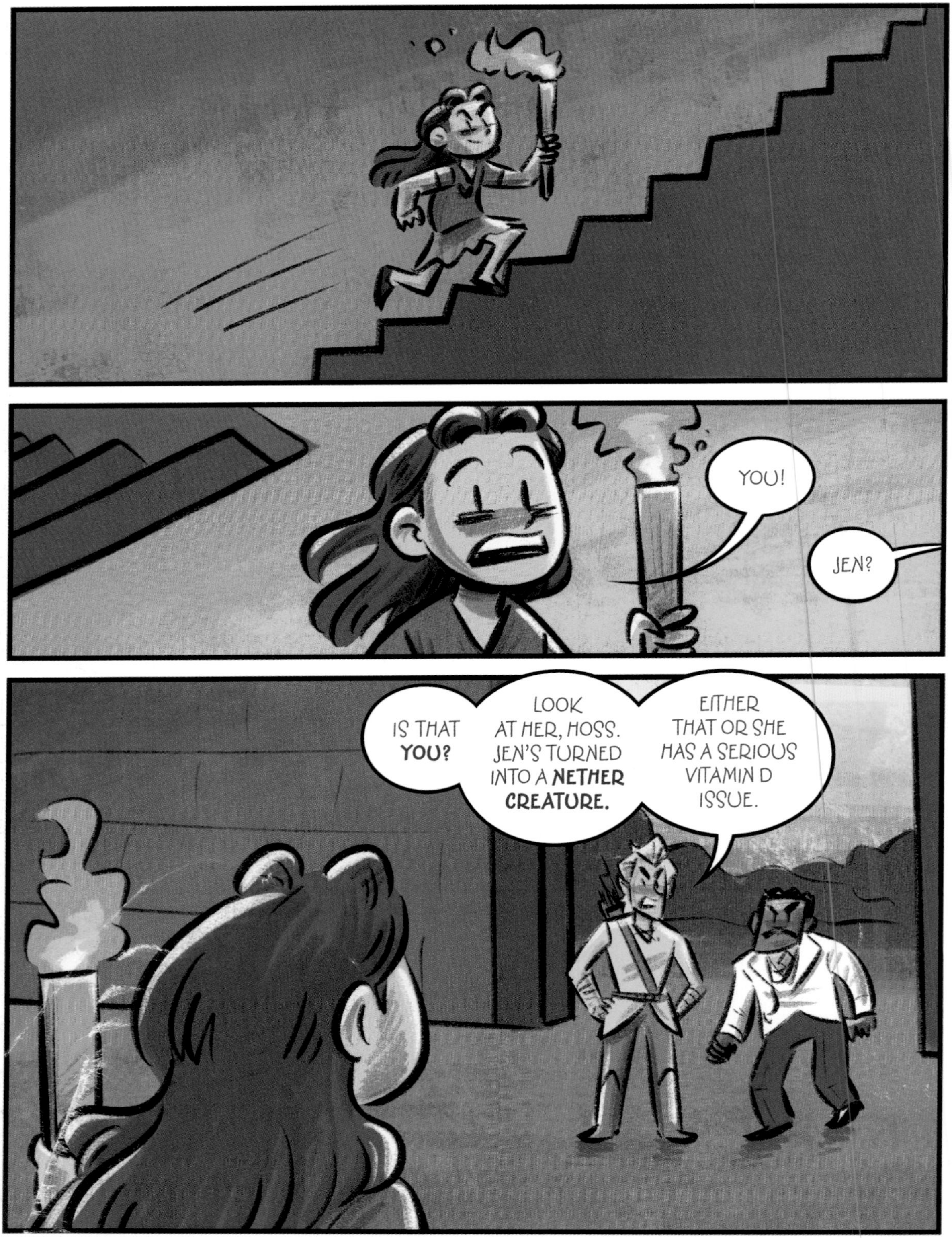
YOU!
JEN?
IS THAT **YOU?**
LOOK AT HER, HOSS. JEN'S TURNED INTO A **NETHER CREATURE.**
EITHER THAT OR SHE HAS A SERIOUS VITAMIN D ISSUE.

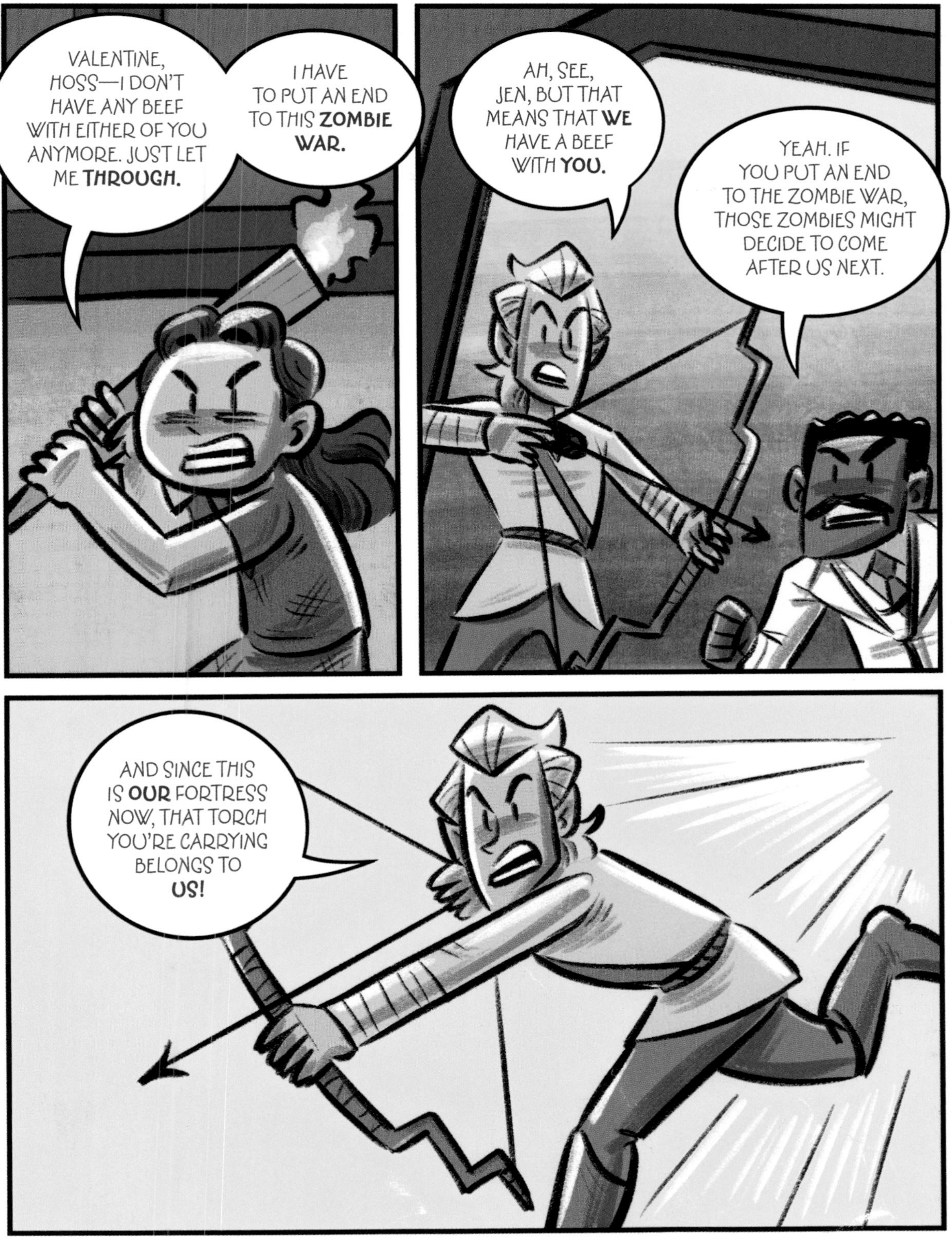
VALENTINE, HOSS—I DON'T HAVE ANY BEEF WITH EITHER OF YOU ANYMORE. JUST LET ME THROUGH.
I HAVE TO PUT AN END TO THIS ZOMBIE WAR.
AH, SEE, JEN, BUT THAT MEANS THAT WE HAVE A BEEF WITH YOU.
YEAH. IF YOU PUT AN END TO THE ZOMBIE WAR, THOSE ZOMBIES MIGHT DECIDE TO COME AFTER US NEXT.
AND SINCE THIS IS OUR FORTRESS NOW, THAT TORCH YOU'RE CARRYING BELONGS TO US!

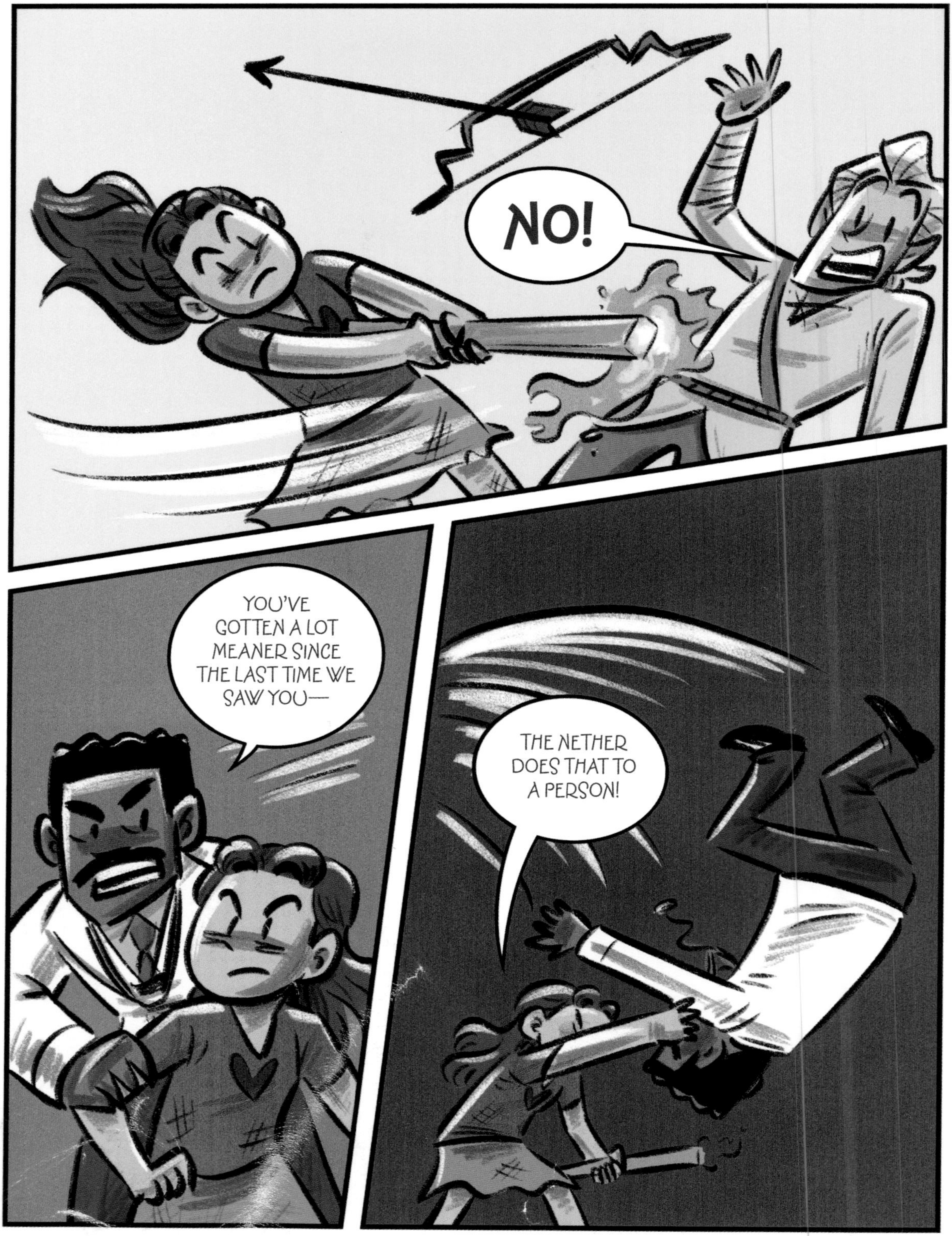
NO!
YOU'VE GOTTEN A LOT MEANER SINCE THE LAST TIME WE SAW YOU—
THE NETHER DOES THAT TO A PERSON!

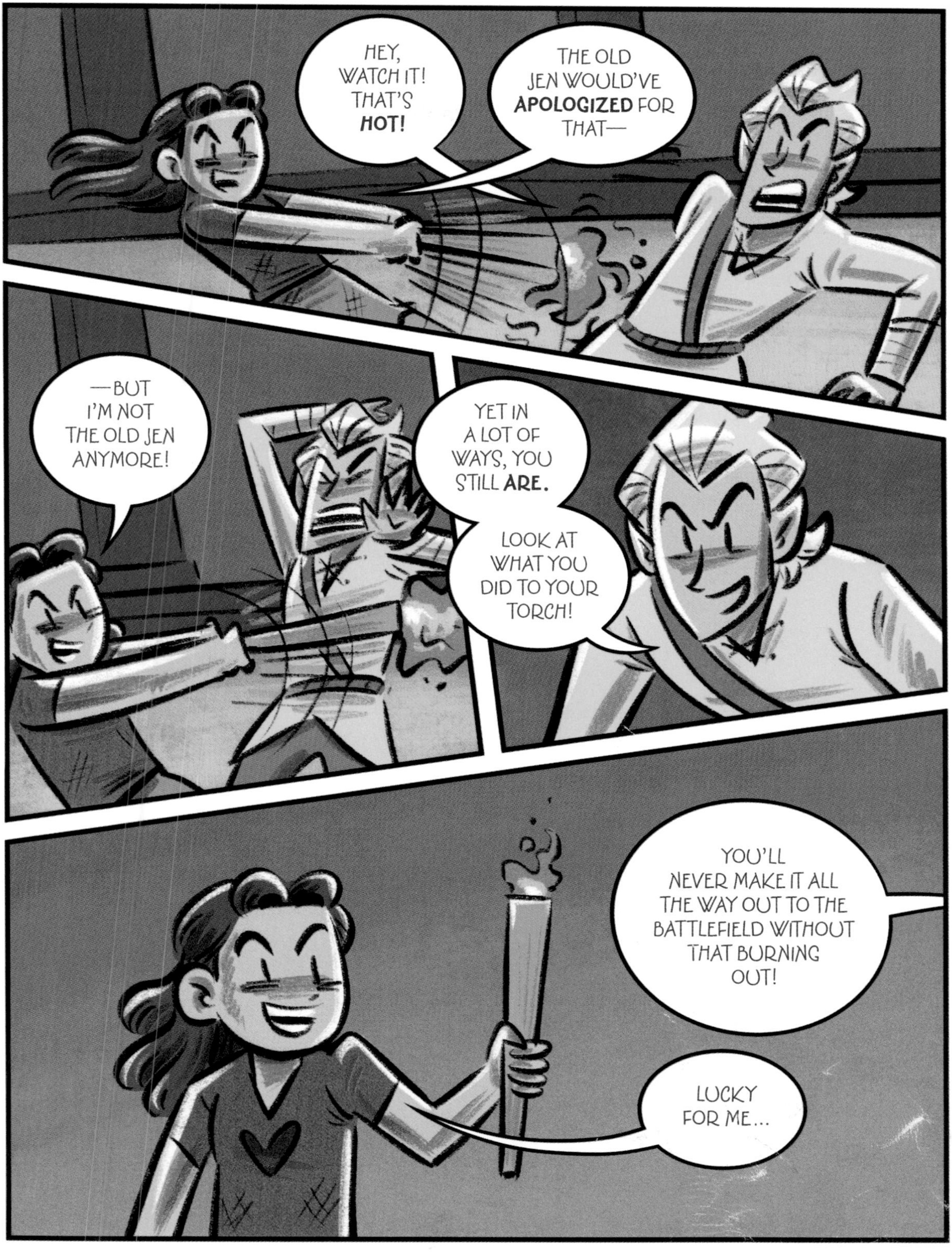
HEY, WATCH IT! THAT'S **HOT!**
THE OLD JEN WOULD'VE **APOLOGIZED** FOR THAT—
—BUT I'M NOT THE OLD JEN ANYMORE!
YET IN A LOT OF WAYS, YOU STILL **ARE.**
LOOK AT WHAT YOU DID TO YOUR TORCH!
YOU'LL NEVER MAKE IT ALL THE WAY OUT TO THE BATTLEFIELD WITHOUT THAT BURNING OUT!
LUCKY FOR ME...

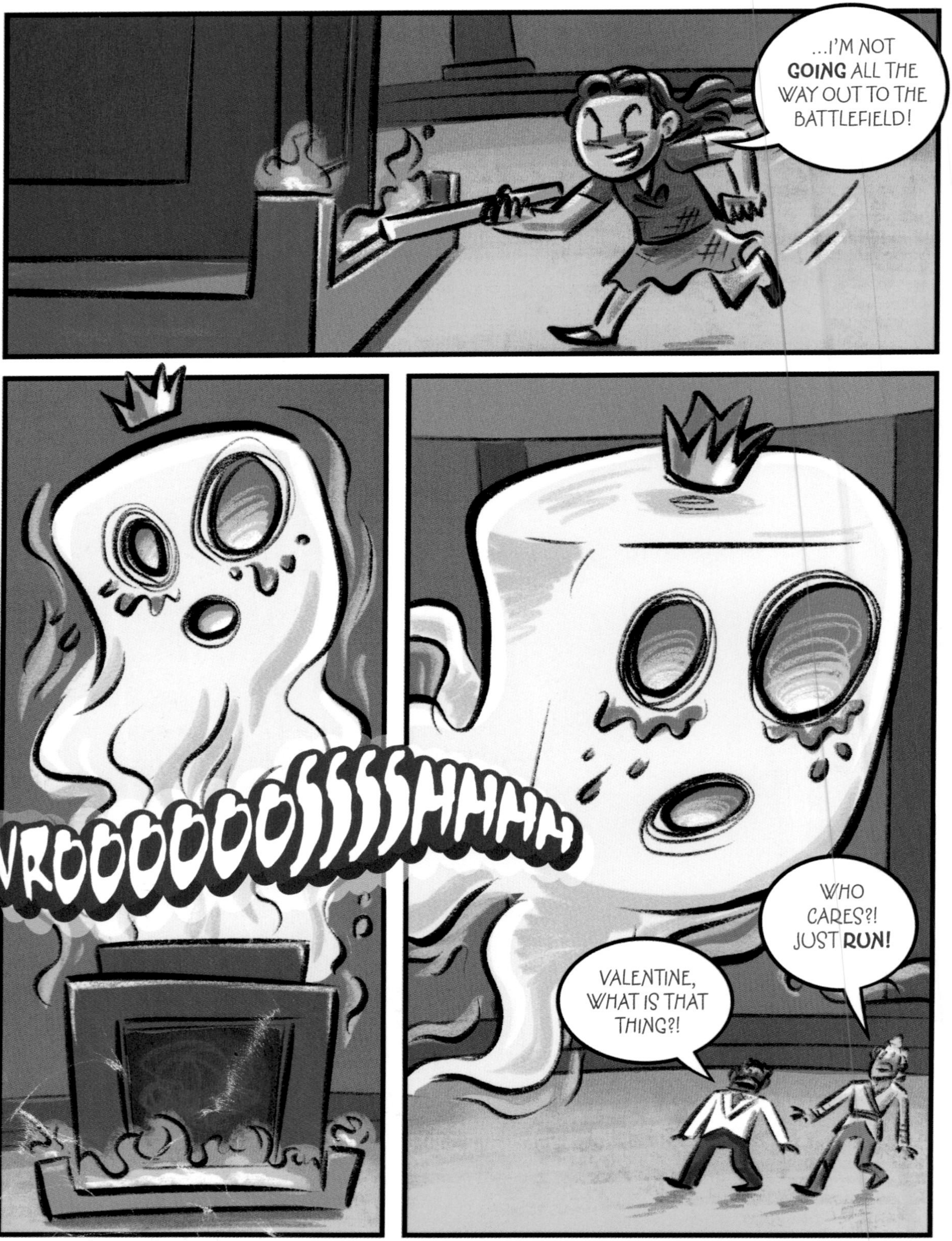
...I'M NOT **GOING** ALL THE WAY OUT TO THE BATTLEFIELD!
VROOOOOOOOSSSSSHHHHH
VALENTINE, WHAT IS THAT THING?!
WHO CARES?! JUST **RUN!**

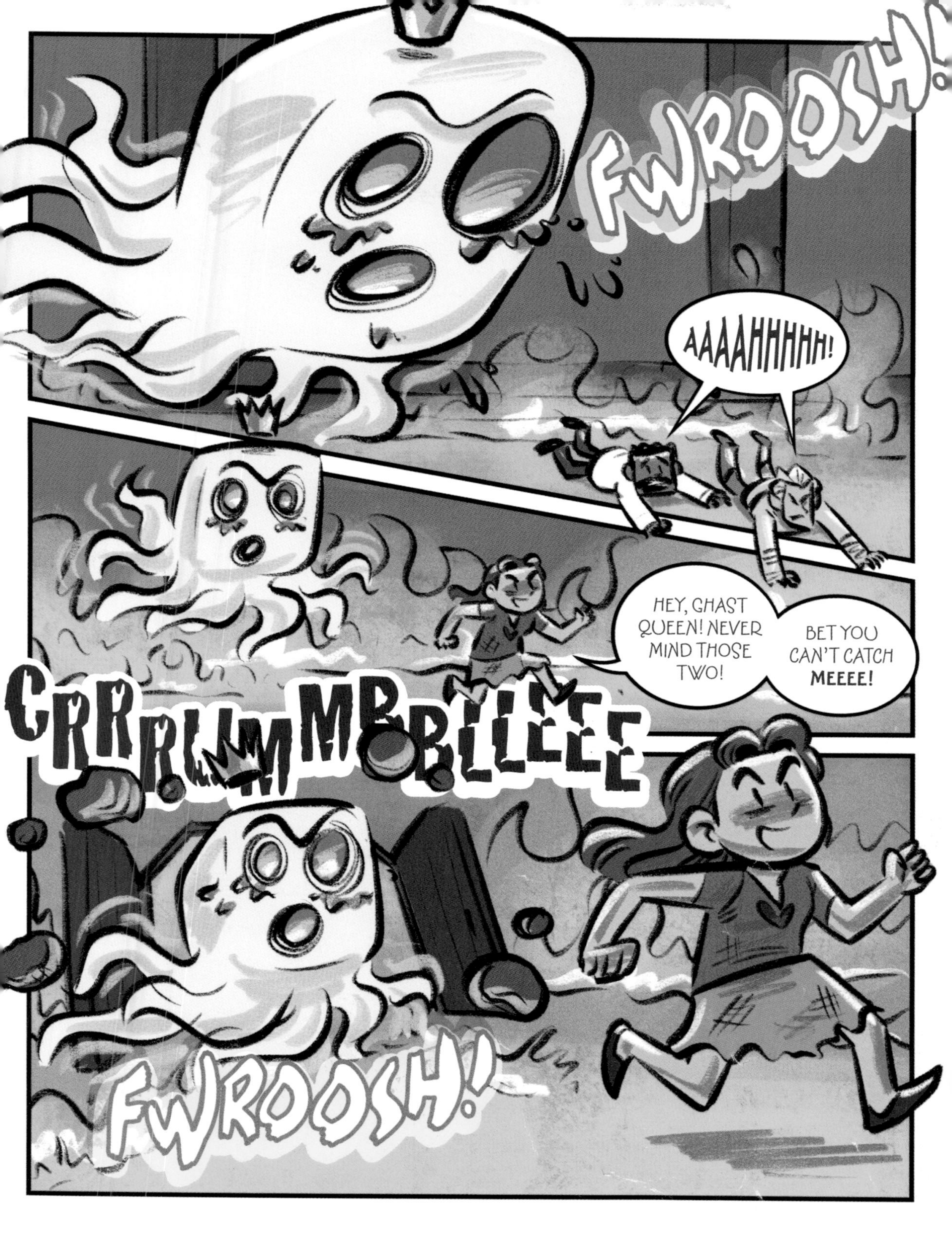
FWROOSH!
AAAAHHHHH!
HEY, GHAST QUEEN! NEVER MIND THOSE TWO!
BET YOU CAN'T CATCH **MEEEE!**
CRRRUMMBLEEE
FWROOSH!

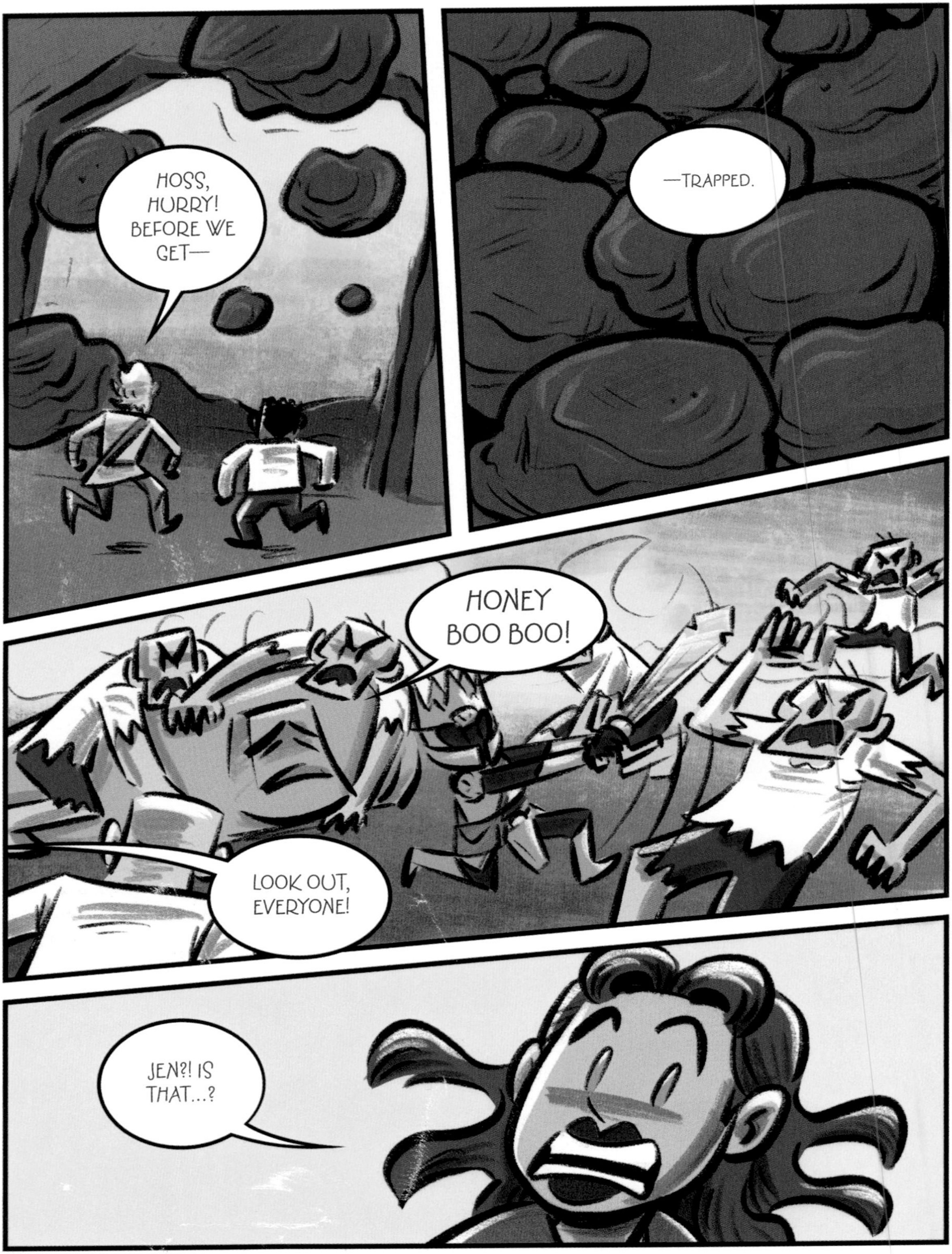
HOSS, HURRY! BEFORE WE GET—
—TRAPPED.
HONEY BOO BOO!
LOOK OUT, EVERYONE!
JEN?! IS THAT...?

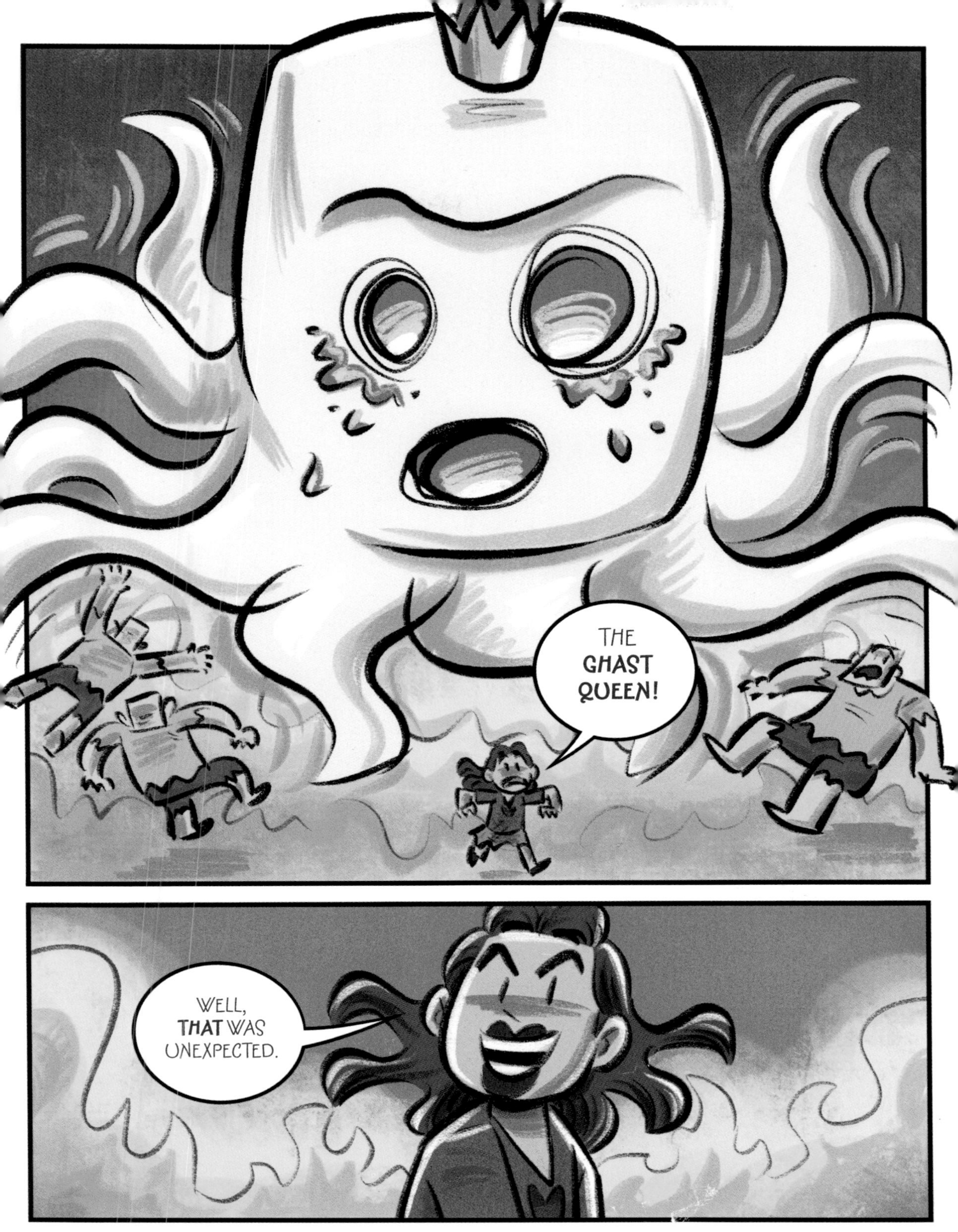
THE GHAST QUEEN!
WELL, THAT WAS UNEXPECTED.

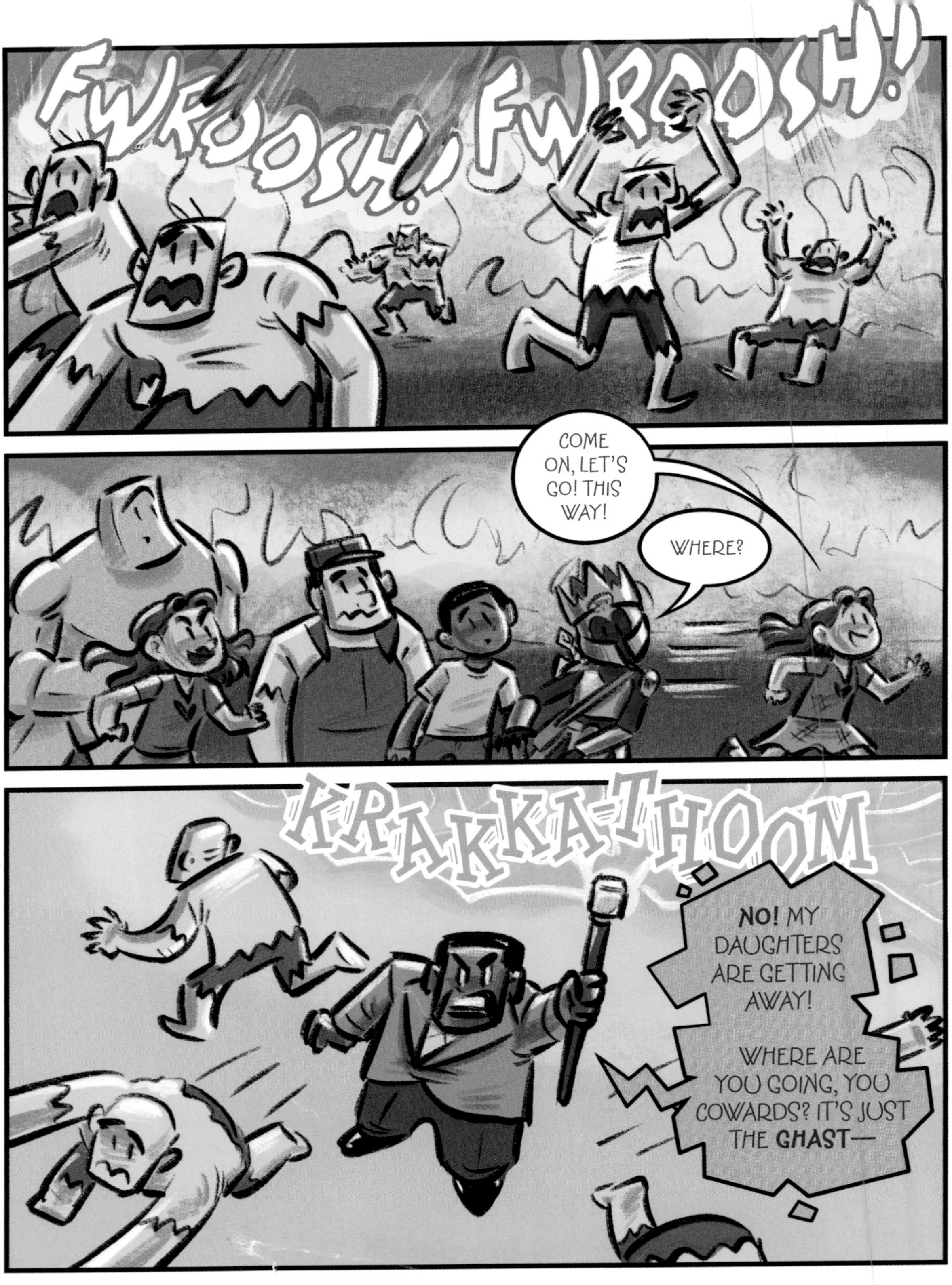
FWROOSH! FWROOSH!
COME ON, LET'S GO! THIS WAY!
WHERE?
KRAKKA-THOOM
NO! MY DAUGHTERS ARE GETTING AWAY!
WHERE ARE YOU GOING, YOU COWARDS? IT'S JUST THE GHAST—

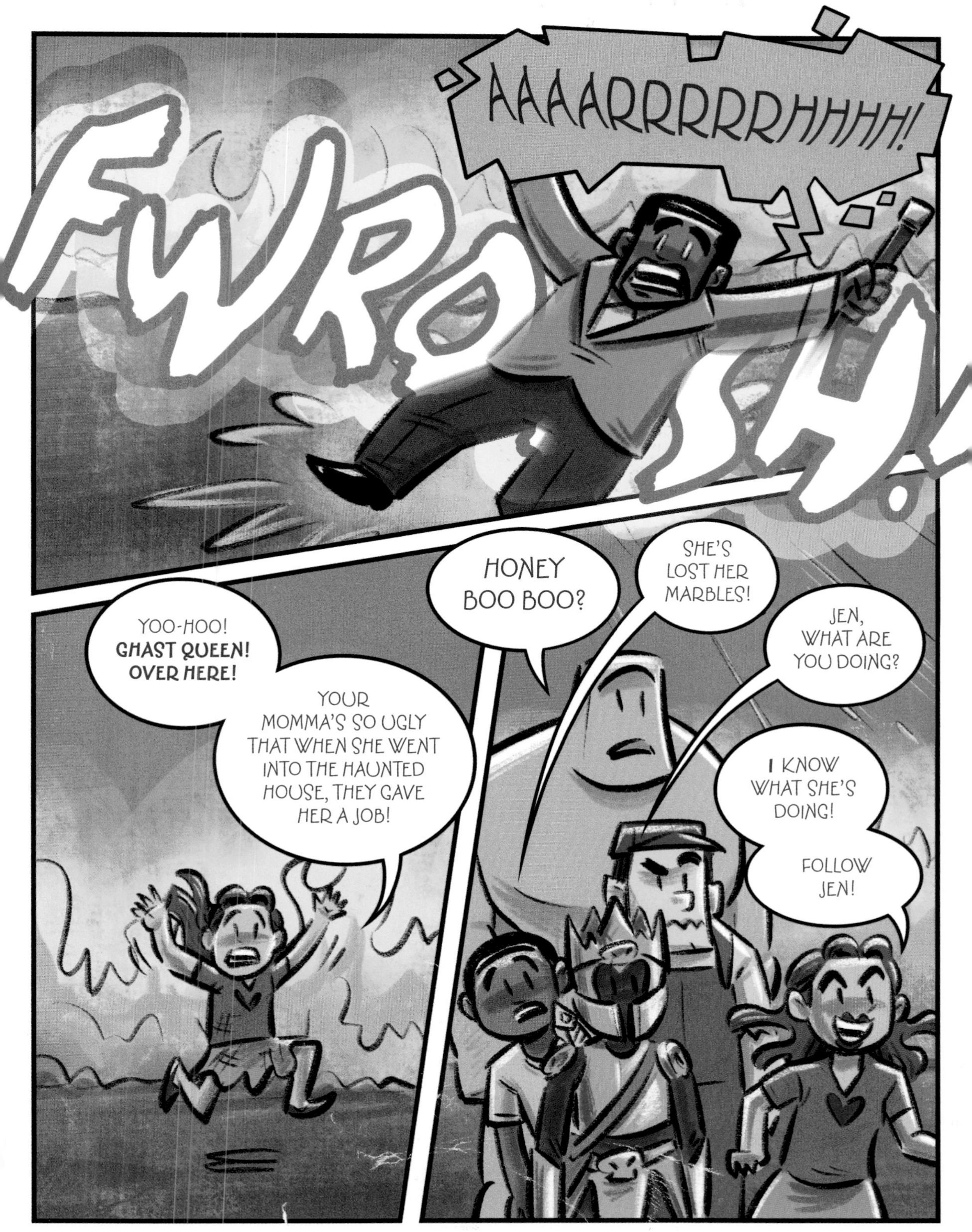
AAAARRRRRHHHH!
FWROOSH!
YOO-HOO! GHAST QUEEN! OVER HERE!
YOUR MOMMA'S SO UGLY THAT WHEN SHE WENT INTO THE HAUNTED HOUSE, THEY GAVE HER A JOB!
HONEY BOO BOO?
SHE'S LOST HER MARBLES!
JEN, WHAT ARE YOU DOING?
I KNOW WHAT SHE'S DOING!
FOLLOW JEN!

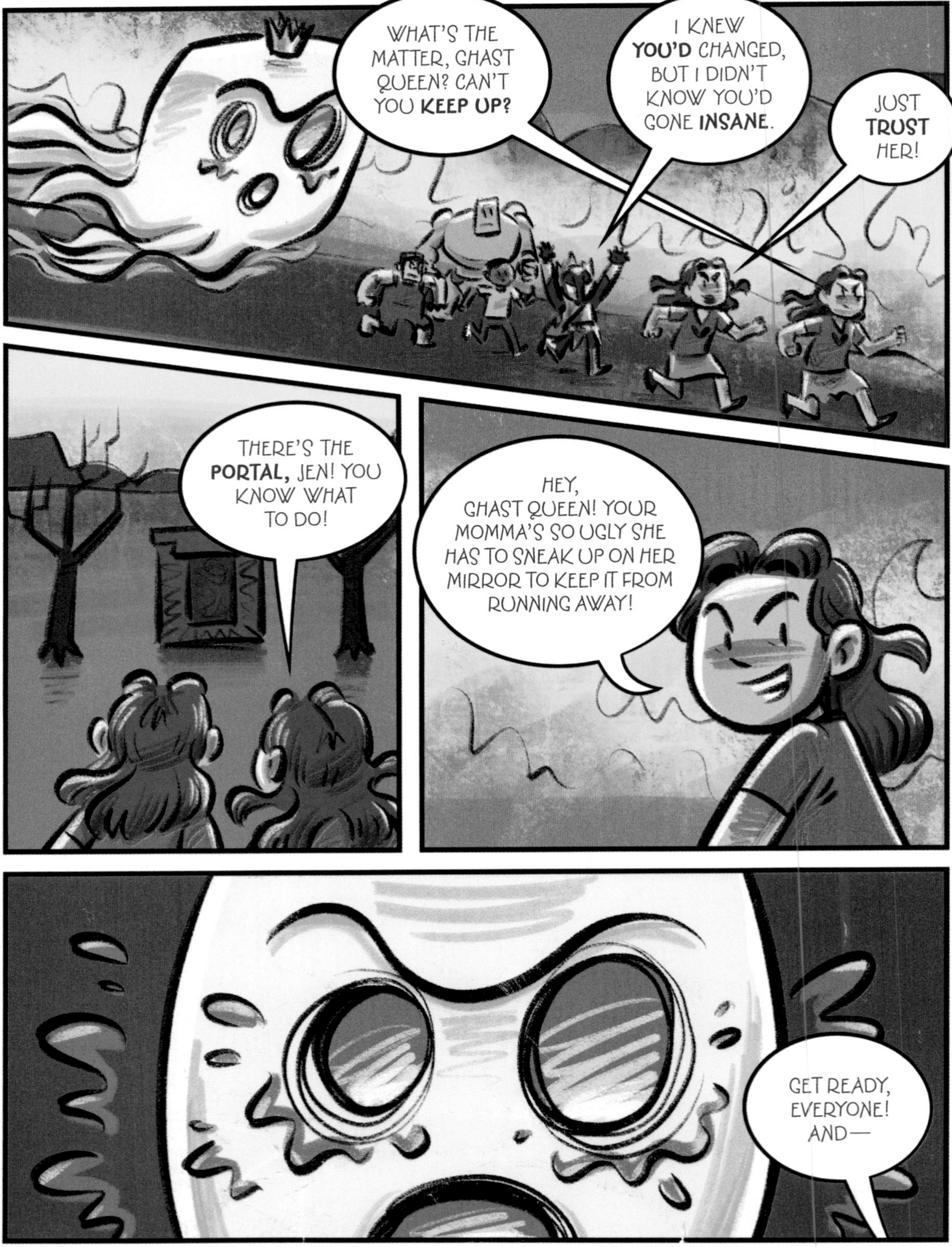
WHAT'S THE MATTER, GHAST QUEEN? CAN'T YOU KEEP UP?
I KNEW YOU'D CHANGED, BUT I DIDN'T KNOW YOU'D GONE INSANE.
JUST TRUST HER!
THERE'S THE PORTAL, JEN! YOU KNOW WHAT TO DO!
HEY, GHAST QUEEN! YOUR MOMMA'S SO UGLY SHE HAS TO SNEAK UP ON HER MIRROR TO KEEP IT FROM RUNNING AWAY!
GET READY, EVERYONE! AND—

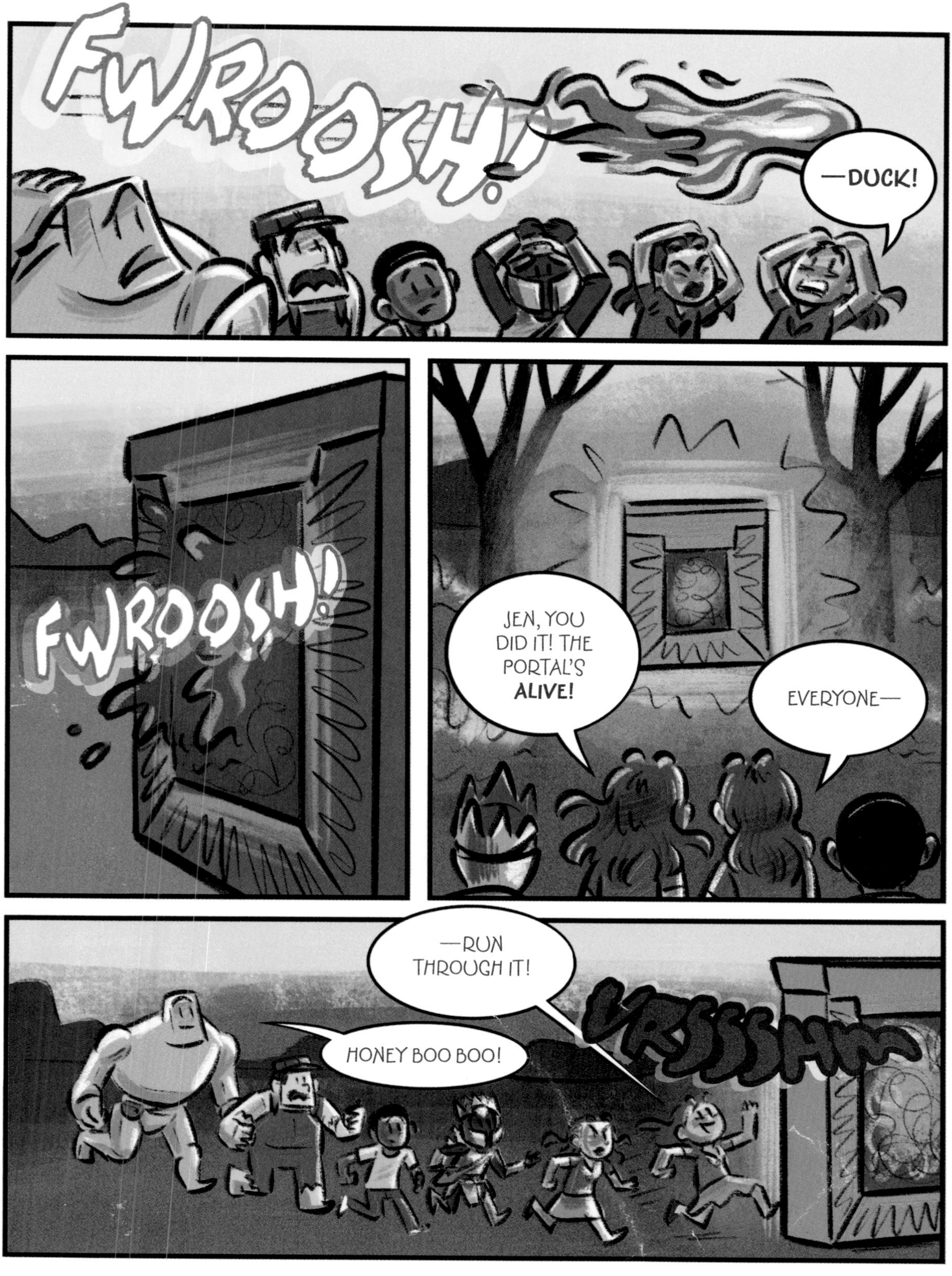
FWROOSH!
—DUCK!
FWROOSH!
JEN, YOU DID IT! THE PORTAL'S **ALIVE!**
EVERYONE—
—RUN THROUGH IT!
HONEY BOO BOO!
VRSSSHM

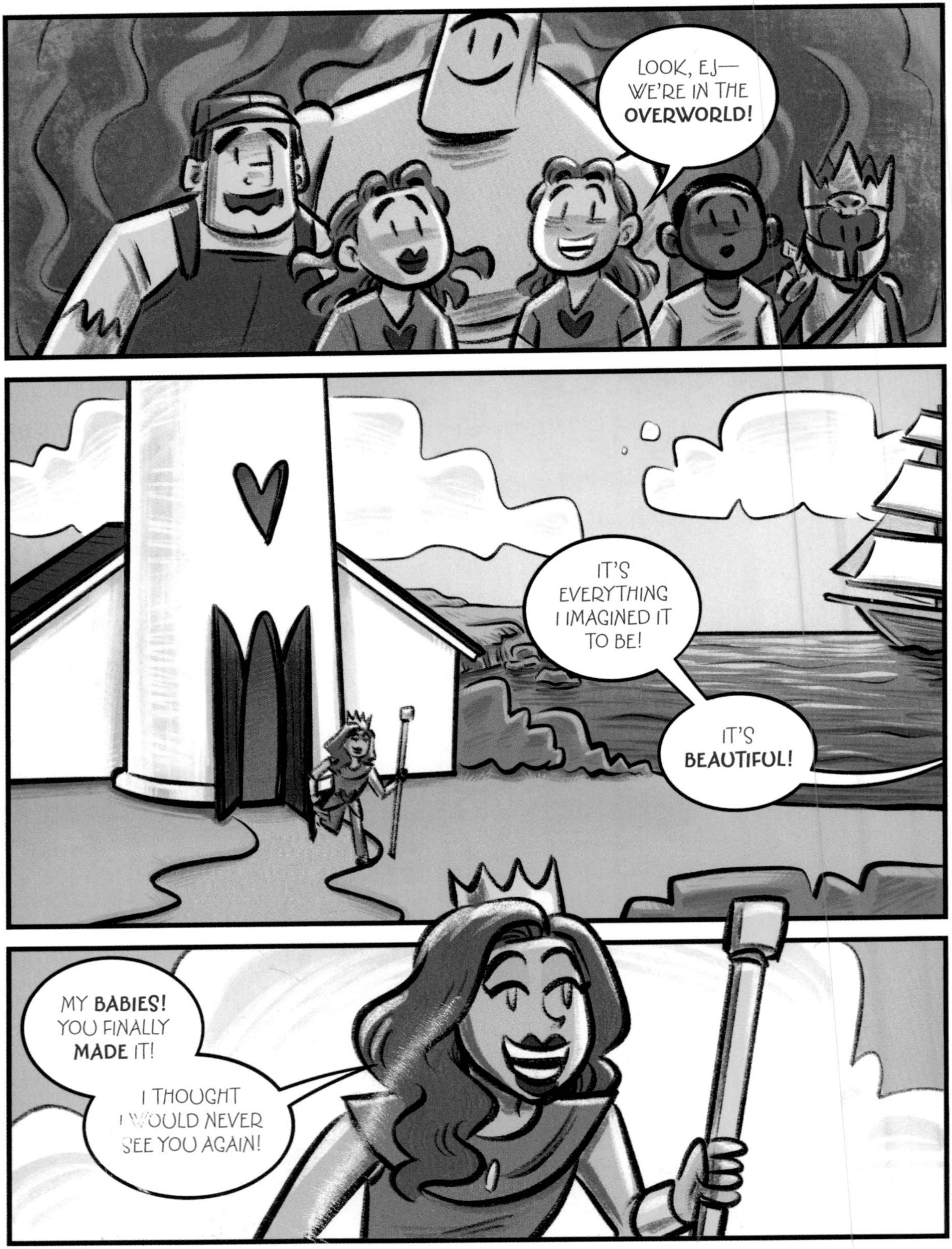
LOOK, EJ— WE'RE IN THE **OVERWORLD!**
IT'S EVERYTHING I IMAGINED IT TO BE!
IT'S **BEAUTIFUL!**
MY **BABIES!** YOU FINALLY **MADE** IT!
I THOUGHT I WOULD NEVER SEE YOU AGAIN!

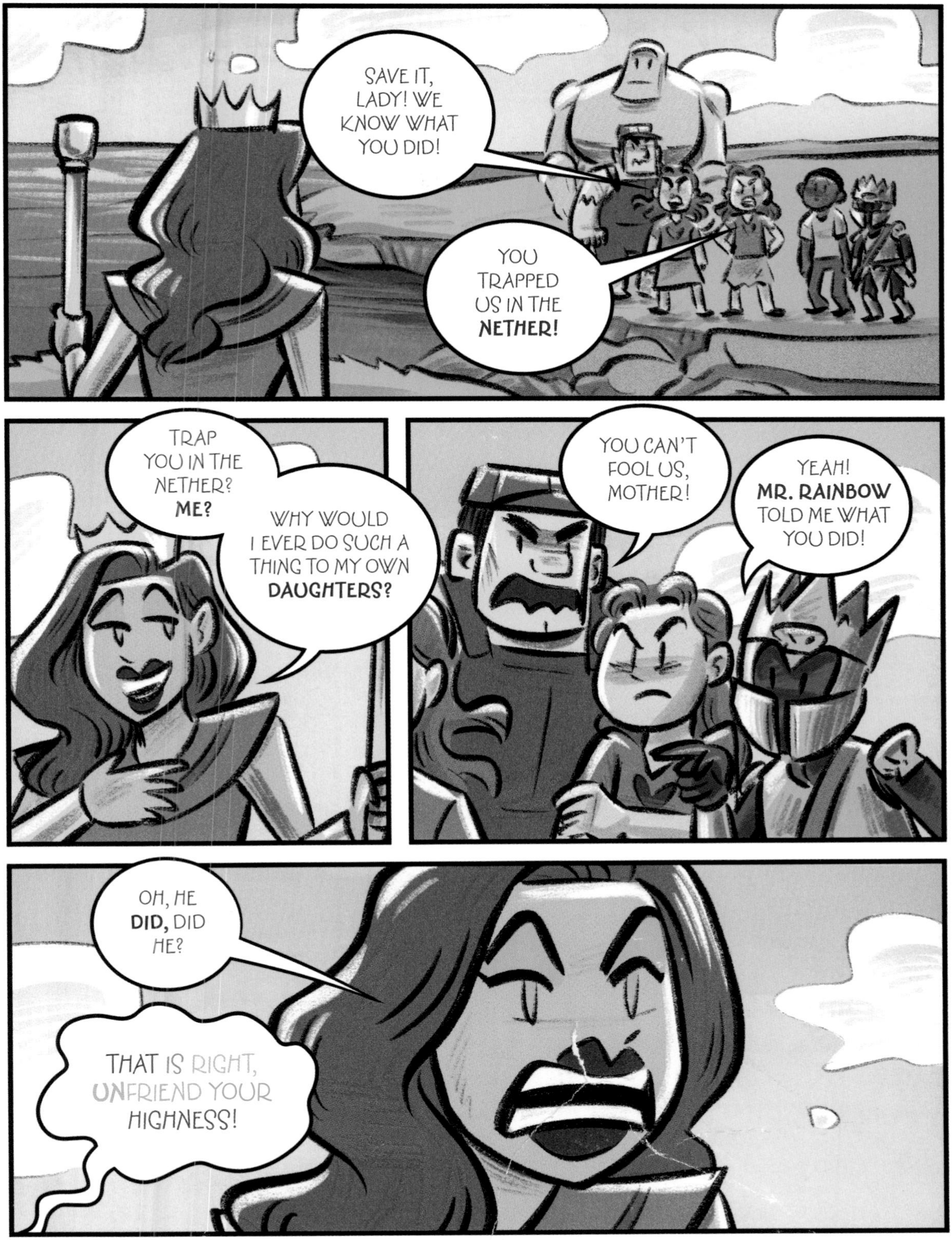
SAVE IT, LADY! WE KNOW WHAT YOU DID!
YOU TRAPPED US IN THE **NETHER!**
TRAP YOU IN THE NETHER? **ME?**
WHY WOULD I EVER DO SUCH A THING TO MY OWN **DAUGHTERS?**
YOU CAN'T FOOL US, MOTHER!
YEAH! **MR. RAINBOW** TOLD ME WHAT YOU DID!
OH, HE **DID,** DID HE?
THAT IS RIGHT, UNFRIEND YOUR HIGHNESS!

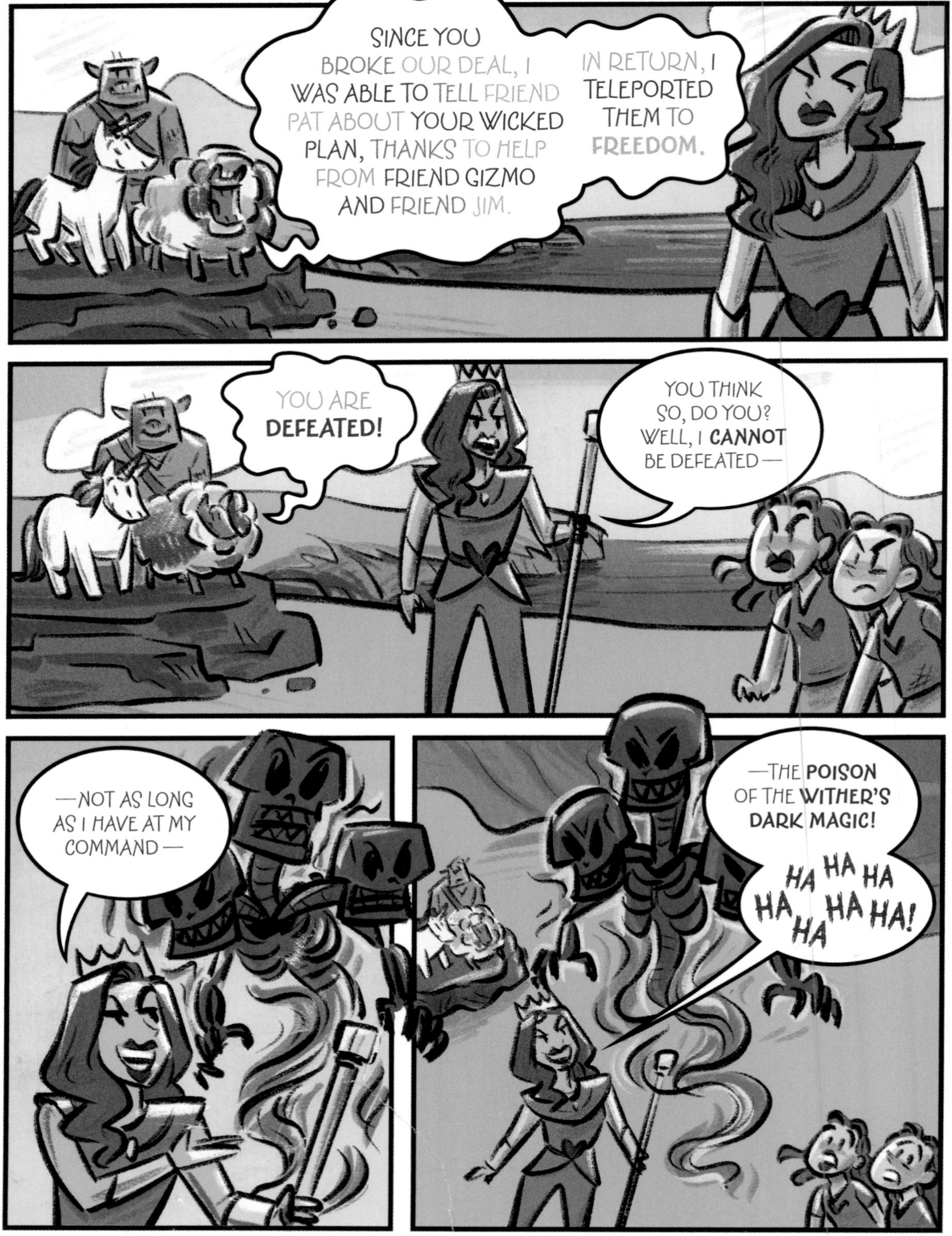
SINCE YOU BROKE OUR DEAL, I WAS ABLE TO TELL FRIEND PAT ABOUT YOUR WICKED PLAN, THANKS TO HELP FROM FRIEND GIZMO AND FRIEND JIM.
IN RETURN, I TELEPORTED THEM TO FREEDOM.
YOU ARE DEFEATED!
YOU THINK SO, DO YOU? WELL, I CANNOT BE DEFEATED—
—NOT AS LONG AS I HAVE AT MY COMMAND—
—THE POISON OF THE WITHER'S DARK MAGIC!
HA HA HA HA HA HA HA!

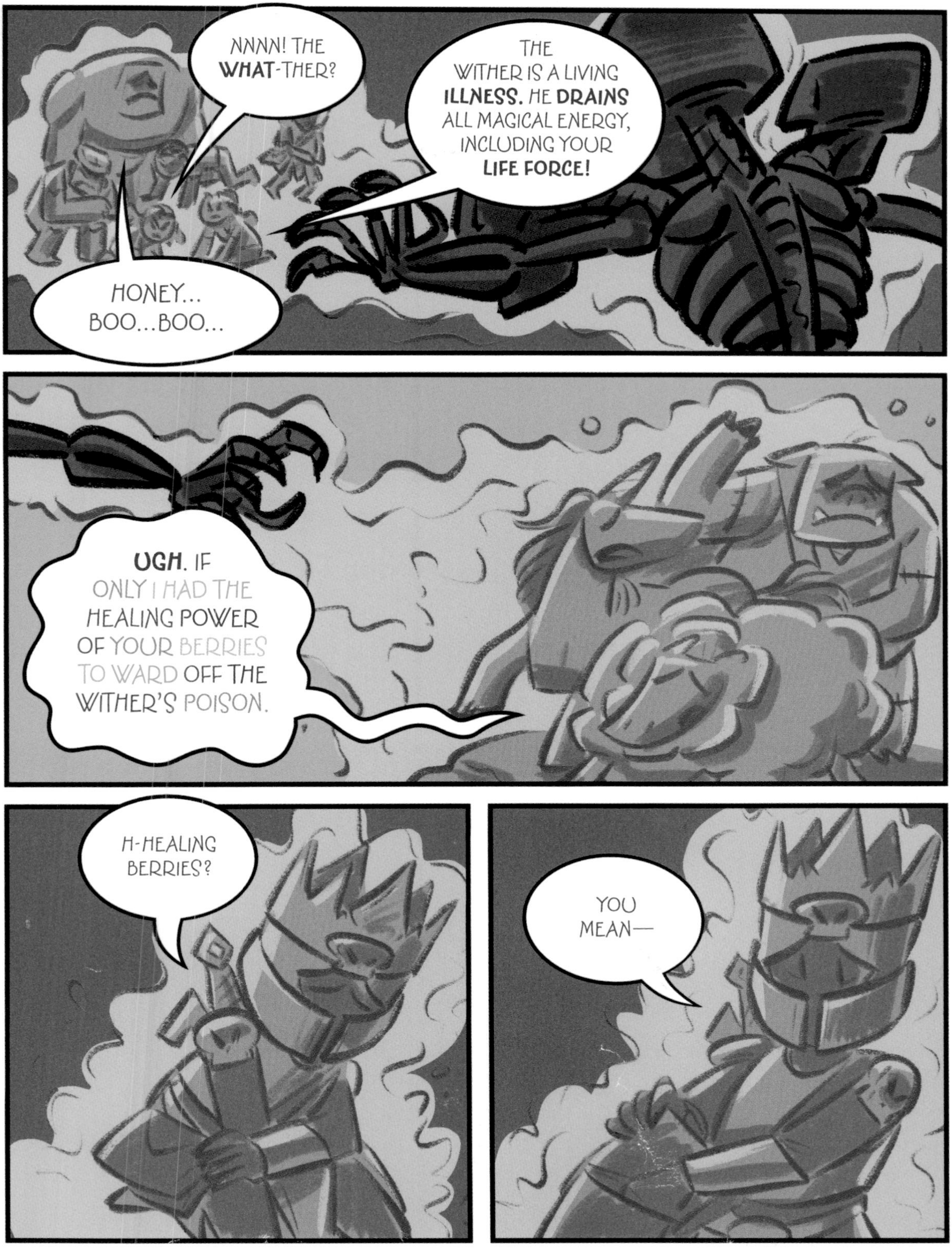
NNNN! THE WHAT-THER?
THE WITHER IS A LIVING ILLNESS. HE DRAINS ALL MAGICAL ENERGY, INCLUDING YOUR LIFE FORCE!
HONEY... BOO...BOO...
UGH. IF ONLY I HAD THE HEALING POWER OF YOUR BERRIES TO WARD OFF THE WITHER'S POISON.
H-HEALING BERRIES?
YOU MEAN—

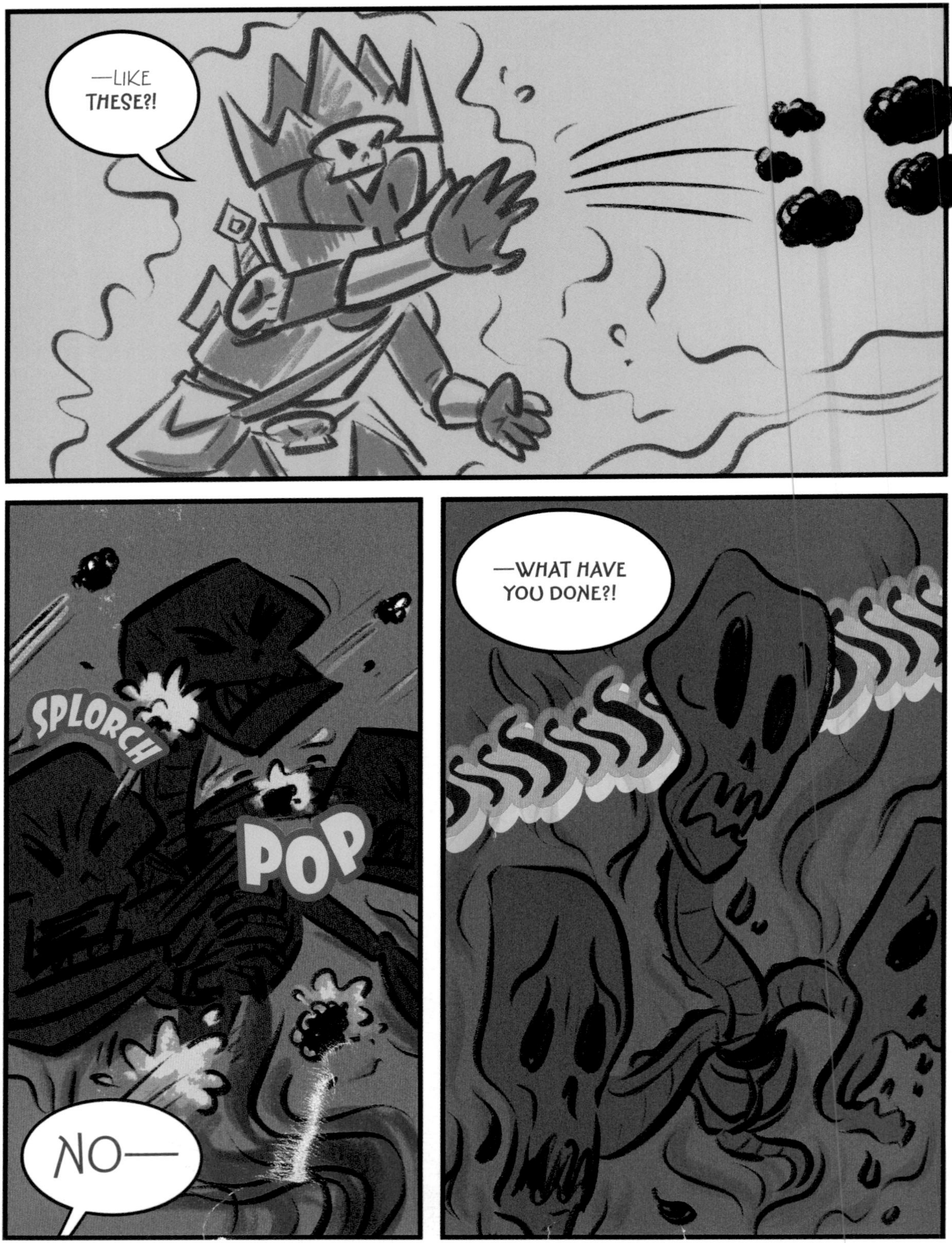
—LIKE
THESE?!
SPLORCH
POP
NO—
—WHAT HAVE
YOU DONE?!

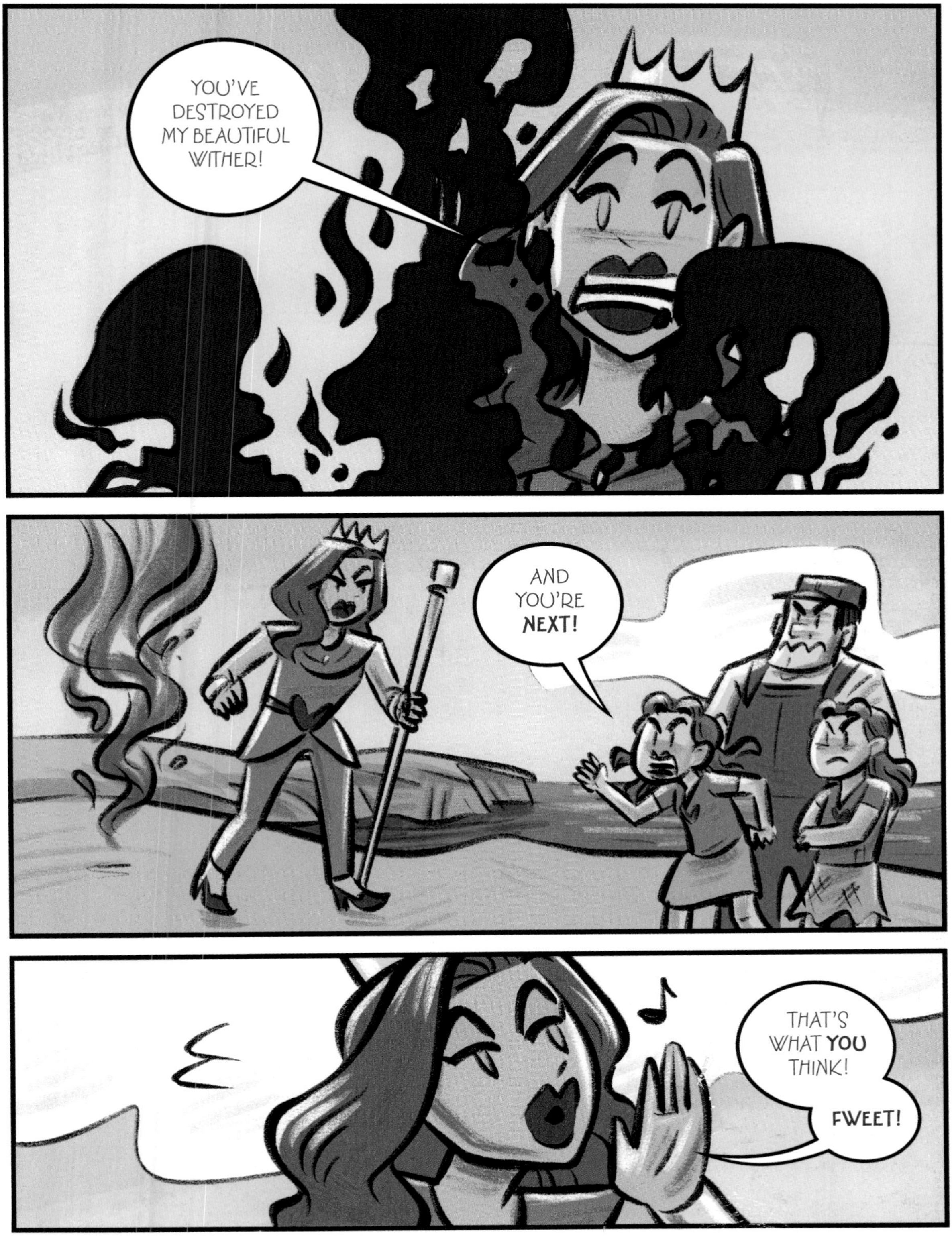
YOU'VE DESTROYED MY BEAUTIFUL WITHER!
AND YOU'RE **NEXT!**
THAT'S WHAT **YOU** THINK!
FWEET!

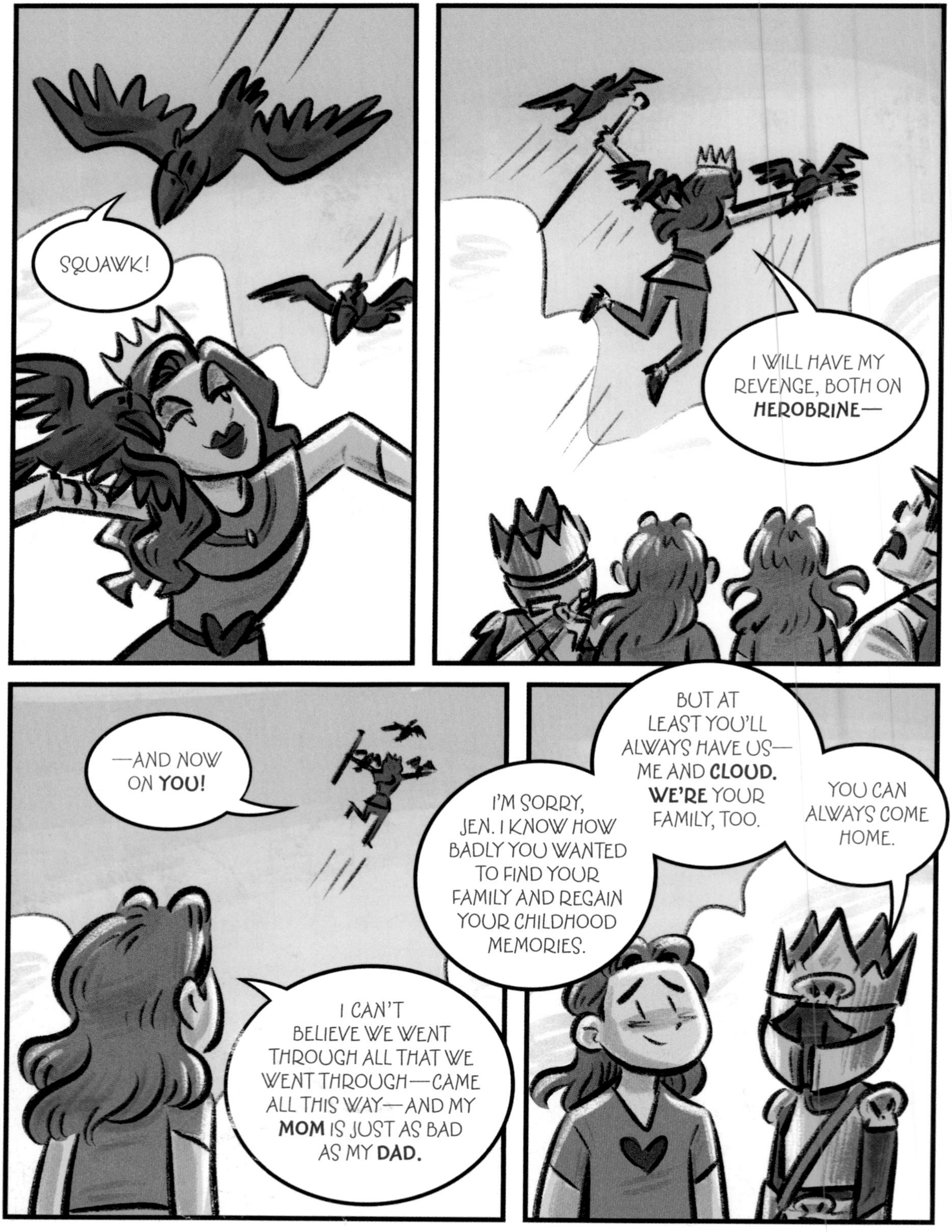
SQUAWK!
I WILL HAVE MY REVENGE, BOTH ON **HEROBRINE**—
—AND NOW ON **YOU!**
I CAN'T BELIEVE WE WENT THROUGH ALL THAT WE WENT THROUGH—CAME ALL THIS WAY—AND MY **MOM** IS JUST AS BAD AS MY **DAD.**
I'M SORRY, JEN. I KNOW HOW BADLY YOU WANTED TO FIND YOUR FAMILY AND REGAIN YOUR CHILDHOOD MEMORIES.
BUT AT LEAST YOU'LL ALWAYS HAVE US— ME AND **CLOUD. WE'RE** YOUR FAMILY, TOO.
YOU CAN ALWAYS COME HOME.

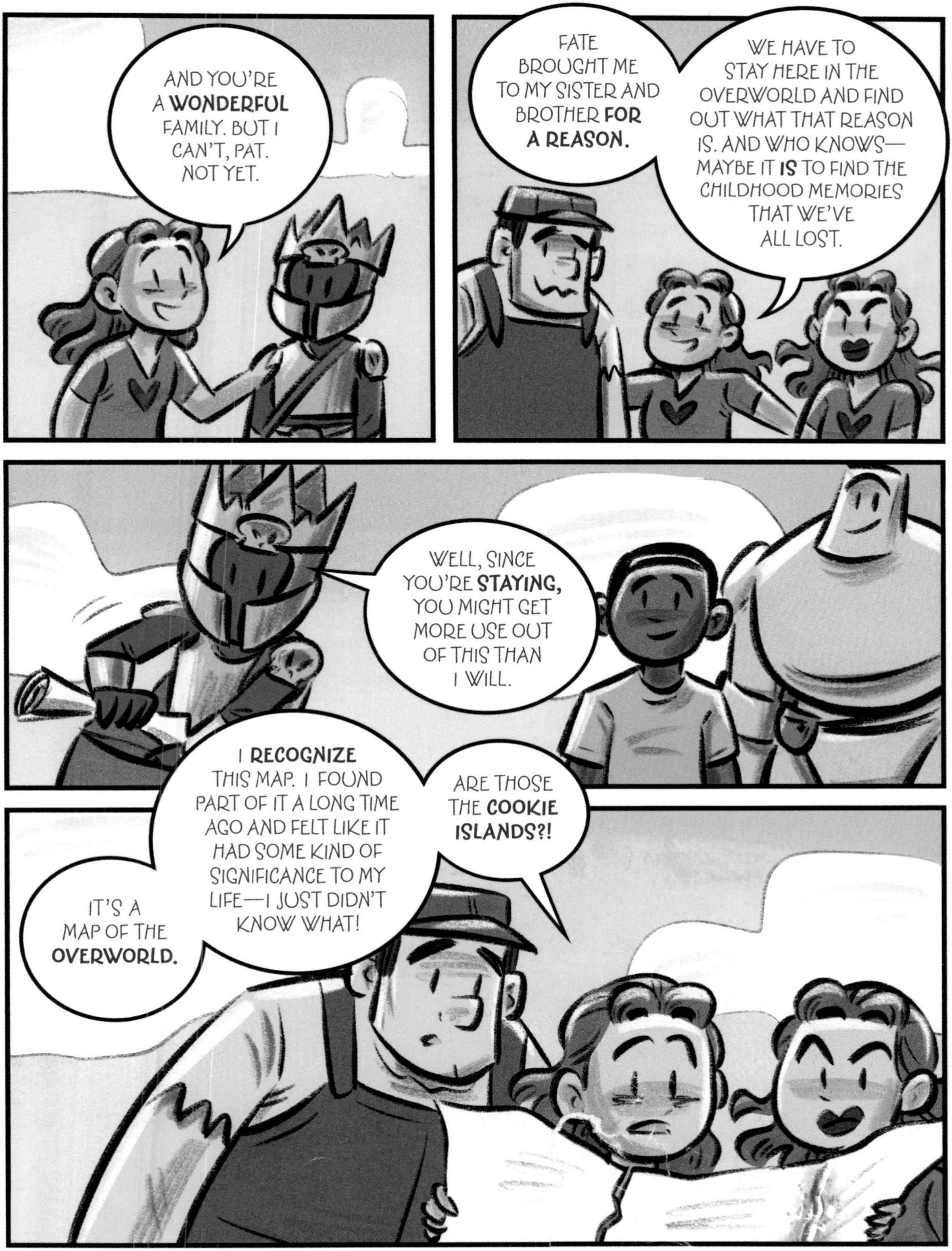
AND YOU'RE A WONDERFUL FAMILY. BUT I CAN'T, PAT. NOT YET.
FATE BROUGHT ME TO MY SISTER AND BROTHER FOR A REASON.
WE HAVE TO STAY HERE IN THE OVERWORLD AND FIND OUT WHAT THAT REASON IS. AND WHO KNOWS—MAYBE IT IS TO FIND THE CHILDHOOD MEMORIES THAT WE'VE ALL LOST.
WELL, SINCE YOU'RE STAYING, YOU MIGHT GET MORE USE OUT OF THIS THAN I WILL.
IT'S A MAP OF THE OVERWORLD.
I RECOGNIZE THIS MAP. I FOUND PART OF IT A LONG TIME AGO AND FELT LIKE IT HAD SOME KIND OF SIGNIFICANCE TO MY LIFE—I JUST DIDN'T KNOW WHAT!
ARE THOSE THE COOKIE ISLANDS?!

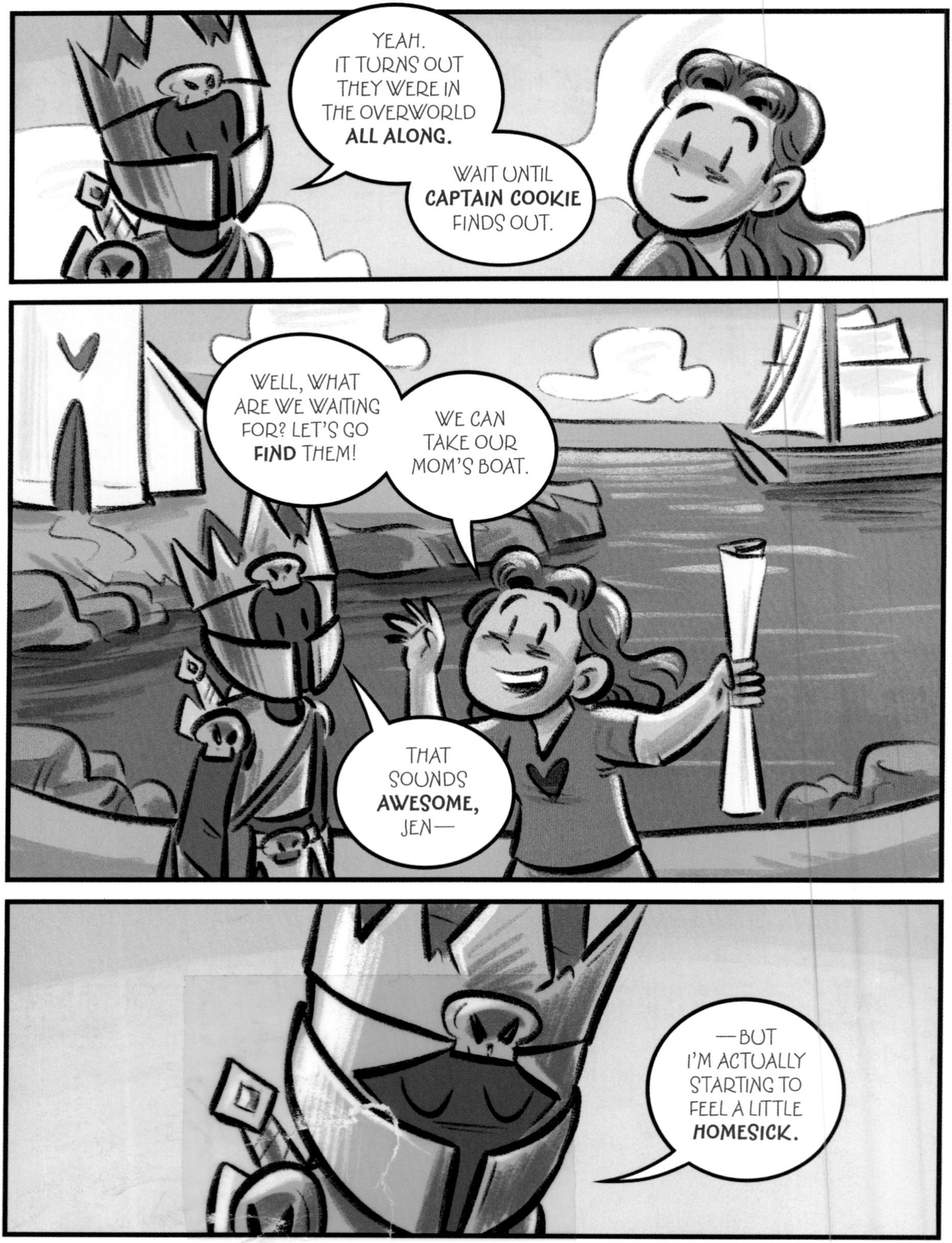
YEAH. IT TURNS OUT THEY WERE IN THE OVERWORLD **ALL ALONG.**
WAIT UNTIL **CAPTAIN COOKIE** FINDS OUT.
WELL, WHAT ARE WE WAITING FOR? LET'S GO **FIND** THEM!
WE CAN TAKE OUR MOM'S BOAT.
THAT SOUNDS **AWESOME,** JEN—
—BUT I'M ACTUALLY STARTING TO FEEL A LITTLE **HOMESICK.**

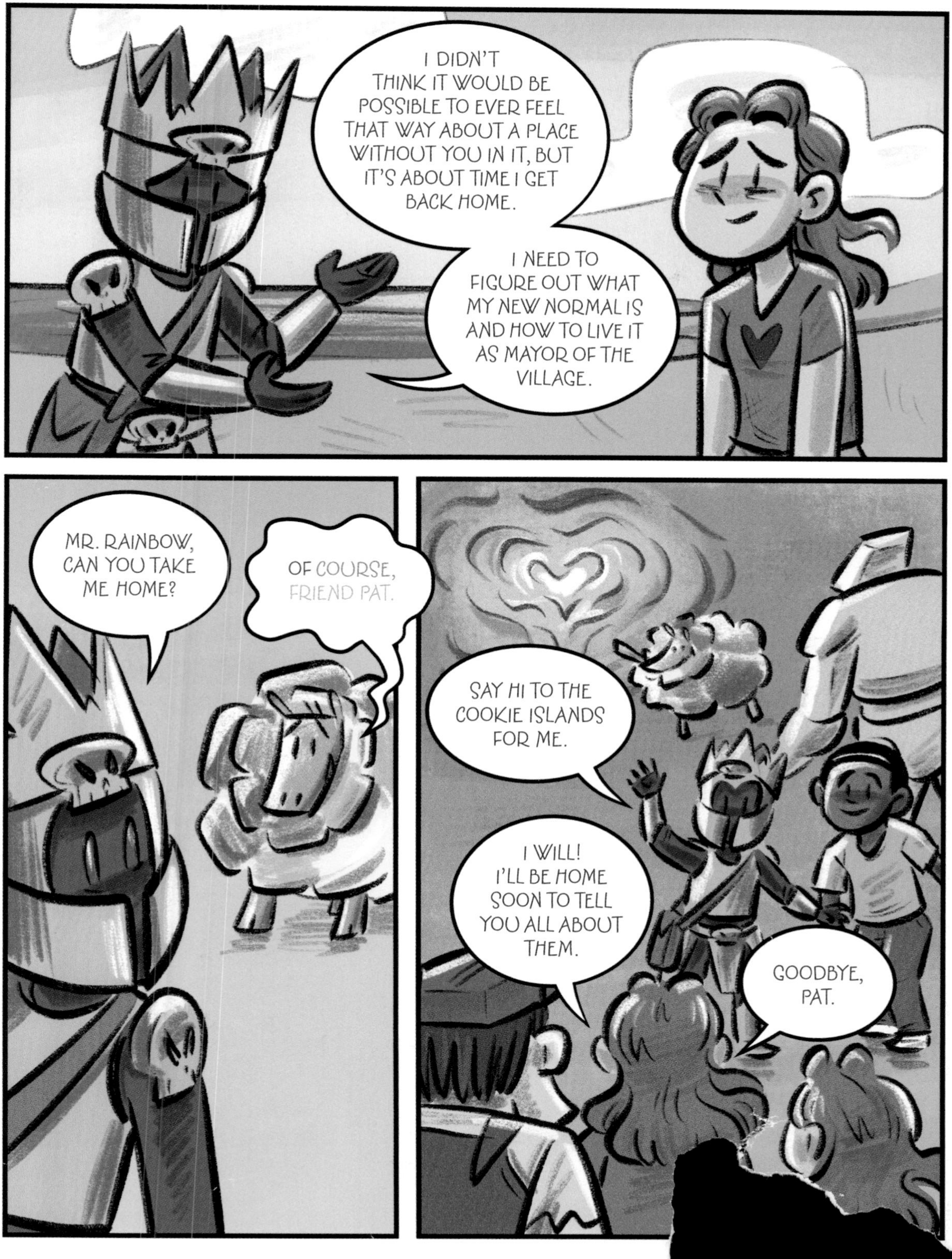
I DIDN'T THINK IT WOULD BE POSSIBLE TO EVER FEEL THAT WAY ABOUT A PLACE WITHOUT YOU IN IT, BUT IT'S ABOUT TIME I GET BACK HOME.
I NEED TO FIGURE OUT WHAT MY NEW NORMAL IS AND HOW TO LIVE IT AS MAYOR OF THE VILLAGE.
MR. RAINBOW, CAN YOU TAKE ME HOME?
OF COURSE, FRIEND PAT.
SAY HI TO THE COOKIE ISLANDS FOR ME.
I WILL! I'LL BE HOME SOON TO TELL YOU ALL ABOUT THEM.
GOODBYE, PAT.

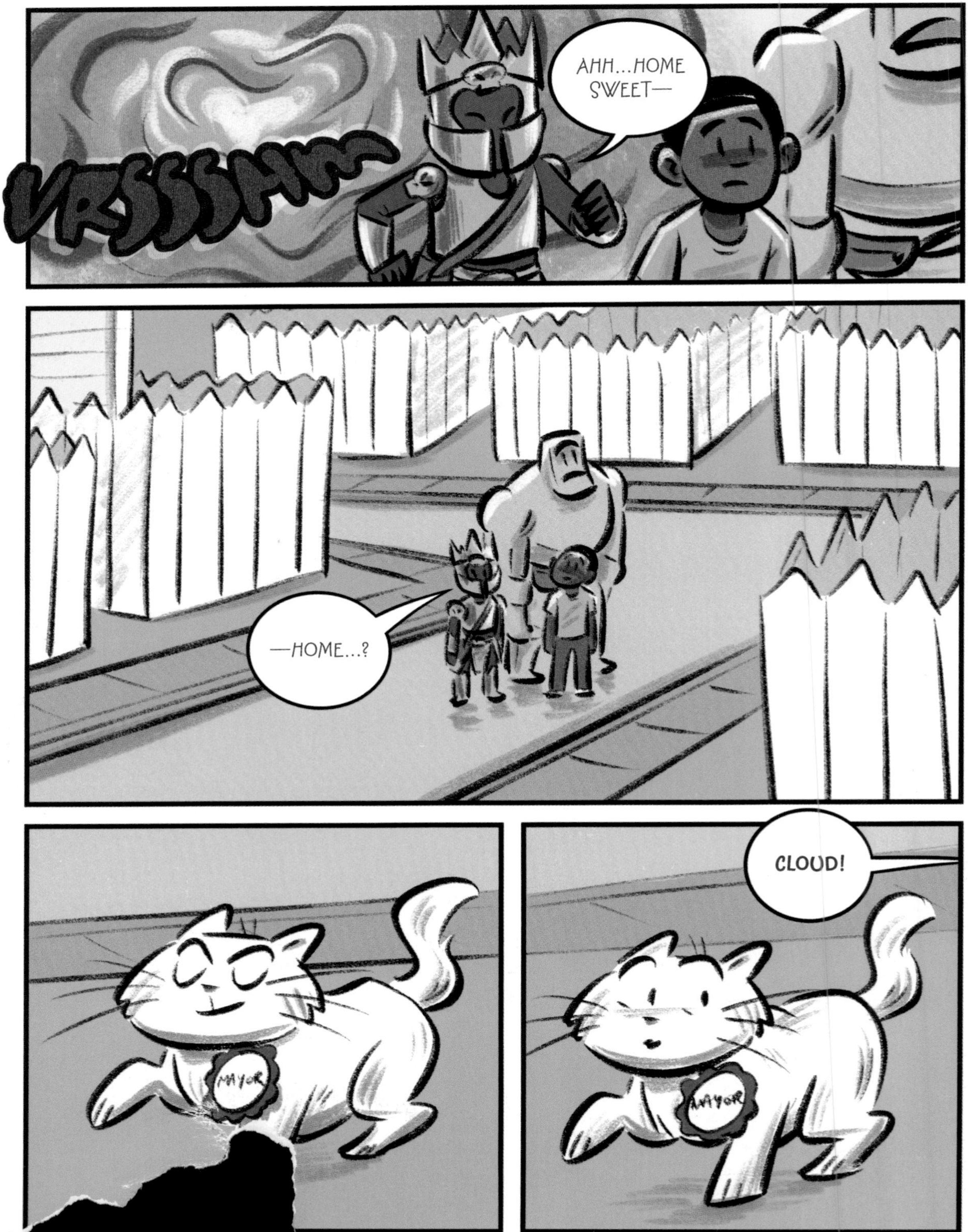
AHH...HOME SWEET—
—HOME...?
MAYOR
CLOUD!

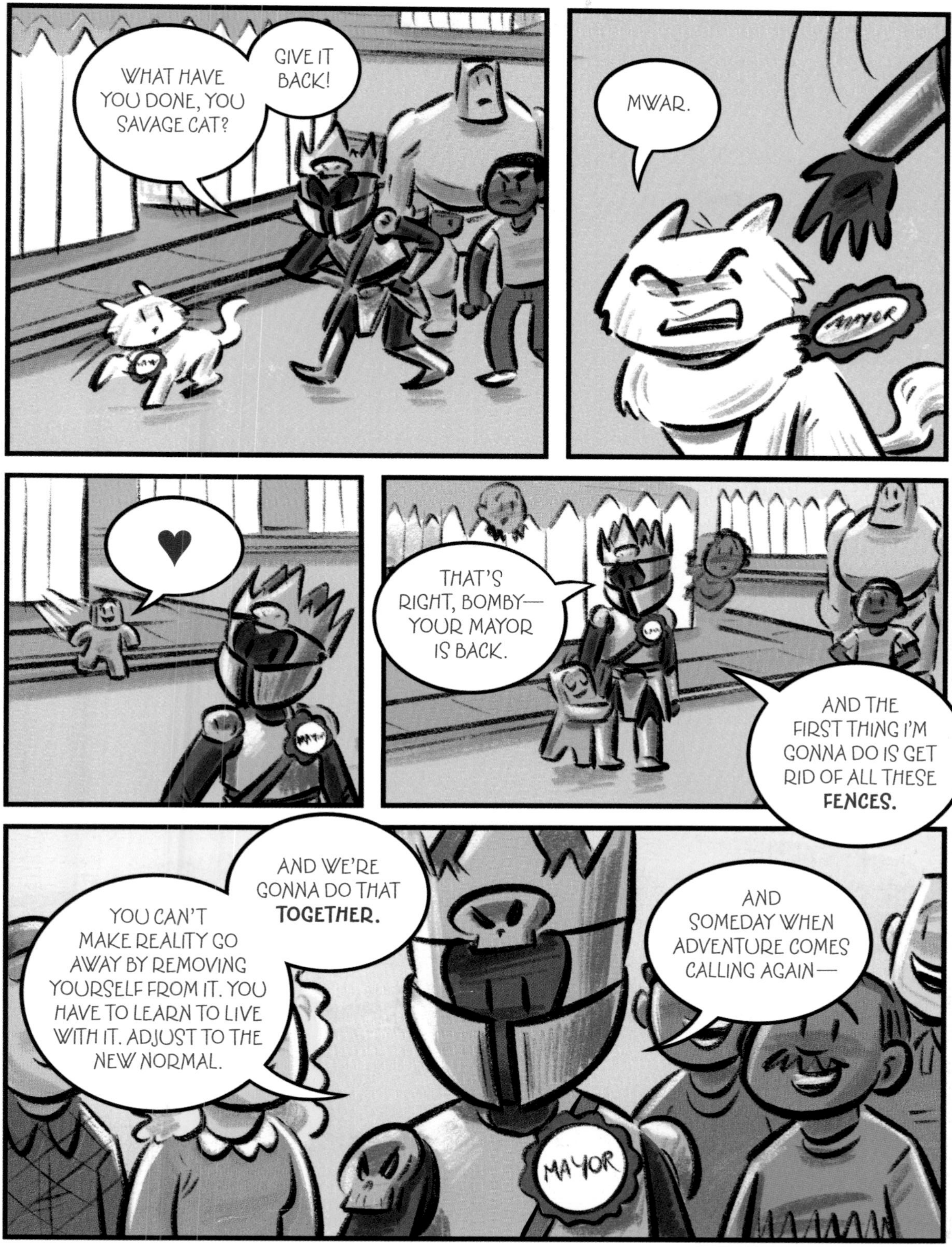

WHAT HAVE YOU DONE, YOU SAVAGE CAT?
GIVE IT BACK!
MWAR.
MAYOR
♥
THAT'S RIGHT, BOMBY— YOUR MAYOR IS BACK.
AND THE FIRST THING I'M GONNA DO IS GET RID OF ALL THESE **FENCES.**
YOU CAN'T MAKE REALITY GO AWAY BY REMOVING YOURSELF FROM IT. YOU HAVE TO LEARN TO LIVE WITH IT. ADJUST TO THE NEW NORMAL.
AND WE'RE GONNA DO THAT **TOGETHER.**
AND SOMEDAY WHEN ADVENTURE COMES CALLING AGAIN—
MAYOR

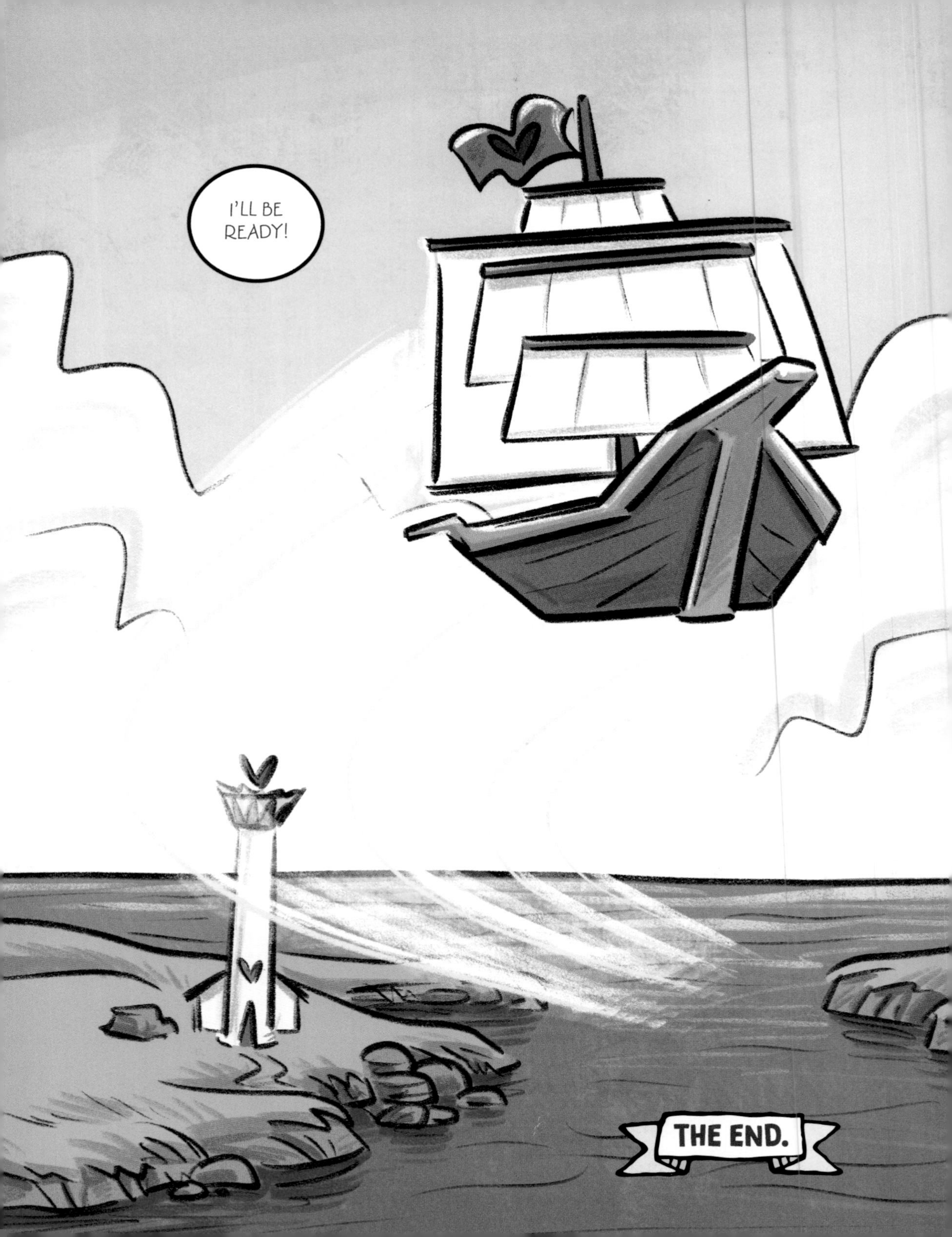
I'LL BE READY!
THE END.